# DIANA

## OF THE CROSSWAYS

*George Meredith aet. 72.*

# DIANA
## OF THE CROSSWAYS

A NOVEL

GEORGE MEREDITH

Quality Paperback Book Club
New York

*Diana of the Crossways* was first published in 1885.

This edition was especially created in 2003 for Quality Paperback Book Club, 1271 Avenue of the Americas, New York, NY 10020. This edition copyright © 2003 by Bookspan. All rights reserved.

www.qpb.com

Printed in the United States of America

DEDICATED TO

SIR FREDERICK POLLOCK
Bart.

# CONTENTS

# CONTENTS

A lady of high distinction for wit and beauty, the daughter of an illustrious Irish House, came under the shadow of a calumny. It has latterly been examined and exposed as baseless. The story of Diana of the Crossways is to be read as fiction.

# DIANA OF THE CROSSWAYS

## CHAPTER I

### OF DIARIES AND DIARISTS TOUCHING THE HEROINE

AMONG the Diaries beginning with the second quarter of our century, there is frequent mention of a lady then becoming famous for her beauty and her wit : ' an unusual combination,' in the deliberate syllables of one of the writers, who is, however, not disposed to personal irony when speaking of her.  It is otherwise in his case : and a general fling at the sex we may deem pardonable, for doing as little harm to womankind as the stone of an urchin cast upon the bosom of mother Earth ; though men must look some day to have it returned to them, which is a certainty ;—and indeed full surely will our idle-handed youngster too, in his riper season, be heard complaining of a strange assault of wanton missiles, coming on him he knows not whence ; for we are all of us distinctly marked to get back what we give, even from the thing named inanimate nature.

The ' LEAVES FROM THE DIARY OF HENRY WILMERS ' are studded with examples of the dinner-table wit of the time, not always worth quotation twice ; for smart remarks have their measured distances, many requiring to be à brûle pourpoint, or within throw of the pistol, to make it hit ; in other words, the majority of them are addressed directly to our muscular system, and they have

A

no effect when we stand beyond the range. On the contrary, they reflect sombrely on the springs of hilarity in the generation preceding us ;—with due reserve of credit, of course, to an animal vivaciousness that seems to have wanted so small an incitement. Our old yeomanry farmers returning to their beds over ferny commons under bright moonlight from a neighbour's harvest-home, eased their bubbling breasts with a ready roar not unakin to it. Still the promptness to laugh is an excellent progenitorial foundation for the wit to come in a people ; and undoubtedly the diarial record of an imputed piece of wit is witness to the spouting of laughter. This should comfort us while we skim the sparkling passages of the 'Leaves.' When a nation has acknowledged that it is as yet but in the fisticuff stage of the art of condensing our purest sense to golden sentences, a readier appreciation will be extended to the gift : which is to strike not the dazzled eyes, the unanticipating nose, the ribs, the sides, and stun us, twirl us, hoodwink, mystify, tickle and twitch, by dexterities of lingual sparring and shuffling, but to strike roots in the mind, the Hesperides of good things.

We shall then set a price on the ' unusual combination.' A witty woman is a treasure ; a witty Beauty is a power. Has she actual beauty, actual wit ?—not simply a tidal material beauty that passes current any pretty flippancy or staggering pretentiousness ? Grant the combination, she will appear a veritable queen of her period, fit for homage ; at least meriting a disposition to believe the best of her, in the teeth of foul rumour ; because the well of true wit is truth itself, the gathering of the precious drops of right reason, wisdom's lightning ; and no soul possessing and dispensing it can justly be a target for the world, however well armed the world confronting her. Our temporary world, that Old Credulity and stone-hurling urchin in one, supposes it possible for a woman to be mentally active up to the point of spiritual clarity and also fleshly vile ; a guide to life and a biter at the fruits of death ; both open mind and hypocrite. It has not yet been taught to appreciate a quality certifying to sound citizenship as authoritatively as acres of land in fee simple, or coffers of bonds, shares and stocks, and a more imperishable guarantee. The multitude of evil reports which it takes for proof, are marshalled against her without question of the nature of the victim, her temptress beauty being a sufficiently presumptive delinquent. It does not pretend to know the whole, or naked body of the facts ; it knows enough for its fumy dubiousness ; and excepting the sentimental of men, a rocket-headed horde, ever at the heels of fair faces for ignition, and up starring away at a hint of tearfulness ;— excepting further by chance a solid champion man, or some generous woman capable of faith in the pelted solitary of her sex, our temporary world blows direct East on her shivering person. The scandal is warrant for that ; the circumstances of the scandal emphasize the warrant. And how clever she is ! Cleverness is an attribute of the selecter missionary lieutenants of Satan. We pray to be defended from her cleverness : she flashes bits of speech that catch men in their unguarded corner. The wary stuff their ears, the stolid bid her best sayings rebound on her reputation. Nevertheless the world, as Christian, remembers its professions, and a portion of it joins the burly in morals by extending to her a rough old charitable mercifulness ; better than sentimental ointment, but the heaviest blow she has to bear, to a character swimming for life.

That the lady in question was much quoted, the Diaries and Memoirs testify. Hearsay as well as hearing was at work to produce the abundance ; and it was a novelty in England, where (in company) the men are the pointed talkers, and the women conversationally fair Circassians. They are, or they know that they should be ; it comes to the same. Happily our civilization has not prescribed the veil to them. The mutes have here and there a sketch or label attached to their names : they are ' strikingly handsome ' ; they are ' very good-looking ' ; occasionally they are noted as ' extremely entertaining ' : in what manner, is inquired by a curious posterity, that in so many matters is left unendingly to jump the empty and gaping figure of interrogation over its own full stop. Great ladies must they be, at the web of politics, for us to hear them cited discoursing. Henry Wilmers is not content to quote the beautiful Mrs. Warwick, he attempts a portrait. Mrs. Warwick is ' quite Grecian.' She might ' pose for a statue.' He presents her in carpenter's lines, with a dab of school-box colours, effective to those whom the Keepsake fashion can stir. She has a straight nose, red lips, raven hair, black eyes, rich complexion, a remarkably fine bust, and she walks well, and has an agreeable voice ; likewise ' delicate extremities.' The writer was created for popularity, had he chosen to bring his art into our literary market.

Perry Wilkinson is not so elaborate : he describes her in his ' Recollections ' as a splendid brune, eclipsing all the blondes coming near her : and ' what is more, the beautiful creature can talk.' He wondered, for she was young, new to society. Subsequently he is rather ashamed of his wonderment, and accounts for it by ' not having known she was Irish.' She ' turns out to be Dan Merion's daughter.'

We may assume that he would have heard if she had any whiff of a brogue. Her sounding of the letter R a trifle scrupulously is noticed by Lady Pennon : ' And last, not least, the lovely Mrs. Warwick, twenty minutes behind the dinner-hour, and *r-r-really* fearing she was late.'

After alluding to the soft influence of her beauty and ingenuousness on the vexed hostess, the kindly old marchioness adds, that it was no wonder she was late, ' for just before starting from home she had broken loose from her husband for good, and she entered the room absolutely houseless ! ' She was not the less ' astonishingly brilliant.' Her observations were often ' so unexpectedly droll I laughed till I cried.' Lady Pennon became in consequence one of the stanch supporters of Mrs. Warwick.

Others were not so easily won. Perry Wilkinson holds a balance when it goes beyond a question of her wit and beauty. Henry Wilmers puts the case aside, and takes her as he finds her. His cousin, the clever and cynical Dorset Wilmers, whose method of conveying his opinions without stating them was famous, repeats on two occasions when her name appears in his pages, ' handsome, lively, witty ' ; and the stressed repetition of calculated brevity while a fiery scandal was abroad concerning the lady, implies weighty substance—the reservation of a constable's truncheon, that could legally have knocked her character down to the pavement. We have not to ask what he judged. But Dorset Wilmers was a political opponent of the eminent Peer who yields the second name to the scandal, and politics in his day flushed the conceptions of men. His short references to ' that Warwick-Dannisburgh affair ' are not verbally malicious. He gets wind of the terms of Lord Dannisburgh's will and testament, noting them without comment. The oddness of the instrument in one respect may have served his turn ; we have no grounds for thinking him malignant. The death of his enemy closes his allusions to Mrs. Warwick. He was growing ancient, and gout narrowed the circle he whirled in. Had he known this ' handsome, lively, witty ' apparition as a woman having political and social views of

her own, he would not, one fancies, have been so stingless.
Our England exposes a sorry figure in his Reminiscences.
He struck heavily, round and about him, wherever he
moved ; he had by nature a tarnishing eye that cast dis-
colouration. His unadorned harsh substantive state-
ments, excluding the adjectives, give his Memoirs the
appearance of a body of facts, attractive to the historic
Muse, which has learnt to esteem those brawny sturdy
giants marching club on shoulder, independent of henchman, in preference to your panoplied knights with their
puffy squires, once her favourites, and wind-filling to her
columns, ultimately found indigestible.

His exhibition of his enemy Lord Dannisburgh, is of the
class of noble portraits we see swinging over inn-portals,
grossly unlike in likeness. The possibility of the man's
doing or saying this and that adumbrates the improba-
bility : he had something of the character capable of it,
too much good sense for the performance. We would
think so, and still the shadow is round our thoughts.
Lord Dannisburgh was a man of ministerial tact, official
ability, Pagan morality ; an excellent general manager,
if no genius in statecraft. But he was careless of social
opinion, unbuttoned, and a laugher. We know that he
could be chivalrous toward women, notwithstanding the
perplexities he brought on them, and this the Dorset-
Diary does not show.

His chronicle is less mischievous as regards Mrs.
Warwick than the paragraphs of Perry Wilkinson, a
gossip presenting an image of perpetual chatter, like the
waxen-faced street advertizements of light and easy
dentistry. He has no belief, no disbelief ; names the
pro-party and the con ; recites the case, and discreetly,
over-discreetly ; and pictures the trial, tells the list of
witnesses, records the verdict : so the case went, and
some thought one thing, some another thing : only it is

reported for positive that a miniature of the incriminated lady was cleverly smuggled over to the jury, and juries sitting upon these cases, ever since their bedazzlement by Phryne, as you know. . . . And then he relates an anecdote of the husband, said to have been not a bad fellow before he married his Diana ;—and the naming of the Goddess reminds him that the second person in the indictment is now everywhere called ' The elderly shepherd ' ;—but immediately after the bridal bells this husband became sour and insupportable ; and either she had the trick of putting him publicly in the wrong, or he lost all shame in playing the churlish domestic tyrant. The instances are incredible of a gentleman. Perry Wilkinson gives us two or three ; one on the authority of a personal friend who witnessed the scene ; at the Warwick whist-table, where the fair Diana would let loose her silvery laugh in the intervals. She was hardly out of her teens, and should have been dancing instead of fastened to a table. A difference of fifteen years in the ages of the wedded pair accounts poorly for the husband's conduct, however solemn a business the game of whist. We read that he burst out at last, with bitter mimicry, ' yang—yang—yang ! ' and killed the bright laugh, shot it dead. She had outraged the decorum of the square-table only while the cards were making. Perhaps her too-dead ensuing silence, as of one striving to bring back the throbs to a slain bird in her bosom, allowed the gap between the wedded pair to be visible, for it was dated back to prophecy as soon as the trumpet proclaimed it.

But a multiplication of similar instances, which can serve no other purpose than that of an apology, is a miserable vindication of innocence. The more we have of them the darker the inference. In delicate situations the chatterer is noxious. Mrs. Warwick had numerous apologists. Those trusting to her perfect rectitude were rarer.

The liberty she allowed herself in speech and action must
have been trying to her defenders in a land like ours ; for
here, and able to throw its shadow on our giddy upper-
circle, the rigour of the game of life, relaxed though it
may sometimes appear, would satisfy the staidest whist-
player.  She did not wish it the reverse, even when claiming a space for laughter : ' the breath of her soul,' as she
called it, and as it may be felt in the early youth of a
lively nature.  She, especially, with her multitude of
quick perceptions and imaginative avenues, her rapid
summaries, her sense of the comic, demanded this aërial
freedom.

We have it from Perry Wilkinson that the union of the
divergent couple was likened to another union always in
a Court of Law.  There was a distinction ; most analogies
will furnish one ;  and here we see England and Ireland
changeing their parts, until later, after the breach, when
the Englishman and Irishwoman resumed a certain
resemblance to the yoked Islands.

Henry Wilmers, I have said, deals exclusively with
the wit and charm of the woman.  He treats the scandal
as we might do in like manner if her story had not to be
told.  But these are not reporting columns ; very little
of it shall trouble them.  The position is faced, and that
is all.  The position is one of the battles incident to
women, their hardest.  It asks for more than justice from
men, for generosity, our civilization not being yet of the
purest.  That cry of hounds at her disrobing by Law is
instinctive.  She runs, and they give tongue ; she is a
creature of the chase.  Let her escape unmangled, it will
pass in the record that she did once publicly run, and
some old dogs will persist in thinking her cunninger than
the virtuous, which never put themselves in such positions,
but ply the distaff at home.  Never should reputation of
woman trail a scent !  How true !  and true also that the

women of waxwork never do ; and that the women of
happy marriages do not ; nor the women of holy nun-
neries ; nor the women lucky in their arts.  It is a test
of the civilized to see and hear, and add no yapping to
the spectacle.

Thousands have reflected on a Diarist's power to cancel
our Burial Service.  Not alone the cleric's good work is
upset by him, but the sexton's as well.  He howks the
graves, and transforms the quiet worms, busy on a single
poor peaceable body, into winged serpents that disorder
sky and earth with a deadly flight of zig-zags, like military rockets, among the living.  And if these are given to
cry too much, to have their tender sentiments considered,
it cannot be said that History requires the flaying of them.
A gouty Diarist, a sheer gossip Diarist, may thus, in the
bequest of a trail of reminiscences, explode our temples (for
our very temples have powder in store), our treasuries,
our homesteads, alive with dynamitic stuff ; nay, disconcert our inherited veneration, dislocate the intimate
connexion between the tugged flaxen forelock and a title.

No similar blame is incurred by Henry Wilmers.  No
blame whatever, one would say, if he had been less
copious, or not so subservient, in recording the lady's
utterances ; for though the wit of a woman may be terse,
quite spontaneous, as this lady's assuredly was here and
there, she is apt to spin it out of a museful mind, at her
toilette, or by the lonely fire, and sometimes it is imitative ;
admirers should beware of holding it up to the withering
glare of print : she herself, quoting an obscure maxim-
monger, says of these lapidary sentences, that they have
merely ' *the value of chalk-eggs, which lure the thinker to sit,*'
and tempt the vacuous to strain for the like, one might
add ; besides flattering the world to imagine itself richer
than it is in eggs that are golden.  Henry Wilmers notes
a multitude of them.  ' The talk fell upon our being

creatures of habit, and how far it was good : She said :—
It is there that we see ourselves crutched between love
grown old and indifference ageing to love.' Critic ears
not present at the conversation catch an echo of maxims
and aphorisms overchannel, notwithstanding a feminine
thrill in the irony of ' ageing to love.' The quotation
ranks rather among the testimonies to her charm.

She is fresher when speaking of the war of the sexes.
For one sentence out of many, though we find it to be but
the clever literary clothing of a common accusation :—
' *Men may have rounded Seraglio Point : they have not yet
doubled Cape Turk.*'

It is war, and on the male side, Ottoman war : her
experience reduced her to think so positively. Her main
personal experience was in the social class which is primi-
tively venatorial still, canine under its polish.

She held a brief for her beloved Ireland. She closes a
discussion upon Irish agitation by saying rather neatly :
' *You have taught them it is English as well as common
human nature to feel an interest in the dog that has bitten
you.*'

The dog periodically puts on madness to win attention ;
we gather then that England, in an angry tremour, tries
him with water-gruel to prove him sane.

Of the Irish priest (and she was not of his retinue),
when he was deemed a revolutionary, Henry Wilmers
notes her saying : ' Be in tune with him ; he is in the
key-note for harmony. He is shepherd, doctor, nurse,
comforter, anecdotist and fun-maker to his poor flock ;
and you wonder they see the burning gateway of their
heaven in him ? Conciliate the priest.'

It has been partly done, done late, when the poor flock
have found their doctoring and shepherding at other
hands : their ' bulb-food and fiddle,' that she petitioned
for, to keep them from a complete shaving off their

patch of bog and scrub soil, without any perception of
the tremendous transatlantic magnification of the fiddle,
and the splitting discord of its latest inspiriting jig.

And she will not have the consequences of the ' weariful
old Irish duel between Honour and Hunger judged by
bread and butter juries.'

She had need to be beautiful to be tolerable in days
when Englishmen stood more openly for the strong arm
to maintain the Union. Her troop of enemies was of her
summoning.

Ordinarily her topics were of wider range, and those of
a woman who mixed hearing with reading, and observation with her musings. She has no doleful ejaculatory
notes, of the kind peculiar to women at war, containing
one-third of speculative substance to two of sentimental
—a feminine plea for comprehension and a squire; and it
was probably the reason (as there is no reason to suppose
an emotional cause) why she exercised her evident sway
over the mind of so plain and straightforward an Englishman as Henry Wilmers. She told him that she read
rapidly, ' a great deal at one gulp,' and thought in flashes
—a way with the makers of phrases. She wrote, she confessed, laboriously. The desire to prune, compress, over-
charge, was a torment to the nervous woman writing
under a sharp necessity for payment. Her songs were
shot off on the impulsion; prose was the heavy task.
' To be pointedly rational,' she said, ' is a greater difficulty for me than a fine delirium.' She did not talk as
if it would have been so, he remarks. One is not astonished at her appearing an ' actress ' to the flat-minded.
But the basis of her woman's nature was pointed flame.
In the fulness of her history we perceive nothing his-
trionic. Capricious or enthusiastic in her youth, she
never trifled with feeling; and if she did so with some
showy phrases and occasionally proffered commonplaces

in gilt, as she was much excited to do, her moods of reflection were direct, always large and honest, universal as well as feminine.

Her saying that ' A woman in the pillory restores the original bark of brotherhood to mankind,' is no more than a cry of personal anguish. She has golden apples in her apron. She says of life : '*When I fail to cherish it in every fibre the fires within are waning,*' and that drives like rain to the roots. She says of the world, generously, if with tapering idea : ' From the point of vision of the angels, this ugly monster, only half out of slime, must appear our one constant hero.'

It can be read maliciously, but abstain.

She says of Romance : ' *The young who avoid that region escape the title of Fool at the cost of a celestial crown.*' Of Poetry : ' *Those that have souls meet their fellows there.*'

But she would have us away with sentimentalism. Sentimental people, in her phrase, ' *fiddle harmonics on the strings of sensualism,*' to the delight of a world gaping for marvels of musical execution rather than for music. For our world is all but a sensational world at present, in maternal travail of a soberer, a braver, a brighter-eyed. Her reflections are thus to be interpreted, it seems to me. She says, ' The vices of the world's nobler half in this day are feminine.' We have to guard against ' half-conceptions of wisdom, hysterical goodness, an impatient charity '—against the elementary state of the altruistic virtues, distinguishable as the sickness and writhings of our egoism to cast its first slough. Idea is there. The funny part of it is our finding it in books of fiction composed for payment. Manifestly this lady did not ' chameleon ' her pen from the colour of her audience : she was not of the uniformed rank and file marching to drum and fife as gallant interpreters of popular appetite, and going or gone to soundlessness and the icy shades.

Touches inward are not absent : ' To have the sense
of the eternal in life is a short flight for the soul.  To have
had it, is the soul's vitality.'

And also : ' Palliation of a sin is the hunted creature's
refuge and final temptation.  Our battle is ever between
spirit and flesh.  Spirit must brand the flesh, that it may
live.'

You are entreated to repress alarm.  She was by
preference light-handed ; and her saying of oratory, that
' *It is always the more impressive for the spice of temper
which renders it untrustworthy,*' is light enough.

On Politics she is rhetorical and swings : she wrote to
spur a junior politician : ' It is the first business of men,
the school to mediocrity, to the covetously ambitious a
sty, to the dullard his amphitheatre, arms of Titans to
the desperately enterprising, Olympus to the genius.'

What a woman thinks of women, is the test of her
nature.  She saw their existing posture clearly, yet
believed, as men disincline to do, that they grow.  She
says, that ' In their judgements upon women men are
females, voices of the present (sexual) dilemma.'  They
desire to have ' a still woman, who can make a constant
society of her pins and needles.'  They create by stoppage
a volcano, and are amazed at its eruptiveness.  ' We live
alone, and do not much feel it till we are visited.'  Love
is presumeably the visitor.  Of the greater loneliness of
women, she says : ' It is due to the prescribed circum-
scription of their minds, of which they become aware in
agitation.  Were the walls about them beaten down, they
would understand that solitariness is a common human
fate and the one chance of growth, like space for timber.'
As to the sensations of women after the beating down
of the walls, she owns that the multitude of the timorous
would yearn in shivering affright for the old prison-nest,
according to the sage prognostic of men ; but the flying

of a valiant few would form a vanguard.  And we are
informed that the beginning of a motive life with women
must be in the head, equally with men (by no means a
truism when she wrote).  Also that ' men do not so much
fear to lose the hearts of thoughtful women as their strict
attention to their graces.'  The present market is what
men are for preserving : an observation of still reverberating force.  Generally in her character of the feminine combatant there is a turn of phrase, like a dimple
near the lips, showing her knowledge that she was uttering but a tart measure of the truth.  She had always
too much lambent humour to be the dupe of the passion
wherewith, as she says, ' we lash ourselves into the
persuasive speech distinguishing us from the animals.'

The instances of her drollery are rather hinted by the
Diarists for the benefit of those who had met her and
could inhale the atmosphere at a word.  Drolleries,
humours, reputed witticisms, are like odours of roast
meats, past with the picking of the joint.  Idea is the
only vital breath.  They have it rarely, or it eludes the
chronicler.  To say of the great erratic and forsaken
Lady A****, after she had accepted the consolations of
Bacchus, that her name was properly signified in asterisks ;
' as she was now nightly an Ariadne in heaven through
her God,' sounds to us a roundabout, with wit somewhere
and fun nowhere.  Sitting at the roast we might have
thought differently.  Perry Wilkinson is not happier in
citing her reply to his compliment on the reviewers' un-
animous eulogy of her humour and pathos :—the ' merry
clown and poor pantaloon demanded of us in every work
of fiction,' she says, lamenting the writer's compulsion
to go on producing them for applause until it is extremest
age that knocks their knees.  We are informed by Lady
Pennon of ' the most amusing description of the first
impressions of a pretty English simpleton in Paris ' ;

and here is an opportunity for ludicrous contrast of the French and English styles of pushing flatteries—'piping to the charmed animal,' as Mrs. Warwick terms it in another place : but Lady Pennon was acquainted with the silly woman of the piece, and found her amusement in the ' wonderful truth ' of that representation.

Diarists of amusing passages are under an obligation to paint us a realistic revival of the time, or we miss the relish. The odour of the roast, and more, a slice of it is required, unless the humorous thing be preternaturally spirited to walk the earth as one immortal among a number less numerous than the mythic Gods. ' He gives good dinners,' a candid old critic said, when asked how it was that he could praise a certain poet. In an island of chills and fogs, cœlum crebris imbribus ac nebulis fœdum, the comic and other perceptions are dependent on the stirring of the gastric juices. And such a revival by any of us would be impolitic, were it a possible attempt, before our systems shall have been fortified by philosophy. Then may it be allowed to the Diarist simply to relate, and we can copy from him.

Then, ah ! then, moreover, will the novelist's Art, now neither blushless infant nor executive man, have attained its majority. We can then be veraciously historical, honestly transcriptive. Rose-pink and dirty drab will alike have passed away. Philosophy is the foe of both, and their silly cancelling contest, perpetually renewed in a shuffle of extremes, as it always is where a phantasm falseness reigns, will no longer baffle the contemplation of natural flesh, smother no longer the soul issuing out of our incessant strife. Philosophy bids us to see that we are not so pretty as rose-pink, not so repulsive as dirty drab ; and that instead of everlastingly shifting those barren aspects, the sight of ourselves is wholesome, bearable, fructifying, finally a delight. Do but perceive that we are coming to philosophy, the stride toward it will be a giant's—a century a day. And imagine the celestial refreshment of having a pure decency in the place of sham ; real flesh ; a soul born active, wind-beaten, but ascending. Honourable will fiction then appear ; honourable, a fount of life, an aid to life, quick with our blood. Why, when you behold it you love it—and you will not encourage it ?—or only when presented by dead hands ? Worse than that alternative dirty drab, your recurring rose-pink is rebuked by hideous revelations of the filthy foul ; for nature will force her way, and if you try to stifle her by drowning, she comes up, not the fairest part of her uppermost ! Peruse your Realists—really your castigators for not having yet embraced Philosophy. As she grows in the flesh when discreetly tended, nature is unimpeachable, flower-like, yet not too decoratively a flower ; you must have her with the stem, the thorns, the roots, and the fat bedding of roses. In this fashion she grew, says historical fiction ; thus does she flourish now, would say the modern transcript, reading the inner as well as exhibiting the outer.

And how may you know that you have reached to Philosophy ? You touch her skirts when you share her hatred of the sham decent, her derision of sentimentalism. You are one with her when—but I would not have you a thousand years older ! Get to her, if in no other way, by the sentimental route :—that very winding path, which again and again brings you round to the point of original impetus, where you have to be unwound for another whirl ; your point of original impetus being the grossly material, not at all the spiritual. It is most true that sentimentalism springs from the former, merely and badly aping the latter ;—fine flower, or pinnacle flame-spire, of sensualism that it is, could it do other ?— and accompanying the former it traverses tracts of desert, here and there couching in a garden, catching with one hand at fruits, with another at colours ; imagining a secret ahead, and goaded by an appetite, sustained by sheer gratifications. Fiddle in harmonics as it may, it will have these gratifications at all costs. Should none be discoverable, at once you are at the Cave of Despair, beneath the funereal orb of Glaucoma, in the thick midst of poniarded, slit-throat, rope-dependant figures, placarded across the bosom Disillusioned, Infidel, Agnostic, Miserrimus. That is the sentimental route to advancement. Spirituality does not light it ; evanescent dreams are its oil-lamps, often with wick askant in the socket.

A thousand years ! You may count full many a thousand by this route before you are one with divine Philosophy. Whereas a single flight of brains will reach and embrace her ; give you the savour of Truth, the right use of the senses, Reality's infinite sweetness ; for these things are in philosophy ; and the fiction which is the summary of actual Life, the within and without of us, is, prose or verse, plodding or soaring, philosophy's elect handmaiden. To such an end let us bend our aim to work, knowing that every form of labour, even this flimsiest, as you esteem it, should minister to growth. If in any branch of us we fail in growth, there is, you are aware, an unfailing aboriginal democratic old monster that waits to pull us down ; certainly the branch, possibly the tree ; and for the welfare of Life we fall. You are acutely conscious of yonder old monster when he is mouthing at you in politics. Be wary of him in the heart ; especially be wary of the disrelish of brainstuff. You must feed on something. Matter that is not nourishing to brains can help to constitute nothing but the bodies which are pitched on rubbish heaps. Brainstuff is not lean stuff ; the brainstuff of fiction is internal history, and to suppose it dull is the profoundest of errors ; how deep, you will understand when I tell you that it is the very football of the holiday-afternoon imps below. They kick it for pastime; they are intelligences perverted. The comic of it, the adventurous, the tragic, they make devilish, to kindle their Ogygian hilarity. But sharply comic, adventurous, instructively tragic, it is in the interwinding with human affairs, to give a flavour of the modern day reviving that of our Poet, between whom and us yawn Time's most hollow jaws. Surely we owe a little to Time, to cheer his progress; a little to posterity, and to our country. Dozens of writers will be in at yonder yawning breach, if only perusers will rally to the philosophic standard. They are sick of the woodeny puppetry they dispense, as on a race-course to the roaring frivolous. Well, if not dozens, half-dozens; gallant pens are alive; one can speak of them in the plural. I venture to say that they would be satisfied with a dozen for audience, for a commencement. They would perish of inanition, unfed, unapplauded, amenable to the laws perchance for an assault on their last remaining pair of ears or heels, to hold them fast. But the example is the thing; sacrifices must be expected. The example might, one hopes, create a taste. A great modern writer, of clearest eye and head, now departed, capable in activity of presenting thoughtful women, thinking men, groaned over his puppetry, that he dared not animate them, flesh though they were, with the fires of positive brainstuff. He could have done it, and he is of the departed! Had he dared, he would (for he was Titan enough) have raised the Art in dignity on a level with History, to an interest surpassing the narrative of public deeds as vividly as man's heart and brain in their union excel his plain lines of action to eruption. The everlasting pantomime, suggested by Mrs. Warwick in her exclamation to Perry Wilkinson, is derided, not unrighteously, by our graver

seniors. They name this Art the pasture of idiots, a
method for idiotizing the entire population which has
taken to reading ; and which soon discovers that it can
write likewise, *that* sort of stuff at least. The forecast
may be hazarded, that if we do not speedily embrace
Philosophy in fiction, the Art is doomed to extinction,
under the shining multitude of its professors. They are
fast capping the candle. Instead, therefore, of objur-
gating the timid intrusions of Philosophy, invoke her
presence, I pray you. History without her is the skeleton
map of events : Fiction a picture of figures modelled on
no skeleton-anatomy. But each, with Philosophy in
aid, blooms, and is humanly shapely. To demand of
us truth to nature, excluding Philosophy, is really to
bid a pumpkin caper. As much as legs are wanted for
the dance, Philosophy is required to make our human
nature credible and acceptable. Fiction implores you
to heave a bigger breast and take her in with this heavenly
preservative helpmate, her inspiration and her essence.
You have to teach your imagination of the feminine
image you have set up to bend your civilized knees to,
that it must temper its fastidiousness, shun the grossness
of the overdainty. Or, to speak in the philosophic tongue,
you must turn on *yourself*, resolutely track and seize that
burrower, and scrub and cleanse him ; by which process,
during the course of it, you will arrive at the conception
of the right heroical woman for *you* to worship : and if
you prove to be of some spiritual stature, you may reach
to an ideal of the heroical feminine type for the worship of
mankind, an image as yet in poetic outline only, on our
upper skies.

' So well do we know ourselves, that we one and all
determine to know a purer,' says the heroine of my
columns. Philosophy in fiction tells, among various
other matters, of the perils of this intimate acquaintance

with a flattering familiar in the ' purer '—a person who more than ceases to be of use to us after his ideal shall have led up men from their flint and arrowhead caverns to inter-communicative daylight. For when the fictitious creature has performed that service of helping to civilize the world, it becomes the most dangerous of delusions, causing first the individual to despise the mass, and then to join the mass in crushing the individual. Wherewith let us to our story, the froth being out of the bottle.

## CHAPTER II

### AN IRISH BALL

IN the Assembly Rooms of the capital city of the Sister Island there was a public Ball, to celebrate the return to Erin of a British hero of Irish blood, after his victorious Indian campaign ; a mighty struggle splendidly ended ; and truly could it be said that all Erin danced to meet him ; but this was the pick of the dancing, past dispute the pick of the supping. Outside those halls the supping was done in Lazarus fashion, mainly through an excessive straining of the organs of hearing and vision, which imparted the readiness for more, declared by physicians to be the state inducing to sound digestion. Some one spied the figure of the hero at a window and was fed ; some only to hear the tale chewed the cud of it ; some told of having seen him mount the steps ; and sure it was that at an hour of the night, no matter when, and never mind a drop or two of cloud, he would come down them again, and have an Irish cheer to freshen his pillow. For 'tis Ireland gives England her soldiers, her generals too. Farther away, over field and bogland,

the whiskies did their excellent ancient service of water-
ing the dry and drying the damp, to the toast of 'Lord
Larrian, God bless him! he's an honour to the old
country!' and a bit of a sigh to follow, hints of a story,
and loud laughter, a drink, a deeper sigh, settling into
conversation upon the brave Lord Larrian's deeds, and
an Irish regiment he favoured—had no taste for the
enemy without the backing of his 'boys.' Not he.
Why, he'd never march to battle and they not handy;
because when he struck he struck hard, he said. And
he has a wound on the right hip and two fingers off his
left hand; has bled for England, to show her what
Irishmen are when they're well treated.

The fine old warrior standing at the upper end of the
long saloon, tall, straight, grey-haired, martial in his
aspect and decorations, was worthy to be the flag-pole
for enthusiasm. His large grey eyes lightened from
time to time as he ranged them over the floating couples,
and dropped a word of inquiry to his aide, Captain Sir
Lukin Dunstane, a good model of a cavalry officer,
though somewhat a giant, equally happy with his chief
in passing the troops of animated ladies under review.
He named as many as were known to him. Reviewing
women exquisitely attired for inspection, all variously
and charmingly smiling, is a relief after the monotonous
regiments of men. Ireland had done her best to present
the hero of her blood an agreeable change; and he too
expressed a patriotic satisfaction on hearing that the
faces most admired by him were of the native isle. He
looked upon one that came whirling up to him on a
young officer's arm and swept off into the crowd of tops,
for a considerable while before he put his customary
question. She was returning on the spin when he
said,

'Who is she?'

Sir Lukin did not know. 'She's a new bird; she nodded to my wife; I'll ask.'

He manœuvred a few steps cleverly to where his wife reposed. The information he gathered for the behoof of his chief was, that the handsome creature answered to the name of Miss Merion; Irish; aged somewhere between eighteen and nineteen; a dear friend of his wife's, and he ought to have remembered her; but she was a child when he saw her last.

'Dan Merion died, I remember, about the day of my sailing for India,' said the General. 'She may be his daughter.'

The bright cynosure rounded up to him in the web of the waltz, with her dark eyes for Lady Dunstane, and vanished again among the twisting columns.

He made his way, handsomely bumped by an apologetic pair, to Lady Dunstane, beside whom a seat was vacated for him; and he trusted she had not over-fatigued herself.

'Confess,' she replied, 'you are perishing to know more than Lukin has been able to tell you. Let me hear that you admire her: it pleases me; and you shall hear what will please you as much, I promise you, General.'

'I do. Who wouldn't?' said he frankly.

'She crossed the Channel expressly to dance here to-night at the public Ball in honour of you.'

'Where she appears, the first person falls to second rank, and accepts it humbly.'

'That is grandly spoken.'

'She makes everything in the room dust round a blazing jewel.'

'She makes a poet of a soldier. Well, that you may understand how pleased I am, she is my dearest friend, though she is younger than I, as may be seen; she is the only friend I have. I nursed her when she was an infant; my father and Mr. Dan Merion were chums. We were parted by my marriage and the voyage to India. We have not yet exchanged a syllable : she was snapped up, of course, the moment she entered the room. I knew she would be a taking girl : how lovely, I did not guess. You are right, she extinguishes the others. She used to be the sprightliest of living creatures, and to judge by her letters, that has not faded. She 's in the market, General.'

Lord Larrian nodded to everything he heard, concluding with a mock doleful shake of the head. 'My poorest subaltern ! ' he sighed, in the theatrical but cordially melancholy style of green age viewing Cytherea's market.

His poorest subaltern was richer than he in the wherewithal to bid for such prizes.

'What is her name in addition to Merion ? '

'Diana Antonia Merion. Tony to me, Diana to the world.'

'She lives over there ? '

'In England, or anywhere ; wherever she is taken in. She will live, I hope, chiefly with me.'

'And honest Irish ? '

'Oh, she 's Irish.'

'Ah ! ' the General was Irish to the heels that night.

Before further could be said the fair object of the dialogue came darting on a trip of little runs, both hands out, all her face one tender sparkle of a smile ; and her cry proved the quality of her blood : 'Emmy ! Emmy ! my heart ! '

'My dear Tony ! I should not have come but for the hope of seeing you here.'

Lord Larrian rose and received a hurried acknowledgement of his courtesy from the usurper of his place.

'Emmy ! we might kiss and hug ; we 're in Ireland. I burn to ! But you 're not still ill, dear ? Say no ! That Indian fever must have gone. You do look a dash pale, my own ; you 're tired.'

' One dance has tired me. Why were you so late ? '

' To give the others a chance ? To produce a greater impression by suspense ? No and no. I wrote you I was with the Pettigrews. We caught the coach, we caught the boat, we were only two hours late for the Ball ; so we did wonders. And good Mrs. Pettigrew is pining somewhere to complete her adornment. I was in the crush, spying for Emmy, when Mr. Mayor informed me it was the duty of every Irishwoman to dance her toes off, if she 'd be known for what she is. And twirl! a man had me by the waist, and I dying to find you.'

' Who was the man ? '

' Not to save these limbs from the lighted stake could I tell you ! '

' You are to perform a ceremonious bow to Lord Larrian.'

' Chatter first ! a little ! '

The plea for chatter was disregarded. It was visible that the hero of the night hung listening and in expectation. He and the Beauty were named to one another, and they chatted through a quadrille. Sir Lukin introduced a fellow-Harrovian of old days, Mr. Thomas Redworth, to his wife.

' Our weather-prophet, meteorologist,' he remarked, to set them going ; ' you remember, in India, my pointing to you his name in a newspaper-letter on the subject. He was generally safe for the cricketing days.'

Lady Dunstane kindly appeared to call it to mind, and she led upon the theme—queried at times by an abrupt ' Eh ? ' and ' I beg pardon,' for manifestly his gaze and one of his ears, if not the pair, were given to the young lady discoursing with Lord Larrian. Beauty is rare ; luckily is it rare, or, judging from its effect on men, and the very stoutest of them, our world would be internally a more distracted planet than we see, to the perversion

of business, courtesy, rights of property, and the rest.
She perceived an incipient victim, of the hundreds she
anticipated, and she very tolerantly talked on : ' The
weather and women have some resemblance they say.
Is it true that he who reads the one can read the other ? '

Lord Larrian here burst into a brave old laugh, exclaiming, ' Oh ! good ! '

Mr. Redworth knitted his thick brows. ' I beg
pardon ? Ah ! women ! Weather and women ? No ;
the one point more variable in women makes all the
difference.'

' Can you tell me what the General laughed at ? '

The honest Englishman entered the trap with prompti-
tude. ' She said :—who is she, may I ask you ? '

Lady Dunstane mentioned her name.

Daughter of the famous Dan Merion ? The young lady
merited examination for her father's sake. But when
reminded of her laughter-moving speech, Mr. Redworth
bungled it ; he owned he spoilt it, and candidly stated his
inability to see the fun. ' She said, St. George's Channel
in a gale ought to be called St. Patrick's—something—I
missed some point. That quadrille-tune, the Pastourelle,
or something . . .'

' She had experience of the Channel last night,' Lady
Dunstane pursued, and they both, while in seeming converse, caught snatches from their neighbours, during a
pause of the dance.

The sparkling Diana said to Lord Larrian, ' You
really decline to make any of us proud women by dancing
to-night ? '

The General answered : ' I might do it on two stilts ; I
can't on one.' He touched his veteran leg.

' But surely,' said she, ' there 's always an inspiration
coming to it from its partner in motion, if one of them
takes the step.'

He signified a woeful negative. ' My dear young lady,
you say dark things to grey hairs ! '

She rejoined : ' If we were over in England, and you
fixed on me the stigma of saying dark things, I should
never speak without being thought obscure.'

' It 's because you flash too brightly for them.'

' I think it is rather the reminiscence of the tooth that
once received a stone when it expected candy.'

Again the General laughed ; he looked pleased and
warmed. ' Yes, that 's their way, that 's their way ! '
and he repeated her words to himself, diminishing their
importance as he stamped them on his memory, but so
heartily admiring the lovely speaker, that he considered
her wit an honour to the old country, and told her so.
Irish prevailed up to boiling-point.

Lady Dunstane, not less gratified, glanced up at Mr.
Redworth, whose brows bore the knot of perplexity over
a strong stare. He, too, stamped the words on his
memory, to see subsequently whether they had a vestige
of meaning. Terrifically precocious, he thought her.
Lady Dunstane, in her quick sympathy with her friend,
read the adverse mind in his face. And her reading of
the mind was right, wrong altogether her deduction of the
corresponding sentiment.

Music was resumed to confuse the hearing of the eaves-
droppers.

They beheld a quaint spectacle : a gentleman, obvi-
ously an Englishman, approached, with the evident
intention of reminding the Beauty of the night of her
engagement to him, and claiming her, as it were, in the
lion's jaws. He advanced a foot, withdrew it, advanced,
withdrew ; eager for his prize, not over-enterprising ;
in awe of the illustrious General she entertained—presumeably quite unaware of the pretender's presence ;
whereupon a voice was heard : ' Oh ! if it was minuetting

you meant before the lady, I 'd never have disputed your
right to perform, sir.' For it seemed that there were two
claimants in the field, an Irishman and an Englishman ;
and the former, having a livelier sense of the situation,
hung aloof in waiting for her eye ; the latter directed
himself to strike bluntly at his prey ; and he continued
minuetting, now rapidly blinking, flushed, angry,
conscious of awkwardness and a tangle, incapable of
extrication. He began to blink horribly under the
raillery of his rival. The General observed him, but
as an object remote and minute, a fly or gnat. The face
of the brilliant Diana was entirely devoted to him she
amused.

Lady Dunstane had the faint lines of a decorous laugh
on her lips, as she said : ' How odd it is that our men
show to such disadvantage in a Ball-room. I have seen
them in danger, and there they shine first of any, and
one is proud of them. They should always be facing
the elements or in action.' She glanced at the minuet,
which had become a petrified figure, still palpitating, bent
forward, an interrogative reminder.

Mr. Redworth reserved his assent to the proclamation
of any English disadvantage. A whiff of Celtic hostility
in the atmosphere put him on his mettle. ' Wherever
the *man* is tried,' he said.

' My lady ! ' the Irish gentleman bowed to Lady Dunstane. ' I had the honour . . . Sullivan Smith . . . at
the castle . . .'

She responded to the salute, and Mr. Sullivan Smith
proceeded to tell her, half in speech, half in dots most
luminous, of a civil contention between the English
gentleman and himself, as to the possession of the loveliest
of partners for this particular ensuing dance, and that they
had simultaneously made a rush from the Lower Courts,
namely, their cards, to the Upper, being the lady ; and

Mr. Sullivan Smith partly founded his preferable claim
on her Irish descent, and on his acquaintance with her
eminent defunct father—one of the ever-radiating stars
of his quenchless country.

Lady Dunstane sympathized with him for his not intruding his claim when the young lady stood pre-engaged,
as well as in humorous appreciation of his imaginative
logic.

' There will be dancing enough after supper,' she said.

' If I could score one dance with her, I 'd go home
supperless and feasted,' said he.   ' And that 's not saying
much among the hordes of hungry troopers tip-toe for the
signal to the buffet.   See, my lady, the gentleman, as we
call him ;  there he is working his gamut perpetually up
to da capo.   Oh !  but it 's a sheep trying to be wolf ;
he 's sheep-eyed and he 's wolf-fanged, pathetic and
larcenous !  Oh, now !  who 'd believe it !—the man has
dared . . . I 'd as soon think of committing sacrilege
in a cathedral ! '

The man was actually, to quote his indignant rival,
' breaching the fortress,' and pointing out to Diana Merion
' her name on his dirty scrap of paper ' :  a shocking sight
when the lady's recollection was the sole point to be
aimed at, and the only umpire.   ' As if all of us couldn't
have written that, and hadn't done it ! '   Mr. Sullivan
Smith groaned disgusted.   He hated bad manners, particularly in cases involving ladies ;  and the bad manners
of a Saxon fired his antagonism to the race ;  individual
members of which he boasted of forgiving and embracing,
honouring.   So the man blackened the race for him, and
the race was excused in the man.   But his hatred of bad
manners was vehement, and would have extended to a
fellow-countryman.   His own were of the antecedent
century, therefore venerable.

Diana turned from her pursuer with a comic woeful

lifting of the brows at her friend.  Lady Dunstane
motioned her fan, and Diana came, bending head.

' Are you bound in honour ? '

' I don't think I am.  And I do want to go on talking
with the General.  He is so delightful and modest—my
dream of a true soldier !—telling me of his last big battle,
bit by bit, to my fishing.'

' Put off this person for a square dance down the list,
and take out Mr. Redworth—Miss Diana Merion, Mr. Redworth : he will bring you back to the General, who must
not totally absorb you, or he will forfeit his popularity.'

Diana instantly struck a treaty with the pertinacious
advocate of his claims, to whom, on his relinquishing her,
Mr. Sullivan Smith remarked : ' Oh ! sir, the law of it,
where a lady 's concerned !  You 're one for evictions, I
should guess, and the anti-human process.  It 's that
letter of the law that stands between you and me and
mine and yours.  But you 've got your congee, and my
blessing on ye ! '

' It was a positive engagement,' said the enemy.

Mr. Sullivan Smith derided him.  ' And a pretty
partner you 've pickled for yourself when she keeps her
positive engagement ! '

He besought Lady Dunstane to console him with a
turn.  She pleaded weariness.  He proposed to sit beside
her and divert her.  She smiled, but warned him that
she was English in every vein.  He interjected : ' Irish
men and English women ! though it 's putting the cart
before the horse—the copper pennies where the gold
guineas should be.  So here 's the gentleman who takes
the oyster, like the lawyer of the fable.  English is he ?
But we read, the last shall be first.  And English women
and Irish men make the finest coupling in the universe.'

' Well, you must submit to see an Irish woman led out
by an English man,' said Lady Dunstane, at the same

time informing the obedient Diana, then bestowing her
hand on Mr. Redworth to please her friend, that he was a
schoolfellow of her husband's.

' Favour can't help coming by rotation, except in very
extraordinary circumstances, and he was ahead of me
with you, and takes my due, and 'twould be hard on me
if I weren't thoroughly indemnified.'   Mr. Sullivan Smith
bowed.   ' You gave them just the start over the frozen
minute for conversation ;  they were total strangers, and
he doesn't appear a bad sort of fellow for a temporary
mate, though he 's not perfectly sure of his legs.   And
that we 'll excuse to any man leading out such a fresh
young beauty of a Bright Eyes—like the stars of a
winter's night in the frosty season over Columkill, or
where you will, so that 's in Ireland, to be sure of the
likeness to her.'

' Her mother was half English.'

' Of course she was.   And what was my observation
about the coupling ?   Dan Merion would make her Irish
all over.   And she has a vein of Spanish blood in her ;
for he had ;  and she 's got the colour.—But you spoke of
their coupling—or I did.   Oh, a man can hold his own
with an English roly-poly mate : he 's not stifled !   But
a woman hasn't his power of resistance to dead weight.
She 's volatile, she 's frivolous, a rattler and gabbler—
haven't I heard what they say of Irish girls over there ?
She marries, and it 's the end of her sparkling.   She must
choose at home for a perfect harmonious partner.'

Lady Dunstane expressed her opinion that her couple
danced excellently together.

' It 'd be a bitter thing to see, if the fellow couldn't
dance, after leading her out ! ' sighed Mr. Sullivan Smith.
' I heard of her over there.   They call her the Black Pearl,
and the Irish Lily—because she 's dark.   They rack their
poor brains to get the laugh of us.'

' And I listen to you,' said Lady Dunstane.

' Ah ! if all England, half, a quarter, the smallest piece of the land were like you, my lady, I 'd be loyal to the finger-nails. Now, is she engaged ?—when I get a word with her ? '

' She is nineteen, or nearly, and she ought to have five good years of freedom, I think.'

' And five good years of serfdom I 'd serve to win her ! '

A look at him under the eyelids assured Lady Dunstane that there would be small chance for Mr. Sullivan Smith, after a life of bondage, if she knew her Diana, in spite of his tongue, his tact, his lively features, and breadth of shoulders.

Up he sprang. Diana was on Mr. Redworth's arm. ' No refreshments,' she said ; and ' this is my refreshment,' taking the seat of Mr. Sullivan Smith, who ejaculated,

' I must go and have that gentleman's name.' He wanted a foe.

' You know you are ready to coquette with the General at any moment, Tony,' said her friend.

' Yes, with the General ! '

' He is a noble old man.'

' Superb. And don't say " old man." With his uniform and his height and his grey head, he is like a glorious October day just before the brown leaves fall.'

Diana hummed a little of the air of Planxty Kelly, the favourite of her childhood, as Lady Dunstane well remembered, and they smiled together at the scenes and times it recalled.

' Do you still write verses, Tony ? '

' I could about him. At one part of the fight he thought he would be beaten. He was overmatched in artillery, and it was a cavalry charge he thundered on them, riding across the field to give the word of command to the couple of regiments, riddled to threads, that gained the day.   That is life—when we dare death to live !   I wonder at men, who are *men*, being anything but soldiers !   I told you, madre, my own Emmy, I forgave you for marrying, because it was a soldier.'

'Perhaps a soldier is to be the happy man.   But you have not told me a word of yourself.   What has been done with the old Crossways ? '

'The house, you know, is mine.   And it's all I have : ten acres and the house, furnished, and let for less than two hundred a year.   Oh ! how I long to evict the tenants !   They can't have my feeling for the place where I was born.   They're people of tolerably good connections, middling wealthy, I suppose, of the name of Warwick, and, as far as I can understand, they stick there to be near the Sussex Downs, for a nephew, who likes to ride on them.   I've a half engagement, barely legible, to visit them on an indefinite day, and can't bear the idea of strangers masters in the old house.   I must be driven there for shelter, for a roof, some month.   And I could make a pilgrimage in rain or snow just to doat on the outside of it.   That's your Tony.'

'She's my darling.'

'I hear myself speak !   But your voice or mine, madre, it's one soul.   Be sure I am giving up the ghost when I cease to be one soul with you, dear and dearest !   No secrets, never a shadow of a deception, or else I shall feel I am not fit to live.   Was I a bad correspondent when you were in India ? '

'Pretty well.   Copious letters when you did write.'

'I was shy.   I knew I should be writing to Emmy and *another*, and only when I came to the flow could I forget him.   He is very finely built ; and I dare say he has a head.   I read of his deeds in India and quivered.   But he was just a bit in the way.   Men are the barriers to perfect naturalness, at least, with girls, I think. You wrote to me in the same tone as ever, and at first I had a struggle to reply. And I, who have such pride in being always myself ! '

Two staring semi-circles had formed, one to front the Hero, the other the Beauty. These half moons imperceptibly dissolved to replenish, and became a fixed obstruction.

' Yes, they look,' Diana made answer to Lady Dunstane's comment on the curious impertinence. She was getting used to it, and her friend had a gratification in seeing how little this affected her perfect naturalness.

' You are often in the world—dinners, dances ? ' she said.

' People are kind.'

' Any proposals ? '

' Nibbles.'

' Quite heart-free ? '

' Absolutely.'

Diana's unshadowed bright face defied all menace of an eclipse.

The block of sturdy gazers began to melt. The General had dispersed his group of satellites by a movement with the Mayoress on his arm, construed as the signal for procession to the supper-table.


## CHAPTER III

### THE INTERIOR OF MR. REDWORTH AND THE EXTERIOR OF MR. SULLIVAN SMITH

' It may be as well to take Mr. Redworth's arm ; you will escape the crush for you,' said Lady Dunstane to Diana. ' I don't sup. Yes ! go ! You must eat, and he is handiest to conduct you.'

Diana thought of her chaperon and the lateness of the hour. She murmured, to soften her conscience, ' Poor Mrs. Pettigrew ! '

And once more Mr. Redworth, outwardly imperturbable, was in the maëlstrom of a happiness resembling tempest. He talked, and knew not what he uttered. To give this matchless girl the best to eat and drink was his business, and he performed it. Oddly, for a man who had no loaded design, marshalling the troops in his active and capacious cranium, he fell upon calculations of his income, present and prospective, while she sat at the table and he stood behind her. Others were wrangling for places, chairs, plates, glasses, game-pie, champagne : she had them ; the lady under his charge to a certainty would have them ; so far good ; and he had seven hundred pounds per annum—seven hundred and fifty, in a favourable aspect, at a stretch. . . .

' Yes, the pleasantest thing to me after working all day is an opera of Carini's,' she said, in full accord with her taste, ' and Tellio for tenor, certainly.'

—A fair enough sum for a bachelor : four hundred personal income, and a prospect of higher dividends to increase it ; three hundred odd from his office, and no immediate prospects of an increase there ; no one died there, no elderly martyr for the advancement of his juniors could be persuaded to die ; they were too tough to think of retiring. Say, seven hundred and fifty . . . eight hundred, if the commerce of the country fortified the Bank his property was embarked in ; or eight-fifty : or nine, ten. . . .

' I could call him my poet also,' Mr. Redworth agreed with her taste in poets. ' His letters are among the best ever written—or ever published : the raciest English I know. Frank, straight out : capital descriptions. The best English letter-writers are as good as the French—

You don't think so ?—in their way, of course. I dare
say we don't sufficiently cultivate the art. We require
the supple tongue a closer intercourse of society gives.'

—Eight or ten hundred. Comfortable enough for a
man in chambers. To dream of entering as a householder on that sum, in these days, would be stark nonsense : and a man two removes from a baronetcy has no
right to set his reckoning on deaths :—if he does, he
becomes a sort of meditative assassin. But what were
the Fates about when they planted a man of the ability
of Tom Redworth in a Government office ! Clearly they
intended him to remain a bachelor for life. And they sent
him over to Ireland on inspection duty for a month to
have sight of an Irish Beauty. . . .

'Think war the finest subject for poets ? ' he exclaimed. 'Flatly no : I don't think it. I think exactly
the reverse. It brings out the noblest traits in human
character ? I won't own that even. It brings out some :
but under excitement, when you have not always the real
man.—Pray don't sneer at domestic life. Well, there
was a suspicion of disdain.—Yes, I can respect the hero,
military or civil ; with this distinction, that the military
hero aims at personal reward—'

'He braves wounds and death,' interposed Diana.

'Whereas the civilian hero—'

'Pardon me, let me deny that the soldier-hero aims at
a personal reward,' she again interposed.

'He gets it.'

'If he is not beaten.'

'And then he is no longer a hero.'

'He is to me.'

She had a woman's inveterate admiration of the profession of arms. Mr. Redworth endeavoured to render practicable an opening in her mind to reason. He admitted
the grandeur of the poetry of Homer. We are a few

centuries in advance of Homer. We do not slay damsels for
a sacrifice to propitiate celestial wrath ; nor do we revel in
details of slaughter. He reasoned with her ; he repeated
stories known to him of civilian heroes, and won her assent
to the heroical title for their deeds, but it was languid, or
not so bright as the deeds deserved—or as the young lady
could look ; and he insisted on the civilian hero, impelled
by some unconscious motive to make her see the thing
he thought, also the thing he was—his plain mind and
matter-of-fact nature. Possibly she caught a glimpse of
that. After a turn of fencing, in which he was impressed
by the vibration of her tones when speaking of military
heroes, she quitted the table, saying : ' An argument between one at supper and another handing plates, is rather
unequal if eloquence is needed. As Pat said to the constable when his hands were tied, You beat me with the
fists, but my spirit is towering and kicks freely.'

—Eight hundred ? a thousand a year, two thousand,
are as nothing in the calculation of a householder who
means that the mistress of the house shall have the
choicest of the fruits and flowers of the Four Quarters ;
and Thomas Redworth had vowed at his first outlook on
the world of women, that never should one of the sisterhood coming under his charge complain of not having
them in profusion. Consequently he was a settled
bachelor. In the character of disengaged and unaspiring
philosophical bachelor, he reviewed the revelations of
her character betrayed by the beautiful virgin devoted
to the sanguine coat. The thrill of her voice in speaking
of soldier-heroes shot him to the yonder side of a gulf.
Not knowing why, for he had no scheme, desperate or
other, in his head, the least affrighted of men was frightened by her tastes, and by her aplomb, her inoffensiveness
in freedom of manner and self-sufficiency—sign of purest
breeding : and by her easy, peerless vivacity, her proofs

of descent from the blood of Dan Merion—a wildish
blood.  The candour of the look of her eyes in speaking,
her power of looking forthright at men, and looking the
thing she spoke, and the play of her voluble lips, the
significant repose of her lips in silence, her weighing of the
words he uttered, for a moment before the prompt appo-
site reply, down to her simple quotation of Pat, alarmed
him ;  he did not ask himself why.  His manly self was
not intruded on his cogitations.  A mere eight hundred
or thousand per annum had no place in that midst.  He
beheld her quietly selecting the position of dignity to suit
her : an eminent military man, or statesman, or wealthy
nobleman : she had but to choose.  A war would offer
her the decorated soldier she wanted.  A war !  Such
are women of this kind !  The thought revolted him, and
pricked his appetite for supper.  He did service by Mrs.
Pettigrew, to which lady Miss Merion, as she said, pro-
moted him, at the table, and then began to refresh in
person, standing.

'Malkin ! that 's the fellow's name ' ; he heard close
at his ear.

Mr. Sullivan Smith had drained a champagne-glass,
bottle in hand, and was priming the successor to it.  He
cocked his eye at Mr. Redworth's quick stare.  'Malkin !
And now we 'll see whether the interior of him is grey,
or black, or tabby, or tortoise-shell, or any other colour
of the Malkin breed.'

He explained to Mr. Redworth that he had summoned
Mr. Malkin to answer to him as a gentleman for calling
Miss Merion a jilt.  'The man, sir, said in my hearing,
she jilted him, and that 's to call the lady a jilt.  There 's
not a point of difference, not a shade.  I overheard him.
I happened by the blessing of Providence to be by when
he named her publicly jilt.  And it 's enough that she 's a
lady to have me for her champion.  The same if she had

been an Esquimaux squaw. I 'll never live to hear a
lady insulted.'

' You don't mean to say you 're the donkey to provoke
a duel ! ' Mr. Redworth burst out gruffly, through turkey
and stuffing.

' And an Irish lady, the young Beauty of Erin ! ' Mr.
Sullivan Smith was flowing on. He became frigid, he
politely bowed : ' Two, sir, if you haven't the grace to
withdraw the offensive term before it cools and can't be
obliterated.'

' Fiddle ! and go to the deuce ! ' Mr. Redworth cried.

' Would a soft slap o' the cheek persuade you, sir ? '

' Try it outside, and don't bother me with nonsense of
that sort at my supper. If I 'm struck, I strike back. I
keep my pistols for bandits and law-breakers. Here,'
said Mr. Redworth, better inspired as to the way of treating an ultra of the isle ; ' touch glasses : you 're a gentleman, and won't disturb good company. By-and-by.'

The pleasing prospect of by-and-by renewed in Mr.
Sullivan Smith his composure. They touched the foam-
ing glasses : upon which, in a friendly manner, Mr. Sullivan Smith proposed that they should go outside as soon
as Mr. Redworth had finished supper—*quite* finished
supper : for the reason that the term ' donkey ' affixed
to him was like a minster cap of schooldays, ringing bells
on his topknot, and also that it stuck in his gizzard.

Mr. Redworth declared the term to be simply hypo-
thetical. ' *If* you fight, you 're a donkey for doing it.
But you won't fight.'

' But I will fight.'

' He won't fight.'

' Then for the honour of your country you must. But
I 'd rather have him first, for I haven't drunk with him,
and it should be a case of necessity to put a bullet or a
couple of inches of steel through the man you 've drunk

with. And what 's in your favour, she danced with ye. She seemed to take to ye, and the man she has the smallest sugar-melting for is sacred if he 's not sweet to me. *If* he retracts ! '

' Hypothetically, No.'

' But supposititiously ? '

' Certainly.'

' Then we grasp hands on it. It 's Malkin or nothing ! ' said Mr. Sullivan Smith, swinging his heel moodily to wander in search of the foe. How one sane man could name another a donkey for fighting to clear an innocent young lady's reputation, passed his rational conception.

Sir Lukin hastened to Mr. Redworth to have a talk over old schooldays and fellows.

' I 'll tell you what,' said the civilian, ' There are Irishmen and Irishmen. I 've met cool heads and long heads among them, and you and I knew Jack Derry, who was good at most things. But the burlesque Irishman can't be caricatured. Nature strained herself in a fit of absurdity to produce him, and all that Art can do is to copy.'

This was his prelude to an account of Mr. Sullivan Smith, whom, as a specimen, he rejoiced to have met.

' There 's a chance of mischief,' said Sir Lukin. ' I know nothing of the man he calls Malkin. I 'll inquire presently.'

He talked of his prospects, and of the women. Fair ones, in his opinion, besides Miss Merion were parading ; he sketched two or three of his partners with a broad brush of epithets.

' It won't do for Miss Merion's name to be mixed up in a duel,' said Redworth.

' Not if she 's to make her fortune in England,' said Sir Lukin. ' It 's probably all smoke.'

The remark had hardly escaped him when a wreath of

metaphorical smoke, and fire, and no mean report,
startled the company of supping gentlemen. At the
pitch of his voice, Mr. Sullivan Smith denounced Mr.
Malkin in presence for a cur masquerading as a cat.

'And that is not the scoundrel's prime offence. For
what d'ye think? He trumps up an engagement to
dance with a beautiful lady, and because she can't remember, binds her to an oath for a dance to come, and
then, holding her prisoner to 'm, he sulks, the dirty dog-
cat goes and sulks, and he won't dance and won't do
anything but screech up in corners that he's jilted. He
said the word. Dozens of gentlemen heard the word.
And I demand an apology of Misterr Malkin—*or* . . !
And none of your guerrier nodding and bravado, Mister
Malkin, at me, if you please. The case is for settlement
between gentlemen.'

The harassed gentleman of the name of Malkin, driven
to extremity by the worrying, stood in braced preparation
for the English attitude of defence. His tormentor drew
closer to him.

'Mind, I give you warning, if you lay a finger on me
I'll knock you down,' said he.

Most joyfully Mr. Sullivan Smith uttered a low melodious cry. 'For a specimen of manners, in an assembly
of ladies and gentlemen . . . I ask ye!' he addressed
the ring about him, to put his adversary entirely in the
wrong before provoking the act of war. And then, as
one intending gently to remonstrate, he was on the point
of stretching out his finger to the shoulder of Mr. Malkin,
when Redworth seized his arm, saying: 'I'm your man:
me first: you're due to me.'

Mr. Sullivan Smith beheld the vanishing of his foe in a
cloud of faces. Now was he wroth on patently reasonable
grounds. He threatened Saxondom. Man up, man
down, he challenged the race of short-legged, thickset,

wooden-pated curmudgeons : and let it be pugilism if
their white livers shivered at the notion of powder and
ball. Redworth, in the struggle to haul him away, received a blow from him. 'And you 've got it ! you
would have it ! ' roared the Celt.

'Excuse yourself to the company for a misdirected
effort,' Redworth said ; and he observed generally : ' No
Irish gentleman strikes a blow in good company.'

'But that 's true as Writ ! And I offer excuses—if
you 'll come along with me and a couple of friends.
The thing has been done before by torchlight—and
neatly.'

'Come along, and come alone,' said Redworth.

A way was cleared for them. Sir Lukin hurried up to
Redworth, who had no doubt of his ability to manage
Mr. Sullivan Smith.

He managed that fine-hearted but purely sensational
fellow so well that Lady Dunstane and Diana, after hearing in some anxiety of the hubbub below, beheld them
entering the long saloon amicably, with the nods and
looks of gentlemen quietly accordant.

A little later, Lady Dunstane questioned Redworth,
and he smoothed her apprehensions, delivering himself,
much to her comfort, thus : ' In no case would any lady's
name have been raised. The whole affair was nonsensical.
He 's a capital fellow of a kind, capable of behaving like
a man of the world and a gentleman. Only he has, or
thinks he has, like lots of his countrymen, a raw wound
—something that itches to be grazed. Champagne on
that ! . . . Irishmen, as far as I have seen of them, are,
like horses, bundles of nerves ; and you must manage
them, as you do with all nervous creatures, with firmness,
but good temper. You must never get into a fury of the
nerves yourself with them. Spur and whip they don't
want ; they 'll be off with you in a jiffy if you try it.

They want the bridle-rein. That seems to me the secret of Irish character. We English are not bad horsemen. It 's a wonder we blunder so in our management of such a people.'

' I wish you were in a position to put your method to the proof,' said she.

He shrugged. ' There 's little chance of it ! '

To reward him for his practical discretion, she contrived that Diana should give him a final dance ; and the beautiful girl smiled quickly responsive to his appeal. He was, moreover, sensible in her look and speech that he had advanced in her consideration to be no longer the mere spinning stick, a young lady's partner. By which he humbly understood that her friend approved him. A gentle delirium enfolded his brain. A householder's life is often begun on eight hundred a year : on less : on much less :—sometimes on nothing but resolution to make a fitting income, carving out a fortune. Eight hundred may stand as a superior basis. That sum is a distinct point of vantage. If it does not mean a carriage and Parisian millinery and a station for one of the stars of society, it means at any rate security ; and then, the heart of the man being strong and sound . . .

' Yes,' he replied to her, ' I like my experience of Ireland and the Irish ; and better than I thought I should. St. George's Channel ought to be crossed oftener by both of us.'

' I 'm always glad of the signal,' said Diana.

He had implied the people of the two islands. He allowed her interpretation to remain personal, for the sake of a creeping deliciousness that it carried through his blood.

' Shall you soon be returning to England ? ' he ventured to ask.

' I am Lady Dunstane's guest for some months.'

' Then you will.  Sir Lukin has an estate in Surrey.
He talks of quitting the Service.'

' I can't believe it ! '

His thrilled blood was chilled.  She entertained a
sentiment amounting to adoration for the profession of
arms !

Gallantly had the veteran General and Hero held on
into the night, that the festivity might not be dashed by
his departure ; perhaps, to a certain degree, to prolong
his enjoyment of a flattering scene.  At last Sir Lukin
had the word from him, and came to his wife.  Diana
slipped across the floor to her accommodating chaperon,
whom, for the sake of another five minutes with her
beloved Emma, she very agreeably persuaded to walk
in the train of Lord Larrian, and forth they trooped down
a pathway of nodding heads and curtsies, resembling oak
and birch-trees under a tempered gale, even to the shed-
ding of leaves, for here a turban was picked up by Sir
Lukin, there a jewelled ear-ring by the self-constituted
attendant, Mr. Thomas Redworth.  At the portico rang
a wakening cheer, really worth hearing.  The rain it
rained, and hats were formless, as in the first conception of the edifice, backs were damp, boots liquidly
musical, the pipe of consolation smoked with difficulty,
with much pulling at the stem, but the cheer arose magnificently, and multiplied itself, touching at the same
moment the heavens and Diana's heart—at least, drawing
them together ; for she felt exalted, enraptured, as proud
of her countrymen as of their hero.

' That 's the natural shamrock, after the artificial ! '
she heard Mr. Redworth say, behind her.

She turned and sent one of her brilliant glances flying
over him, in gratitude for a timely word well said.  And
she never forgot the remark, nor he the look.

## CHAPTER IV

CONTAINING HINTS OF DIANA'S EXPERIENCES AND OF ·
WHAT THEY LED TO

A FORTNIGHT after this memorable Ball the principal
actors of both sexes had crossed the Channel back to England, and old Ireland was left to her rains from above and
her undrained bogs below ; her physical and her mental
vapours ; her ailments and her bog-bred doctors ; as to
whom the governing country trusted they would be silent
or discourse humorously.

The residence of Sir Lukin Dunstane, in the county of
Surrey, inherited by him during his recent term of Indian
services, was on the hills, where a day of Italian sky, or
better, a day of our breezy South-west, washed from the
showery night, gives distantly a tower to view, and a
murky web, not without colour : the ever-flying banner
of the metropolis, the smoke of the city's chimneys, if
you prefer plain language.  At a first inspection of the
house, Lady Dunstane did not like it, and it was advertized to be let, and the auctioneer proclaimed it in his
dialect.  Her taste was delicate ; she had the sensitiveness of an invalid : twice she read the stalking advertize-
ment of the attractions of Copsley, and hearing Diana
call it ' the plush of speech,' she shuddered ; she decided
that a place where her husband's family had lived ought
not to stand forth meretriciously spangled and daubed,
like a show-booth at a fair, for a bait ; though the grand-
iloquent man of advertizing letters assured Sir Lukin
that a public agape for the big and gaudy mouthful is in
no milder way to be caught ; as it is apparently the case.
She withdrew the trumpeting placard.  Retract we like-

wise ' banner of the metropolis.' That plush of speech
haunts all efforts to swell and illuminate citizen prose
to a princely poetic.

Yet Lady Dunstane herself could name the bank of
smoke, when looking North-eastward from her summer-
house, the flag of London : and she was a person of the
critical mind, well able to distinguish between the simple
metaphor and the superobese. A year of habitation induced her to conceal her dislike of the place in love : cat's
love, she owned. Here, she confessed to Diana, she would
wish to live to her end. It seemed remote, where an
invigorating upper air gave new bloom to her cheeks ;
but she kept one secret from her friend.

Copsley was an estate of nearly twelve hundred acres,
extending across the ridge of the hills to the slopes North
and South. Seven counties rolled their backs under this
commanding height, and it would have tasked a pigeon to
fly within an hour the stretch of country visible at the
Copsley windows. Sunrise to right, sunset leftward, the
borders of the grounds held both flaming horizons. So
much of the heavens and of earth is rarely granted to a
dwelling. The drawback was the structure, which had no
charm, scarce a face. ' It is written that I should live in
barracks,' Lady Dunstane said. The colour of it taught
white to impose a sense of gloom. Her cat's love of the
familiar inside corners was never able to embrace the
outer walls. Her sensitiveness, too, was racked by the
presentation of so pitiably ugly a figure to the landscape.
She likened it to a coarse-featured country wench, whose
cleaning and decorating of her countenance makes complexion grin and ruggedness yawn. Dirty, dilapidated,
hung with weeds and parasites, it would have been more
tolerable. She tried the effect of various creepers, and
they were as a staring paint. What it was like then, she
had no heart to say.

One may, however, fall on a pleasureable resignation in accepting great indemnities, as Diana bade her believe, when the first disgust began to ebb. ' A good hundred over there would think it a Paradise for an asylum ' : she signified London. Her friend bore such reminders meekly. They were readers of books of all sorts, political, philosophical, economical, romantic ; and they mixed the diverse readings in thought, after the fashion of the ardently youthful. Romance affected politics, trans- formed economy, irradiated philosophy. They discussed the knotty question, Why things were not *done*, the things being confessedly to do ; and they cut the knot. Men, men calling themselves statesmen, declined to perform that operation, because, forsooth, other men objected to have it performed on them. And common humanity declared it to be for the common weal ! If so, then it is clearly indicated as a course of action : we shut our eyes against logic and the vaunted laws of economy. They are the knot we cut ; or would cut, had we the sword. Diana did it to the tune of Garryowen or Planxty Kelly. O for a despot ! The cry was for a beneficent despot, naturally : a large-minded benevolent despot. In short, a despot to obey their bidding. Thoughtful young people who think through the heart soon come to this conclusion. The heart is the beneficent despot they would be. He cures those miseries ; he creates the novel harmony. He sees all difficulties through his own sanguine hues. He is the musical poet of the problem, demanding merely to have it solved that he may sing : clear proof of the necessity for solving it immediately.

Thus far in their pursuit of methods for the govern- ment of a nation, to make it happy, Diana was leader. Her fine ardour and resonance, and more than the con- vincing ring of her voice, the girl's impassioned rapidity in rushing through any perceptible avenue of the labyrinth, or beating down obstacles to form one, and coming swiftly to *some* solution, constituted her the chief of the pair of democratic rebels in questions that clamoured for instant solution. By dint of reading solid writers, using the brains they possessed, it was revealed to them gradually that their particular impatience came perhaps of the most earnest desire to get to a comfortable termination of the inquiry :—the heart aching for mankind sought a nest for itself. At this point Lady Dunstane took the lead. Diana had to be tugged to follow. She could not accept a ' perhaps ' that cast dubiousness on her disinterested championship. She protested a perfect certainty of the single aim of her heart outward. But she reflected. She discovered that her friend had gone ahead of her.

The discovery was reached, and even acknowledged, before she could persuade herself to swallow the repulsive truth. O self ! self ! self ! are we eternally masking in a domino that reveals your hideous old face when we could be most positive we had escaped you ? Eternally ! the desolating answer knelled. Nevertheless the poor, the starving, the overtaxed in labour, *they* have a right to the cry of Now ! now ! They have ; and if a cry could conduct us to the secret of aiding, healing, feeding, elevating them, we might swell the cry. As it is, we must lay it on our wits patiently to track and find the secret ; and meantime do what the individual with his poor pittance can. A miserable contribution ! sighed the girl. Old Self was perceived in the sigh. She was haunted.

After all, one must live one's life. Placing her on a lower pedestal in her self-esteem, the philosophy of youth revived her ; and if the abatement of her personal pride was dispiriting, she began to see an advantage in getting inward eyes.

' It 's infinitely better I should know it, Emmy—I 'm

a reptile ! Pleasure here, pleasure there, I 'm always
thinking of pleasure. I shall give up thinking and take
to drifting. Neither of us can do more than open purses ;
and mine 's lean. If the old Crossways had no tenant, it
would be a purse all mouth. And charity is haunted, like
everything we do. Only I say with my whole strength
—yes, I am sure, in spite of the men professing that they
are practical, the rich will not move without a goad. I
have and hold—you shall hunger and covet, until you
are strong enough to force my hand :—that 's the speech
of the wealthy. And they are Christians. In name.
Well, I thank heaven I 'm at war with myself.'

' You always manage to strike out a sentence worth
remembering, Tony,' said Lady Dunstane. ' At war with
ourselves, means the best happiness we can have.'

It suited her, frail as her health was, and her wisdom
striving to the spiritual of happiness. War with herself
was far from happiness in the bosom of Diana. She
wanted external life, action, fields for energies, to vary the
struggle. It fretted and rendered her ill at ease. In her
solitary rides with Sir Lukin through a long winter season,
she appalled that excellent but conventionally-minded
gentleman by starting, nay supporting, theories next to
profane in the consideration of a land-owner. She spoke
of Reform : of the Repeal of the Corn Laws as the simple
beginning of the grants due to the people. She had her
ideas, of course, from that fellow Redworth, an occasional
visitor at Copsley ; and a man might be a donkey and
think what he pleased, since he had a vocabulary to
back his opinions. A woman, Sir Lukin held, was by
nature a mute in politics. Of the thing called a Radical
woman, he could not believe that she was less than monstrous : ' with a nose,' he said ; and doubtless, horse
teeth, hatchet jaws, slatternly in the gown, slipshod,
awful. As for a girl, an unmarried, handsome girl, ad-

mittedly beautiful, her interjections, echoing a man, were
ridiculous, and not a little annoying now and then, for
she could be piercingly sarcastic. Her vocabulary in
irony was a quiverful. He admired her and liked her
immensely ; complaining only of her turn for unfeminine
topics. He pardoned her on the score of the petty difference rankling between them in reference to his abandonment of his Profession, for here she was patriotically
wrong-headed. Everybody knew that he had sold out
in order to look after his estates of Copsley and Dunena,
secondly : and in the first place, to nurse and be a companion to his wife. He had left her but four times in
five months ; he had spent just three weeks of that time
away from her in London. No one could doubt of his
having kept his pledge, although his wife occupied herself with books and notions and subjects foreign to his
taste—his understanding, too, he owned. And Redworth had approved of his retirement, had a contempt
for soldiering. ' Quite as great as yours for civilians, I
can tell you,' Sir Lukin said, dashing out of politics to
the vexatious personal subject. Her unexpressed disdain
was ruffling.

' Mr. Redworth recommends work : he respects the
working soldier,' said Diana.

Sir Lukin exclaimed that he had been a working
soldier ; he was ready to serve if his country wanted him.
He directed her to anathematize Peace, instead of scorning a fellow for doing the duties next about him : and the
mention of Peace fetched him at a bound back to politics.
He quoted a distinguished Tory orator, to the effect,
that any lengthened term of peace bred maggots in the
heads of the people.

' Mr. Redworth spoke of it : he translated something
from Aristophanes for a retort,' said Diana.

' Well, we 're friends, eh ? ' Sir Lukin put forth a hand.

She looked at him surprised at the unnecessary call for
a show of friendship ; she touched his hand with two tips
of her fingers, remarking, ' I should think so, indeed.'

He deemed it prudent to hint to his wife that Diana
Merion appeared to be meditating upon Mr. Redworth.

' That is a serious misfortune, if true,' said Lady
Dunstane. She thought so for two reasons : Mr. Redworth generally disagreed in opinion with Diana, and
contradicted her so flatly as to produce the impression of
his not even sharing the popular admiration of her beauty ;
and, further, she hoped for Diana to make a splendid
marriage. The nibbles threatened to be snaps and bites.
There had been a proposal, in an epistle, a quaint effusion,
from a gentleman avowing that he had seen her and had
*not* danced with her on the night of the Irish ball. He
was rejected, but Diana groaned over the task of replying
to the unfortunate applicant, so as not to wound him.
' Shall I have to do this often, I wonder ? ' she said.

' Unless you capitulate,' said her friend.

Diana's exclamation : ' May I be heart-free for another
ten years ! ' encouraged Lady Dunstane to suppose her
husband quite mistaken.

In the Spring Diana went on a first pilgrimage to her
old home, The Crossways, and was kindly entertained by
the uncle and aunt of a treasured nephew, Mr. Augustus
Warwick. She rode with him on the Downs. A visit of
a week humanized her view of the intruders. She wrote
almost tenderly of her host and hostess to Lady Dunstane ;
they had but ' the one fault of spoiling their nephew.'
Him she described as a ' gentlemanly official,' a picture of
him. His age was thirty-four. He seemed ' fond of her
scenery.' Then her pen swept over the Downs like a
flying horse. Lady Dunstane thought no more of the
gentlemanly official. He was a barrister who did not
practise : in nothing the man for Diana. Letters came

from the house of the Pettigrews in Kent ; from London ; from Halford Manor in Hertfordshire ; from Lockton Grange in Lincolnshire : after which they ceased to be the thrice weekly ; and reading the latest of them, Lady Dunstane imagined a flustered quill. The letter succeeding the omission contained no excuse, and it was brief. There was a strange interjection, as to the wearifulness of constantly wandering, like a leaf off the tree. Diana spoke of looking for a return of the dear winter days at Copsley. That was her station. Either she must have had some disturbing experience, or Copsley was dear for a Redworth reason, thought the anxious peruser ; musing, dreaming, putting together divers shreds of correspondence and testing them with her intimate knowledge of Diana's character, Lady Dunstane conceived that the unprotected beautiful girl had suffered a persecution, it might be an insult. She spelt over the names of the guests at the houses. Lord Wroxeter was of evil report : Captain Rampan, a Turf captain, had the like notoriety. And it is impossible in a great house for the hostess to spread her ægis to cover every dame and damsel present. She has to depend on the women being discreet, the men civilized.

'How brutal men can be !' was one of Diana's incidental remarks, in a subsequent letter, relating simply to masculine habits. In those days the famous ancestral plea of ' the passion for his charmer ' had not been altogether socially quashed down among the provinces, where the bottle maintained a sort of sway, and the beauty which inflamed the sons of men was held to be in coy expectation of violent effects upon their boiling blood. There were, one hears that there still are, remnants of the pristine male, who, if resisted in their suing, conclude that they are scorned, and it infuriates them : some also whose ' passion for the charmer ' is an instinct to pull

down the standard of the sex, by a bully imposition of
sheer physical ascendancy, whenever they see it flying
with an air of gallant independence : and some who
dedicate their lives to a study of the arts of the Lord of
Reptiles, until they have worked the crisis for a display
of him in person. Assault or siege, they have achieved
their triumphs ; they have dominated a frailer system of
nerves, and a young woman without father, or brother,
or husband, to defend her, is cryingly a weak one, therefore inviting to such an order of heroes. Lady Dunstane
was quick-witted and had a talkative husband ; she knew
a little of the upper social world of her time. She was
heartily glad to have Diana by her side again.

Not a word of any serious experience was uttered.
Only on one occasion while they conversed, something
being mentioned of her tolerance, a flush of swarthy
crimson shot over Diana, and she frowned, with the outcry, ' Oh ! I have discovered that I can be a tigress ! '

Her friend pressed her hand, saying, ' The cause a good
one ! '

' Women have to fight.'

Diana said no more. There had been a bad experience
of her isolated position in the world.

Lady Dunstane now indulged a partial hope that Mr.
Redworth might see in this unprotected beautiful girl a
person worthy of his esteem. He had his opportunities,
and evidently he liked her. She appeared to take more
cordially to him. She valued the sterling nature of the
man. But they were a hopeless couple, they were so
friendly. Both ladies noticed in him an abstractedness
of look, often when conversing, as of a man in calculation ;
they put it down to an ambitious mind. Yet Diana said
then, and said always, that it was he who had first taught
her the art of observing. On the whole, the brilliant marriage seemed a fairer prospect for her ; how reasonable to

anticipate, Lady Dunstane often thought when admiring the advance of Diana's beauty in queenliness, for never did woman carry her head more grandly, more thrillingly make her presence felt; and if only she had been an actress showing herself nightly on a London stage, she would before now have met the superb appreciation, melancholy to reflect upon!

Diana regained her happy composure at Copsley. She had, as she imagined, no ambition. The dulness of the place conveyed a charm to a nature recovering from disturbance to its clear smooth flow. Air, light, books, and her friend, these good things she had; they were all she wanted. She rode, she walked, with Sir Lukin or Mr. Redworth, for companion; or with Saturday and Sunday guests, Lord Larrian, her declared admirer, among them. ' Twenty years younger!' he said to her, shrugging, with a merry smile drawn a little at the corners to sober sourness; and she vowed to her friend that she would not have had the heart to refuse him. 'Though,' said she, ' speaking generally, I cannot tell you what a foreign animal a husband would appear in my kingdom.' Her experience had wakened a sexual aversion, of some slight kind, enough to make her feminine pride stipulate for perfect independence, that she might have the calm out of which imagination spreads wing. Imagination had become her broader life, and on such an earth, under such skies, a husband who is not the fountain of it, certainly is a foreign animal: he is a discordant note. He contracts the ethereal world, deadens radiancy. He is gross fact, a leash, a muzzle, harness, a hood, whatever is detestable to the free limbs and senses. It amused Lady Dunstane to hear Diana say, one evening when their conversation fell by hazard on her future, that the idea of a convent was more welcome to her than the most splendid marriage. 'For,' she added, ' as I am sure I

shall never know anything of this love they rattle about
and rave about, I shall do well to keep to my good single
path ; and I have a warning within me that a step out
of it will be a wrong one—for me, dearest ! '

She wished her view of the yoke to be considered purely
personal, drawn from no examples and comparisons.
The excellent Sir Lukin was passing a great deal of his
time in London.   His wife had not a word of blame for
him ;  he was a respectful husband, and attentive when
present ;  but so uncertain, owing to the sudden pressure
of engagements, that Diana, bound on a second visit to
The Crossways, doubted whether she would be able to
quit her friend, whose condition did not allow of her being
left solitary at Copsley.   He came nevertheless a day
before Diana's appointed departure on her round of visits.
She was pleased with him, and let him see it, for the
encouragement of a husband in the observance of his
duties.   One of the horses had fallen lame, so they went
out for a walk, at Lady Dunstane's request.   It was a
delicious afternoon of Spring, with the full red disk of sun
dropping behind the brown beech-twigs.   She remembered long afterward the sweet simpleness of her feelings
as she took in the scent of wild flowers along the lanes
and entered the woods—jaws of another monstrous and
blackening experience.   He fell into the sentimental vein,
and a man coming from that heated London life to these
glorified woods, might be excused for doing so, though
it sounded to her just a little ludicrous in him.   She
played tolerantly second to it ;  she quoted a snatch of
poetry, and his whole face was bent to her, with the
petition that she would repeat the verse.   Much struck
was this giant ex-dragoon.   Ah ! how fine ! grand !   He
would rather hear that than any opera : it was diviner !
' Yes, the best poetry is,' she assented.   ' On your lips,' he
said.   She laughed.   ' I am not a particularly melodious

reciter.' He vowed he could listen to her eternally, eternally. His face, on a screw of the neck and shoulders, was now perpetually three-quarters fronting. Ah! she was going to leave.—' Yes, and you will find my return quite early enough,' said Diana, stepping a trifle more briskly. His fist was raised on the length of the arm, as if in invocation. ' Not in the whole of London is there a woman worthy to fasten your shoe-buckles! My oath on it! I look; I can't spy one.' Such was his flattering eloquence.

She told him not to think it necessary to pay her compliments. ' And here, of all places! ' They were in the heart of the woods. She found her hand seized—her waist. Even then, so impossible is it to conceive the unimaginable even when the apparition of it smites us, she expected some protesting absurdity, or that he had seen something in her path.—What did she hear? And from her friend's husband!

If stricken idiotic, he was a gentleman; the tigress she had detected in her composition did not require to be called forth; half-a-dozen words, direct, sharp as fangs and teeth, with the eyes burning over them, sufficed for the work of defence.—' The man who swore loyalty to Emma!' Her reproachful repulsion of eyes was unmistakeable, withering; as masterful as a superior force on his muscles.—What thing had he been taking her for? —She asked it within: and he of himself, in a reflective gasp. Those eyes of hers appeared as in a cloud, with the wrath above: she had the look of a Goddess in anger. He stammered, pleaded across her flying shoulder—Oh! horrible, loathsome, pitiable to hear! . . . ' A momentary aberration . . . her beauty . . . he deserved to be shot! . . . could not help admiring . . . quite lost his head . . . on his honour! never again! '

Once in the roadway, and Copsley visible, she checked

her arrowy pace for breath, and almost commiserated the
dejected wretch in her thankfulness to him for silence.
Nothing exonerated him, but at least he had the grace
not to beg secresy. That would have been an intolerable
whine of a poltroon, adding to her humiliation. He
abstained ; he stood at her mercy without appealing.

She was not the woman to take poor vengeance. But,
Oh ! she was profoundly humiliated, shamed through and
through. The question, was I guilty of any lightness—
anything to bring this on me ? would not be laid. And
how she pitied her friend ! This house, her heart's home,
was now a wreck to her : nay, worse, a hostile citadel.
The burden of the task of meeting Emma with an open
face, crushed her like very guilt. Yet she succeeded.
After an hour in her bedchamber she managed to lock up
her heart and summon the sprite of acting to her tongue
and features : which ready attendant on the suffering
female host performed his liveliest throughout the evening, to Emma's amusement, and to the culprit ex-
dragoon's astonishment ; in whom, to tell the truth of
him, her sparkle and fun kindled the sense of his being
less criminal than he had supposed, with a dim vision of
himself as the real proven donkey for not having been a
harmless dash more so. But, to be just as well as penetrating, this was only the effect of her personal charm on
his nature. So it spurred him a moment, when it struck
this doleful man that to have secured one kiss of those
fresh and witty sparkling lips he would endure forfeits,
pangs, anything save the hanging of his culprit's head
before his Emma. Reflection washed him clean. Secresy
is not a medical restorative, by no means a good thing for
the baffled amorously-adventurous cavalier, unless the
lady's character shall have been firmly established in or
over his hazy wagging noddle. Reflection informed him
that the honourable, generous, proud girl spared him

for the sake of the house she loved. After a night of tossing, he rose right heartily repentant. He showed it in the best manner, not dramatically. On her accepting his offer to drive her down to the valley to meet the coach, a genuine illumination of pure gratitude made a better man of him, both to look at and in feeling. She did not hesitate to consent ; and he had half expected a refusal. She talked on the way quite as usual, cheerfully, if not altogether so spiritedly. A flash of her matchless wit now and then reduced him to that abject state of man beside the fair person he has treated high cavalierly, which one craves permission to describe as pulp. He was utterly beaten.

The sight of Redworth on the valley road was a relief to them both. He had slept in one of the houses of the valley, and spoke of having had the intention to mount to Copsley. Sir Lukin proposed to drive him back. He glanced at Diana, still with that calculating abstract air of his ; and he was rallied. He confessed to being absorbed in railways, the new lines of railways projected to thread the land and fast mapping it.

'You 've not embarked money in them ? ' said Sir Lukin.

The answer was : ' I have ; all I possess.' And Redworth for a sharp instant set his eyes on Diana, indifferent to Sir Lukin's bellow of stupefaction at such gambling on the part of a prudent fellow.

He asked her where she was to be met, where written to, during the Summer, in case of his wishing to send her news.

She replied : ' Copsley will be the surest. I am always in communication with Lady Dunstane.' She coloured deeply. The recollection of the change of her feeling for Copsley suffused her maiden mind.

The strange blush prompted an impulse in Redworth to speak to her at once of his venture in railways. But what would she understand of them, as connected with the mighty stake he was playing for ? He delayed. The coach came at a trot of the horses, admired by Sir Lukin, round a corner. She entered it, her maid followed, the door banged, the horses trotted. She was off.

Her destiny of the Crossways tied a knot, barred a gate, and pointed to a new direction of the road on that fine spring morning, when beech-buds were near the burst, cowslips yellowed the meadow-flats, and skylarks quivered upward.

For many long years Redworth had in his memory, for a comment on procrastination and excessive scrupulousness in his calculating faculty, the blue back of a coach.

He declined the vacated place beside Sir Lukin, promising to come and spend a couple of days at Copsley in a fortnight—Saturday week. He wanted, he said, to have a talk with Lady Dunstane. Evidently he had railways on the brain, and Sir Lukin warned his wife to be guarded against the speculative mania, and advise the man, if she could.

## CHAPTER V

### CONCERNING THE SCRUPULOUS GENTLEMAN WHO CAME TOO LATE

On the Saturday of his appointment Redworth arrived at Copsley, with a shade deeper of the calculating look under his thick brows, habitual to him latterly. He found Lady Dunstane at her desk, pen in hand, the paper untouched ; and there was an appearance of trouble about her somewhat resembling his own, as he would have observed, had he been open-minded enough to notice anything, except that she was writing a letter. He begged her to continue it; he proposed to read a book till she was at leisure.

'I have to write, and scarcely know how,' said she, clearing her face to make the guest at home, and taking a chair by the fire, ' I would rather chat for half an hour.'

She spoke of the weather, frosty, but tonic ; bad for the last days of hunting, good for the farmer and the country, let us hope.

Redworth nodded assent. It might be surmised that he was brooding over those railways, in which he had embarked his fortune. Ah ! those railways ! She was not long coming to the wailful exclamation upon them, both to express her personal sorrow at the disfigurement of our dear England, and lead to a little, modest, offering of a woman's counsel to the rash adventurer ; for thus could she serviceably put aside her perplexity awhile. Those railways ! When would there be peace in the land ? Where one single nook of shelter and escape from them ! And the English, blunt as their senses are to noise and hubbub, would be revelling in hisses, shrieks, puffings and screeches, so that travelling would become an intolerable affliction. ' I speak rather as an invalid,' she admitted ; ' I conjure up all sorts of horrors, the whistle in the night beneath one's windows, and the smoke of trains defacing the landscape ; hideous accidents too. They will be wholesale and past help. Imagine a collision ! I have borne many changes with equanimity, I pretend to a certain degree of philosophy, but this mania for cutting up the land does really cause me to pity those who are to follow us. They will not see the England we have seen. It will be patched and scored, disfigured . . . a sort of barbarous Maori visage—England in a New Zealand mask. You may call it the sentimental view. In this case, I am decidedly sentimental : I love my country. I do love quiet, rural England. Well, and I

love beauty, I love simplicity. All that will be destroyed
by the refuse of the towns flooding the land—barring
accidents, as Lukin says. There seems nothing else to
save us.'

Redworth acquiesced. 'Nothing.'

'And you do not regret it ? ' he was asked.

'Not a bit. We have already exchanged opinions on
the subject. Simplicity must go, and the townsman meet
his equal in the countryman. As for beauty, I would
sacrifice that to circulate gumption. A bushelful of
nonsense is talked pro and con : it always is at an inno-
vation. What we are now doing, is to take a longer and
a quicker stride, that is all.'

'And establishing a new field for the speculator.'

'Yes, and I am one, and this is the matter I wanted to
discuss with you, Lady Dunstane,' said Redworth, bending forward, the whole man devoted to the point of
business.

She declared she was complimented ; she felt the
compliment, and trusted her advice might be useful,
faintly remarking that she had a woman's head : and
' not less ' was implied as much as ' not more,' in order to
give strength to her prospective opposition.

All his money, she heard, was down on the railway
table. He might within a year have a tolerable fortune :
and, of course, he *might* be ruined. He did not expect
it ; still he fronted the risks. 'And now,' said he, ' I
come to you for counsel. I am not held among my
acquaintances to be a marrying man, as it 's called.'

He paused. Lady Dunstane thought it an occasion to
praise him for his considerateness.

' You involve no one but yourself, you mean ? ' Her
eyes shed approval. ' Still the day may come . . . I
say only that it may : and the wish to marry is a rosy
colouring . . . equal to a flying chariot in conducting us

across difficulties and obstructions to the deed. And
then one may have to regret a previous rashness.'

These practical men are sometimes obtuse : she dwelt
on that vision of the future.

He listened, and resumed : ' My view of marriage is,
that no man should ask a woman to be his wife unless he
is well able to support her in the comforts, not to say
luxuries, she is accustomed to.' His gaze had wandered
to the desk ; it fixed there. ' That is Miss Merion's
writing,' he said.

' The letter ? ' said Lady Dunstane, and she stretched
out her hand to press down a leaf of it. ' Yes ; it is from
her.'

' Is she quite well ? '

' I suppose she is. She does not speak of her health.'

He looked pertinaciously in the direction of the letter,
and it was not rightly mannered. That letter, of all
others, was covert and sacred to the friend. It contained the weightiest of secrets.

' I have not written to her,' said Redworth.

He was astonishing : ' To whom ? To Diana ? You
could very well have done so, only I fancy she knows
nothing, has never given a thought to railway stocks and
shares ; she has a loathing for speculation.'

' And speculators too, I dare say.'

' It is extremely probable.' Lady Dunstane spoke
with an emphasis, for the man liked Diana, and would
be moved by the idea of forfeiting her esteem.

' She might blame me if I did anything dishonourable.'

' She certainly would.'

' She will have no cause.'

Lady Dunstane began to look, as at a cloud charged
with remote explosions : and still for the moment she
was unsuspecting. But it was a flitting moment. When
he went on, and very singularly droning to her ear : ' The

more a man loves a woman, the more he should be positive, before asking her, that she will not have to consent to a loss of position, and I would rather lose her than fail to give her all—not be sure, as far as a man can be sure, of giving her all I think she 's worthy of ' : then the cloud shot a lightning flash, and the doors of her understanding swung wide to the entry of a great wonderment. A shock of pain succeeded it. Her sympathy was roused so acutely that she slipped over the reflective rebuke she would have addressed to her silly delusion concerning his purpose in speaking of his affairs to a woman. Though he did not mention Diana by name, Diana was clearly the person. And why had he delayed to speak to her ?—Because of this venture of his money to make him a fortune, for the assurance of her future comfort ! Here was the best of men for the girl, not displeasing to her ; a good, strong, trustworthy man, pleasant to hear and to see, only erring in being a trifle too scrupulous in love : and a fortnight back she would have imagined he had no chance ; and now she knew that the chance was excellent in those days, with this revelation in Diana's letter, which said that all chance was over.

'The courtship of a woman,' he droned away, ' is in my mind not fair to her until a man has to the full enough to sanction his asking her to marry him. And if he throws all he possesses on a stake . . . to win her—give her what she has a right to claim, he ought. . . . Only at present the prospect seems good. . . . He ought of course to wait. Well, the value of the stock I hold has doubled, and it increases. I am a careful watcher of the market. I have friends—brokers and railway Directors. I can rely on them.'

'Pray,' interposed Lady Dunstane, ' specify—I am rather in a mist—the exact point upon which you do me the honour to consult me.' She ridiculed herself for

having imagined that such a man would come to consult
her upon a point of business.

'It is,' he replied, ' this : whether, as affairs now stand
with me—I have an income from my office, and personal
property . . . say between thirteen and fourteen hundred a year to start with—whether you think me justi-
fied in asking a lady to share my lot ? '

'Why not ?  But will you name the lady ? '

' Then I may write at once ?  In your judgement . . .
Yes, the lady.  I have not named her.  I had no right.
Besides, the general question first, in fairness to the
petitioner.  You might reasonably stipulate for more
for a friend.  She could make a match, as you have
said . . .' he muttered of ' brilliant,' and ' the highest ' ;
and his humbleness of the honest man enamoured touched
Lady Dunstane.  She saw him now as the man of strength
that she would have selected from a thousand suitors to
guide her dear friend.

She caught at a straw : ' Tell me, it is not Diana ? '

' Diana Merion ! '

As soon as he had said it he perceived pity, and he drew
himself tight for the stroke.  ' She 's in love with some
one ? '

' She is engaged.'

He bore it well.  He was a big-chested fellow, and that
excruciating twist within of the revolution of the wheels of
the brain snapping their course to grind the contrary to
that of the heart, was revealed in one short lift and gasp,
a compression of the tremendous change he underwent.

' Why did you not speak before ? ' said Lady Dunstane.
Her words were tremulous.

' I should have had no justification.'

' You might have won her ! '  She could have wept ; her
sympathy and her self-condolence under disappointment
at Diana's conduct joined to swell the feminine flood.

The poor fellow's quick breathing and blinking reminded her of cruelty in a restropect.  She generalized, to ease her spirit of regret, by hinting it without hurting : ' Women really are not puppets.  They are not so excessively luxurious.  It is good for young women in the early days of marriage to rough it a little.'  She found herself droning, as he had done.

He had ears for nothing but the fact.

' Then I am too late ! '

' I have heard it to-day.'

' She is engaged !  Positively ? '

Lady Dunstane glanced backward at the letter on her desk.  She had to answer the strangest of letters that had ever come to her, and it was from her dear Tony, the baldest intimation of the weightiest piece of intelligence which a woman can communicate to her heart's friend. The task of answering it was now doubled.  ' I fear so, I fancy so,' she said, and she longed to cast eye over the letter again, to see if there might possibly be a loophole behind the lines.

' Then I must make my mind up to it,' said Redworth. ' I think I 'll take a walk.'

She smiled kindly.  ' It will be our secret.'

' I thank you with all my heart, Lady Dunstane.'

He was not a weaver of phrases in distress.  His blunt reserve was eloquent of it to her, and she liked him the better ;  could have thanked him, too, for leaving her promptly.

When she was alone she took in the contents of the letter at a hasty glimpse.  It was of one paragraph, and fired its shot like a cannon with the muzzle at her breast :—

' MY OWN EMMY,—I have been asked in marriage by Mr. Warwick, and have accepted him.  Signify your approval, for I have decided that it is the wisest thing a

waif can do. We are to live at The Crossways for four
months of the year, so I shall have Dada in his best days
and all my youngest dreams, my sunrise and morning dew,
surrounding me ; my old home for my new one. I write
in haste, to you first, burning to hear from you. Send
your blessing to yours in life and death, through all
transformations,

                                                    ' TONY.'

That was all. Not a word of the lover about to be decorated with the title of husband. No confession of love,
nor a single supplicating word to her friend, in excuse
for the abrupt decision to so grave a step. Her previous
description of him, as a ' gentlemanly official ' in his
appearance, conjured him up most distastefully. True,
she might have made a more lamentable choice ;—a silly
lordling, or a hero of scandals ; but if a gentlemanly
official was of stabler mould, he failed to harmonize quite
so well with the idea of a creature like Tony. Perhaps
Mr. Redworth also failed in something. Where was the
man fitly to mate her ! Mr. Redworth, however, was
manly and trustworthy, of the finest Saxon type in build
and in character. He had great qualities, and his excess
of scrupulousness was most pitiable.

She read : ' The wisest thing a waif can do.' It bore a
sound of desperation. Avowedly Tony had accepted
him without being in love. Or was she masking the
passion ? No : had it been a case of love, she would have
written very differently to her friend.

Lady Dunstane controlled the pricking of the wound
inflicted by Diana's novel exercise in laconics where the
fullest flow was due to tenderness, and despatched felici-
tations upon the text of the initial line : ' Wonders are
always happening.' She wrote to hide vexation beneath
surprise ; naturally betraying it. ' I must hope and pray

E

that you have not been precipitate.' Her curiosity to inspect the happiest of men, the most genuine part of her letter, was expressed coldly. When she had finished the composition she perused it, and did not recognize herself in her language, though she had been so guarded to cover the wound her Tony dealt their friendship—in some degree injuring their sex. For it might now, after such an example, verily seem that women are incapable of a translucent perfect confidence :—their impulses, caprices, desperations, tricks of concealment, trip a heart-whole friendship. Well, to-morrow, if not to-day, the tripping may be expected ! Lady Dunstane resigned herself sadly to a lowered view of her Tony's character. This was her unconscious act of reprisal. Her brilliant beloved Tony, dazzling but in beauty and the gifted mind, stood as one essentially with the common order of women. She wished to be settled, Mr. Warwick proposed, and for the sake of living at The Crossways she accepted him—she, the lofty scorner of loveless marriages ! who had said—how many times ! that nothing save love excused it ! She degraded their mutual high standard of womankind. Diana was in eclipse, full three parts. The bulk of the gentlemanly official she had chosen obscured her. But I have written very carefully, thought Lady Dunstane, dropping her answer into the post-bag. She had, indeed, been so careful, that to cloak her feelings, she had written as another person. Women with otiose husbands have a task to preserve friendship.

Redworth carried his burden through the frosty air at a pace to melt icicles in Greenland. He walked unthinkingly, right ahead, to the red West, as he discovered when pausing to consult his watch. Time was left to return at the same pace and dress for dinner ; he swung round and picked up remembrances of sensations he had strewn by the way. She knew these woods ; he was walking in her footprints ; she was engaged to be married. Yes, his principle, never to ask a woman to marry him, never to court her, without bank-book assurance of his ability to support her in cordial comfort, was right. He maintained it, and owned himself a donkey for having stuck to it. Between him and his excellent principle there was war, without the slightest division. Warned of the danger of losing her, he would have done the same again, confessing himself donkey for his pains. The principle was right, because it was due to the woman. His rigid adherence to the principle set him belabouring his donkey-ribs, as the proper due to himself. For he might have had a chance, all through two Winters. The opportunities had been numberless. Here, in this beech wood ; near that thorn-bush ; on the juniper slope ; from the corner of chalk and sand in junction, to the corner of clay and chalk ; all the length of the wooded ridge he had reminders of her presence and his priceless chances : and still the standard of his conduct said No, while his heart bled.

He felt that a chance had been. More sagacious than Lady Dunstane, from his not nursing a wound, he divined in the abruptness of Diana's resolution to accept a suitor, a sober reason, and a fitting one, for the wish that she might be settled. And had he spoken !—If he had spoken to her, she might have given her hand to him, to a dis-honourable brute ! A blissful brute. But a worse than donkey. Yes, his principle was right, and he lashed with it, and prodded with it, drove himself out into the sour wilds where bachelordom crops noxious weeds without a hallowing luminary, and clung to it, bruised and bleeding though he was.

The gentleness of Lady Dunstane soothed him during the term of a visit that was rather like purgatory sweet-ened by angelical tears. He was glad to go, wretched in having gone. She diverted the incessant conflict between his insubordinate self and his castigating, but avowedly sovereign, principle. Away from her, he was the victim of a flagellation so dire that it almost drove him to revolt against the lord he served, and somehow the many memories at Copsley kept him away. Sir Lukin, when speaking of Diana's 'engagement to that fellow Warwick,' exalted her with an extraordinary enthusiasm, exceedingly hard for the silly beast who had lost her to bear. For the present the place dearest to Redworth of all places on earth was unendurable.

Meanwhile the value of railway investments rose in the market, fast as asparagus-heads for cutting : a circumstance that added stings to reflection. Had he been only a little bolder, a little less the fanatical devotee of his rule of masculine honour, less the slave to the letter of success. . . . But why reflect at all ? Here was a goodly income approaching, perhaps a seat in Parliament ; a station for the airing of his opinions—and a social status for the wife now denied to him. The wife was denied to him ; he could conceive of no other. The tyrant-ridden, reticent, tenacious creature had thoroughly wedded her in mind ; her view of things had a throne beside his own, even in their differences. He perceived, agreeing or disagreeing, the motions of her brain, as he did with none other of women ; and this it is which stamps character on her, divides her from them, upraises and enspheres. He declined to live with any other of the sex.

Before he could hear of the sort of man Mr. Warwick was—a perpetual object of his quest—the bridal bells had rung, and Diana Antonia Merion lost her maiden name. She became the Mrs. Warwick of our footballing world.

Why she married, she never told. Possibly, in amazement at herself subsequently, she forgot the specific reason. That which weighs heavily in youth, and commits us to desperate action, will be a trifle under older

eyes, to blunter senses, a more enlightened understanding.
Her friend Emma probed for the reason vainly. It was
partly revealed to Redworth, by guess-work and a putting
together of pieces, yet quite luminously, as it were by
touch of tentacle-feelers—one evening that he passed
with Sir Lukin Dunstane, when the lachrymose ex-
dragoon and son of Idlesse, had rather more than dined.

## CHAPTER VI

### THE COUPLE

SIX months a married woman, Diana came to Copsley to
introduce her husband. They had run over Italy : ' the
Italian Peninsula,' she quoted him in a letter to Lady
Dunstane : and were furnishing their London house.
Her first letters from Italy appeared to have a little bloom
of sentiment. Augustus was mentioned as liking this and
that in the land of beauty. He patronized Art, and it
was a pleasure to hear him speak upon pictures and
sculptures ; he knew a great deal about them. ' He is
an authority.' Her humour soon began to play round
the fortunate man, who did not seem, to the reader's
mind, to bear so well a sentimental clothing. His pride
was in being very English on the Continent, and Diana's
instances of his lofty appreciations of the garden of Art
and Nature, and statuesque walk through it, would have
been more amusing if her friend could have harmonized
her idea of the couple. A description of 'a bit of a wrangle
between us ' at Lucca, where an Italian post-master on
a journey of inspection, claimed a share of their carriage
and audaciously attempted entry, was laughable, but
jarred. Would she some day lose her relish for ridicule,

and see him at a distance ?    He was generous, Diana said :
she saw fine qualities in him.    It might be that he was
lavish on his bridal tour.    She said he was unselfish, kind,
affable with his equals ;   he was cordial to the acquaintances he met.    Perhaps his worst fault was an affected
superciliousness before the foreigner, not uncommon in
those days.    ' You are to know, dear Emmy, that we
English are the aristocracy of Europeans.'    Lady Dunstane inclined to think we were ;   nevertheless, in the
mouth of a ' gentlemanly official ' the frigid arrogance
added a stroke of caricature to his deportment.    On the
other hand, the reports of him gleaned by Sir Lukin
sounded favourable.    He was not taken to be preternaturally stiff, nor bright, but a goodish sort of fellow ;
good horseman, good shot, good character.    In short, the
average Englishman, excelling as a cavalier, a slayer,
and an orderly subject.    That was a somewhat elevated
standard to the patriotic Emma.    Only she would never
have stipulated for an average to espouse Diana.    Would
he understand her, and value the best in her ?    Another
and unanswered question was, how could she have conde-
scended to wed with an average ?    There was transparently some secret not confided to her friend.

He appeared.    Lady Dunstane's first impression of him
recurred on his departure.    Her unanswered question
drummed at her ears, though she remembered that Tony's
art in leading him out had moderated her rigidly judicial
summary of the union during a greater part of the visit.
But his requiring to be led out, was against him.    Considering the subjects, his talk was passable.    The subjects treated of politics, pictures, Continental travel, our
manufactures, our wealth and the reasons for it—excellent
reasons well-weighed.    He was handsome, as men go ;
rather tall, not too stout, precise in the modern fashion
of his dress, and the pair of whiskers encasing a colourless

depression up to a long, thin, straight nose, and closed
lips indicating an aperture. The contraction of his
mouth expressed an intelligence in the attitude of the
firmly negative. The lips opened to smile, the teeth
were faultless : an effect was produced, if a cold one—
the colder for the unparticipating northern eyes ; eyes
of that half cloud and blue, which make a kind of hueless
grey, and are chiefly striking in an authoritative stare.
Without contradicting, for he was exactly polite, his look
signified a person conscious of being born to command :
in fine, an aristocrat among the ' aristocracy of Europeans.' His differences of opinion were prefaced by a
' Pardon me,' and pausing smile of the teeth ; then a
succinctly worded sentence or two, a perfect settlement
of the dispute. He disliked argumentation. He said so,
and Diana remarked it of him, speaking as a wife who
merely noted a characteristic. Inside his boundary, he
had neat phrases, opinions in packets. Beyond it, apparently the world was void of any particular interest. Sir
Lukin, whose boundary would have shown a narrower
limitation had it been defined, stood no chance with him.
Tory versus Whig, he tried a wrestle, and was thrown.
They agreed on the topic of Wine. Mr. Warwick had a
fine taste in wine. Their after-dinner sittings were
devoted to this and the alliterative cognate theme,
equally dear to the gallant ex-dragoon, from which it
resulted that Lady Dunstane received satisfactory information in a man's judgement of him. ' Warwick is a
clever fellow, and a thorough man of the world, I can tell
you, Emmy.' Sir Lukin further observed that he was a
gentlemanly fellow. ' A gentlemanly official ! ' Diana's
primary dash of portraiture stuck to him, so true it was !
As for her, she seemed to have forgotten it. Not only
did she strive to show him to advantage by leading him
out ; she played second to him, subserviently, fondly ;

she quite submerged herself, content to be dull if he might shine ; and her talk of her husband in her friend's blue-chamber boudoir of the golden stars, where they had discussed the world and taken counsel in her maiden days, implied admiration of his merits.  He rode superbly : he knew Law : he was prepared for any position : he could speak really eloquently ; she had heard him at a local meeting.  And he loved the old Crossways almost as much as she did.  ' He has promised me he will never ask me to sell it,' she said, with a simpleness that could hardly have been acted.

When she was gone, Lady Dunstane thought she had worn a mask, in the natural manner of women trying to make the best of their choice ; and she excused her poor Tony for the artful presentation of him at her own cost. But she could not excuse her for having married the man. Her first and her final impression likened him to a house locked up and empty :—a London house conventionally furnished and decorated by the upholsterer, and empty of inhabitants.  How a brilliant and beautiful girl could have committed this rashness, was the perplexing riddle : the knottier because the man was idle : and Diana had ambition ; she despised and dreaded idleness in men.— Empty of inhabitants even to the ghost !  Both human and spiritual were wanting.  The mind contemplating him became reflectively stagnant.

I must not be unjust ! Lady Dunstane hastened to ex-claim, at a whisper that he had at least proved his appre-ciation of Tony ; whom he preferred to call Diana, as she gladly remembered : and the two were bound together for a moment warmly by her recollection of her beloved Tony's touching little petition : ' You will invite us again ? ' and then there had flashed in Tony's dear dark eyes the look of their old love drowning.  They were not to be thought of separately.  She admitted that the introduction to a woman of her friend's husband is crucially trying to him : he may well show worse than he is. Yet his appreciation of Tony in espousing her, was rather marred by Sir Lukin's report of him as a desperate admirer of beautiful woman. It might be for her beauty only, not for her spiritual qualities ! At present he did not seem aware of their existence. But, to be entirely just, she had hardly exhibited them or a sign of them during the first interview : and sitting with his hostess alone, he had seized the occasion to say, that he was the happiest of men. He said it with the nearest approach to fervour she had noticed. Perhaps the very fact of his not producing a highly favourable impression, should be set to plead on his behalf. Such as he was, he was himself, no simulator. She longed for Mr. Redworth's report of him.

Her compassion for Redworth's feelings when beholding the woman he loved another man's wife, did not soften the urgency of her injunction that he should go speedily, and see as much of them as he could. ' Because,' she gave her reason, ' I wish Diana to know she has not lost a single friend through her marriage, and is only one the richer.'

Redworth buckled himself to the task. He belonged to the class of his countrymen who have a dungeon-vault for feelings that should not be suffered to cry abroad, and into this oubliette he cast them, letting them feed as they might, or perish. It was his heart down below, and in no voluntary musings did he listen to it, to sustain the thing. Grimly lord of himself, he stood emotionless before the world. Some worthy fellows resemble him, and they are called deep-hearted. He was dungeon-deep. The prisoner underneath might clamour and leap ; none heard him or knew of him ; nor did he ever view the day. Diana's frank : ' Ah, Mr. Redworth, how glad I am to

see you ! ' was met by the calmest formalism of the wish
for her happiness.  He became a guest at her London
house, and his report of the domesticity there, and notably
of the lord of the house, pleased Lady Dunstane more
than her husband's.  He saw the kind of man accurately,
as far as men are to be seen on the surface ; and she could
say assentingly, without anxiety : ' Yes, yes,' to his remarks upon Mr. Warwick, indicative of a man of capable
head in worldly affairs, commonplace beside his wife.
The noble gentleman for Diana was yet unborn, they
tacitly agreed.  Meantime one must not put a mortal
husband to the fiery ordeal of his wife's deserts, they
agreed likewise.  ' You may be sure she is a constant
friend,' Lady Dunstane said for his comfort ; and she
reminded herself subsequently of a shade of disappointment at his imperturbable rejoinder : ' I could calculate
on it.'  For though not at all desiring to witness the sentimental fit, she wished to see that he held an image of Diana :
—surely a woman to kindle poets and heroes, the princes
of the race ; and it was a curious perversity that the two
men she had moved were merely excellent, emotionless,
ordinary men, with heads for business.  Elsewhere, out
of England, Diana would have been a woman for a place
in song, exalted to the skies.  Here she had the destiny
to inflame Mr. Redworth and Mr. Warwick, two railway
Directors, bent upon scoring the country to the likeness
of a child's lines of hop-scotch in a gravel-yard.

As with all invalids, the pleasure of living backward
was haunted by the tortures it evoked, and two years later
she recalled this outcry against the Fates.  She would
then have prayed for Diana to inflame none but such men
as those two.  The original error was, of course, that rash
and most inexplicable marriage, a step never alluded to by
the driven victim of it.  Lady Dunstane heard rumours of
dissensions.  Diana did not mention them.  She spoke

of her husband as unlucky in railway ventures, and of a
household necessity for money, nothing further.    One day
she wrote of a Government appointment her husband had
received, ending the letter : ' So there is the end of our
troubles.' Her friend rejoiced, and afterward looking
back at her satisfaction, saw the dire beginning of
them.

Lord Dannisburgh's name, as one of the admirers of
Mrs. Warwick, was dropped once or twice by Sir Lukin.
He had dined with the Warwicks, and met the eminent
member of the Cabinet at their table.    There is no harm
in admiration, especially on the part of one of a crowd
observing a star.    No harm can be imputed when the
husband of a beautiful woman accepts an appointment
from the potent Minister admiring her.    So Lady Dunstane thought, for she was sure of Diana to her inmost
soul.    But she soon perceived in Sir Lukin that the old
Dog-world was preparing to yelp on a scent.    He of his
nature belonged to the hunting pack, and with a cordial
feeling for the quarry, he was quite with his world in expecting to see her run, and readiness to join the chase.
No great scandal had occurred for several months.    The
world was in want of it ; and he, too, with a very cordial
feeling for the quarry, piously hoping she would escape,
already had his nose to ground, collecting testimony in
the track of her.    He said little to his wife, but his world
was getting so noisy that he could not help half pursing
his lips, as with the soft whistle of an innuendo at the heels
of it.    Redworth was in America, engaged in carving up
that hemisphere.    She had no source of information but
her husband's chance gossip ; and London was death to
her ; and Diana, writing faithfully twice a week, kept
silence as to Lord Dannisburgh, except in naming him
among her guests.    She wrote this, which might have a
secret personal signification : ' We women are the verbs

passive of the alliance, we have to learn, and if we take
to activity, with the best intentions, we conjugate a
frightful disturbance. We are to run on lines, like the
steam-trains, or we come to no station, dash to fragments.
I have the misfortune to know I was born an active. I
take my chance.'

Once she coupled the names of Lord Larrian and Lord
Dannisburgh, remarking that she had a fatal attraction
for antiques.

The death of her husband's uncle and illness of his aunt
withdrew her to The Crossways, where she remained
nursing for several months, reading diligently, as her
letters showed, and watching the approaches of the de-
stroyer. She wrote like her former self, subdued by
meditation in the presence of that inevitable. The world
ceased barking. Lady Dunstane could suppose Mr.
Warwick to have now a reconciling experience of his
wife's noble qualities. He probably did value them
more. He spoke of her to Sir Lukin in London with
commendation. 'She is an attentive nurse.' He inherited a considerable increase of income when he and
his wife were the sole tenants of The Crossways, but disliking the house, for reasons hard to explain by a man
previously professing to share her attachment to it, he
wished to sell or let the place, and his wife would do
neither. She proposed to continue living in their small
London house rather than be cut off from The Crossways,
which, he said, was ludicrous : people should live up to
their position ; and he sneered at the place, and slightly
wounded her, for she was open to a wound when the cold
fire of a renewed attempt at warmth between them was
crackling and showing bits of flame, after she had given
proof of her power to serve. Service to himself and his
relatives affected him. He deferred to her craze for The
Crossways, and they lived in a larger London house, ' up

to their position,' which means ever a trifle beyond it,
and gave choice dinner-parties to the most eminent.
His jealousy slumbered. Having ideas of a seat in
Parliament at this period, and preferment superior to the
post he held, Mr. Warwick deemed it sagacious to court
the potent patron Lord Dannisburgh could be ; and his
wife had his interests at heart, the fork-tongued world
said. The cry revived. Stories of Lord D. and Mrs. W.
whipped the hot pursuit. The moral repute of the great
Whig lord and the beauty of the lady composed inflammable material.

' Are you altogether cautious ? ' Lady Dunstane wrote
to Diana ; and her friend sent a copious reply : ' You
have the fullest right to ask your Tony anything, and I
will answer as at the Judgement bar. You allude to Lord
Dannisburgh. He is near what Dada's age would have
been, and is, I think I can affirm, next to my dead father
and my Emmy, my dearest friend. I love him. I could
say it in the streets without shame ; and you do not
imagine me shameless. Whatever his character in his
younger days, he can be honestly a woman's friend,
believe me. I see straight to his heart ; he has no disguise ; and unless I am to suppose that marriage is the
end of me, I must keep him among my treasures. I see
him almost daily ; it is not possible to think I can be
deceived ; and as long as he does me the honour to
esteem my poor portion of brains by coming to me for
what he is good enough to call my counsel, I shall let
the world wag its tongue. Between ourselves, I trust
to be doing some good. I know I am of use in various
ways. No doubt there is a danger of a woman's head
being turned, when she reflects that a powerful Minister
governing a kingdom has not considered her too insignificant to advise him ; and I am sensible of it. I am,
I assure you, dearest, on my guard against it. That

would not attach me to him, as his homely friendliness
does. He is the most amiable, cheerful, *benignant* of
men ; he has no feeling of an enemy, though naturally
his enemies are numerous and venomous. He is full of
observation and humour. How he would amuse you !
In many respects accord with you. And I should not
have a spark of jealousy. Some day I shall beg permission to bring him to Copsley. At present, during
the Session, he is too busy, as you know. Me—his
" crystal spring of wisdom "—he can favour with no more
than an hour in the afternoon, or a few minutes at night.
Or I get a pencilled note from the benches of the House,
with an anecdote, or news of a Division. I am sure to
be enlivened.

' So I have written to you fully, simply, frankly. Have
perfect faith in your Tony, who would, she vows to
heaven, die rather than disturb it and her heart's
beloved.'

The letter terminated with one of Lord Dannisburgh's
anecdotes, exciting to merriment in the season of its
freshness ;—and a postscript of information : ' Augustus
expects a mission—about a month ; uncertain whether
I accompany him.'

Mr. Warwick departed on his mission. Diana remained
in London. Lady Dunstane wrote entreating her to pass
the month—her favourite time of the violet yielding to
the cowslip—at Copsley. The invitation could not be
accepted, but the next day Diana sent word that she
had a surprise for the following Sunday, and would bring
a friend to lunch, if Sir Lukin would meet them at the
corner of the road in the valley leading up to the heights,
at a stated hour.

Lady Dunstane gave the listless baronet his directions,
observing : ' It 's odd, she never will come alone since
her marriage.'

' Queer,' said he of the serenest absence of conscience ;
and that there must be something not entirely right going
on, he strongly inclined to think.

## CHAPTER VII

### THE CRISIS

IT was a confirmed suspicion when he beheld Lord
Dannisburgh on the box of a four-in-hand, and the peerless Diana beside him, cockaded lackeys in plain livery
and the lady's maid to the rear.   But Lord Dannisburgh's
visit was a compliment, and the freak of his driving down
under the beams of Aurora on a sober Sunday morning
capital fun ;  so with a gaiety that was kept alive for the
invalid Emma to partake of it, they rattled away to the
heights, and climbed them, and Diana rushed to the arms
of her friend, whispering and cooing for pardon if she
startled her, guilty of a little whiff of blarney :—Lord
Dannisburgh wanted so much to be introduced to her,
and she so much wanted her to know him, and she hoped
to be graciously excused for thus bringing them together,
' that she might be chorus to them ! '   Chorus was a
pretty fiction on the part of the thrilling and topping
voice.   She was the very radiant Diana of her earliest
opening day, both in look and speech, a queenly comrade,
and a spirit leaping and shining like a mountain water.
She did not seduce, she ravished.   The judgement was
taken captive and flowed with her.   As to the prank of
the visit, Emma heartily enjoyed it and hugged it for a
holiday of her own, and doating on the beautiful, dark-
eyed, fresh creature, who bore the name of the divine
Huntress, she thought her a true Dian in stature, step, and
attributes, the genius of laughter superadded.   None

else on earth so sweetly laughed, none so spontaneously, victoriously provoked the healthful openness. Her delicious chatter, and her museful sparkle in listening, equally quickened every sense of life. Adorable as she was to her friend Emma at all times, she that day struck a new fountain in memory. And it was pleasant to see the great lord's admiration of this wonder. One could firmly believe in their friendship, and his winning ideas from the abounding bubbling well. A recurrent smile beamed on his face when hearing and observing her. Certain dishes provided at the table were Diana's favourites, and he relished them, asking for a second help, and remarking that her taste was good in that as in all things. They lunched, eating like boys. They walked over the grounds of Copsley, and into the lanes and across the meadows of the cowslip, rattling, chatting, enlivening the frosty air, happy as children biting to the juices of ripe apples off the tree. But Tony was the tree, the dispenser of the rosy gifts. She had a moment of reflection, only a moment, and Emma felt the pause as though a cloud had shadowed them and a spirit had been shut away. Both spoke of their happiness at the kiss of parting. That melancholy note at the top of the wave to human hearts conscious of its enforced decline was repeated by them, and Diana's eyelids blinked to dismiss a tear.

'You have no troubles?' Emma said.

'Only the pain of the good-bye to my beloved,' said Diana. 'I have never been happier—never shall be! Now you know him you think with me? I knew you would. You have seen him as he always is—except when he is armed for battle. He is the kindest of souls. And soul I say. He is the one man among men who gives me notions of a soul in men.'

The eulogy was exalted. Lady Dunstane made a little

mouth for Oh, in correction of the transcendental touch,
though she remembered their foregone conversations upon
men—strange beings that they are !—and understood
Diana's meaning.

' Really ! really ! honour ! ' Diana emphasized her ex-
travagant praise, to print it fast. ' Hear him speak of
Ireland.'

' Would he not speak of Ireland in a tone to catch
the Irishwoman ? '

' He is past thoughts of catching, dearest. At that age
men are pools of fish, or what you will : they are not
anglers. Next year, if you invite us, we will come again.'

' But you will come to stay in the Winter ? '

' Certainly. But I am speaking of one of my holidays.'

They kissed fervently. The lady mounted ; the grey
and portly lord followed her ; Sir Lukin flourished his
whip, and Emma was left to brood over her friend's
last words : ' One of my holidays.' Not a hint to the
detriment of her husband had passed. The stray beam
balefully illuminating her marriage slipped from her
involuntarily. Sir Lukin was troublesome with his
ejaculations that evening, and kept speculating on the
time of the arrival of the four-in-hand in London ; upon
which he thought a great deal depended. They had
driven out of town early, and if they drove back late they
would not be seen, as all the cacklers were sure then to
be dressing for dinner, and he would not pass the Clubs.
' I couldn't suggest it,' he said. ' But Dannisburgh's
an old hand. But they say he snaps his fingers at tattle,
and laughs. Well, it doesn't matter for *him*, perhaps, but
a game of two. . . . Oh ! it 'll be all right. They can't
reach London before dusk. And the cat 's away.'

' It 's more than ever incomprehensible to me how she
could have married that man,' said his wife.

' I 've long since given it up,' said he.

F

Diana wrote her thanks for the delightful welcome,
telling of her drive home to smoke and solitude, with a
new host of romantic sensations to keep her company.
She wrote thrice in the week, and the same addition of one
to the ordinary number next week. Then for three
weeks not a line. Sir Lukin brought news from London
that Warwick had returned, nothing to explain the
silence. A letter addressed to The Crossways was likewise unnoticed. The supposition that they must be
visiting on a round, appeared rational ; but many weeks
elapsed, until Sir Lukin received a printed sheet in the
superscription of a former military comrade, who had
marked a paragraph. It was one of those journals, now
barely credible, dedicated to the putrid of the upper circle,
wherein initials raised sewer-lamps, and Asmodeus lifted
a roof, leering hideously. Thousands detested it, and
fattened their crops on it. Domesticated beasts of
superior habits to the common will indulge themselves
with a luxurious roll in carrion, for a revival of their
original instincts. Society was largely a purchaser. The
ghastly thing was dreaded as a scourge, hailed as a refreshment, nourished as a parasite. It professed un-
daunted honesty, and operated in the fashion of the
worms bred of decay. Success was its boasted justification. The animal world, when not rigorously watched,
will always crown with success the machine supplying its
appetites. The old dog-world took signal from it. The
one-legged devil-god waved his wooden hoof, and the
creatures in view, the hunt was uproarious. Why should
we seem better than we are ?—down with hypocrisy,
cried the censor morum, spicing the lamentable dere-
lictions of this and that great person, male and female.
The plea of corruption of blood in the world, to excuse
the public chafing of a grievous itch, is not less old than
sin ; and it offers a merry day of frisky truant running to

the animal made unashamed by another and another
stripped, branded, and stretched flat. Sir Lukin read
of Mr. and Mrs. W. and a distinguished Peer of the realm.
The paragraph was brief ; it had a flavour. Promise of
more to come, pricked curiosity. He read it enraged,
feeling for his wife ; and again indignant, feeling for
Diana. His third reading found him out : he felt for
both, but as a member of the whispering world, much
behind the scenes, he had a longing for the promised
insinuations, just to know what they could say, or dared
say. The paper was not shown to Lady Dunstane. A
run to London put him in the tide of the broken dam of
gossip. The names were openly spoken and swept from
mouth to mouth of the scandalmongers, gathering
matter as they flew. He knocked at Diana's door, where
he was informed that the mistress of the house was absent.
More than official gravity accompanied the announcement.
Her address was unknown. Sir Lukin thought it now
time to tell his wife. He began with a hesitating circum-
locution, in order to prepare her mind for bad news. She
divined immediately that it concerned Diana, and forcing
him to speak to the point, she had the story jerked out
to her in a sentence. It stopped her heart.

The chill of death was tasted in that wavering ascent
from oblivion to recollection. Why had not Diana come
to her, she asked herself, and asked her husband ; who,
as usual, was absolutely unable to say. Under compulsory squeezing, he would have answered, that she did
not come because she could not fib so easily to her bosom
friend : and this he thought, notwithstanding his personal experience of Diana's generosity. But he had
other personal experiences of her sex, and her sex plucked
at the bright star and drowned it.

The happy day of Lord Dannisburgh's visit settled in
Emma's belief as the cause of Mr. Warwick's unpardon-

able suspicions and cruelty. Arguing from her own
sensations of a day that had been like the return of sweet
health to her frame, she could see nothing but the loveliest freakish innocence in Diana's conduct, and she recalled her looks, her words, every fleeting gesture, even
to the ingenuousness of the noble statesman's admiration
of her, for the confusion of her unmanly and unworthy
husband. And Emma was nevertheless a thoughtful
person ; only her heart was at the head of her thoughts,
and led the file, whose reasoning was accurate on erratic
tracks. All night her heart went at fever pace. She
brought the repentant husband to his knees, and then
doubted, strongly doubted, whether she would, whether
in consideration for her friend she could, intercede with
Diana to forgive him. In the morning she slept heavily.
Sir Lukin had gone to London early for further tidings.
She awoke about midday, and found a letter on her
pillow. It was Diana's. Then while her fingers eagerly
tore it open, her heart, the champion rider over-night,
sank. It needed support of facts, and feared them : not
in distrust of that dear persecuted soul, but because the
very bravest of hearts is of its nature a shivering defender,
sensitive in the presence of any hostile array, much craving for material support, until the mind and spirit dis-
place it, depute it to second them instead of leading.

She read by a dull November fog-light a mixture of the
dreadful and the comforting, and dwelt upon the latter in
abandonment, hugged it, though conscious of evil and
the little that there was to veritably console.

The close of the letter struck the blow. After bluntly
stating that Mr. Warwick had served her with a process,
and that he had no case without suborning witnesses,
Diana said : ' But I leave the case, and him, to the world.
Ireland, or else America, it is a guiltless kind of suicide to
bury myself abroad. He has my letters. They are such

as I can own to you, and ask you to kiss me—and kiss
me when you have heard all the evidence, all that I can
add to it, kiss me. You know me too well to think I
would ask you to kiss criminal lips. But I cannot face
the world. In the dock, yes. Not where I am expected
to smile and sparkle, on pain of incurring suspicion if
I show a sign of oppression. I cannot do that. I see
myself wearing a false grin—your Tony! No, I do well
to go. This is my resolution ; and in consequence, my
beloved! my only truly loved on earth! I do not come
to you, to grieve you, as I surely should. Nor would
it soothe me, dearest. This will be to you the best of
reasons. It could not soothe me to see myself giving
pain to Emma. I am like a pestilence, and let me swing
away to the desert, for there I do no harm. I know I
am right. I have questioned myself—it is not cowardice.
I do not quail. I abhor the part of actress. I should do
it well—too well ; destroy my soul in the performance.
Is a good name before such a world as this worth that
sacrifice ?    A convent and self-quenching ;—cloisters
would seem to me like holy dew. But that would be
sleep, and I feel the powers of life. Never have I felt them
so mightily. If it were not for being called on to act and
mew, I would stay, fight, meet a bayonet-hedge of charges
and rebut them. I have my natural weapons and my
cause. It must be confessed that I have also more knowledge of men and the secret contempt—it must be—the
best of them entertain for us. Oh! and we confirm it
if we trust them. But they have been at a wicked school.

' I will write. From whatever place, you shall have
letters, and constant. I write no more now. In my
present mood I find no alternative between rageing and
drivelling. I am henceforth dead to the world. Never
dead to Emma till my breath is gone—poor flame! I

blow at a bed-room candle, by which I write in a brown
fog, and behold what I am—though not even serving to
write such a tangled scrawl as this. I am of no mortal
service. In two days I shall be out of England. Within
a week you shall hear where. I long for your heart on
mine, your dear eyes. You have faith in me, and I fly
from you!—I must be mad. Yet I feel calmly reasonable.
I know that this is the thing to do. Some years hence
a grey woman may return, to hear of a butterfly Diana,
that had her day and disappeared. Better than a mew-
ing and courtseying simulacrum of the woman—I drivel
again. Adieu. I suppose I am not liable to capture
and imprisonment until the day when my name is cited
to appear. I have left London. This letter and I quit
the scene by different routes—I would they were one.
My beloved! I have an ache—I think I am wronging
you. I am not mistress of myself, and do as something
within me, wiser than I, dictates.—You will write kindly.
Write your whole heart. It is not compassion I want, I
want you. I can bear stripes from you. Let me hear
Emma's voice—the true voice. This running away
merits your reproaches. It will look like—. I have more
to confess : the *tigress* in me wishes it were ! I should
then have a reckless passion to fold me about, and the
glory—infernal, if you name it so, and so it would be—
of suffering for and *with* some one else. As it is, I am
utterly solitary, sustained neither from above nor below,
except within myself, and that is all fire and smoke, like
their new engines.—I kiss this miserable sheet of paper.—
Yes, I judge that I have run off a line—and what a line !—
which hardly shows a trace for breathing things to follow
until they feel the transgression in wreck. How immensely nature seems to prefer men to women !—But
this paper is happier than the writer.

‘ Your Tony.’

That was the end. Emma kissed it in tears. They had often talked of the possibility of a classic friendship between women, the alliance of a mutual devotedness men choose to doubt of. She caught herself accusing Tony of the lapse from friendship. Hither should the true friend have flown unerringly.

The blunt ending of the letter likewise dealt a wound. She reperused it, perused and meditated. The flight of Mrs. Warwick! She heard that cry—fatal! But she had no means of putting a hand on her.—'Your Tony.' The coldness might be set down to exhaustion : it might, yet her not coming to her friend for counsel and love was a positive weight in the indifferent scale. She read the letter backwards, and by snatches here and there ; many perusals and hours passed before the scattered creature exhibited in its pages came to her out of the flying threads of the web as her living Tony, whom she loved and prized and was ready to defend against the world. By that time the fog had lifted ; she saw the sky on the borders of milky cloudfolds. Her invalid's chill sensitiveness conceived a sympathy in the baring heavens, and lying on her sofa in the drawing-room she gained strength of meditative vision, weak though she was to help, through ceasing to brood on her wound and herself. She cast herself into her dear Tony's feelings ; and thus it came, that she imagined Tony would visit The Crossways, where she kept souvenirs of her father, his cane, and his writing-desk, and a precious miniature of him hanging above it, before leaving England for ever. The fancy sprang to certainty ; every speculation confirmed it. Had Sir Lukin been at home she would have despatched him to The Crossways at once. The West wind blew, and gave her a view of the Downs beyond the weald from her southern window. She thought it even possible to drive there and reach the place, on the chance of her vivid suggestion, some time after nightfall ; but a walk across the room to try her forces was too convincing of her inability. She walked with an ebony silver-mounted stick, a present from Mr. Redworth. She was leaning on it when the card of Thomas Redworth was handed to her.

## CHAPTER VIII

IN WHICH IS EXHIBITED HOW A PRACTICAL MAN AND A DIVINING WOMAN LEARN TO RESPECT ONE ANOTHER

' You see, you are my crutch,' Lady Dunstane said to him, raising the stick in reminder of the present.

He offered his arm and hurriedly informed her, to dispose of dull personal matter, that he had just landed. She looked at the clock. ' Lukin is in town. You know the song : " Alas, I scarce can go or creep While *Lukin* is away." I do not doubt you have succeeded in your business over there. Ah ! Now I suppose you have confidence in your success. I should have predicted it, had you come to me.' She stood, either musing or in weakness, and said abruptly : ' Will you object to lunching at One o'clock ? '

' The sooner the better,' said Redworth. She had sighed : her voice betrayed some agitation, strange in so serenely-minded a person.

His partial acquaintance with the Herculean Sir Lukin's reputation in town inspired a fear of his being about to receive admission to the distressful confidences of the wife, and he asked if Mrs. Warwick was well. The answer sounded ominous, with its accompaniment of evident pain : ' I think her health is good.'

Had they quarrelled ? He said he had not heard a word of Mrs. Warwick for several months.

' I heard from her this morning,' said Lady Dunstane, and motioned him to a chair beside the sofa, where she half reclined, closing her eyes.  The sight of tears on the eyelashes frightened him.  She roused herself to look at the clock.  ' Providence or accident, you are here,' she said.  ' I could not have prayed for the coming of a truer man.  Mrs. Warwick is in great danger. . . . You know our love.  She is the best of me, heart and soul.  Her husband has chosen to act on vile suspicions—baseless, I could hold my hand in the fire and swear.  She has enemies, or the jealous fury is on the man—I know little of him.  He has commenced an action against her.  He will rue it.  But she . . . you understand this of women at least ;—they are not cowards in all things !—but the horror of facing a public scandal :—my poor girl writes of the hatefulness of having to act the complacent—put on her accustomed self !  She would have to go about, a mark for the talkers, and behave as if nothing were in the air—full of darts !  Oh, that general whisper !—it makes a coup de massue—a gale to sink the bravest vessel :— and a woman must preserve her smoothest front ; chat, smile—or else !—Well, she shrinks from it.  I should too.  She is leaving the country.'

' Wrong ! ' cried Redworth.

' Wrong indeed.  She writes, that in two days she will be out of it.  Judge her as I do, though you are a man, I pray.  You have seen the hunted hare.  It is our education—we have something of the hare in us when the hounds are full cry.  Our bravest, our best, have an impulse to run.  " By this, poor Wat far off upon a hill." Shakespeare would have the divine comprehension.  I have thought all round it and come back to him.  She is one of Shakespeare's women : another character, but one of his own :—another Hermione !  I dream of him—seeing her with that eye of steady flame.  The bravest and

best of us at bay in the world need an eye like his, to read
deep and not be baffled by inconsistencies.'

Insensibly Redworth blinked. His consciousness of an
exalted compassion for the lady was heated by these
flights of advocacy to feel that he was almost seated
beside the sovereign poet thus eulogized, and he was of a
modest nature.

'But you are practical,' pursued Lady Dunstane, observing signs that she took for impatience. 'You are
thinking of what can be done. If Lukin were here I
would send him to The Crossways without a moment's
delay, on the chance, the mere chance :—it shines to me !
If I were only a little stronger ! I fear I might break
down, and it would be unfair to my husband. He has
trouble enough with my premature infirmities already. I
am certain she will go to The Crossways. Tony is one of
the women who burn to give last kisses to things they
love. And she has her little treasures hoarded there.
She was born there. Her father died there. She is three
parts Irish—superstitious in affection. I know her so
well. At this moment I *see* her there. If not, she has
grown unlike herself.'

'Have you a stout horse in the stables ? ' Redworth
asked.

'You remember the mare Bertha; you have ridden her.'

'The mare would do, and better than a dozen horses.'
He consulted his watch. 'Let me mount Bertha, I en-
gage to deliver a letter at The Crossways to-night.'

Lady Dunstane half inclined to act hesitation in accepting the aid she sought, but said : 'Will you find your
way ? '

He spoke of three hours of daylight and a moon to rise.
'She has often pointed out to me from your ridges where
The Crossways lies, about three miles from the Downs,
near a village named Storling, on the road to Brasted.

The house has a small plantation of firs behind it, and a bit of river—rare for Sussex—to the right. An old straggling red brick house at Crossways, a stone's throw from a fingerpost on a square of green : roads to Brasted, London, Wickford, Riddlehurst. I shall find it. Write what you have to say, my lady, and confide it to me. She shall have it to-night, if she 's where you suppose. I 'll go, with your permission, and take a look at the mare. Sussex roads are heavy in this damp weather, and the frost coming on won't improve them for a tired beast. We haven't our rails laid down there yet.'

'You make me admit some virtues in the practical,' said Lady Dunstane ; and had the poor fellow vollied forth a tale of the everlastingness of his passion for Diana, it would have touched her far less than his exact memory of Diana's description of her loved birthplace.

She wrote :

'I trust my messenger to tell you how I hang on you. I see my ship making for the rocks. You break your Emma's heart. It will be *the second* wrong step. I shall not survive it. The threat has made me incapable of rushing to you, as I might have had strength to do yesterday. I am shattered, and I wait panting for Mr. Redworth's return *with you*. He has called, by accident, as we say. Trust to him. If ever heaven was active to avert a fatal mischance it is to-day. You will not stand against my supplication. It is my life I cry for. I have no more time. He starts. He leaves me to pray—like the mother seeing her child on the edge of the cliff. Come. This is your breast, my Tony ! And your soul warns you it is *right* to come. Do rightly. Scorn other counsel— the coward's. Come with our friend—the one man known to me who can be a friend of women.

'Your EMMA.'

Redworth was in the room. ' The mare 'll do it well,'
he said. ' She has had her feed, and in five minutes will
be saddled at the door.'

' But you must eat, dear friend,' said the hostess.

' I 'll munch at a packet of sandwiches on the way. There
seems a chance, and the time for lunching may miss it.'

' You understand . . . ? '

' Everything, I fancy.'

' If she is there ! '

' One break in the run will turn her back.'

The sensitive invalid felt a blow in his following up
the simile of the hunted hare for her friend, but it had a
promise of hopefulness. And this was all that could be
done by earthly agents, under direction of spiritual, as
her imagination encouraged her to believe.

She saw him start, after fortifying him with a tumbler
of choice Bordeaux, thinking how Tony would have said
she was like a lady arming her knight for battle. On the
back of the mare he passed her window, after lifting his
hat, and he thumped at his breast-pocket, to show her
where the letter housed safely. The packet of provision
bulged on his hip, absurdly and blessedly to her sight, not
unlike the man, in his combination of robust serviceable
qualities, as she reflected during the later hours, until the
sun fell on smouldering November woods, and sensations
of the frost he foretold bade her remember that he had
gone forth riding like a huntsman. His great-coat lay
on a chair in the hall, and his travelling-bag was beside it.
He had carried it up from the valley, expecting hospitality, and she had sent him forth half naked to weather
a frosty November night ! She called in the groom,
whose derision of a great-coat for any gentleman upon
Bertha, meaning work for the mare, appeased her remorse-
fulness. Brisby, the groom, reckoned how long the mare
would take to do the distance to Storling, with a rider like

Mr. Redworth on her back. By seven, Brisby calculated, Mr. Redworth would be knocking at the door of the
Three Ravens Inn, at Storling, when the mare would have
a decent grooming, and Mr. Redworth was not the gentleman to let her be fed out of his eye. More than that,
Brisby had some acquaintance with the people of the inn.
He begged to inform her ladyship that he was half a
Sussex man, though not exactly born in the county ; his
parents had removed to Sussex after the great event ; and
the Downs were his first field of horse-exercise, and no
place in the world was like them, fair weather or foul,
Summer or Winter, and snow ten feet deep in the gullies.
The grandest air in England, he had heard say.

His mistress kept him to the discourse, for the comfort
of hearing hard bald matter-of-fact ; and she was amused
and rebuked by his assumption that she must be entertaining an anxiety about master's favourite mare. But,
ah ! that Diana had delayed in choosing a mate ; had
avoided her disastrous union with perhaps a more imposing man, to see the true beauty of masculine character
in Mr. Redworth, as he showed himself to-day. How
could he have doubted succeeding ? One grain more of
faith in his energy, and Diana might have been mated to
the right husband for her—an open-minded clear-faced
English gentleman. Her speculative ethereal mind
clung to bald matter-of-fact to-day. She would have
vowed that it was the sole potentially heroical. Even
Brisby partook of the reflected rays, and he was very
benevolently considered by her. She dismissed him only
when his recounting of the stages of Bertha's journey
began to fatigue her and deaden the medical efficacy of
him and his like. Stretched on the sofa, she watched
the early sinking sun in South-western cloud, and the
changes from saffron to intensest crimson, the crown of a
November evening, and one of frost.

Redworth struck on a southward line from chalk-ridge to sand, where he had a pleasant footing in familiar country, under beeches that browned the ways, along beside a meadow-brook fed by the heights, through pines and across deep sand-ruts to full view of weald and Downs. Diana had been with him here in her maiden days. The coloured back of a coach put an end to that dream. He lightened his pocket, surveying the land as he munched. A favourable land for rails : and she had looked over it : and he was now becoming a wealthy man : and she was a married woman straining the leash. His errand would not bear examination, it seemed such a desperate long shot. He shut his inner vision on it, and pricked forward. When the burning sunset shot waves above the juniper and yews behind him, he was far on the weald, trotting down an interminable road. That the people opposing railways were not people of business, was his reflection, and it returned persistently : for practical men, even the most devoted among them, will think for themselves ; their army, which is the rational, calls them to its banners, in opposition to the sentimental ; and Redworth joined it in the abstract, summoning the horrible state of the roads to testify against an enemy wanting almost in common humaneness. A slip of his excellent stepper in one of the half-frozen pits of the highway was the principal cause of his confusion of logic ; she was half on her knees. Beyond the market town the roads were so bad that he quitted them, and with the indifference of an engineer, struck a line of his own South-eastward over fields and ditches, favoured by a round horizon moon on his left. So for a couple of hours he went ahead over rolling fallow land to the meadow-flats and a pale shining of freshets ; then hit on a lane skirting the water, and reached an amphibious village ; five miles from Storling, he was informed, and a clear traverse of lanes, not to be mistaken,

' if he kept a sharp eye open.' The sharpness of his eyes was divided between the sword-belt of the starry Hunter and the shifting lanes that zig-zagged his course below. The Downs were softly illumined ; still it amazed him to think of a woman like Diana Warwick having an attachment to this district, so hard of yield, mucky, featureless, fit but for the rails she sided with her friend in detesting. Reasonable women, too ! The moon stood high on her march as he entered Storling. He led his good beast to the stables of The Three Ravens, thanking her and caressing her. The ostler conjectured from the look of the mare that he had been out with the hounds and lost his way. It appeared to Redworth singularly, that near the ending of a wild goose chase, his plight was pretty well described by the fellow. However, he had to knock at the door of The Crossways now, in the silent night time, a certainly empty house, to his fancy. He fed on a snack of cold meat and tea, standing, and set forth, clearly directed, ' if he kept a sharp eye open.' Hitherto he had proved his capacity, and he rather smiled at the repetition of the formula to him, of all men. A turning to the right was taken, one to the left, and through the churchyard, out of the gate, round to the right, and on. By this route, after an hour, he found himself passing beneath the bare chestnuts of the churchyard wall of Storling, and the sparkle of the edges of the dead chestnut-leaves at his feet reminded him of the very ideas he had entertained when treading them. The loss of an hour strung him to pursue the chase in earnest, and he had a beating of the heart as he thought that it might be serious. He recollected thinking it so at Copsley. The long ride, and nightfall, with nothing in view, had obscured his mind to the possible behind the thick obstruction of the probable ; again the possible waved its marsh-light. To help in saving her from a fatal step, supposing a dozen combinations of the conditional mood, became his fixed object, since here he was—of that there was no doubt ; and he was not here to play the fool, though the errand were foolish. He entered the church-yard, crossed the shadow of the tower, and hastened along the path, fancying he beheld a couple of figures vanishing before him. He shouted ; he hoped to obtain directions from these natives : the moon was bright, the gravestones legible ; but no answer came back, and the place appeared to belong entirely to the dead. ' I 've frightened them,' he thought. They left a queerish sensation in his frame. A ride down to Sussex to see ghosts would be an odd experience ; but an undigested dinner of tea is the very grandmother of ghosts ; and he accused it of confusing him, sight and mind. Out of the gate, now for the turning to the right, and on. He turned. He must have previously turned wrongly some-where—and where ? A light in a cottage invited him to apply for the needed directions. The door was opened by a woman, who had never heard tell of The Crossways, nor had her husband, nor any of the children crowding round them. A voice within ejaculated : ' Crassways ! ' and soon upon the grating of a chair, an old man, whom the woman named her lodger, by way of introduction, pre-sented himself with his hat on, saying : ' I knows the spot they calls Crassways,' and he led. Redworth understood the intention that a job was to be made of it, and submitting, said : ' To the right, I think.' He was bidden to come along, if he wanted ' they Crassways,' and from the right they turned to the left, and further sharp round, and on to a turn, where the old man, other-wise incommunicative, said : ' There, down thik theer road, and a post in the middle.'

' I want a house, not a post ! ' roared Redworth, spy-ing a bare space.

The old man despatched a finger travelling to his nob. 'Naw, there's ne'er a house. But that's crassways for four roads, if it's crassways you wants.'

They journeyed backward. They were in such a maze of lanes that the old man was master, and Redworth vowed to be rid of him at the first cottage. This, however, they were long in reaching, and the old man was promptly through the garden-gate, hailing the people and securing information, before Redworth could well hear. He smiled at the dogged astuteness of a dense-headed old creature determined to establish a claim to his fee. They struck a lane sharp to the left.

'You're Sussex?' Redworth asked him, and was answered: 'Naw; the Sheers.'

Emerging from deliberation, the old man said: 'Ah'm a Hampshireman.'

'A capital county!'

'Heigh!' The old man heaved his chest. 'Once!'

'Why, what has happened to it?'

'Once it were a capital county, I say. Hah! you asks me what have happened to it. You take and go and look at it now. And down heer'll be no better soon, I tells 'em. When ah was a boy, old Hampshire was a proud country, wi' the old coaches and the old squires, and Harvest Homes, and Christmas merryings.—Cutting up the land! There's no pride in livin' theer, nor anywhere, as I sees, now.'

'You mean the railways.'

'It's the Devil come up and abroad ower all England!' exclaimed the melancholy ancient patriot.

A little cheering was tried on him, but vainly. He saw with unerring distinctness the triumph of the Foul Potentate, nay his personal appearance 'in they theer puffin' engines.' The country which had produced Andrew Hedger, as he stated his name to be, would never show

the same old cricketing commons it did when he was a
boy.  Old England, he declared, was done for.

When Redworth applied to his watch under the brilliant
moonbeams, he discovered that he had been listening to
this natural outcry of a decaying and shunted class full
three-quarters of an hour, and The Crossways was not in
sight.  He remonstrated.  The old man plodded along.
' We must do as we 're directed,' he said.

Further walking brought them to a turn.  Any turn
seemed hopeful.  Another turn offered the welcome sight
of a blazing doorway on a rise of ground off the road.
Approaching it, the old man requested him to ' bide a bit,'
and stalked the ascent at long strides.  A vigorous old
fellow.  Redworth waited below, observing how he
joined the group at the lighted door, and, as it was apparent, put his question of the whereabout of The Crossways.  Finally, in extreme impatience, he walked up to
the group of spectators.  They were all, and Andrew
Hedger among them, the most entranced and profoundly
reverent, observing the dissection of a pig.

Unable to awaken his hearing, Redworth jogged his
arm, and the shake was ineffective until it grew in force.

' I 've no time to lose ;  have they told you the way ? '

Andrew Hedger yielded his arm.  He slowly withdrew
his intent fond gaze from the fair outstretched white
carcase, and with drooping eyelids, he said :  ' Ah could
eat hog a solid hower ! '

He had forgotten to ask the way, intoxicated by the
aspect of the pig ;  and when he did ask it, he was hard of
understanding, given wholly to his last glimpses.

Redworth got the directions.  He would have dismissed Mr. Andrew Hedger, but there was no doing so.
' I 'll show ye on to the Crossways *House*,' the latter said,
implying that he had already earned something by showing him the Crossways post.

' Hog 's my feed,' said Andrew Hedger. The gastric springs of eloquence moved him to discourse, and he unburdened himself between succulent pauses. ' They 've killed him early. He 's fat ; and he might ha' been fatter. But he 's fat. They 've got their Christmas ready, that they have. Lord ! you should see the chitterlings, and the sausages hung up to and along the beams. That 's a crown for any dwellin' ! They runs 'em round the top of the room—it 's like a May-day wreath in old times. Home-fed hog ! They 've a treat in store, they have. And snap your fingers at the world for many a long day. And the hams ! They cure their own hams at that house. Old style ! That 's what I say of a hog. He 's good from end to end, and beats a Christian hollow. Everybody knows it and owns it.'

Redworth was getting tired. In sympathy with current conversation, he said a word for the railways : they would certainly make the flesh of swine cheaper, bring a heap of hams into the market. But Andrew Hedger remarked with contempt that he had not much opinion of foreign hams : nobody knew what they fed on. Hog, he said, would feed on anything, where there was no choice— they had wonderful stomachs for food. Only, when they had a choice, they left the worst for last, and home-fed filled them with stuff to make good meat and fat—' what we calls prime bacon.' As it is not right to damp a native enthusiasm, Redworth let him dilate on his theme, and mused on his boast to eat hog a *solid hour*, which roused some distant classic recollection :—an odd jumble.

They crossed the wooden bridge of a flooded stream.

' Now ye have it,' said the hog-worshipper ; ' that may be the house, I reckon.'

A dark mass of building, with the moon behind it, shining in spires through a mound of firs, met Redworth's gaze. The windows all were blind, no smoke rose from

the chimneys.   He noted the dusky square of green, and
the finger-post signalling the centre of the four roads.
Andrew Hedger repeated that it was the Crossways house,
ne'er a doubt.   Redworth paid him his expected fee,
whereupon Andrew, shouldering off, wished him a hearty
good night, and forthwith departed at high pedestrian
pace, manifestly to have a concluding look at the beloved
anatomy.

There stood the house.   Absolutely empty ! thought
Redworth.   The sound of the gate-bell he rang was like
an echo to him.   The gate was unlocked.   He felt a return
of his queer churchyard sensation when walking up the
garden-path, in the shadow of the house.   Here she was
born : here her father died : and this was the station of
her dreams, as a girl at school near London and in Paris.
Her heart was here.   He looked at the windows facing
the Downs with dead eyes.   The vivid idea of her was a
phantom presence, and cold, assuring him that the bodily
Diana was absent.   Had Lady Dunstane guessed rightly,
he might perhaps have been of service !

Anticipating the blank silence, he rang the house-bell.
It seemed to set wagging a weariful tongue in a corpse.
The bell did its duty to the last note, and one thin revival
stroke, for a finish, as in days when it responded livingly
to the guest.   He pulled, and had the reply, just the
same, with the faint terminal touch, resembling exactly a
' There ! ' at the close of a voluble delivery in the negative.   Absolutely empty.   He pulled and pulled.   The
bell wagged, wagged.   This had been a house of a witty
host, a merry girl, junketting guests ; a house of hilarious
thunders, lightnings of fun and fancy.   Death never
seemed more voiceful than in that wagging of the bell.

For conscience' sake, as became a trusty emissary, he
walked round to the back of the house, to verify the total
emptiness.   His apprehensive despondency had said that

it was absolutely empty, but upon consideration he supposed the house must have some guardian : likely enough, an old gardener and his wife, lost in deafness double-shotted by sleep ! There was no sign of them. The night air waxed sensibly crisper. He thumped the back-doors. Blank hollowness retorted on the blow. He banged and kicked. The violent altercation with wood and wall lasted several minutes, ending as it had begun. Flesh may worry, but is sure to be worsted in such an argument.

' Well, my dear lady ! '—Redworth addressed Lady Dunstane aloud, while driving his hands into his pockets for warmth—' we 've done what we could. The next best thing is to go to bed and see what morning brings us.'

The temptation to glance at the wild divinings of dreamy-witted women from the point of view of the practical man, was aided by the intense frigidity of the atmosphere in leading him to criticize a sex not much used to the exercise of brains. ' And they hate railways ! ' He associated them, in the matter of intelligence, with Andrew Hedger and Company. They sank to the level of the temperature in his esteem—as regarded their intellects. He approved their warmth of heart. The nipping of the victim's toes and finger-tips testified powerfully to that.

Round to the front of the house at a trot, he stood in moonlight. Then, for involuntarily he now did everything running, with a dash up the steps he seized the sullen pendant bell-handle, and worked it pumpwise, till he perceived a smaller bell-knob beside the door, at which he worked piston-wise. Pump and piston, the hurly-burly and the tinkler created an alarm to scare cat and mouse and Cardinal spider, all that run or weave in desolate houses, with the good result of a certain degree of heat to his frame. He ceased, panting. No stir within, nor

light.   That white stare of windows at the moon was
undisturbed.

The Downs were like a wavy robe of shadowy grey silk.
No wonder that she had loved to look on them !

And it was no wonder that Andrew Hedger enjoyed
prime bacon.   Bacon frizzling, fat rashers of real home-
fed on the fire—none of your foreign—suggested a genial
refreshment and resistance to antagonistic elements.   Nor
was it, granting health, granting a sharp night—the
temperature at least fifteen below zero—an excessive
boast for a man to say he could go on eating for a solid
hour.

These were notions darting through a half nourished
gentleman nipped in the frame by a severely frosty night.
Truly a most beautiful night !   She would have delighted
to see it here.   The Downs were like floating islands, like
fairy-laden vapours ;   solid, as Andrew Hedger's hour of
eating ;   visionary, as too often his desire !

Redworth muttered to himself, after taking the picture
of the house and surrounding country from the sward,
that he thought it about the sharpest night he had ever
encountered in England.   He was cold, hungry, dis-
pirited, and astoundingly stricken with an incapacity to
separate any of his thoughts from old Andrew Hedger.
Nature was at her pranks upon him.

He left the garden briskly, as to the legs, and reluctantly.   He would have liked to know whether Diana
had recently visited the house, or was expected.   It
could be learnt in the morning ;   but his mission was
urgent and he on the wings of it.   He was vexed and
saddened.

Scarcely had he closed the garden-gate when the noise
of an opening window arrested him, and he called.   The
answer was in a feminine voice, youngish, not disagree-
able, though not Diana's.

He heard none of the words, but rejoined in a bawl :
' Mrs. Warwick !—Mr. Redworth ! '

That was loud enough for the deaf or the dead.

The window closed.  He went to the door and waited.
It swung wide to him ; and, O marvel of a woman's
divination of a woman ! there stood Diana.

## CHAPTER  IX

SHOWS  HOW  A  POSITION  OF  DELICACY  FOR  A  LADY  AND
   GENTLEMAN  WAS  MET  IN  SIMPLE  FASHION  WITHOUT
   HURT  TO  EITHER

REDWORTH'S impulse was to laugh for very gladness of
heart, as he proffered excuses for his tremendous alarums :
and in doing so, the worthy gentleman imagined he must
have persisted in clamouring for admission because he
suspected, that if at home, she would require a violent
summons to betray herself.  It was necessary to him to
follow his abashed sagacity up to the mark of his happy
animation.

' Had I known it was you ! ' said Diana, bidding him
enter the passage.  She wore a black silk mantilla and
was warmly covered.

She called to her maid Danvers, whom Redworth remembered : a firm woman of about forty, wrapped, like
her mistress, in head-covering, cloak, scarf and shawl.
Telling her to scour the kitchen for firewood, Diana led
into a sitting-room.  ' I need not ask—you have come
from Lady Dunstane,' she said.  ' Is she well ? '

' She is deeply anxious.'

' You are cold.  Empty houses are colder than out of
doors.  You shall soon have a fire.'

She begged him to be seated.

The small glow of candle-light made her dark rich colouring orange in shadow.

' House and grounds are open to a tenant,' she resumed. ' I say good-bye to them to-morrow morning. The old couple who are in charge sleep in the village to-night. I did not want them here. You have quitted the Government service, I think ? '

' A year or so since.'

' When did you return from America ? '

' Two days back.'

' And paid your visit to Copsley immediately ? '

' As early as I could.'

' That was true friendliness. You have a letter for me ? '

' I have.'

He put his hand to his pocket for the letter.

' Presently,' she said. She divined the contents, and nursed her resolution to withstand them. Danvers had brought firewood and coal. Orders were given to her, and in spite of the opposition of the maid and intervention of the gentleman, Diana knelt at the grate, observing : ' Allow me to do this. I can lay and light a fire.'

He was obliged to look on : she was a woman who spoke her meaning. She knelt, handling paper, firewood and matches, like a housemaid. Danvers proceeded on her mission, and Redworth eyed Diana in the first fire-glow. He could have imagined a Madonna on an old black Spanish canvas.

The act of service was beautiful in gracefulness, and her simplicity in doing the work touched it spiritually. He thought, as she knelt there, that never had he seen how lovely and how charged with mystery her features were ; the dark large eyes full on the brows ; the proud line of a straight nose in right measure to the bow of the

lips ; reposeful red lips, shut, and their curve of the
slumber-smile at the corners.  Her forehead was broad ;
the chin of a sufficient firmness to sustain that noble
square ;  the brows marked by a soft thick brush to the
temples ;  her black hair plainly drawn along her head
to the knot, revealed by the mantilla fallen on her neck.

Elegant in plainness, the classic poet would have said
of her hair and dress.  She was of the women whose wits
are quick in everything they do.  That which was proper
to her position, complexion, and the hour, surely marked
her appearance.  Unaccountably this night, the fair
fleshly presence over-weighted her intellectual distinction,
to an observer bent on vindicating her innocence.  Or
rather, he saw the hidden in the visible.

Owner of such a woman, and to lose her !  Redworth
pitied the husband.

The crackling flames reddened her whole person.  Gazing, he remembered Lady Dunstane saying of her once,
that in anger she had the nostrils of a war-horse.  The
nostrils now were faintly alive under some sensitive impression of her musings.  The olive cheeks, pale as she
stood in the doorway, were flushed by the fire-beams,
though no longer with their swarthy central rose, tropic
flower of a pure and abounding blood, as it had seemed.
She was now beset by battle.  His pity for her, and his
eager championship, overwhelmed the spirit of compassion for the foolish wretched husband.  Dolt, the man
must be, Redworth thought ;  and he asked inwardly, Did
the miserable tyrant suppose of a woman like this, that
she would be content to shine as a candle in a grated
lanthorn ?  The generosity of men speculating upon
other men's possessions is known.  Yet the man who
loves a woman has to the full the husband's jealousy of
her good name.  And a lover, that without the claims
of the alliance, can be wounded on her behalf, is less

distracted in his homage by the personal luminary, to which
man's manufacture of balm and incense is mainly drawn
when his love is wounded. That contemplation of her
incomparable beauty, with the multitude of his ideas
fluttering round it, did somewhat shake the personal
luminary in Redworth. He was conscious of pangs.
The question bit him : How far had she been indiscreet
or wilful ? and the bite of it was a keen acid to his nerves.
A woman doubted by her husband, is always, and even to
her champions in the first hours of the noxious rumour,
until they have solidified in confidence through service,
a creature of the wilds, marked for our ancient running.
Nay, more than a cynical world, these latter will be sensible
of it. The doubt casts her forth, the general yelp drags
her down ; she runs like the prey of the forest under
spotting branches ; clear if we can think so, but it has
to be thought in devotedness : her character is abroad.
Redworth bore a strong resemblance to his fellowmen,
except for his power of faith in this woman. Nevertheless
it required the superbness of her beauty and the contrasting charm of her humble posture of kneeling by the fire,
to set him on his right track of mind. He knew and was
sure of her. He dispersed the unhallowed fry in attendance upon any stirring of the reptile part of us, to look at
her with the eyes of a friend. And if . . . !—a little
mouse of a thought scampered out of one of the chambers
of his head and darted along the passages, fetching a
sweat to his brows. Well, whatsoever the fact, his
heart was hers ! He hoped he could be charitable to
women.

She rose from her knees and said : ' Now, please, give
me the letter.'

He was entreated to excuse her for consigning him to
firelight when she left the room.

Danvers brought in a dismal tallow candle, remarking

that her mistress had not expected visitors : her mistress
had nothing but tea and bread and butter to offer him.
Danvers uttered no complaint of her sufferings ; happy
in being the picture of them.

' I 'm not hungry,' said he.

A plate of Andrew Hedger's own would not have
tempted him.  The foolish frizzle of bacon sang in his
ears as he walked from end to end of the room ; an
illusion of his fancy pricked by a frost-edged appetite.
But the anticipated contest with Diana checked and
numbed the craving.

Was Warwick a man to proceed to extremities on a
mad suspicion ?—What kind of proof had he ?

Redworth summoned the portrait of Mr. Warwick
before him, and beheld a sweeping of close eyes in cloud,
a long upper lip in cloud ; the rest of him was all cloud.
As usual with these conjurations of a face, the index of
the nature conceived by him displayed itself, and no
more ; but he took it for the whole physiognomy, and
pronounced of the husband thus delineated, that those
close eyes of the long upper lip would both suspect and
proceed madly.

He was invited by Danvers to enter the dining-room.

There Diana joined him.

' The best of a dinner on bread and butter is, that one
is ready for supper soon after it,' she said, swimming to
the tea-tray.  ' You have dined ? '

' At the inn,' he replied.

' The Three Ravens !  When my father's guests from
London flooded The Crossways, The Three Ravens provided the overflow with beds.  On nights like this I have
got up and scraped the frost from my window-panes to
see them step into the old fly, singing some song of his.
The inn had a good reputation for hospitality in those
days.  I hope they treated you well ? '

'Excellently,' said Redworth, taking an enormous mouthful, while his heart sank to see that she who smiled to encourage his eating had been weeping. But she also consumed her bread and butter.

'That poor maid of mine is an instance of a woman able to do things against the grain,' she said. 'Danvers is a foster-child of luxury. She loves it ; great houses, plentiful meals, and the crowd of twinkling footmen's calves. Yet you see her here in a desolate house, consenting to cold, and I know not what, terrors of ghosts ! poor soul. I have some mysterious attraction for her. She would not let me come alone. I should have had to hire some old Storling grannam, or retain the tattling keepers of the house. She loves her native country too, and disdains the foreigner. My tea you may trust.'

Redworth had not a doubt of it. He was becoming a tea-taster. The merit of warmth pertained to the beverage. 'I think you get your tea from Scoppin's, in the City,' he said.

That was the warehouse for Mrs. Warwick's tea. They conversed of Teas ; the black, the green, the mixtures ; each thinking of the attack to come, and the defence. Meantime, the cut bread and butter having flown, Redworth attacked the loaf. He apologized.

'Oh ! pay me a practical compliment,' Diana said, and looked really happy at his unfeigned relish of her simple fare.

She had given him one opportunity in speaking of her maid's love of native country. But it came too early.

'They say that bread and butter is fattening,' he remarked.

'You preserve the mean,' said she.

He admitted that his health was good. For some little time, to his vexation at the absurdity, she kept him talking of himself. So flowing was she, and so sweet the

motion of her mouth in utterance, that he followed her
lead, and he said odd things and corrected them.  He
had to describe his ride to her.

'Yes ! the view of the Downs from Dewhurst,' she
exclaimed.  ' Or any point along the ridge.  Emma and
I once drove there in Summer, with clotted cream from
her dairy, and we bought fresh-plucked wortleberries, and
stewed them in a hollow of the furzes, and ate them with
ground biscuits and the clotted cream iced, and thought
it a luncheon for seraphs.  Then you dropped to the road
round under the sand-heights—and meditated railways ! '

' Just a notion or two.'

' You have been very successful in America ? '

' Successful ; perhaps ; we exclude extremes in our calculations of the still problematical.'

' I am sure,' said she, ' you always have faith in your
calculations.'

Her innocent archness dealt him a stab sharper than any
he had known since the day of his hearing of her engagement.  He muttered of his calculations being human ;
he was as much of a fool as other men—more !

' Oh ! no,' said she.

' Positively.'

' I cannot think it.'

' I know it.'

' Mr. Redworth, you will never persuade me to believe it.'

He knocked a rising groan on the head, and rejoined :
' I hope I may not have to say so to-night.'

Diana felt the edge of the dart.  ' And meditating railways, you scored our poor land of herds and flocks ; and
night fell, and the moon sprang up, and on you came.  It
was clever of you to find your way by the moonbeams.'

' That 's about the one thing I seem fit for ! '

' But what delusion is this, in the mind of a man succeeding in everything he does ! ' cried Diana, curious

despite her wariness. 'Is there to be the revelation of a
hairshirt ultimately ?—a Journal of Confessions ? You
succeeded in everything you aimed at, and broke your
heart over one chance miss ? '

'My heart is not of the stuff to break,' he said, and
laughed off her fortuitous thrust straight into it.
'Another cup, yes. I came . . .'

'By night,' said she, 'and cleverly found your way,
and dined at The Three Ravens, and walked to The
Crossways, and met no ghosts.'

'On the contrary—or at least I saw a couple.'

'Tell me of them ; we breed them here. We sell them
periodically to the newspapers.'

'Well, I started them in their natal locality. I saw
them, going down the churchyard, and bellowed after
them with all my lungs. I wanted directions to The
Crossways ; I had missed my way at some turning. In
an instant they were vapour.'

Diana smiled. 'It was indeed a voice to startle
delicate apparitions ! So do roar Hyrcanean tigers,
Pyramus and Thisbe-slaying lions ! One of your ghosts
carried a loaf of bread, and dropped it in fright ; one
carried a pound of fresh butter for home consumption.
They were in the churchyard for one in passing to kneel
at her father's grave and kiss his tombstone.'

She bowed her head, forgetful of her guard.

The pause presented an opening. Redworth left his
chair and walked to the mantelpiece. It was easier to
him to speak, not facing her.

'You have read Lady Dunstane's letter,' he began.

She nodded. 'I have.'

'Can you resist her appeal to you ? '

'I must.'

'She is not in a condition to bear it well. You will
pardon me, Mrs. Warwick . . .'

'Fully! Fully!'

'I venture to offer merely practical advice. You have thought of it all, but have not felt it. In these cases, the one thing to do is to make a stand. Lady Dunstane has a clear head. She sees what has to be endured by you. Consider : she appeals to me to bring you her letter. Would she have chosen me, or any man, for her messenger, if it had not appeared to her a matter of life and death ?— You count me among your friends.'

'One of the truest.'

'Here are two, then, and your own good sense. For I do not believe it to be a question of courage.'

'He has commenced. Let him carry it out,' said Diana.

Her desperation could have added the cry—And give me freedom ! That was the secret in her heart. She had struck on the hope for the detested yoke to be broken at any cost.

'I decline to meet his charges. I despise them. If my friends have faith in me—and they may !—I want nothing more.'

'Well, I won't talk commonplaces about the world,' said Redworth. 'We can none of us afford to have it against us. Consider a moment : to your friends you are the Diana Merion they knew, and they will not suffer an injury to your good name without a struggle. But if you fly ? You leave the dearest you have to the whole brunt of it.'

'They will, if they love me.'

'They will. But think of the shock to her. Lady Dunstane reads you . . .'

'Not quite. No, not if she even wishes me to stay !' said Diana.

He was too intent on his pleading to perceive a signification.

'She reads you as clearly in the dark as if you were present with her.'

'Oh! why am I not ten years older!' Diana cried, and tried to face round to him, and stopped paralyzed. 'Ten years older, I could discuss my situation, as an old woman of the world, and use my wits to defend myself.'

'And then you would not dream of flight before it!'

'No, she does not read me: no! She saw that I might come to The Crossways. She—no one but myself can see the wisdom of my holding aloof, in contempt of this baseness.'

'And of allowing her to sink under that which your presence would arrest. Her strength will not support it.'

'Emma! Oh, cruel!' Diana sprang up to give play to her limbs. She dropped on another chair. 'Go I must, I cannot turn back. She saw my old attachment to this place. It was not difficult to guess . . . Who but I can see the wisest course for me!'

'It comes to this, that the blow aimed at you in your absence will strike her, and mortally,' said Redworth.

'Then I say it is terrible to have a friend,' said Diana, with her bosom heaving.

'Friendship, I fancy, means one heart between two.'

His unstressed observation hit a bell in her head, and set it reverberating. She and Emma had spoken, written, the very words. She drew forth her Emma's letter from under her left breast, and read some half-blinded lines.

Redworth immediately prepared to leave her to her feelings—trustier guides than her judgement in this crisis.

'Adieu, for the night, Mrs. Warwick,' he said, and was guilty of eulogizing the judgement he thought erratic for the moment. 'Night is a calm adviser. Let me presume to come again in the morning. I dare not go back without you.'

She looked up. As they faced together each saw that

the other had passed through a furnace, scorching enough
to him, though hers was the delicacy exposed.  The reflection had its weight with her during the night.

' Danvers is getting ready a bed for you ; she is airing
linen,' Diana said.  But the bed was declined, and the
hospitality was not pressed.  The offer of it seemed to him
significant of an unwary cordiality and thoughtlessness of
tattlers that might account possibly for many things—
supposing a fool or madman, or malignants, to interpret
them.

' Then, good night,' said she.

They joined hands.  He exacted no promise that she
would be present in the morning to receive him ; and it
was a consolation to her desire for freedom, until she
reflected on the perfect confidence it implied, and felt as a
quivering butterfly impalpably pinned.

## CHAPTER X

### THE CONFLICT OF THE NIGHT

HER brain was a steam-wheel throughout the night ;
everything that could be thought of was tossed, nothing
grasped.

The unfriendliness of the friends who sought to retain
her recurred.  For look—to fly could not be interpreted
as a flight.  It was but a stepping aside, a disdain of
defending herself, and a wrapping herself in her dignity.
Women would be with her.  She called on the noblest of
them to justify the course she chose, and they did, in an
almost audible murmur.

And O the rich reward.  A black archway-gate swung
open to the glittering fields of freedom.

Emma was not of the chorus.  Emma meditated as an invalid.  How often had Emma bewailed to her that the most grievous burden of her malady was her fatal tendency to brood sickly upon human complications!  She could not see the blessedness of the prospect of freedom to a woman abominably yoked.  What if a miserable woman were dragged through mire to reach it!  Married, the mire was her portion, whatever she might do.  That man—but pass him!

And that other—the dear, the kind, careless, high-hearted old friend.  He could honestly protest his guiltlessness, and would smilingly leave the case to go its ways. Of this she was sure, that her decision and her pleasure would be his.  They were tied to the stake.  She had already tasted some of the mortal agony.  Did it matter whether the flames consumed her?

Reflecting on the interview with Redworth, though she had performed her part in it placidly, her skin burned. It was the beginning of tortures if she stayed in England.

By staying to defend herself she forfeited her attitude of dignity and lost all chance of her reward.  And name the sort of world it is, dear friends, for which we are to sacrifice our one hope of freedom, that we may preserve our fair fame in it!

Diana cried aloud, ' My freedom!' feeling as a butterfly flown out of a box to stretches of sunny earth beneath spacious heavens.  Her bitter marriage, joyless in all its chapters, indefensible where the man was right as well as where insensately wrong, had been imprisonment.  She excused him down to his last madness, if only the bonds were broken.  Here, too, in this very house of her happiness with her father, she had bound herself to the man : voluntarily, quite inexplicably.  Voluntarily, as we say. But there must be a spell upon us at times.  Upon young women there certainly is.

The wild brain of Diana, armed by her later enlightenment as to the laws of life and nature, dashed in revolt at
the laws of the world when she thought of the forces,
natural and social, urging young women to marry and be
bound to the end.

It should be a spotless world which is thus ruthless.

But were the world impeccable it would behave more
generously.

The world is ruthless, dear friends, because the world is
hypocrite ! The world cannot afford to be magnani-
mous, or even just.

Her dissensions with her husband, their differences of
opinion, and puny wranglings, hoistings of two standards,
reconciliations for the sake of decency, breaches of the
truce, and his detested meanness, the man behind the
mask ; and glimpses of herself too, the half-known, half-
suspected, developing creature claiming to be Diana, and
unlike her dreamed Diana, deformed by marriage, irrit-
able, acerb, rebellious, constantly justifiable against him,
but not in her own mind, and therefore accusing him of
the double crime of provoking her and perverting her—
these were the troops defiling through her head while she
did battle with the hypocrite world.

One painful sting was caused by the feeling that she
could have loved—whom ? An ideal. Had he, the
imagined but unvisioned, been her yoke-fellow, would she
now lie raising caged-beast cries in execration of the yoke ?
She would not now be seeing herself as hare, serpent,
tigress ! The hypothesis was reviewed in negatives : she
had barely a sense of softness, just a single little heave of
the bosom, quivering upward and leadenly sinking, when
she glanced at a married Diana heartily mated. The
regrets of the youthful for a life sailing away under
medical sentence of death in the sad eyes of relatives resemble it. She could have loved. Good-bye to that !

A woman's brutallest tussle with the world was upon her. She was in the arena of the savage claws, flung there by the man who of all others should have protected her from them. And what had she done to deserve it ? She listened to the advocate pleading her case ; she primed him to admit the charges, to say the worst, in contempt of legal prudence, and thereby expose her transparent honesty. The very things awakening a mad suspicion proved her innocence. But was she this utterly simple person ? Oh, no ! She was the Diana of the pride in her power of fencing with evil—by no means of the order of those ninny young women who realize the popular conception of the purely innocent. She had fenced and kept her guard. Of this it was her angry glory to have the knowledge. But she had been compelled to fence. Such are men in the world of facts, that when a woman steps out of her domestic tangle to assert, because it is a tangle, her rights to partial independence, they sight her for their prey, or at least they complacently suppose her accessible. Wretched at home, a woman ought to bury herself in her wretchedness, else may she be assured that not the cleverest, wariest guard will cover her character.

Against the husband her cause was triumphant. Against herself she decided not to plead it, for this reason, that the preceding Court, which was the public and only positive one, had entirely and justly exonerated her. But the holding of her hand by the friend half a minute too long for friendship, and the overfriendliness of looks, letters, frequency of visits, would speak within her. She had a darting view of her husband's estimation of them in his present mood. She quenched it ; they were trifles, things that women of the world have to combat. The revelation to a fair-minded young woman of the majority of men being naught other than men, and some of the friendliest of men betraying confidence under the excuse of temptation, is one of the shocks to simplicity which leave her the alternative of misanthropy or philosophy. Diana had not the heart to hate her kind, so she resigned herself to pardon, and to the recognition of the state of duel between the sexes—active enough in her sphere of society. The circle hummed with it ; many lived for it. Could she pretend to ignore it ? Her personal experience might have instigated a less clear and less intrepid nature to take advantage of the opportunity for playing the popular innocent, who runs about with astonished eyes to find herself in so hunting a world, and wins general compassion, if not shelter in unsuspected and unlicenced places. There is perpetually the inducement to act the hypocrite before the hypocrite world, unless a woman submits to be the humbly knitting housewife, unquestioningly worshipful of her lord ; for the world is. ever gracious to an hypocrisy that pays homage to the mask of virtue by copying it ; the world is hostile to the face of an innocence not conventionally simpering and quite surprised ; the world prefers decorum to honesty. ' Let me be myself, whatever the martyrdom ! ' she cried, in that phase of young sensation when, to the blooming woman, the putting on of a mask appears to wither her and reduce her to the show she parades. Yet, in common with her sisterhood, she owned she had worn a sort of mask ; the world demands it of them as the price of their station. That she had never worn it consentingly, was the plea for now casting it off altogether, showing herself as she was, accepting martyrdom, becoming the first martyr of the modern woman's cause— a grand position ! and one imaginable to an excited mind in the dark, which does not conjure a critical humour, as light does, to correct the feverish sublimity. She was, then, this martyr, a woman capable of telling the world she knew it, and of confessing that she had behaved in disdain of its rigider rules, according to her own ideas of her immunities. O brave!

But was she holding the position by flight? It involved the challenge of consequences, not an evasion of them.

She moaned; her mental steam-wheel stopped; fatigue brought sleep.

She had sensationally led her rebellious wits to the Crossways, distilling much poison from thoughts on the way; and there, for the luxury of a still seeming indecision, she sank into oblivion.


## CHAPTER XI

RECOUNTS THE JOURNEY IN A CHARIOT, WITH A CERTAIN
AMOUNT OF DIALOGUE, AND A SMALL INCIDENT ON
THE ROAD

IN the morning the fight was over. She looked at the signpost of The Crossways whilst dressing, and submitted to follow, obediently as a puppet, the road recommended by friends, though a voice within, that she took for the intimations of her reason, protested that they were wrong, that they were judging of her case in the general, and unwisely—disastrously for her.

The mistaking of her desires for her reason was peculiar to her situation.

'So I suppose I shall some day see The Crossways again,' she said, to conceive a compensation in the abandonment of freedom. The night's red vision of martyrdom was reserved to console her secretly, among the unopened lockers in her treasury of thoughts. It helped to sustain her; and she was too conscious of things necessary for her sustainment to bring it to the light of day and examine it. She had a pitiful bit of pleasure in the gratification she imparted to Danvers, by informing her that the journey of the day was backward to Copsley.

'If I may venture to say so, ma'am, I am very glad,' said her maid.

'You must be prepared for the questions of lawyers, Danvers.'

'Oh, ma'am! they 'll get nothing out of me, and their wigs won't frighten me.'

'It is usually their baldness that is most frightening, my poor Danvers.'

'Nor their baldness, ma'am,' said the literal maid; 'I never cared for their heads, or them. I 've been in a Case before.'

'Indeed!' exclaimed her mistress; and she had a chill.

Danvers mentioned a notorious Case, adding, 'They got nothing out of me.'

'In my Case you will please to speak the truth,' said Diana, and beheld in the looking-glass the primming of her maid's mouth. The sight shot a sting.

'Understand that there is to be no hesitation about telling the truth of what you know of me,' said Diana; and the answer was, 'No, ma'am.'

For Danvers could remark to herself that she *knew* little, and was not a person to hesitate. She was a maid of the world, with the quality of faithfulness, by nature, to a good mistress.

Redworth's further difficulties were confined to the hiring of a conveyance for the travellers, and hot-water bottles, together with a postillion not addicted to drunkenness. He procured a posting-chariot, an ancient and musty, of a late autumnal yellow unrefreshed by paint; the only bottles to be had were Dutch schiedam. His

postillion, inspected at Storling, carried the flag of
habitual inebriation on his nose, and he deemed it adviseable to ride the mare in accompaniment as far as
Riddlehurst, notwithstanding the postillion's vows upon
his honour that he was no *drinker*. The emphasis, to a
gentleman acquainted with his countrymen, was not
reassuring. He had hopes of enlisting a trustier fellow
at Riddlehurst, but he was disappointed ; and while
debating upon what to do, for he shrank from leaving
two women to the conduct of that inflamed trough-
snout, Brisby, despatched to Storling by an afterthought
of Lady Dunstane's, rushed out of the Riddlehurst inn
taproom, and relieved him of the charge of the mare. He
was accommodated with a seat on a stool in the chariot,
'My triumphal car,' said his captive. She was very
amusing about her postillion ; Danvers had to beg pardon
for laughing. 'You are happy,' observed her mistress.
But Redworth laughed too, and he could not boast of any
happiness beyond the temporary satisfaction, nor could
she who sprang the laughter boast of that little. She
said to herself, in the midst of the hilarity, ' Wherever
I go now, in all weathers, I am perfectly naked ! ' And
remembering her readings of a certain wonderful old
quarto book in her father's library, by an eccentric old
Scottish nobleman, wherein the wearing of garments and
sleeping in houses is accused as the cause of human de-
generacy, she took a forced merry stand on her return to
the primitive healthful state of man and woman, and
affected scorn of our modern ways of dressing and thinking. Whence it came that she had some of her wildest
seizures of iridescent humour. Danvers attributed the
fun to her mistress's gladness in not having pursued her
bent to quit the country. Redworth saw deeper, and
was nevertheless amazed by the airy hawk-poise and
pounce-down of her wit, as she ranged high and low, now

capriciously generalizing, now dropping bolt upon things
of passage—the postillion jogging from rum to gin, the
rustics baconly agape, the horse-kneed ostlers. She
touched them to the life in similes and phrases ; and
next she was aloft, derisively philosophizing, but with
a comic afflatus that dispersed the sharpness of her
irony in mocking laughter. The afternoon refreshments
at the inn of the county market-town, and the English
idea of public hospitality, as to manner and the substance
provided for wayfarers, were among the themes she made
memorable to him. She spoke of everything tolerantly,
just naming it in a simple sentence, that fell with a ring
and chimed : their host's ready acquiescence in receiving
orders, his contemptuous disclaimer of stuff he did not
keep, his flat indifference to the sheep he sheared, and
the phantom half-crown flickering in one eye of the anticipatory waiter ; the pervading and confounding smell
of stale beer over all the apartments ; the prevalent
notion of bread, butter, tea, milk, sugar, as mattter for
the exercise of a native inventive genius—these were
reviewed in quips of metaphor.

'Come, we can do better at an inn or two known to me,'
said Redworth.

'Surely this is the best that can be done for us, when
we strike them with the magic wand of a postillion ? '
said she.

'It depends, as elsewhere, on the individuals entertaining us.'

'Yet you admit that your railways are rapidly " polishing off " the individual.'

'They will spread the metropolitan idea of comfort.'

'I fear they will feed us on nothing but that big word.
It booms—a curfew bell—for every poor little light that
we would read by.'

Seeing their beacon-nosed postillion preparing to

mount and failing in his jump, Redworth was apprehensive, and questioned the fellow concerning potation.

'Lord, sir, they call me half a horse, but I can't 'bide
water,' was the reply, with the assurance that he had not
'taken a pailful.'

Habit enabled him to gain his seat.

'It seems to us unnecessary to heap on coal when the
chimney is afire; but he may know the proper course,'
Diana said, convulsing Danvers; and there was discern-
ibly to Redworth, under the influence of her phrases, a
likeness of the flaming 'half-horse,' with the animals all
smoking in the frost, to a railway engine. 'Your
wrinkled centaur,' she named the man. Of course he
had to play second to her, and not unwillingly; but he
reflected passingly on the instinctive push of her rich
and sparkling voluble fancy to the initiative, which
women do not like in a woman, and men prefer to distantly admire. English women and men feel toward the
quick-witted of their species as to aliens, having the
demerits of aliens—wordiness, vanity, obscurity, shallow-
ness, an empty glitter, the sin of posturing. A quick-
witted woman exerting her wit is both a foreigner and
potentially a criminal. She is incandescent to a breath of
rumour. It accounted for her having detractors; a
heavy counterpoise to her enthusiastic friends. It might
account for her husband's discontent—the reduction of
him to a state of mere masculine antagonism. What is
the husband of a vanward woman? He feels himself
but a diminished man. The English husband of a voluble
woman relapses into a dreary mute. Ah, for the choice
of places! Redworth would have yielded her the loquent
lead for the smallest of the privileges due to him who
now rejected all, except the public scourging of her. The
conviction was in his mind that the husband of this
woman sought rather to punish than be rid of her.

But a part of his own emotion went to form the judgement.

Furthermore, Lady Dunstane's allusion to her ' enemies ' made him set down her growing crop of back-biters to the trick she had of ridiculing things English. If the English do it themselves, it is in a professionally robust, a jocose, kindly way, always with a glance at the other things, great things, they excel in ; and it is done to have the credit of doing it. They are keen to catch an inimical tone ; they will find occasion to chastise the presumptuous individual, unless it be the leader of a party, therefore a power ; for they respect a power. Redworth knew their quaintnesses ; without overlooking them he winced at the acid of an irony that seemed to spring from aversion, and regretted it, for her sake. He had to recollect that she was in a sharp-strung mood, bitterly surexcited ; moreover he reminded himself of her many and memorable phrases of enthusiasm for England —Shakespeareland, as she would sometimes perversely term it, to sink the country in the poet. English forti-tude, English integrity, the English disposition to do justice to dependents, adolescent English ingenuousness, she was always ready to laud. Only her enthusiasm re-quired rousing by circumstances ; it was less at the brim than her satire. Hence she made enemies among a placable people.

He felt that he could have helped her under happier conditions. The beautiful vision she had been on the night of the Irish Ball swept before him, and he looked at her, smiling.

' Why do you smile ? ' she said.

' I was thinking of Mr. Sullivan Smith.'

' Ah ! my dear compatriot ! And think, too, of Lord Larrian.'

She caught her breath. Instead of recreation, the

names brought on a fit of sadness. It deepened ; she
neither smiled nor rattled any more. She gazed across
the hedgeways at the white meadows and bare-twigged
copses showing their last leaves in the frost.

' I remember your words : " Observation is the most
enduring of the pleasures of life " ; and so I have found
it,' she said. There was a brightness along her under-
eyelids that caused him to look away.

The expected catastrophe occurred on the descent of a
cutting in the sand, where their cordial postillion at a trot
bumped the chariot against the sturdy wheels of a waggon,
which sent it reclining for support upon a beech-tree's
huge intertwisted serpent roots, amid strips of brown
bracken and pendant weeds, while he exhibited one short
stump of leg, all boot, in air. No one was hurt. Diana
disengaged herself from the shoulder of Danvers, and
mildly said :

' That reminds me, I forgot to ask why we came in a
chariot.'

Redworth was excited on her behalf, but the broken
glass had done no damage, nor had Danvers fainted.
The remark was unintelligible to him, apart from the
comforting it had been designed to give. He jumped
out, and held a hand for them to do the same. ' I never
foresaw an event more positively,' said he.

' And it was nothing but a back view that inspired you
all the way,' said Diana.

A waggoner held the horses, another assisted Redworth
to right the chariot. The postillion had hastily recovered
possession of his official seat, that he might as soon as
possible feel himself again where he was most intelligent,
and was gay in stupidity, indifferent to what happened
behind him. Diana heard him counselling the waggoner
as to the common sense of meeting small accidents with a
cheerful soul.

'Lord!' he cried, 'I been pitched a somerset in my time, and taken up for dead, and that didn't beat me!'

Disasters of the present kind could hardly affect such a veteran. But he was painfully disconcerted by Redworth's determination not to entrust the ladies any farther to his guidance. Danvers had implored for permission to walk the mile to the town, and thence take a fly to Copsley. Her mistress rather sided with the postillion, who begged them to spare him the disgrace of riding in and delivering a box at the Red Lion.

'What 'll they say? And they know Arthur Dance well there,' he groaned. 'What! Arthur! chariotin' a box! And me a better man to his work now than I been for many a long season, fit for double the journey! A bit of a shake always braces me up. I could read a newspaper right off, small print and all. Come along, sir, and hand the ladies in.'

Danvers vowed her thanks to Mr. Redworth for refusing. They walked ahead; the postillion communicated his mixture of professional and human feelings to the waggoners, and walked his horses in the rear, meditating on the weak-heartedness of gentryfolk, and the means for escaping being chaffed out of his boots at the Old Red Lion, where he was to eat, drink, and sleep that night. Ladies might be fearsome after a bit of a shake; he would not have supposed it of a gentleman. He jogged himself into an arithmetic of the number of nips of liquor he had taken to soothe him on the road, in spite of the gentleman. 'For some of 'em are sworn enemies of poor men, as yonder one, ne'er a doubt.'

Diana enjoyed her walk beneath the lingering brownred of the frosty November sunset, with the scent of sand-earth strong in the air.

'I had to hire a chariot because there was no two-horse

carriage,' said Redworth, ' and I wished to reach Copsley as early as possible.'

She replied, smiling, that accidents were fated. As a certain marriage had been ! The comparison forced itself on her reflections.

' But this is quite an adventure,' said she, reanimated by the brisker flow of her blood. ' We ought really to be thankful for it, in days when nothing happens.'

Redworth accused her of getting that idea from the perusal of romances.

' Yes, our lives require compression, like romances, to be interesting, and we object to the process,' she said. ' Real happiness is a state of dulness. When we taste it consciously it becomes mortal—a thing of the Seasons. But I like my walk. How long these November sunsets burn, and what hues they have ! There is a scientific reason, only don't tell it me. Now I understand why you always used to choose your holidays in November.'

She thrilled him with her friendly recollection of his customs.

' As to happiness, the looking forward is happiness,' he remarked.

' Oh, the looking back ! back ! ' she cried.

' Forward ! that is life.'

' And backward, death, if you will ; and still it is happiness. Death, and our postillion ! '

' Ay ; I wonder why the fellow hangs to the rear,' said Redworth, turning about.

' It 's his cunning strategy, poor creature, so that he may be thought to have delivered us at the head of the town, for us to make a purchase or two, if we go to the inn on foot,' said Diana. ' We 'll let the manœuvre succeed.'

Redworth declared that she had a head for everything, and she was flattered to hear him.

So passing from the southern into the western road, they saw the town-lights beneath an amber sky burning out sombrely over the woods of Copsley, and entered the town, the postillion following.

## CHAPTER XII

### BETWEEN EMMA AND DIANA

DIANA was in the arms of her friend at a late hour of the evening, and Danvers breathed the amiable atmosphere of footmen once more, professing herself perished.  This maid of the world, who could endure hardships and loss of society for the mistress to whom she was attached, no sooner saw herself surrounded by the comforts befitting her station, than she indulged in the luxury of a wailful dejectedness, the better to appreciate them.  She was unaffectedly astonished to find her outcries against the cold and the journeyings to and fro interpreted as a serving-woman's muffled comments on her mistress's behaviour.  Lady Dunstane's maid Bartlett, and Mrs. Bridges the housekeeper, and Foster the butler, contrived to let her know that they could speak an if they would ; and they expressed their pity of her to assist her to begin the speaking.  She bowed in acceptance of Foster's offer of a glass of wine after supper, but treated him and the other two immediately as though they had been interrogating bigwigs.

' They wormed nothing out of me,' she said to her mistress at night, undressing her.  ' But what a set they are !  They 've got such comfortable places, they 've all their days and hours for talk of the doings of their superiors.  They read the vilest of those town papers, and they put their two and two together of what is happening in and about. And not one of the footmen thinks of staying, because it's so dull; and they and the maids object—did one ever hear ?—to the three uppers retiring, when they've done dining, to the private room to dessert.'

'That is the custom ? ' observed her mistress.

'Foster carries the decanter, ma'am, and Mrs. Bridges the biscuits, and Bartlett the plate of fruit, and they march out in order.'

'The man at the head of the procession, probably.'

'Oh yes. And the others, though they have everything except the wine and dessert, don't like it. When I was here last they were new, and hadn't a word against it. Now they say it's invidious ! Lady Dunstane will be left without an under-servant at Copsley soon. I was asked about your boxes, ma'am, and the moment I said they were at Dover, that instant all three peeped. They let out a mouse to me. They do love to talk ! '

Her mistress could have added, ' And you too, my good Danvers ! ' trustworthy though she knew the creature to be in the main.

'Now go, and be sure you have bedclothes enough before you drop asleep,' she said ; and Danvers directed her steps to gossip with Bartlett.

Diana wrapped herself in a dressing-gown Lady Dunstane had sent her, and sat by the fire, thinking of the powder of tattle stored in servants' halls to explode beneath her : and but for her choice of roads she might have been among strangers. The liking of strangers best is a curious exemplification of innocence.

'Yes, I was in a muse,' she said, raising her head to Emma, whom she expected and sat armed to meet, unaccountably iron-nerved. ' I was questioning whether I could be quite as blameless as I fancy, if I sit and shiver to be in England. You will tell me I have taken the right road. I doubt it. But the road is taken, and here I am. But any road that leads me to you is homeward, my darling ! ' She tried to melt, determining to be at least open with her.

' I have not praised you enough for coming,' said Emma, when they had embraced again.

' Praise a little your " truest friend of women." Your letter gave the tug. I might have resisted it.'

' He came straight from heaven ! But, cruel Tony ! where is your love ? '

' It is unequal to yours, dear, I see. I could have wrestled with anything abstract and distant, from being certain—. But here I am.'

' But, my own dear girl, you never could have allowed this infamous charge to be undefended ? '

' I think so. I 've an odd apathy as to my character ; rather like death, when one dreams of flying the soul. What does it matter ? I should have left the flies and wasps to worry a corpse. And then—good-bye gentility ! I should have worked for my bread. I had thoughts of America. I fancy I can write ; and Americans, one hears, are gentle to women.'

' Ah, Tony ! there 's the looking back. And, of all women, you ! '

' Or else, dear—well, perhaps once on foreign soil, in a different air, I might—might have looked back, and seen my whole self, not shattered, as I feel it now, and come home again compassionate to the poor persecuted animal to defend her. Perhaps that was what I was running away for. I fled on the instinct, often a good thing to trust.'

' I *saw* you at The Crossways.'

' I remembered I had the dread that you would, though I did not imagine you would reach me so swiftly. My going there was an instinct, too. I suppose we are all

I

instinct when we have the world at our heels. Forgive
me if I generalize without any longer the right to be
included in the common human sum. " Pariah " and
" taboo " are words we borrow from barbarous tribes ;
they stick to me.'

' My Tony, you look as bright as ever, and you speak
despairingly.'

' Call me enigma. I am that to myself, Emmy.'

' You are not quite yourself to your friend.'

' Since the blow I have been bewildered ; I see nothing
upright. It came on me suddenly ; stunned me. A bolt
out of a clear sky, as they say. He spared me a scene.
There had been threats, and yet the sky was clear, or
seemed. When we have a man for arbiter, he is our
sky.'

Emma pressed her Tony's unresponsive hand, feeling
strangely that her friend ebbed from her.

' Has he . . . to mislead him ? ' she said, colouring at
the breach in the question.

' Proofs ?   He has the proofs he supposes.'

' Not to justify suspicion ? '

' He broke open my desk and took my letters.'

' Horrible !  But the letters ? '   Emma shook with a
nervous revulsion.

' You might read them.'

' Basest of men !  That is the unpardonable cowardice ! ' exclaimed Emma.

' The world will read them, dear,' said Diana, and
struck herself to ice.

She broke from the bitter frigidity in fury.   ' They are
letters—none very long—sometimes two short sentences
—he wrote at any spare moment.  On my honour, as a
woman, I feel for him most.  The letters—I would bear
any accusation rather than that exposure.  Letters of a
man of his age to a young woman he rates too highly !

The world reads them.  Do you hear it saying it could
have excused her for that fiddle-faddle with a younger—
a young lover ?  And had I thought of a lover ! . . . I
had no thought of loving or being loved.  I confess I was
flattered.  To you, Emma, I will confess. . . . You see
the public ridicule !—and half his age, he and I would
have appeared a romantic couple !  Confess, I said.
Well, dear, the stake is lighted for a trial of its effect on
me.  It is this :  he was never a dishonourable friend ;
but men appear to be capable of friendship with women
only for as long as we keep out of pulling distance of that
line where friendship ceases.  *They* may step on it ; *we*
must hold back a league.  I have learnt it.  You will
judge whether he disrespects me.  As for him, he is a
man ;  at his worst, not one of the worst ;  at his best,
better than very many.  There, now, Emma, you have
me stripped and burning ;  there is my full confession.
Except for this—yes, one thing further—that I do rage
at the ridicule, and could choose, but for you, to have
given the world cause to revile me, or think me romantic.
Something or somebody to suffer for would really be
agreeable.  It is a singular fact, I have not known what
this love is, that they talk about.  And behold me
marched into Smithfield !—society's heretic, if you
please.  I must own I think it hard.'

Emma chafed her cold hand softly.

' It is hard ;  I understand it,' she murmured.  ' And
is your Sunday visit to us in the list of offences ? '

' An item.'

' You gave me a happy day.'

' Then it counts for me in heaven.'

' He set spies on you ? '

' So we may presume.'

Emma went through a sphere of tenuious reflections in
a flash.

'He will rue it. Perhaps now . . . he may now be regretting his wretched frenzy. And Tony could pardon ; she has the power of pardoning in her heart.'

'Oh! certainly, dear. But tell me why it is you speak to-night rather unlike the sedate, philosophical Emma ; in a tone—well, tolerably sentimental ? '

'I am unaware of it,' said Emma, who could have retorted with a like reproach. 'I am anxious, I will not say at present for your happiness, for your peace ; and I have a hope that possibly a timely word from some friend—Lukin or another—might induce him to consider.'

'To pardon *me*, do you mean ? ' cried Diana, flushing sternly.

'Not pardon. Suppose a case of faults on both sides.'

'You address a faulty person, my dear. But do you know that you are hinting at a reconcilement ? '

'Might it not be ? '

'Open your eyes to what it involves. I trust I can pardon. Let him go his ways, do his darkest, or repent. But return to the roof of the " basest of men," who was guilty of " the unpardonable cowardice " ? You expect me to be superhuman. When I consent to that, I shall be out of my woman's skin, which he has branded. Go back to him ! ' She was taken with a shudder of head and limbs. 'No ; I really have the power of pardoning, and I am bound to ; for among my debts to him, this present exemption, that is like liberty dragging a chain, or, say, an escaped felon wearing his manacles, should count. I am sensible of my obligation. The price I pay for it is an immoveable patch—attractive to male idiots, I have heard, and a mark of scorn to females. Between the two the remainder of my days will be lively. " Out, out, damned spot ! " But it will not. And not on the

hand—on the forehead ! We 'll talk of it no longer. I
have sent a note, with an enclosure, to my lawyers. I
sell The Crossways, if I have the married woman's
right to any scrap of property, for money to scatter
fees.'

'My purse, dear Tony !' exclaimed Emma. 'My
house ! You will stay with me ? Why do you shake
your head ? With me you are safe.' She spied at the
shadows in her friend's face. ' Ever since your marriage,
Tony, you have been strange in your trick of refusing to
stay with me. And you and I made our friendship the
pledge of a belief in eternity ! We vowed it. Come, I
do talk sentimentally, but my heart is in it. I beg you—
all the reasons are with me—to make my house your
home. You will. You know I am rather lonely.'

Diana struggled to keep her resolution from being
broken by tenderness. And doubtless poor Sir Lukin
had learnt his lesson ; still, her defensive instincts could
never quite slumber under his roof ; not because of any
further fear that they would have to be summoned ; it
was chiefly owing to the consequences of his treacherous
foolishness. For this half-home with her friend thence-
forward denied to her, she had accepted a protector,
called husband—rashly, past credence, in the retrospect ;
but it had been her propelling motive ; and the loathings
roused by her marriage helped to sicken her at the idea
of a lengthened stay where she had suffered the shock
precipitating her to an act of insanity.

' I do not forget you were an heiress, Emmy, and I will
come to you if I need money to keep my head up. As for
staying, two reasons are against it. If I am to fight my
battle, I must be seen ; I must go about—wherever I am
received. So my field is London. That is obvious.
And I shall rest better in a house where my story is not
known.'

Two or three questions ensued. Diana had to fortify her fictitious objection by alluding to her maid's prattle of the household below ; and she excused the hapless, overfed, idle people of those regions.

To Emma it seemed a not unnatural sensitiveness. She came to a settled resolve in her thoughts, as she said, 'They want a change. London is their element.'

Feeling that she deceived this true heart, however lightly and necessarily, Diana warmed to her, forgiving her at last for having netted and dragged her back to front the enemy ; an imposition of horrors, of which the scene and the travelling with Redworth, the talking of her case with her most intimate friend as well, had been a distempering foretaste.

They stood up and kissed, parting for the night.

An odd world, where for the sin we have not participated in we must fib and continue fibbing, she reflected. She did not entirely cheat her clearer mind, for she perceived that her step in flight had been urged both by a weak despondency and a blind desperation ; also that the world of a fluid civilization is perforce artificial. But her mind was in the background of her fevered senses, and when she looked in the glass and mused on uttering the word, 'Liar ! ' to the lovely image, her senses were refreshed, her mind somewhat relieved, the face appeared so sovereignly defiant of abasement.

Thus did a nature distraught by pain obtain some short lull of repose. Thus, moreover, by closely reading herself, whom she scourged to excess that she might in justice be comforted, she gathered an increasing knowledge of our human constitution, and stored matter for the brain.

## CHAPTER XIII

### TOUCHING THE FIRST DAYS OF HER PROBATION

THE result of her sleeping was, that Diana's humour, locked up over-night, insisted on an excursion, as she lay with half-buried head and open eyelids, thinking of the firm of lawyers she had to see ; and to whom, and to the legal profession generally, she would be, under outward courtesies, nothing other than ' the woman Warwick.' She pursued the woman Warwick unmercifully through a series of interviews with her decorous and crudely-minded defenders ; accurately perusing them behind their senior staidness.   Her scorching sensitiveness sharpened her intelligence in regard to the estimate of discarded wives entertained by men of business and plain men of the world, and she drove the woman Warwick down their ranks, amazed by the vision of a puppet so unlike to herself in reality, though identical in situation.   That woman, reciting her side of the case, gained a gradual resemblance to Danvers ;  she spoke primly ;  perpetually the creature aired her handkerchief ; she was bent on softening those sugarloaves, the hard business-men applying to her for facts.   Facts were treated as unworthy of her ;  mere stuff of the dustheap, mutton-bones, old shoes ; she swam above them in a cocoon of her spinning, sylphidine, unseizable ;  and between perplexing and mollifying the slaves of facts, she saw them at their heels, a tearful fry, abjectly imitative of her melodramatic performances. The spectacle was presented of a band of legal gentlemen vociferating mightily for swords and the onset, like the Austrian empress's Magyars, to vindicate her just and holy cause.   Our Law-courts failing, they threatened

Parliament, and for a last resort, the country ! We are
not going to be the woman Warwick without a stir, my
brethren.

Emma, an early riser that morning, for the purpose
of a private consultation with Mr. Redworth, found her
lying placidly wakeful, to judge by appearances.

' You have not slept, my dear child ? '

' Perfectly,' said Diana, giving her hand and offering
the lips. ' I 'm only having a warm morning bath in
bed,' she added, in explanation of a chill moisture that
the touch of her exposed skin betrayed ; for whatever
the fun of the woman Warwick, there had been sympathetic feminine horrors in the frame of the sentient
woman.

Emma fancied she kissed a quiet sufferer. A few remarks very soon set her wildly laughing. Both were
laughing when Danvers entered the room, rather guilty,
being late ; and the sight of the prim-visaged maid she
had been driving among the lawyers kindled Diana's
comic imagination to such a pitch that she ran riot
in drolleries, carrying her friend headlong on the
tide.

' I have not laughed so much since you were married,'
said Emma.

' Nor I, dear ;—proving that the bar to it was the
ceremony,' said Diana.

She promised to remain at Copsley three days. ' Then
for the campaign in Mr. Redworth's metropolis. I
wonder whether I may ask him to get me lodgings : a
sitting-room and two bedrooms. The Crossways has a
board up for letting. I should prefer to be my own
tenant ; only it would give me a hundred pounds more
to get a substitute's money. I should like to be at work
writing instantly. Ink is my opium, and the pen
my nigger, and he must dig up gold for me. It is

written. Danvers, you can make ready to dress me when I ring.'

Emma helped the beautiful woman to her dressing-gown and the step from her bed. She had her thoughts, and went down to Redworth at the breakfast-table, marvelling that any husband other than a madman could cast such a jewel away. The material loveliness eclipses intellectual qualities in such reflections.

' He must be mad,' she said, compelled to disburden herself in a congenial atmosphere ; which, however, she infrigidated by her overflow of exclamatory wonderment —a curtain that shook voluminous folds, luring Redworth to dreams of the treasure forfeited. He became rigidly practical.

' Provision will have to be made for her. Lukin must see Mr. Warwick. She will do wisely to stay with friends in town, mix in company. Women are the best allies for such cases. Who are her solicitors ? '

' They are mine : Braddock, Thorpe, and Simnel.'

' A good firm. She is in safe hands with them. I dare say they may come to an arrangement.'

' I should wish it. She will never consent.'

Redworth shrugged. A woman's ' never ' fell far short of outstripping the sturdy pedestrian Time, to his mind.

Diana saw him drive off to catch the coach in the valley, regulated to meet the train, and much though she liked him, she was not sorry that he had gone. She felt the better clad for it. She would have rejoiced to witness the departure on wings of all her friends, except Emma, to whom her coldness overnight had bound her anew warmly in contrition. And yet her friends were well-beloved by her ; but her emotions were distraught.

Emma told her that Mr. Redworth had undertaken to hire a suite of convenient rooms, and to these she looked forward, the nest among strangers, where she could begin

to write, earning bread : an idea that, with the pride of
independence, conjured the pleasant morning smell of a
bakery about her.

She passed three peaceable days at Copsley, at war only
with the luxury of the house.   On the fourth, a letter to
Lady Dunstane from Redworth gave the address of the
best lodgings he could find, and Diana started for London.

She had during a couple of weeks, besides the first fresh
exercising of her pen, as well as the severe gratification of
economy, a savage exultation in passing through the
streets on foot and unknown.   Save for the plunges into
the office of her solicitors, she could seem to herself a
woman who had never submitted to the yoke.   What a
pleasure it was, after finishing a number of pages, to start
Eastward toward the lawyer-regions, full of imaginary
cropping incidents, and from that churchyard Westward,
against smoky sunsets, or in welcome fogs, an atom of the
crowd !   She had an affection for the crowd.   They
clothed her.   She laughed at the gloomy forebodings of
Danvers concerning the perils environing ladies in the
streets after dark alone.   The lights in the streets after
dark, and the quick running of her blood, combined to
strike sparks of fancy and inspirit the task of composition
at night.   This new, strange, solitary life, cut off from
her adulatory society, both by the shock that made the
abyss and by the utter foreignness, threw her in upon her
natural forces, recasting her, and thinning away her
memory of her past days, excepting girlhood, into the
remote.   She lived with her girlhood as with a simple
little sister.   They were two in one, and she corrected
the dreams of the younger, protected and counselled her
very sagely, advising her to love Truth and look always
to Reality for her refreshment.   She was ready to say,
that no habitable spot on our planet was healthier and
pleasanter than London.   As to the perils haunting the

head of Danvers, her experiences assured her of a perfect
immunity from them ; and the maligned thoroughfares
of a great city, she was ready to affirm, contrasted
favourably with certain hospitable halls.

The long-suffering Fates permitted her for a term to
enjoy the generous delusion.    Subsequently a sweet surprise alleviated the shock she had sustained.    Emma
Dunstane's carriage was at her door, and Emma entered
her sitting-room, to tell her of having hired a house in the
neighbourhood, looking on the park.    She begged to
have her for guest, sorrowfully anticipating the refusal.
At least they were to be near one another.

'You really like this life in lodgings ? ' asked Emma,
to whom the stiff furniture and narrow apartments were
a dreariness, the miserably small fire of the sitting-room
an aspect of cheerless winter.

'I do,' said Diana ; ' yes,' she added with some reserve,
and smiled at her damped enthusiasm, ' I can eat when I
like, walk, work—and I am working !   My legs and my
pen demand it.   Let me be independent !   Besides, I
begin to learn something of the bigger world outside the
one I know, and I crush my mincing tastes.   In return for
that, I get a sense of strength I had not when I was a
drawing-room exotic.   Much is repulsive.   But I am
taken with a passion for reality.'

They spoke of the lawyers, and the calculated period of
the trial ; of the husband too, and his inciting belief in
the falseness of his wife.   ' That is his excuse,' Diana
said, her closed mouth meditatively dimpling the corners
over thoughts of his grounds for fury.   He had them,
though none for the incriminating charge.   The Sphinx
mouth of the married woman at war and at bay must be
left unriddled.   She and the law differed in their interpretation of the dues of wedlock.

But matters referring to her case were secondary with

Diana beside the importance of her storing impressions.
Her mind required to hunger for something, and this
Reality which frequently she was forced to loathe, she
forced herself proudly to accept, despite her youthfulness.
Her philosophy swallowed it in the lump, as the great
serpent his meal ; she hoped to digest it sleeping likewise.
Her visits of curiosity to the Law Courts, where she stood
spying and listening behind a veil, gave her a great deal
of tough substance to digest.   There she watched the
process of the tortures to be applied to herself, and
hardened her senses for the ordeal.   She saw there the
ribbed and shanked old skeleton world on which our fair
fleshly is moulded.   After all, your Fool's Paradise is not
a garden to grow in.   Charon's ferry-boat is not thicker
with phantoms.   They do not live in mind or soul.
Chiefly women people it : a certain class of limp men ;
women for the most part : they are sown there.   And
put their garden under the magnifying glass of intimacy,
what do we behold ?   A world not better than the world
it curtains, only foolisher.

Her conversations with Lady Dunstane brought her at
last to the point of her damped enthusiasm.   She related
an incident or two occurring in her career of independence,
and they discussed our state of civilization plainly and
gravely, save for the laughing peals her phrases occasionally provoked ; as when she named the intruders and
disturbers of solitarily-faring ladies, ' Cupid's footpads.'
Her humour was created to swim on waters where a
prescribed and cultivated prudery should pretend to be
drowning.

' I was getting an exalted idea of English gentlemen,
Emmy.   " Rich and rare were the gems she wore."   I
was ready to vow that one might traverse the larger island
similarly respected.   I praised their chivalry.   I thought
it a privilege to live in such a land.   I cannot describe to

you how delightful it was to me to walk out and home
generally protected.  I might have been seriously annoyed
but that one of the clerks—" articled," he called himself—
of our lawyers happened to be by.  He offered to guard
me, and was amusing with his modest tiptoe air.  No,
I trust to the English common man more than ever.  He
is a man of honour.  I am convinced he is matchless in
any other country, except Ireland.  The English gentleman trades on his reputation.'

He was condemned by an afflicted delicacy, the sharpest
of critical tribunals.

Emma bade her not to be too sweeping from a bad
example.

' It is not a single one,' said Diana.  ' What vexes me
and frets me is, that I must be a prisoner, or allow
Danvers to mount guard.  And I can't see the end of it.
And Danvers is no magician.  She seems to know her
countrymen, though.  She warded one of them off, by
saying to me :  " This is the crossing, *my lady*."  He fled.'

Lady Dunstane affixed the popular title to the latter
kind of gentleman.  She was irritated on her friend's
behalf, and against the worrying of her sisterhood, thinking in her heart, nevertheless, that the passing of a face
and figure like Diana's might inspire honourable emotions,
pitiable for being hapless.

' If you were with me, dear, you would have none of
these annoyances,' she said, pleading forlornly.

Diana smiled to herself.  ' No ! I should relapse into
softness.  This life exactly suits my present temper.  My
landlady is respectful and attentive ;  the little housemaid
is a willing slave ;  Danvers does not despise them pug-
naciously ;  they make a home for me, and I am learning
daily.  Do you know, the less ignorant I become, the
more considerate I am for the ignorance of others—I love
them for it.'  She squeezed Emma's hand with more

meaning than her friend apprehended. ' So I win my
advantage from the trifles I have to endure. They are
really trifles, and I should once have thought them
mountains ! '

For the moment Diana stipulated that she might not
have to encounter friends or others at Lady Dunstane's
dinner-table, and the season not being favourable to those
gatherings planned by Lady Dunstane in her project of
winning supporters, there was a respite, during which
Sir Lukin worked manfully at his three Clubs to vindicate
Diana's name from the hummers and hawers, gaining
half a dozen hot adherents, and a body of lukewarm,
sufficiently stirred to be desirous to see the lady. He
worked with true champion zeal, although an interview
granted him by the husband settled his opinion as to any
possibility of the two ever coming to terms. Also it
struck him that if he by misadventure had been a woman
and the wife of such a fellow, by Jove ! . . .—his apostrophe to the father of the gods of pagandom signifying
the amount of matter Warwick would have had reason to
complain of in earnest. By ricochet his military mind
rebounded from his knowledge of himself to an ardent
faith in Mrs. Warwick's innocence ; for, as there was no
resemblance between them, there must, he deduced, be a
difference in their capacity for enduring the perpetual
company of a prig, a stick, a petrified poser. Moreover,
the novel act of advocacy, and the nature of the advocacy,
had effect on him. And then he recalled the scene in the
winter beech-woods, and Diana's wild-deer eyes ; her
perfect generosity to a traitor and fool. How could he
have doubted her ? Glimpses of the corrupting cause for
it partly penetrated his density : a conqueror of ladies,
in mid career, doubts them all. Of course he had meant
no harm, nothing worse than some pretty philandering
with the loveliest woman of her time. And, by Jove !

it was worth the rebuff to behold the Beauty in her
wrath.

The reflections of Lothario, however much tending
tardily to do justice to a particular lady, cannot terminate
wholesomely. But he became a gallant partisan. His
portrayal of Mr. Warwick to his wife and his friends was
fine caricature. ' The fellow had his hand up at my first
word—stood like a sentinel under inspection. " Understand, Sir Lukin, that I receive you simply as an acquaintance. As an intermediary, permit me to state that
you are taking superfluous trouble. The case must
proceed. It is final. She is at liberty, in the meantime,
to draw on my bankers for the provision she may need,
at the rate of five hundred pounds per annum." He
spoke of " the lady now bearing my name." He was
within an inch of saying " dishonouring." I swear I
heard the " dis," and he caught himself up. He " again
declined any attempt towards reconciliation." It could
" only be founded on evasion of the truth to be made
patent on the day of trial." Half his talk was lawyers'
lingo. The fellow's teeth looked like frost. If Lot's wife
had a brother, his name 's Warwick. How Diana Merion,
who could have had the pick of the best of us, ever came
to marry a fellow like that, passes my comprehension,
queer creatures as women are ! He can ride ; that 's
about all he can do. I told him Mrs. Warwick had no
thought of reconciliation. " Then, Sir Lukin, you will
perceive that we have no standpoint for a discussion." I
told him the point was, for a man of honour not to drag
his wife before the public, as he had no case to stand on—
less than nothing. You should have seen the fellow's
face. He shot a sneer up to his eyelids, and flung his
head back. So I said, "Good-day." He marches me to
the door, " with his compliments to Lady Dunstane."
I could have floored him for that. Bless my soul, what

fellows the world is made of, when here 's a man, calling
himself a gentleman, who, just because he gets in a rage
with his wife for one thing or another—and past all competition the handsomest woman of her day, and the
cleverest, the nicest, the best of the whole boiling—has her
out for a public horsewhipping, and sets all the idiots of
the kingdom against her ! I tried to reason with him.
He made as if he were going to sleep standing.'

Sir Lukin gratified Lady Dunstane by his honest championship of Diana. And now, in his altered mood (the
thrice indebted rogue was just cloudily conscious of a
desire to propitiate his dear wife by serving her friend),
he began a crusade against the scandal-newspapers, going
with an Irish military comrade straight to the editorial
offices, and leaving his card and a warning that the chastisement for print of the name of the lady in their columns
would be personal and condign. Captain Carew Mahony,
albeit unacquainted with Mrs. Warwick, had espoused
her cause. She was a woman, she was an Irishwoman,
she was a beautiful woman. She had, therefore, three
positive claims on him as a soldier and a man. Other
Irish gentlemen, animated by the same swelling degrees
were awaking to the intimation that they might be wanted.
Some words were dropped here and there by General Lord
Larrian : he regretted his age and infirmities. A goodly
regiment for a bodyguard might have been selected to
protect her steps in the public streets, when it was bruited
that the General had sent her a present of his great New-
foundland dog, Leander, to attend on her and impose a
required respect. But as it chanced that her address
was unknown to the volunteer constabulary, they had
to assuage their ardour by thinking the dog luckier than
they.

The report of the dog was a fact. He arrived one morning at Diana's lodgings, with a soldier to lead him, and a

card to introduce : the Hercules of dogs, a very ideal of
the species, toweringly big, benevolent, reputed a rescuer
of lives, disdainful of dog-fighting, devoted to his guardian's office, with a majestic paw to give and the noblest
satisfaction in receiving caresses ever expressed by mortal
male enfolded about the head, kissed, patted, hugged,
snuggled, informed that he was his new mistress's one
love and darling.

She despatched a thrilling note of thanks to Lord
Larrian, sure of her touch upon an Irish heart.

The dog Leander soon responded to the attachment of
a mistress enamoured of him. ' He is my husband,' she
said to Emma, and started a tear in the eyes of her smiling
friend ; ' he promises to trust me, and never to have the
law of me, and to love my friends as his own ; so we are
certain to agree.' In rain, snow, sunshine, through the
parks and the streets, he was the shadow of Diana, commanding, on the whole, apart from some desperate attempts to make him serve as introducer, a civilized behaviour in the legions of Cupid's footpads. But he helped,
innocently enough, to create an enemy.

## CHAPTER XIV

### GIVING GLIMPSES OF DIANA UNDER HER CLOUD BEFORE THE WORLD AND OF HER FURTHER APPRENTICESHIP

As the day of her trial became more closely calculable,
Diana's anticipated alarms receded with the deadening of
her heart to meet the shock. She fancied she had put on
proof-armour, unconscious that it was the turning of the
inward flutterer to steel which supplied her cuirass and
shield. The necessity to brave society, in the character

K

of honest Defendant, caused but a momentary twitch of the nerves. Her heart beat regularly, like a serviceable clock ; none of her faculties abandoned her save songfulness, and none belied her, excepting a disposition to tartness almost venomous in the sarcastic shafts she let fly at friends interceding with Mr. Warwick to spare his wife, when she had determined to be tried. A strange fit of childishness overcame her powers of thinking, and was betrayed in her manner of speaking, though to herself her dwindled humour allowed her to appear the towering Britomart. She pouted contemptuously on hearing that a Mr. Sullivan Smith (a remotely recollected figure) had besought Mr. Warwick for an interview, and gained it, by stratagem, ' to bring the man to his senses ' : but an ultra-Irishman did not compromise her battle-front, as the busybody supplications of a personal friend like Mr. Redworth did ; and that the latter, without consulting her, should be ' one of the plaintive crew whining about the heels of the Plaintiff for a mercy she disdained and rejected ' was bitter to her taste.

' He does not see that unless I go through the fire there is no justification for this wretched character of mine ! ' she exclaimed. Truce, treaty, withdrawal, signified publicly pardon, not exoneration by any means ; and now that she was in armour she had no dread of the public. So she said. Redworth's being then engaged upon the canvass of a borough, added to the absurdity of his meddling with the dilemmas of a woman. ' Dear me, Emma ! think of stepping aside from the parliamentary road to entreat a husband to relent, and arrange the domestic alliance of a contrary couple ! Quixottry is agreeable reading, a silly performance.' Lady Dunstane pleaded his friendship. She had to quit the field where such darts were showering.

The first dinner-party was aristocratic, easy to

encounter.   Lord and Lady Crane, Lady Pennon, Lord
and Lady Esquart, Lord Larrian, Mr. and Mrs. Montvert
of Halford Manor, Lady Singleby, Sir Walter Capperston :
friends, admirers of Diana ; patrons, in the phrase of the
time, of her father, were the guests.   Lady Pennon expected to be amused, and was gratified, for Diana had
only to open her mouth to set the great lady laughing.
She petitioned to have Mrs. Warwick at her table that
day week, because the marquis was dying to make her
acquaintance, and begged to have all her sayings repeated to him ; vowed she must be salt in the desert.
' And remember, I back you through thick and thin,'
said Lady Pennon.   To which Diana replied : ' If I am
salt in the desert, you are the spring ' ; and the old lady
protested she must put that down for her book.   The
witty Mrs. Warwick, of whom wit was expected, had
many incitements to be guilty of cheap wit ; and the
beautiful Mrs. Warwick, being able to pass anything she
uttered, gave good and bad alike, under the impulsion
to give out something, that the stripped and shivering
Mrs. Warwick might find a cover in applause.   She discovered the social uses of cheap wit ; she laid ambushes
for anecdotes, a telling form of it among a people of no
conversational interlocution, especially in the circles de-
pending for dialogue upon perpetual fresh supplies of
scandal ; which have plentiful crops, yet not sufficient.
The old dinner and supper tables at The Crossways furnished her with an abundant store ; and recollection
failing, she invented.   Irish anecdotes are always popular
in England, as promoting, besides the wholesome shake
of the sides, a kindly sense of superiority.   Anecdotes
also are portable, unlike the lightning flash, which will
not go into the pocket ; they can be carried home, they
are disbursable at other tables.   These were Diana's
weapons.   She was perforce the actress of her part.

In happier times, when light of heart and natural, her
vogue had not been so enrapturing.   Doubtless Cleopatra in her simple Egyptian uniform would hardly have
won such plaudits as her stress of barbaric Oriental
splendours evoked for her on the swan and serpent Nile-
barge—not from posterity at least.   It is a terrible decree,
that all must act who would prevail ; and the more extended the audience, the greater need for the mask and
buskin.

From Lady Pennon's table Diana passed to Lady
Crane's, Lady Esquart's, Lady Singleby's, the Duchess
of Raby's, warmly clad in the admiration she excited.
She appeared at Princess Thérèse Paryli's first ball of the
season, and had her circle, not of worshippers only.   She
did not dance.   The princess, a fair Austrian, benevolent
to her sisterhood, an admirer of Diana's contrasting complexion, would have had her dance once in a quadrille
of her forming, but yielded to the mute expression of
the refusal.   Wherever Mrs. Warwick went, her arts of
charming were addressed to the women.   Men may be
counted on for falling bowled over by a handsome face
and pointed tongue ; women require some wooing from
their ensphered and charioted sister, particularly if she
is clouded ; and old women—excellent buttresses—must
be suavely courted.   Now, to woo the swimming matron
and court the settled dowager, she had to win forgiveness
for her beauty ; and this was done, easily done, by for-
bearing to angle with it in the press of nibblers.   They
ranged about her, individually unnoticed.   Seeming
unaware of its effect where it kindled, she smote a number
of musical female chords, compassion among them.   A
general grave affability of her eyes and smiles was taken
for quiet pleasure in the scene.   Her fitful intentness of
look when conversing with the older ladies told of the
mind within at work upon what they said, and she was

careful that plain dialogue should make her comprehensible to them.  Nature taught her these arts, through
which her wit became extolled entirely on the strength of
her reputation, and her beauty did her service by never
taking aim abroad.  They are the woman's arts of self-
defence, as legitimately and honourably hers as the manful use of the fists with a coarser sex.  If it had not been
nature that taught her the practice of them in extremity,
the sagacious dowagers would have seen brazenness
rather than innocence—or an excuseable indiscretion—
in the part she was performing.  They are not lightly
duped by one of their sex.  Few tasks are more difficult
than for a young woman under a cloud to hoodwink old
women of the world.  They are the prey of financiers ;
but Time has presented them a magic ancient glass to
scan their sex in.

At Princess Paryli's Ball two young men of singular
elegance were observed by Diana, little though she con-
centered her attention on any figures of the groups.  She
had the woman's faculty (transiently bestowed by per-
fervid jealousy upon men) of distinguishing minutely in
the calmest of indifferent glances.  She could see without
looking ; and when her eyes were wide they had not to
dwell to be detective.  It did not escape her that the
Englishman of the two hurried for the chance of an introduction, nor that he suddenly, after putting a question
to a man beside him, retired.  She spoke of them to
Emma as they drove home.  ' The princess's partner in
the first quadrille . . . Hungarian, I suppose ?  He
was like a Tartar modelled by a Greek : supple as the
Scythian's bow, braced as the string !  He has the air
of a born horseman, and valses perfectly.  I won't say
he was handsomer than a young Englishman there,
but he. had the advantage of soldierly training.  How
different is that quick springy figure from our young

men's lounging style! It comes of military exercise and discipline.'

'That was Count Jochany, a cousin of the princess, and a cavalry officer,' said Emma. 'You don't know the other? I am sure the one you mean must be Percy Dacier.'

His retiring was explained : the Hon. Percy Dacier was the nephew of Lord Dannisburgh, often extolled to her as the promising youngster of his day, with the reserve that he wasted his youth : for the young gentleman was decorous and studious ; ambitious, according to report ; a politician taking to politics much too seriously and exclusively to suit his uncle's pattern for the early period of life. Uncle and nephew went their separate ways, rarely meeting, though their exchange of esteem was cordial.

Thinking over his abrupt retirement from the crowded semicircle, Diana felt her position pinch her, she knew not why.

Lady Dunstane was as indefatigable by day as by night in the business of acting goddess to her beloved Tony, whom she assured that the service, instead of exhausting, gave her such healthfulness as she had imagined herself to have lost for ever. The word was passed, and invitations poured in to choice conversational breakfasts, private afternoon concerts, all the humming season's assemblies. Mr. Warwick's treatment of his wife was taken by implication for lunatic ; wherever she was heard or seen, he had no case ; a jury of some hundreds of both sexes, ready to be sworn, pronounced against him. Only the personal enemies of the lord in the suit presumed to doubt, and they exercised the discretion of a minority.

But there is an upper middle class below the aristocratic, boasting an aristocracy of morals, and eminently persuasive of public opinion, if not commanding it.

Previous to the relaxation, by amendment, of a certain
legal process, this class was held to represent the austerity
of the country. At present a relaxed austerity is represented; and still the bulk of the members are of fair
repute, though not quite on the level of their pretensions.
They were then, while more sharply divided from the
titular superiors they are socially absorbing, very powerful to brand a woman's character, whatever her rank
might be; having innumerable agencies and avenues
for that high purpose, to say nothing of the printing-press.
Lady Dunstane's anxiety to draw them over to the cause
of her friend set her thinking of the influential Mrs. Cramborne Wathin, with whom she was distantly connected;
the wife of a potent serjeant-at-law fast mounting to the
Bench and knighthood; the centre of a circle, and not
strangely that, despite her deficiency in the arts and
graces, for she had wealth and a cook, a husband proud
of his wine-cellar, and the ambition to rule; all the
rewards, together with the expectations, of the virtuous.
She was a lady of incisive features bound in stale parch-
ment. Complexion she had none, but she had spotless-
ness of skin, and sons and daughters just resembling her,
like cheaper editions of a precious quarto of a perished
type. You discerned the imitation of the type, you
acknowledged the inferior compositor. Mr. Cramborne
Wathin was by birth of a grade beneath his wife; he
sprang (behind a curtain of horror) from tradesmen. The
Bench was in designation for him to wash out the stain,
but his children suffered in large hands and feet, short
legs, excess of bone, prominences misplaced. Their
mother inspired them carefully with the religion she
opposed to the pretensions of a nobler blood, while in-
stilling into them that the blood they drew from her was
territorial, far above the vulgar. Her appearance and
her principles fitted her to stand for the Puritan rich of

the period, emerging by the aid of an extending wealth into luxurious worldliness, and retaining the maxims of their forefathers for the discipline of the poor and erring.

Lady Dunstane called on her, ostensibly to let her know she had taken a house in town for the season, and in the course of the chat Mrs. Cramborne Wathin was invited to dinner. ' You will meet my dear friend, Mrs. Warwick,' she said, and the reply was : ' Oh, I have heard of her.'

The formal consultation with Mr. Cramborne Wathin ended in an agreement to accept Lady Dunstane's kind invitation.

Considering her husband's plenitude of old legal anecdotes, and her own diligent perusal of the funny publications of the day, that she might be on the level of the wits and celebrities she entertained, Mrs. Cramborne Wathin had a right to expect the leading share in the conversation to which she was accustomed. Every honour was paid to them; they met aristocracy in the persons of Lord Larrian, of Lady Rockden, Colonel Purlby, the Pettigrews, but neither of them held the table for a moment; the topics flew, and were no sooner up than down; they were unable to get a shot. They had to eat in silence, occasionally grinning, because a woman labouring under a stigma would rattle-rattle, as if the laughter of the company were her due, and decency beneath her notice. Some one alluded to a dog of Mrs. Warwick's, whereupon she trips out a story of her dog's amazing intelligence.

' And pray,' said Mrs. Cramborne Wathin across the table, merely to slip in a word, ' what is the name of this wonderful dog ? '

' His name is Leander,' said Diana.

' Oh, Leander. I don't think I hear myself calling to a dog in a name of three syllables. Two at the most.'

' No, so I call Hero! if I want him to come immediately,'

said Diana, and the gentlemen, to Mrs. Cramborne
Wathin's astonishment, acclaimed it.    Mr. Redworth,
at her elbow, explained the point, to her disgust.

That was Diana's offence.

If it should seem a small one, let it be remembered that
a snub was intended, and was foiled ; and foiled with an
apparent simplicity, enough to exasperate, had there
been no laughter of men to back the countering stroke.
A woman under a cloud, she talked, pushed to shine ;
she would be heard, would be applauded.    Her chronicler
must likewise admit the error of her giving way to a
petty sentiment of antagonism on first beholding Mrs.
Cramborne Wathin, before whom she at once resolved to
be herself, for a holiday, instead of acting demurely to
conciliate.    Probably it was an antagonism of race, the
shrinking of the skin from the burr.    But when Tremendous Powers are invoked, we should treat any simple
revulsion of our blood as a vice.    The Gods of this world's
contests demand it of us, in relation to them, that the
mind, and not the instincts, shall be at work.    Otherwise
the course of a prudent policy is never to invoke them,
but avoid.

The upper class was gained by her intrepidity, her
charm, and her elsewhere offending wit, however the case
might go.    It is chivalrous, but not, alas, inflammable in
support of innocence.    The class below it is governed in
estimates of character by accepted patterns of conduct ;
yet where innocence under persecution is believed to
exist, the members animated by that belief can be enthusiastic.    Enthusiasm is a heaven-sent steeplechaser, and
takes a flying leap of the ordinary barriers ; it is more
intrusive than chivalry, and has a passion to communicate its ardour.    Two letters from stranger ladies reached
Diana, through her lawyers and Lady Dunstane.    Anonymous letters, not so welcome, being male effusions,

arrived at her lodgings, one of them comical almost over the verge to pathos in its termination : ' To me you will ever be the Goddess Diana—my faith in woman ! '

He was unacquainted with her !

She had not the heart to think the writers donkeys. How they obtained her address was a puzzle ; they stole in to comfort her slightly.  They attached her to her position of Defendant by the thought of what would have been the idea of her character if she had flown—a reflection emanating from inexperience of the resources of sentimentalists.

If she had flown !  She was borne along by the tide like a butterfly that a fish may gobble unless a friendly hand shall intervene.  And could it in nature ?  She was past expectation of release.  The attempt to imagine living with any warmth of blood in her vindicated character, for the sake of zealous friends, consigned her to a cold and empty house upon a foreign earth.  She had to set her mind upon the mysterious enshrouded Twelve, with whom the verdict would soon be hanging, that she might prompt her human combativeness to desire the vindication at such a price as she would have to pay for it. When Emma Dunstane spoke to her of the certainty of triumphing, she suggested a possible dissentient among the fateful Twelve, merely to escape the drumming sound of that hollow big word.  The irreverent imp of her humour came to her relief by calling forth the Twelve, in the tone of the clerk of the Court, and they answered to their names of trades and crafts after the manner of Titania's elves, and were questioned as to their fitness, by education, habits, enlightenment, to pronounce decisively upon the case in dispute, the case being plainly stated. They replied, that the long habit of dealing with scales enabled them to weigh the value of evidence the most delicate.  Moreover, they were Englishmen, and any-

thing short of downright bullet facts went to favour the
woman. For thus we right the balance of legal injustice
toward the sex : we conveniently wink, ma'am. A
rough, old-fashioned way for us ! Is it a Breach of
Promise ?—She may reckon on her damages : we have
daughters of our own. Is it a suit for Divorce ?—Well,
we have wives of our own, and we can lash, or we can
spare ; that 's as it may be ; but we 'll keep the couple
tied, let 'em hate as they like, if they can't furnish pork-
butchers' reasons for sundering ; because the man makes
the money in this country.—My goodness ! what a funny
people, sir !—It 's our way of holding the balance, ma'am.
—But would it not be better to rectify the law and the
social system, dear sir ?—Why, ma'am, we find it com-
fortabler to take cases as they come, in the style of our
fathers.—But don't you see, my good man, that you are
offering scapegoats for the comfort of the majority ?—
Well, ma'am, there always were scapegoats, and always
will be ; we find it comes round pretty square in the end.

' And I may be the scapegoat, Emmy ! It is perfectly
possible. The grocer, the porkbutcher, drysalter,
stationer, tea-merchant, et caetera—they sit on me. I
have studied the faces of the juries, and Mr. Braddock
tells me of their composition. And he admits that they
do justice roughly—a rough and tumble country ! to
quote him—though he says they are honest in intention.'

' More shame to the man who drags you before them—
if he persists ! ' Emma rejoined.

' He will. I know him. I would not have him draw
back now,' said Diana, catching her breath. ' And, dearest, do not abuse him ; for if you do, you set me imagining
guiltiness. Oh, heaven!—suppose me publicly pardoned!
No, I have kinder feelings when we stand opposed. It is
odd, and rather frets my conscience, to think of the little
resentment I feel. Hardly any ! He has not cause to

like his wife. I can own it, and I am sorry for him, heartily. No two have ever come together so naturally antagonistic as we two. We walked a dozen steps in stupefied union, and hit upon crossways. From that moment it was tug and tug; he me, I him. By resisting, I made him a tyrant; and he, by insisting, made me a rebel. And he was the maddest of tyrants—a weak one. My dear, he was also a double-dealer. Or no, perhaps not in design. He was moved at one time by his interests; at another by his idea of his honour. He took what I could get for him, and then turned and drubbed me for getting it.'

'This is the creature you try to excuse!' exclaimed indignant Emma.

'Yes, because—but fancy all the smart things I said being called my "sallies"!—can a woman live with it? —because I behaved . . . I despised him too much, and I showed it. He is not a contemptible man before the world; he is merely a very narrow one under close inspection. I could not—or did not—conceal my feeling. I showed it not only to him, to my friend. Husband grew to mean to me stifler, lung-contractor, iron mask, inquisitor, everything anti-natural. He suffered under my "sallies": and it was the worse for him when he did not perceive their drift. He is an upright man; I have not seen marked meanness. One might build up a respectable figure in negatives. I could add a row of noughts to the single number he cherishes, enough to make a millionnaire of him; but strike away the first, the rest are wind. Which signifies, that if you do not take his estimate of himself, you will think little of his negative virtues. He is not eminently, that is to say, not saliently, selfish; not rancorous, not obtrusive—ta-ta-ta-ta. But dull!—dull as a woollen nightcap over eyes and ears and mouth. Oh! an executioner's black

cap to me. Dull, and suddenly staring awake to the
idea of his honour. I " rendered " him ridiculous—I
had caught a trick of " using men's phrases." Dearest,
now that the day of trial draws nigh—you have never
questioned me, and it was like you to spare me pain—
but now I can speak of him and myself.' Diana dropped
her voice. Here was another confession. The proximity of the trial acted like fire on her faded recollection
of incidents. It may be that partly the shame of alluding to them had blocked her woman's memory. For
one curious operation of the charge of guiltiness upon the
nearly guiltless is to make them paint themselves pure
white, to the obliteration of minor spots, until the whiteness being acknowledged, or the ordeal imminent, the
spots recur and press upon their consciences. She resumed, in a rapid undertone : ' You know that a certain
degree of independence had been, if not granted by him,
conquered by me. I had the habit of it. Obedience
with him is imprisonment—he is a blind wall. He received a commission, greatly to his advantage, and was
absent. He seems to have received information of some
sort. He returned unexpectedly, at a late hour, and
attacked me at once, middling violent. My friend—and
that he is !—was coming from the House for a ten minutes'
talk, as usual, on his way home, to refresh him after the
long sitting and bear-baiting he had nightly to endure.
Now let me confess : I grew frightened ; Mr. Warwick
was " off his head," as they say—crazy, and I could not
bear the thought of those two meeting. While he raged
I threw open the window and put the lamp near it, to
expose the whole interior—cunning as a veteran intriguer :
horrible, but it had to be done to keep them apart. He
asked me what madness possessed me, to sit by an open
window at midnight, in view of the public, with a damp
wind blowing. I complained of want of air and fanned

my forehead. I heard the steps on the pavement; I stung him to retort loudly, and I was relieved; the steps passed on. So the trick succeeded—the trick! It was the worst I was guilty of, but it was a trick, and it branded me trickster. It teaches me to see myself with an abyss in my nature full of infernal possibilities. I think I am hewn in black rock. A woman who can do as I did by instinct, needs to have an angel always near her, if she has not a husband she reveres.'

' We are none of us better than you, dear Tony; only some are more fortunate, and many are cowards,' Emma said. ' You acted prudently in a wretched situation, partly of your own making, partly of the circumstances. But a nature like yours could not sit still and moan. That marriage was to blame! The English notion of women seems to be that we are born white sheep or black; circumstances have nothing to do with our colour. They dread to grant distinctions, and to judge of us discerningly is beyond them. Whether the fiction, that their homes are purer than elsewhere, helps to establish the fact, I do not know: there is a class that does live honestly; and at any rate it springs from a liking for purity; but I am sure that their method of impressing it on women has the dangers of things artificial. They narrow their understanding of human nature, and that is not the way to improve the breed.'

' I suppose we women are taken to be the second thoughts of the Creator; human nature's fringes, mere finishing touches, not a part of the texture,' said Diana; ' the pretty ornamentation. However, I fancy I perceive some tolerance growing in the minds of the dominant sex. Our old lawyer Mr. Braddock, who appears to have no distaste for conversations with me, assures me he expects the day to come when women will be encouraged to work at crafts and professions for their

independence. That is the secret of the opinion of us at
present—our dependency. Give us the means of independence, and we will gain it, and have a turn at judging
you, my lords ! You shall behold a world reversed.
Whenever I am distracted by existing circumstances, I
lay my finger on the material conditions, and I touch
the secret. Individually, it *may* be moral with us ;
collectively, it is material—gross wrongs, gross hungers.
I am a married rebel, and thereof comes the social rebel.
I was once a dancing and singing girl. You remember
the night of the Dublin Ball. A Channel sea in uproar,
stirred by witches, flows between.'

' You are as lovely as you were then—I could say,
lovelier,' said Emma.

' I have unconquerable health, and I wish I could give
you the half of it, dear. I work late into the night, and I
wake early and fresh in the morning. I do not sing, that
is all. A few days more, and my character will be up
before the Bull's Head to face him in the arena. The
worst of a position like mine is, that it causes me incessantly to think and talk of myself. I believe I
think less than I talk, but the subject is growing
stale ; as those who are long dying feel, I dare say—if
they do not take it as the compensation for their
departure.'

The Bull's Head, or British Jury of Twelve, with the
wig on it, was faced during the latter half of a week of
good news. First, Mr. Thomas Redworth was returned
to Parliament by a stout majority for the Borough of
Orrybridge : the Hon. Percy Dacier delivered a brilliant
speech in the House of Commons, necessarily pleasing to
his uncle : Lord Larrian obtained the command of the
Rock : the house of The Crossways was let to a tenant
approved by Mr. Braddock : Diana received the opening
proof-sheets of her little volume, and an instalment of

the modest honorarium : and finally, the Plaintiff in the suit involving her name was adjudged to have not proved his charge.

She heard of it without a change of countenance.

She could not have wished it the reverse ; she was exonerated.  But she was not free ; far from that ; and she revenged herself on the friends who made much of her triumph and overlooked her plight, by showing no sign of satisfaction.  There was in her bosom a revolt at the legal consequences of the verdict—or blunt acquiescence of the Law in the conditions possibly to be imposed on her unless she went straight to the relieving phial ; and the burden of keeping it under, set her wildest humour alight, somewhat as Redworth remembered of her on the journey from The Crossways to Copsley.  This ironic fury, coming of the contrast of the outer and the inner, would have been indulged to the extent of permanent injury to her disposition had not her beloved Emma, immediately after the tension of the struggle ceased, required her tenderest aid.  Lady Dunstane chanted victory, and at night collapsed.  By the advice of her physician she was removed to Copsley, where Diana's labour of anxious nursing restored her through love to a saner spirit.  The hopefulness of life must bloom again in the heart whose prayers are offered for a life dearer than its own to be preserved.  A little return of confidence in Sir Lukin also refreshed her when she saw that the poor creature did honestly, in his shaggy rough male fashion, reverence and cling to the flower of souls he named as his wife.  His piteous groans of self-accusation during the crisis haunted her, and made the conduct and nature of men a bewilderment to her still young understanding.  Save for the knot of her sensations (hardly a mental memory, but a sullen knot) which she did not disentangle to charge him with his complicity in the

blind rashness of her marriage, she might have felt
sisterly, as warmly as she compassionated him.

It was midwinter when Dame Gossip, who keeps the
exotic world alive with her fanning whispers, related that
the lovely Mrs. Warwick had left England on board the
schooner-yacht Clarissa, with Lord and Lady Esquart,
for a voyage in the Mediterranean : and (behind her hand)
that the reason was urgent, inasmuch as she fled to escape
the meshes of the terrific net of the marital law brutally
whirled to capture her by the man her husband.


## CHAPTER XV

### INTRODUCES THE HON. PERCY DACIER

The Gods of this world's contests, against whom our
poor stripped individual is commonly in revolt, are, as we
know, not miners, they are reapers ; and if we appear no
longer on the surface, they cease to bruise us : they will
allow an arena character to be cleansed and made pre-
sentable while enthusiastic friends preserve discretion.   It
is of course less than magnanimity ;  they are not proposed to you for your worship ;  they are little Gods,
temporary as that great wave, their parent human mass
of the hour.   But they have one worshipful element in
them, which is, the divine insistancy upon there being
two sides to a case—to every case.   And the People so
far directed by them may boast of healthfulness.   Let
the individual shriek, the innocent, triumphant, have in
honesty to admit the fact.   One side is vanquished, according to decree of Law, but the superior Council does not
allow it to be extinguished.

Diana's battle was fought shadowily behind her for the

L

space of a week or so, with some advocates on behalf of
the beaten man ; then it became a recollection of a beautiful woman, possibly erring, misvalued by a husband, who
was neither a man of the world nor a gracious yokefellow,
nor anything to match her. She, however, once out of
the public flames, had to recall her scorchings to be gentle
with herself. Under a defeat, she would have been
angrily self-vindicated. The victory of the ashen laurels
drove her mind inward to gird at the hateful yoke, in
compassion for its pair of victims. Quite earnestly by
such means, yet always bearing a comical eye on her
subterfuges, she escaped the extremes of personal blame.
Those advocates of her opponent in and out of court
compelled her honest heart to search within and own to
faults. But were they not natural faults ? It was her
marriage ; it was marriage in the abstract : her own
mistake and the world's clumsy machinery of civilization : these were the capital offenders : not the wife who
would laugh ringingly, and would have friends of the
other sex, and shot her epigrams at the helpless despot,
and was at times—yes, vixenish ; a nature driven to it,
but that was the word. She was too generous to recount
her charges against the vanquished. If his wretched
jealousy had ruined her, the secret high tribunal within
her bosom, which judged her guiltless for putting the
sword between their marriage tie when they stood as
one, because a quarrelling couple could not in honour
play the embracing, pronounced him just pardonable.
She distinguished that he could only suppose, manlikely,
one bad cause for the division.

To this extent she used her unerring brains, more openly
than on her night of debate at The Crossways. The next
moment she was off in vapour, meditating grandly on her
independence of her sex and the passions. Love ! she
did not know it ; she was not acquainted with either the

criminal or the domestic God, and persuaded herself that
she never could be. She was a Diana of coldness, pre-
ferring friendship ; she could be the friend of men. There
was another who could be the friend of women. Her
heart leapt to Redworth. Conjuring up his clear trusty
face, at their grasp of hands when parting, she thought
of her visions of her future about the period of the Dublin
Ball, and acknowledged, despite the erratic step to wedlock, a gain in having met and proved so true a friend.
His face, figure, character, lightest look, lightest word,
all were loyal signs of a man of honour, cold as she ; he
was the man to whom she could have opened her heart
for inspection. Rejoicing in her independence of an
emotional sex, the impulsive woman burned with a regret
that at their parting she had not broken down conventional barriers and given her cheek to his lips in the anti-
insular fashion with a brotherly friend. And why not
when both were cold ? Spirit to spirit, she did, delightfully refreshed by her capacity to do so without a throb.
He had held her hand and looked into her eyes half a
minute, like a dear comrade ; as little arousing her instincts of defensiveness as the clearing heavens ; and
sisterly love for it was his due, a sister's kiss. He needed
a sister, and should have one in her. Emma's recollected
talk of ' Tom Redworth ' painted him from head to foot,
brought the living man over the waters to the deck of
the yacht. A stout champion in the person of Tom
Redworth was left on British land ; but for some reason
past analysis, intermixed, that is, among a swarm of sensations, Diana named her champion to herself with the
formal prefix : perhaps because she knew a man's
Christian name to be dangerous handling. They differed
besides frequently in opinion, when the habit of thinking of him as Mr. Redworth would be best. Women
are bound to such small observances, and especially

the beautiful of the sisterhood, whom the world soon warns that they carry explosives and must particularly guard against the ignition of petty sparks. She was less indiscreet in her thoughts than in her acts, as is the way with the reflective daughter of impulse ; though she had fine mental distinctions : what she could offer to do ' spirit to spirit,' for instance, held nothing to her mind of the intimacy of calling the gentleman plain Tom in mere contemplation of him. Her friend and champion was a volunteer, far from a mercenary, and he deserved the reward, if she could bestow it unalarmed. They were to meet in Egypt. Meanwhile England loomed the home of hostile forces ready to shock, had she been a visible planet, and ready to secrete a virus of her past history, had she been making new.

She was happily away, borne by a whiter than swan's wing on the sapphire Mediterranean. Her letters to Emma were peeps of splendour for the invalid : her way of life on board the yacht, and sketches of her host and hostess as lovers in wedlock on the other side of our perilous forties ; sketches of the bays, the towns, the people—priests, dames, cavaliers, urchins, infants, shifting groups of supple southerners—flashed across the page like a web of silk, and were dashed off, redolent of herself, as lightly as the silvery spray of the blue waves she furrowed ; telling, without allusions to the land behind her, that she had dipped in the wells of blissful oblivion. Emma Dunstane, as is usual with those who receive exhilarating correspondence from makers of books, condemned the authoress in comparison, and now first saw that she had the gift of writing. Only one cry : ' Italy, Eden of exiles ! ' betrayed the seeming of a moan. She wrote of her poet and others immediately. Thither had they fled, with adieu to England !

How many have waved the adieu ! And it is England

nourishing, England protecting them, England clothing
them in the honours they wear. Only the posturing
lower natures, on the level of their buskins, can pluck out
the pocket-knife of sentimental spite to cut themselves
loose from her at heart in earnest. The higher, bleed as
they may, too pressingly feel their debt. Diana had the
Celtic vivid sense of country. In England she was Irish,
by hereditary, and by wilful opposition. Abroad, gazing
along the waters, observing, comparing, reflecting, above
all, reading of the struggles at home, the things done
and attempted, her soul of generosity made her, though
not less Irish, a daughter of Britain. It is at a distance
that striving countries should be seen if we would have
them in the pure idea ; and this young woman of fervid
mind, a reader of public speeches and speculator on the
tides of politics (desirous, further, to feel herself rather
more in the pure idea), began to yearn for England long
before her term of holiday exile had ended. She had been
flattered by her friend, her ' wedded martyr at the stake,'
as she named him, to believe that she could exercise a
judgement in politics—could think, even speak acutely,
on public affairs. The reports of speeches delivered by
the men she knew or knew of, set her thrilling ; and she
fancied the sensibility to be as independent of her sympathy with the orators as her political notions were
sovereignly above a sex devoted to trifles, and the feelings
of a woman who had gone through fire. She fancied it
confidently, notwithstanding a peculiar intuition that the
plunge into the nobler business of the world would be a
haven of safety for a woman with blood and imagination,
when writing to Emma : ' Mr. Redworth's great success
in Parliament is good in itself, whatever his views of
present questions ; and I do not heed them when I
look to what may be done by a man of such power in
striking at unjust laws, which keep the really numerically

better-half of the population in a state of slavery.   If he
had been a lawyer !   It must be a lawyer's initiative—a
lawyer's Bill.   Mr. Percy Dacier also spoke well, as might
have been expected, and his uncle's compliment to him
was merited.   Should you meet him sound him.   He has
read for the Bar, and is younger than Mr. Redworth.   The
very young men and the old are our hope.   The middle-
aged are hard and fast for existing facts.   We pick *our*
leaders on the slopes, the incline and decline of the mountain—not on the upper table-land midway, where all appears to men so solid, so tolerably smooth, save for a few
excrescences, roughnesses, gradually to be levelled at
their leisure ; which induces one to protest that the
middle-age of men is their time of delusion.   It is no
paradox.   They may be publicly useful in a small way,
I do not deny it at all.   They must be near the gates of
life—the opening or the closing—for their *minds* to be
accessible to the urgency of the greater questions.   Otherwise the world presents itself to them under too settled an
aspect—unless, of course, Vesuvian Revolution shakes
the land.   And that touches only their nerves.   I dream
of some old Judge !   There is one—if having caught we
could keep him.   But I dread so tricksy a pilot.   You have
guessed him—the ancient Puck !   We have laughed
all day over the paper telling us of his worrying the Lords.
Lady Esquart congratulates her husband in being out of
it.   Puck *bien ridé* and bewigged might perhaps—except
that at the critical moment he would be sure to plead
allegiance to Oberon.   However, the work will be performed by some one : I am prophetic :—when maidens
are grandmothers !—when your Tony is wearing a perpetual laugh in the unhusbanded regions where there is
no institution of the wedding-tie.'

For the reason that she was not to participate in the result of the old Judge's or young hero's happy champion-

ship of the cause of her sex, she conceived her separateness high aloof, and actually supposed she was a contemplative, simply speculative political spirit, impersonal albeit a woman.  This, as Emma, smiling at the lines, had not to learn, was always her secret pride of fancy— the belief in her possession of a disengaged intellect.

The strange illusion, so clearly exposed to her correspondent, was maintained through a series of letters very slightly descriptive, dated from the Piræus, the Bosphorus, the coasts of the Crimea, all more or less relating to the latest news of the journals received on board the yacht, and of English visitors fresh from the country she now seemed fond of calling ' home.'  Politics, and gentle allusions to the curious exhibition of ' love in marriage ' shown by her amiable host and hostess :—' these dear Esquarts, who are never tired of one another, but courtly courting, tempting me to think it possible that a fortunate selection and a mutual deference may subscribe to human happiness':—filled the paragraphs.  Reviews of her first literary venture were mentioned once: 'I was well advised by Mr. Redworth in putting ANTONIA for authoress. She is a buff jerkin to the stripes, and I suspect that the signature of D. A. M., written in full, would have cawed woefully to hear that her style is affected, her characters nullities, her cleverness forced, etc., etc.  As it is, I have much the same contempt for poor Antonia's performance. Cease penning, little fool!  She writes, " with some comprehension of the passion of love."  I know her to be a stranger to the earliest cry.  So you see, dear, that utter ignorance is the mother of the Art.  Dialogues " occasionally pointed."  She has a sister who may do better.—But why was I not apprenticed to a serviceable profession or a trade ?  I perceive now that a hanger-on of the market had no right to expect a happier fate than mine has been.'

On the Nile, in the winter of the year, Diana met the
Hon. Percy Dacier. He was introduced to her at Cairo by
Redworth. The two gentlemen had struck up a House
of Commons acquaintanceship, and finding themselves
bound for the same destination, had grown friendly.
Redworth's arrival had been pleasantly expected. She
remarked on Dacier's presence to Emma, without sketch
or note of him as other than much esteemed by Lord and
Lady Esquart. These, with Diana, Redworth, Dacier,
the German Eastern traveller Schweizerbarth, and the
French Consul and Egyptologist Duriette, composed a
voyaging party up the river, of which expedition Redworth was Lady Dunstane's chief writer of the records.
His novel perceptiveness and shrewdness of touch made
them amusing ; and his tenderness to the Beauty's
coquettry between the two foreign rivals, moved a deeper
feeling. The German had a guitar, the Frenchman a
voice ; Diana joined them in harmony. They complained apart severally of the accompaniment and the
singer. Our English criticized them apart ; and that is
at any rate to occupy a post, though it contributes nothing
to entertainment. At home the Esquarts had sung duets ;
Diana had assisted Redworth's manly chest-notes at the
piano. Each of them declined to be vocal. Diana sang
alone for the credit of the country, Italian and French
songs, Irish also. She was in her mood of Planxty Kelly
and Garryowen all the way. ' Madame est Irlandaise ? '
Redworth heard the Frenchman say, and he owned to
what was implied in the answering tone of the question.
' We should be dull dogs without the Irish leaven ! ' So
Tony in exile still managed to do something for her
darling Erin. The solitary woman on her heights at
Copsley raised an exclamation of, ' Oh ! that those two
had been or could be united ! ' She was conscious of
a mystic symbolism in the prayer.

She was not apprehensive of any ominous intervention of another.  Writing from Venice, Diana mentioned Mr. Percy Dacier as being engaged to an heiress ; ' A Miss Asper, niece of a mighty shipowner, Mr. Quintin Manx, Lady Esquart tells me : money fabulous, and necessary to a younger son devoured with ambition.  The elder brother, Lord Creedmore, is a common Nimrod, always absent in Hungary, Russia, America, hunting somewhere.  Mr. Dacier will be in the Cabinet with the next Ministry.'  No more of him.  A new work by ANTONIA was progressing.

The Summer in South Tyrol passed like a royal procession before young eyes for Diana, and at the close of it, descending the Stelvio, idling through the Valtelline, Como Lake was reached, Diana full of her work, living the double life of the author.  At Bellagio one afternoon Mr. Percy Dacier appeared.  She remembered subsequently a disappointment she felt in not beholding Mr. Redworth either with him or displacing him.  If engaged to a lady, he was not an ardent suitor; nor was he a pointedly complimentary acquaintance.  His enthusiasm was reserved for Italian scenery.  She had already formed a sort of estimate of his character, as an indifferent observer may do, and any woman previous to the inflaming of her imagination, if that is in store for her ; and she now fell to work resetting the puzzle it became as soon her positive conclusions had to be shaped again.  ' But women never can know young men,' she wrote to Emma, after praising his good repute as one of the brotherhood.  ' He drops pretty sentences now and then : no compliments ; milky nuts.  Of course he has a head, or he would not be where he is—and that seems always to me the most enviable place a young man can occupy.'  She observed in him a singular conflicting of a buoyant animal nature with a curb of studiousness, as if the fardels of age were piling on his shoulders before youth had quitted its pastures.

His build of limbs and his features were those of the finely-
bred English ; he had the English taste for sports, games,
manly diversions ; and in the bloom of life, under thirty,
his head was given to bend. The head bending on a tall
upright figure, where there was breadth of chest, told of
weights working. She recollected his open look, larger
than inquiring, at the introduction to her ; and it recurred
when she uttered anything specially taking. What it
meant was past a guess, though comparing it with the
frank directness of Redworth's eyes, she saw the difference
between a look that accepted her and one that dilated on
two opinions.

Her thought of the gentleman was of a brilliant young
charioteer in the ruck of the race, watchful for his chance
to push to the front ; and she could have said that a dubious consort might spoil a promising career. It flattered
her to think that she sometimes prompted him, sometimes illumined. He repeated sentences she had spoken.
—' I shall be better able to describe Mr. Dacier when you
and I sit together, my Emmy, and a stroke here and there
completes the painting. Set descriptions are good for
puppets. Living men and women are too various in the
mixture fashioning them—even the " external presentment "—to be livingly rendered in a formal sketch. I
may tell you his eyes are pale blue, his features regular,
his hair silky, brownish, his legs long, his head rather
stooping (only the head), his mouth commonly closed ;
these are the facts, and you have seen much the same in
a nursery doll. Such literary craft is of the nursery. So
with landscapes. The art of the pen (we write on darkness) is to rouse the inward vision, instead of labouring
with a Drop-scene brush, as if it were to the eye ; because
our flying minds cannot contain a protracted description.
That is why the poets, who spring imagination with a word
or a phrase, paint lasting pictures. The Shakespearian,

the Dantesque, are in a line, two at most.  He lends
an attentive ear when I speak, agrees or has a quaint
pucker of the eyebrows dissenting inwardly.  He lacks
mental liveliness—cheerfulness, I should say, and is
thankful to have it imparted.  One suspects he would be
a dull domestic companion.  He has a veritable thirst for
hopeful views of the world, and no spiritual distillery of
his own.  He leans to depression.  Why !  The broken
reed you call your Tony carries a cargo, all of her manufacture—she reeks of secret stills ; and here is a young
man—a sapling oak—inclined to droop.  His nature has
an air of imploring me *que je l'arrose* !  I begin to perform
Mrs. Dr. Pangloss on purpose to brighten him—the mind,
the views.  He is not altogether deficient in conversational gaiety, and he shines in exercise.  But the world is
a poor old ball bounding down a hill—to an Irish melody
in the evening generally, by request.  So far of Mr. Percy
Dacier, of whom I have some hopes—distant, perhaps
delusive—that he may be of use to our cause.  He listens.
It is an auspicious commencement.'

Lugano is the Italian lake most lovingly encircled by
mountain arms, and every height about it may be scaled
with ease.  The heights have their nest of waters below
for a home scene, the southern Swiss peaks, with celestial
Monta Rosa, in prospect.  It was there that Diana re-
awakened, after the trance of a deadly draught, to the
glory of the earth and her share in it.  She wakened like
the Princess of the Kiss ;  happily not to kisses ;  to no
sign, touch or call that she could trace backward.  The
change befell her without a warning.  After writing deliberately to her friend Emma, she laid down her pen and
thought of nothing ;  and into this dreamfulness a wine
passed, filling her veins, suffusing her mind, quickening
her soul :—and coming whence ? out of air, out of the
yonder of air.  She could have imagined a seraphic

presence in the room, that bade her arise and live ; take
the cup of the wells of youth arrested at her lips by her marriage ; quit her wintry bondage for warmth, light, space,
the quick of simple being. And the strange pure ecstasy
was not a transient electrification ; it came in waves on a
continuous tide ; looking was living ; walking flying.
She hardly knew that she slept. The heights she had seen
rosy at eve were marked for her ascent in the dawn.
Sleep was one wink, and fresh as the dewy field and rock-
flowers on her way upward, she sprang to more and more
of heaven, insatiable, happily chirruping over her possessions. The threading of the town among the dear common people before others were abroad, was a pleasure :
and pleasant her solitariness threading the gardens at the
base of the rock, only she astir ; and the first rough steps
of the winding footpath, the first closed buds, the sharper
air, the uprising of the mountain with her ascent ; and
pleasant too was her hunger and the nibble at a little loaf
of bread. A linnet sang in her breast, an eagle lifted her
feet. The feet were verily winged, as they are in a season
of youth when the blood leaps to light from the pressure
of the under forces, like a source at the wellheads, and
the whole creature blooms, vital in every energy as a
spirit. To be a girl again was magical. She could fancy
her having risen from the dead. And to be a girl, with a
woman's broader vision and receptiveness of soul, with
knowledge of evil, and winging to ethereal happiness,
this was a revelation of our human powers.

She attributed the change to the influences of nature's
beauty and grandeur. Nor had her woman's consciousness to play the chrysalis in any shy recesses of her heart ;
she was nowhere veiled or torpid ; she was illumined, like
the Salvatore she saw in the evening beams and mounted
in the morning's ; and she had not a spot of secresy ; all
her nature flew and bloomed ; she was bird, flower, flowing

river, a quivering sensibility unweighted, unshrouded. Desires and hopes would surely have weighted and shrouded her. She had none, save for the upper air, the eyes of the mountain.

Which was the dream—her past life or this ethereal existence ? But this ran spontaneously, and the other had often been stimulated—her vivaciousness on the Nile-boat, for a recent example. She had not a doubt that her past life was the dream, or deception : and for the reason that now she was compassionate, large of heart toward all beneath her. Let them but leave her free, they were forgiven, even to prayers for their wellbeing ! The plural number in the case was an involuntary multiplying of the single, coming of her incapacity during this elevation and rapture of the senses to think distinctly of that One who had discoloured her opening life. Freedom to breathe, gaze, climb, grow with the grasses, fly with the clouds, to muse, to sing, to be an unclaimed self, dispersed upon earth, air, sky, to find a keener transfigured self in that radiation—she craved no more.

Bear in mind her beauty, her charm of tongue, her present state of white simplicity in fervour : was there ever so perilous a woman for the most guarded and clearest-eyed of young men to meet at early morn upon a mountain side ?

## CHAPTER XVI

### TREATS OF A MIDNIGHT BELL, AND OF A SCENE OF EARLY MORNING

On a round of the mountains rising from Osteno, Southeastward of Lugano, the Esquart party rose from the natural grotto and headed their carriages up and down the

defiles, halting for a night at Rovio, a little village below
the Generoso, lively with waterfalls and watercourses;
and they fell so in love with the place, that after roaming
along the flowery borderways by moonlight, they resolved to rest there two or three days and try some easy
ascents. In the diurnal course of nature, being pleasantly
tired, they had the avowed intention of sleeping there;
so they went early to their beds, and carelessly wished
one another good-night, none of them supposing slumber
to be anywhere one of the warlike arts, a paradoxical
thing you must battle for and can only win at last when
utterly beaten. Hard by their inn, close enough for a
priestly homily to have been audible, stood a church
campanile, wherein hung a Bell, not ostensibly communi-
cating with the demons of the pit; in daylight rather a
merry comrade. But at night, when the children of
nerves lay stretched, he threw off the mask. As soon as
they had fairly nestled, he smote their pillows a shatter-
ing blow, loud for the retold preluding quarters, incred-
ibly clanging the number ten. Then he waited for
neighbouring campanili to box the ears of slumber's
votaries in turn; whereupon, under pretence of excessive
conscientiousness, or else oblivious of his antecedent
damnable misconduct, or perhaps in actual league and
trapdoor conspiracy with the surging goblin hosts beneath us, he resumed his blaring strokes, a sonorous
recapitulation of the number; all the others likewise.
It was an alarum fit to warn of Attila or Alaric; and not
simply the maniacal noise invaded the fruitful provinces
of sleep like Hun and Vandal, the irrational repetition
ploughed the minds of those unhappy somnivolents,
leaving them worse than sheared by barbarians, disrupt,
as by earthquake, with the unanswerable question to
Providence, Why!—Why twice?

Designing slumberers are such infants. When they

have undressed and stretched themselves flat, it seems
that they have really gone back to their mothers' breasts,
and they fret at whatsoever does not smack of nature, or
custom. The cause of a repetition so senseless in its
violence, and so unnecessary, set them querying and
kicking until the inevitable quarters recommenced. Then
arose an insurgent rabble in their bosoms, it might be the
loosened imps of darkness, urging them to speculate
whether the proximate monster about to dole out the
eleventh hour in uproar would again forget himself and
repeat his dreary arithmetic a second time ; for they
were unaware of his religious obligation, following the
hour of the district, to inform them of the tardy hour of
Rome. They waited in suspense, curiosity enabling
them to bear the first crash callously. His performance
was the same. And now they took him for a crazy
engine whose madness had infected the whole neighbourhood. Now was the moment to fight for sleep in contempt of him, and they began by simulating an entry
into the fortress they were to defend, plunging on their
pillows, battening down their eyelids, breathing with a
dreadful regularity. Alas ! it came to their knowledge
that the Bell was in possession and they the besiegers.
Every resonant quarter was anticipated up to the blow,
without averting its murderous abruptness ; and an
executioner Midnight that sounded, in addition to the
reiterated quarters, four and twenty ringing hammer-
strokes, with the aching pause between the twelves, left
them the prey of the legions of torturers which are
summed, though not described, in the title of a sleepless
night.

From that period the curse was milder, but the victims
raged. They swam on vasty deeps, they knocked at
rusty gates, they shouldered all the weapons of black
Insomnia's armoury and became her soldiery, doing her

will upon themselves. Of her originally sprang the inspired teaching of the doom of men to excruciation in
endlessness. She is the fountain of the infinite ocean
whereon the exceedingly sensitive soul is tumbled everlastingly, with the diversion of hot pincers to appease its
appetite for change.

Dacier was never the best of sleepers. He had taken to
exercise his brains prematurely, not only in learning, but
also in reflection ; and a reflectiveness that is indulged
before we have a rigid mastery of the emotions, or have
slain them, is apt to make a young man more than commonly a child of nerves : nearly as much so as the dissi-
pated, with the difference that they are hilarious while
wasting their treasury, which he is not ; and he may
recover under favouring conditions, which is a point of
vantage denied to them. Physically he had stout reserves, for he had not disgraced the temple. His intemperateness lay in the craving to rise and lead : a
precocious ambition. This apparently modest young
man started with an aim—and if in the distance and with
but a slingstone, like the slender shepherd fronting the
Philistine, all his energies were in his aim—at Government. He had hung on the fringe of an Administration.
His party was out, and he hoped for higher station on
its return to power. Many perplexities were therefore
buzzing about his head ; among them at present one
sufficiently magnified and voracious to swallow the
remainder. He added force to the interrogation as to
why that Bell should sound its inhuman strokes twice,
by asking himself why he was there to hear it ! A
strange suspicion of a bewitchment might have enlightened him if he had been a man accustomed to yield
to the peculiar kind of sorcery issuing from that sex. He
rather despised the power of women over men : and nevertheless he was there, listening to that Bell, instead of

having obeyed the call of his family duties, when the latter were urgent. He had received letters at Lugano, summoning him home, before he set forth on his present expedition. The noisy alarum told him he floundered in quags, like a silly creature chasing a marsh-lamp. But was it so ? Was it not, on the contrary, a serious pursuit of the secret of a woman's character ?—Oh, a woman and her character ! Ordinary women and their characters might set to work to get what relationship and likeness they could. They had no secret to allure. This one had : she had the secret of lake waters under rock, unfathomable in limpidness. He could not think of her without shooting at nature, and nature's very sweetest and subtlest, for comparisons. As to her sex, his active man's contempt of the petticoated secret attractive to boys and graylings, made him believe that in her he hunted the mind and the spirit : perchance a double mind, a twilighted spirit ; but not a mere woman. She bore no resemblance to the bundle of women. Well, she was worth studying ; she had ideas, and could give ear to ideas. Furthermore, a couple of the members of his family inclined to do her injustice. At least, they judged her harshly, owing, he thought, to an inveterate opinion they held regarding Lord Dannisburgh's obliquity in relation to women. He shared it, and did not concur in their verdict upon the woman implicated. That is to say, knowing something of her now, he could see the possibility of her innocence in the special charm that her mere sparkle of features and speech, and her freshness would have for a man like his uncle. The possibility pleaded strongly on her behalf, while the darker possibility weighted by his uncle's reputation plucked at him from below.

She was delightful to hear, delightful to see ; and her friends loved her and had faith in her. So

clever a woman might be too clever for her
friends ! . . .

The circle he moved in hummed of women, prompting
novices as well as veterans to suspect that the multitude
of them, and notably the fairest, yet more the cleverest,
concealed the serpent somewhere.

She certainly had not directed any of her arts upon him.
Besides he was half engaged. And that was a burning
perplexity ; not because of abstract scruples touching the
necessity for love in marriage. The young lady, great
heiress though she was, and willing, as she allowed him
to assume ; graceful too, reputed a beauty ; struck him
cold. He fancied her transparent, only Arctic. Her
transparency displayed to him all the common virtues,
and a serene possession of the inestimable and eminent
one outweighing all ; but charm, wit, ardour, inter-
communicative quickness, and kindling beauty, airy
grace, were qualities that a man, it seemed, had to look
for in women spotted by a doubt of their having the chief
and priceless.

However, he was not absolutely plighted. Nor did it
matter to him whether this or that woman concealed the
tail of the serpent and trail, excepting the singular
interest this woman managed to excite, and so deeply as
set him wondering how that Resurrection Bell might be
affecting her ability to sleep. Was she sleeping ?—or
waking ? His nervous imagination was a torch that
alternately lighted her lying asleep with the innocent,
like a babe, and tossing beneath the overflow of her dark
hair, hounded by haggard memories. She fluttered
before him in either aspect ; and another perplexity now
was to distinguish within himself which was the aspect
he preferred. Great Nature brought him thus to drink
of her beauty, under the delusion that the act was a speculation on her character.

The Bell, with its clash, throb and long swoon of sound, reminded him of her name : Diana !—An attribute ? or a derision ?

It really mattered nothing to him, save for her being maligned ; and if most unfairly, then that face of the varying expressions, and the rich voice, and the remembered gentle and taking words coming from her, appealed to him with a supplicating vividness that pricked his heart to leap.

He was dozing when the Bell burst through the thin division between slumber and wakefulness, recounting what seemed innumerable peals, hard on his cranium. Gray daylight blanched the window and the bed : his watch said five of the morning. He thought of the pleasure of a bath beneath some dashing sprayshowers, and jumped up to dress, feeling a queer sensation of skin in his clothes, the sign of a feverish night ; and yawning he went into the air. Leftward the narrow village street led to the footway along which he could make for the mountain-wall. He cast one look at the head of the campanile, silly as an owlish roysterer's glazed stare at the young Aurora, and hurried his feet to check the yawns coming alarmingly fast, in the place of ideas.

His elevation above the valley was about the kneecap of the Generoso. Waters of past rain-clouds poured down the mountain-sides like veins of metal, here and there flinging off a shower on the busy descent ; only dubiously animate in the lack lustre of the huge bulk piled against a yellow East that wafted fleets of pinky cloudlets overhead. He mounted his path to a level with inviting grassmounds where water circled, running from scoops and cups to curves and brook-streams, and in his fancy calling to him to hear them. To dip in them was his desire. To roll and shiver braced by the icy flow was the spell to break that baleful incantation of the intolerable night ;

so he struck across a ridge of boulders, wreck of a landslip
from the height he had hugged, to the open space of
shadowed undulations, and soon had his feet on turf.
Heights to right and to left, and between them, aloft, a
sky the rosy wheelcourse of the chariot of morn, and
below, among the knolls, choice of sheltered nooks where
waters whispered of secresy to satisfy Diana herself.
They have that whisper and waving of secresy in secret
scenery ; they beckon to the bath ; and they conjure
classic visions of the pudency of the Goddess irate or
unsighted.   The semi-mythological state of mind, built
of old images and favouring haunts, was known to Dacier.
The name of Diana, playing vaguely on his consciousness,
helped to it.   He had no definite thought of the mortal
woman when the highest grass-roll near the rock gave him
view of a bowered source and of a pool under a chain of
cascades, bounded by polished shelves and slabs.   The
very spot for him, he decided at the first peep ; and at
the second, with fingers instinctively loosening his waist-
coat-buttons for a commencement, he shouldered round
and strolled away, though not at a rapid pace, nor far
before he halted.

That it could be no other than she, the figure he had
seen standing beside the pool, he was sure.   Why had he
turned ?   Thoughts thick and swift as a blush in the
cheeks of seventeen overcame him ; and queen of all, the
thought bringing the picture of this mountain-solitude to
vindicate a woman shamefully assailed.—She who found
her pleasure in these haunts of nymph and Goddess, at
the fresh cold bosom of nature, must be clear as day.
She trusted herself to the loneliness here, and to the
honour of men, from a like irreflective sincereness.   She
was unable to imagine danger where her own impelling
thirst was pure. . . .

The thoughts, it will be discerned, were but flashes of

a momentary vivid sensibility. Where a woman's charm
has won half the battle, her character is an advancing
standard and sings victory, let her do no more than take a
quiet morning walk before breakfast.

But why had he turned his back on her ? There was
nothing in his presence to alarm, nothing in her appearance to forbid. The motive and the movement were
equally quaint ; incomprehensible to him ; for after
putting himself out of sight, he understood the absurdity
of the supposition that she would seek the secluded sylvan
bath for the same purpose as he. Yet now he was
debarred from going to meet her. She might have an
impulse to bathe her feet. Her name was Diana. . . .

Yes, and a married woman ; and a proclaimed one !
And notwithstanding those brassy facts, he was ready to
side with the evidence declaring her free from stain ; and
further, to swear that her blood was Diana's !

Nor had Dacier ever been particularly poetical about
women. The present Diana had wakened his curiosity,
had stirred his interest in her, pricked his admiration, but
gradually, until a sleepless night with its flock of raven-
fancies under that dominant Bell, ended by colouring her,
the moment she stood in his eyes, as freshly as the morning heavens. We are much influenced in youth by
sleepless nights : they disarm, they predispose us to
submit to soft occasion ; and in our youth occasion is
always coming.

He heard her voice. She had risen up the grass-mound,
and he hung brooding half-way down. She was dressed
in some texture of the hue of lavender. A violet scarf
loosely knotted over the bosom opened on her throat.
The loop of her black hair curved under a hat of gray
beaver. Memorably radiant was her face.

They met, exchanged greetings, praised the beauty of
the morning, and struck together on the Bell. She

laughed : ' I heard it at ten ; I slept till four.   I never wake later.   I was out in the air by half-past.   Were you disturbed ? '

He alluded to his troubles with the Bell.

' It sounded like a felon's heart in skeleton ribs,' he said.

' Or a proser's tongue in a hollow skull,' said she.

He bowed to her conversible readiness, and at once fell into the background, as he did only with her, to perform accordant bass in their dialogue ; for when a woman lightly caps our strained remarks, we gallantly surrender the leadership, lest she should too cuttingly assert her claim.

Some sweet wild cyclamen flowers were at her breast. She held in her left hand a bunch of buds and blown cups of the pale purple meadow-crocus.   He admired them. She told him to look round.   He confessed to not having noticed them in the grass : what was the name ?   Colchicum, in Botany, she said.

' These are plucked to be sent to a friend ; otherwise I 'm reluctant to take the life of flowers for a whim. Wild flowers, I mean.   I am not sentimental about garden flowers : they are cultivated for decoration, grown for clipping.'

' I suppose they don't carry the same signification,' said Dacier, in the tone of a pupil to such themes.

' They carry no feeling,' said she.   ' And that is my excuse for plucking these, where they seem to spring like our town-dream of happiness.   I believe they are sensible of it too ; but these must do service to my invalid friend, who cannot travel.   Are you ever as much interested in the woes of great ladies as of country damsels ?   I am not —not unless they have natural distinction.   You have met Lady Dunstane ? '

The question sounded artless.   Dacier answered that he

thought he had seen her somewhere once, and Diana shut her lips on a rising under-smile.

'She is the *cœur d'or* of our time ; the one soul I would sacrifice these flowers to.'

'A bit of a blue-stocking, I think I have heard said.'

'She might have been admitted to the Hotel Rambouillet, without being anything of a Précieuse.  She is the woman of the largest heart now beating.'

'Mr. Redworth talked of her.'

'As she deserved, I am sure.'

'Very warmly.'

'He would ! '

'He told me you were the Damon and Pythias of women.'

'Her one fault is an extreme humility that makes her always play second to me ; and as I am apt to gabble, I take the lead ; and I am froth in comparison.  I can reverence my superiors even when tried by intimacy with them.  She is the next heavenly thing to heaven that I know.  Court her, if ever you come across her.  Or have you a man's horror of women with brains ? '

'Am I expressing it ? ' said he.

'Do not breathe London or Paris here on me.'  She fanned the crocuses under her chin.  'The early morning always has this—I wish I had a word !—touch . . . whisper . . . gleam . . . beat of wings—I envy poets now more than ever !—of Eden, I was going to say. Prose can paint evening and moonlight, but poets are needed to sing the dawn.  That is because prose is equal to melancholy stuff.  Gladness requires the finer language.  Otherwise we have it coarse—anything but a reproduction.  You politicians despise the little distinctions " twixt tweedledum and tweedledee," I fancy.'

Of the poetic sort, Dacier's uncle certainly did.  For himself he confessed to not having thought much on them.

' But how divine is utterance ! ' she said. ' As we to the brutes, poets are to us.'

He listened somewhat with the head of the hanged. A beautiful woman choosing to rhapsodize has her way, and is not subjected to the critical commentary within us. He wondered whether she had discoursed in such a fashion to his uncle.

' I can read good poetry,' said he.

' If you would have this valley—or mountain-cleft, one should call it—described, only verse could do it for you,' Diana pursued, and stopped, glanced at his face and smiled. She had spied the end of a towel peeping out of one of his pockets. ' You came out for a bath ! Go back, by all means, and mount that rise of grass where you first saw me ; and down on the other side, a little to the right, you will find the very place for a bath, at a corner of the rock—a natural fountain ; a bubbling pool in a ring of brushwood, with falling water, so tempting that I could have pardoned a push : about five feet deep. Lose no time.'

He begged to assure her that he would rather stroll with her : it had been only a notion of bathing by chance when he pocketed the towel.

' Dear me,' she cried, ' if I had been a man I should have scurried off at a signal of release, quick as a hare I once woke up in a field with my foot on its back.'

Dacier's eyebrows knotted a trifle over her eagerness to dismiss him : he was not used to it, but rather to be courted by women, and to condescend.

' I shall not long, I 'm afraid, have the pleasure of walking beside you and hearing you. I had letters at Lugano. My uncle is unwell, I hear.'

' Lord Dannisburgh ? '

The name sprang from her lips unhesitatingly.

His nodded affirmative altered her face and her voice.

' It is not a grave illness ? '

' They rather fear it.'

' You had the news at Lugano ? '

He answered the implied reproach : ' I can be of no service.'

' But surely ! '

' It 's even doubtful that he would be bothered to receive me. We hold no views in common—excepting one.'

' Could I ? ' she exclaimed. ' O that I might ! If he is really ill ! But if it is actually serious he would perhaps have a wish . . . I can nurse. I know I have the power to cheer him. You ought indeed to be in England.'

Dacier said he had thought it better to wait for later reports. ' I shall drive to Lugano this afternoon, and act on the information I get there. Probably it ends my holiday.'

' Will you do me the favour to write me word ?—and especially tell me if you think he would like to have me near him,' said Diana. ' And let him know that if he wants nursing or cheerful companionship, I am at any moment ready to come.'

The flattery of a beautiful young woman to wait on him would be very agreeable to Lord Dannisburgh, Dacier conceived. Her offer to go was possibly purely charitable. But the prudence of her occupation of the post obscured whatever appeared admirable in her devotedness. Her choice of a man like Lord Dannisburgh for the friend to whom she could sacrifice her good name less falteringly than she gathered those field-flowers was inexplicable ; and she herself a darker riddle at each step of his reading.

He promised curtly to write. ' I will do my best to hit a flying address.'

' Your Club enables me to hit a permanent one that will establish the communication,' said Diana. ' We shall not sleep another night at Rovio. Lady Esquart is the lightest of sleepers, and if you had a restless time, she and her husband must have been in purgatory. Besides, permit me to say, you should be with your party. The times are troublous—not for holidays! Your holiday has had a haunted look, creditably to your conscience as a politician. These Corn Law agitations!'

'Ah, but no politics here!' said Dacier.

'Politics everywhere!—in the Courts of Faëry! They are not discord to me.'

'But not the last day—the last hour!' he pleaded.

'Well! only do not forget your assurance to me that you would give some thoughts to Ireland—and the cause of women. Has it slipped from your memory?'

'If I see the chance of serving you, you may trust to me.'

She sent up an interjection on the misfortune of her not having been born a man.

It was to him the one smart of sourness in her charm as a woman.

Among the boulder-stones of the ascent to the path, he ventured to propose a little masculine assistance in a hand stretched mutely. Although there was no great need for help, her natural kindliness checked the inclination to refuse it. When their hands disjoined she found herself reddening. She cast it on the exertion. Her heart was throbbing. It might be the exertion likewise.

He walked and talked much more airily along the descending pathway, as if he had suddenly become more intimately acquainted with her.

She listened, trying to think of the manner in which he might be taught to serve that cause she had at heart ; and the colour deepened on her cheeks till it set fire to her underlying consciousness : blood to spirit. A tremour of alarm ran through her.

His request for one of the crocuses to keep as a souvenir of the morning was refused. ' They are sacred ; they were all devoted to my friend when I plucked them.'

He pointed to a half-open one, with the petals in disparting pointing to junction, and compared it to the famous tiptoe ballet-posture, arms above head and fingers like swallows meeting in air, of an operatic danseuse of the time.

' I do not see it, because I will not see it,' she said, and she found a personal cooling and consolement in the phrase.—We have this power of resisting invasion of the poetic by the commonplace, the spirit by the blood, if we please, though you men may not think that we have !— Her alarmed sensibilities bristled and made head against him as an enemy. She fancied (for the aforesaid reason —because she chose) that it was on account of the offence to her shy morning pleasure by his Londonizing. At any other moment her natural liveliness and trained social ease would have taken any remark on the eddies of the tide of converse ; and so she told herself, and did not the less feel wounded, adverse, armed. He seemed somehow to have dealt a mortal blow to the happy girl she had become again. The woman she was protested on behalf of the girl, while the girl in her heart bent lowered sad eyelids to the woman ; and which of them was wiser of the truth she could not have said, for she was honestly not aware of the truth, but she knew she was divided in halves, with one half pitying the other, one rebuking : and all because of the incongruous comparison of a wild flower to an opera dancer ! Absurd indeed. We human creatures are the silliest on earth, most certainly.

Dacier had observed the blush, and the check to her flowing tongue did not escape him as they walked back to the inn down the narrow street of black rooms, where the women gossiped at the fountain and the cobbler

threaded on his doorstep.  His novel excitement supplied
the deficiency, sweeping him past minor reflections.  He
was, however, surprised to hear her tell Lady Esquart, as
soon as they were together at the breakfast-table, that he
had the intention of starting for England ; and further
surprised, and slightly stung too, when on the poor lady's
moaning over her recollection of the midnight Bell, and
vowing she could not attempt to sleep another night in the
place, Diana declared her resolve to stay there one day
longer with her maid, and explore the neighbourhood for
the wild flowers in which it abounded.  Lord and Lady
Esquart agreed to anything agreeable to her, after excusing themselves for the necessitated flight, piteously
relating the story of their sufferings.  My lord could have
slept, but he had remained awake to comfort my lady.

'True knightliness ! ' Diana said, in praise of these
long married lovers ; and she asked them what they had
talked of during the night.

'You, my dear, partly,' said Lady Esquart.

'For an opiate ? '

'An invocation of the morning,' said Dacier.

Lady Esquart looked at Diana and at him.  She
thought it was well that her fair friend should stay.  It
was then settled for Diana to rejoin them the next evening at Lugano, thence to proceed to Luino on the Maggiore.

'I fear it is good-bye for me,' Dacier said to her, as he
was about to step into the carriage with the Esquarts.

'If you have not better news of your uncle, it must be,'
she replied, and gave him her hand promptly and formally,
hardly diverting her eyes from Lady Esquart to grace the
temporary gift with a look.  The last of her he saw was a
waving of her arm and a finger pointing triumphantly at
the Bell in the tower.  It said, to an understanding un-
practised in the feminine mysteries : ' I can sleep through
anything.'  What that revealed of her state of conscience

and her nature, his efforts to preserve the lovely optical figure blocked his guessing. He was with her friends, who liked her the more they knew her, and he was compelled to lean to their view of the perplexing woman.

'She is a riddle to the world,' Lady Esquart said, 'but I know that she is good. It is the best of signs when women take to her and are proud to be her friend.'

My lord echoed his wife. She talked in this homely manner to stop any notion of philandering that the young gentleman might be disposed to entertain in regard to a lady so attractive to the pursuit as Diana's beauty and delicate situation might make her seem.

'She is an exceedingly clever person, and handsomer than report, which is uncommon,' said Dacier, becoming voluble on town-topics, Miss Asper incidentally among them. He denied Lady Esquart's charge of an engagement ; the matter hung.

His letters at Lugano summoned him to England instantly.

'I have taken leave of Mrs. Warwick, but tell her I regret, et caetera,' he said ; 'and by the way, as my uncle's illness appears to be serious, the longer she is absent the better, perhaps.'

'It would never do,' said Lady Esquart, understanding his drift immediately. 'We winter in Rome. She will not abandon us—I have her word for it. Next Easter we are in Paris ; and so home, I suppose. There will be no hurry before we are due at Cowes. We seem to have become confirmed wanderers ; for two of us at least it is likely to be our last great tour.'

Dacier informed her that he had pledged his word to write to Mrs. Warwick of his uncle's condition, and the several appointed halting-places of the Esquarts between the lakes and Florence were named to him. Thus all things were openly treated ; all had an air of being on the surface ; the communications passing between Mrs. Warwick and the Hon. Percy Dacier might have been perused by all the world.  None but that portion of it, sage in suspiciousness, which objects to such communications under any circumstances, could have detected in their correspondence a spark of coming fire or that there was common warmth.  She did not feel it, nor did he. The position of the two interdicted it to a couple honourably sensible of social decencies ;  and who were, be it added, kept apart.  The blood is the treacherous element in the story of the nobly civilized, of which secret Diana, a wife and no wife, a prisoner in liberty, a blooming woman imagining herself restored to transcendent maiden ecstasies—the highest youthful poetic—had received some faint intimation when the blush flamed suddenly in her cheeks and her heart knelled like the towers of a city given over to the devourer.  She had no wish to meet him again.  Without telling herself why, she would have shunned the meeting.  Disturbers that thwarted her simple happiness in sublime scenery were best avoided.  She thought so the more for a fitful blur to the simplicity of her sensations, and a task she sometimes had in restoring and toning them, after that sweet morning time in Rovio.

## CHAPTER XVII

### ' THE PRINCESS EGERIA '

LONDON, say what we will of it, is after all the head of the British giant, and if not the liveliest in bubbles, it is past competition the largest broth-pot of brains anywhere

simmering on the hob : over the steadiest of furnaces too.
And the oceans and the continents, as you know, are perpetual and copious contributors, either to the heating
apparatus or to the contents of the pot. Let grander
similes be sought. This one fits for the smoky receptacle
cherishing millions, magnetic to tens of millions more,
with its caked outside of grime, and the inward substance
incessantly kicking the lid, prankish, but never casting it
off. A good stew, you perceive ; not a parlous boiling.
Weak as we may be in our domestic cookery, our political
has been sagaciously adjusted as yet to catch the ardours
of the furnace without being subject to their volcanic
activities.

That the social is also somewhat at fault, we have proof
in occasional outcries over the absence of these or those
particular persons famous for inspiriting. It sticks and
clogs. The improvizing songster is missed, the convivial
essayist, the humorous Dean, the travelled cynic, and he,
the one of his day, the iridescent Irishman, whose remembered repartees are a feast, sharp and ringing, at divers
tables descending from the upper to the fat citizen's,
where, instead of coming in the sequence of talk, they
are exposed by blasting, like fossil teeth of old Deluge
sharks in monotonous walls of our chalk-quarries. Nor
are these the less welcome for the violence of their introduction among a people glad to be set burning rather
briskly awhile by the most unexpected of digs in the ribs.
Dan Merion, to give an example. That was Dan Merion's
joke with the watchman : and he said that other thing
to the Marquis of Kingsbury, when the latter asked him
if he had ever won a donkey-race. And old Dan is dead,
and we are the duller for it ! which leads to the question :
Is genius hereditary ? And the affirmative and negative
are respectively maintained, rather against the Yes in
the dispute, until a member of the audience speaks of

Dan Merion's having left a daughter reputed for a sparkling wit not much below the level of his own.   Why, are
you unaware that the Mrs. Warwick of that scandal case
of Warwick *versus* Dannisburgh was old Dan Merion's girl
and his only child ?   It is true ; for a friend had it from
a man who had it straight from Mr. Braddock, of the
firm of Braddock, Thorpe and Simnel, her solicitors in the
action, who told him he could sit listening to her for hours,
and that she was as innocent as day ;  a wonderful combination of a good woman and a clever woman and a real
beauty.   Only her misfortune was to have a furiously
jealous husband, and they say he went mad after hearing
the verdict.

Diana was talked of in the London circles.   A witty
woman is such salt that where she has once been tasted
she must perforce be missed more than any of the absent,
the dowering heavens not having yet showered her like
very plentifully upon us.   Then it was first heard that
Percy Dacier had been travelling with her.   Miss Asper
heard of it.   Her uncle, Mr. Quintin Manx, the millionnaire, was an acquaintance of the new Judge and titled
dignitary, Sir Cramborne Wathin, and she visited Lady
Wathin, at whose table the report in the journals of the
Nile-boat party was mentioned.   Lady Wathin's table
could dispense with witty women, and, for that matter,
witty men.   The intrusion of the spontaneous on the
stereotyped would have clashed.   She preferred, as
hostess, the old legal anecdotes sure of their laugh, and
the citations from the manufactories of fun in the Press,
which were current and instantly intelligible to all her
guests.   She smiled suavely on an impromptu pun,
because her experience of the humorous appreciation of
it by her guests bade her welcome the upstart.   Nothing
else impromptu was acceptable.   Mrs. Warwick therefore was not missed by Lady Wathin.   ' I have met her,'

she said. 'I confess I am *not* one of the fanatics about
Mrs. Warwick. She has a sort of skill in getting men to
clamour. If you stoop to tickle them, they will applaud.
It is a way of winning a reputation.' When the ladies
were separated from the gentlemen by the stream of Claret,
Miss Asper heard Lady Wathin speak of Mrs. Warwick
again. An allusion to Lord Dannisburgh's fit of illness
in the House of Lords led to her saying that there was
no doubt he had been fascinated, and that, in her opinion,
Mrs. Warwick was a dangerous woman. Sir Cramborne
knew something of Mr. Warwick : 'Poor man !' she
added. A lady present put a question concerning Mrs.
Warwick's beauty. 'Yes,' Lady Wathin said, 'she has
good looks to aid her. Judging from what I hear and
have seen, her thirst is for notoriety. Sooner or later
we shall have her making a noise, you may be certain.
Yes, she *has* the secret of dressing well—in the French
style.'

A simple newspaper report of the expedition of a Nile-
boat party could stir the Powers to take her up and turn
her on their wheel in this manner.

But others of the sons and daughters of London were
regretting her prolonged absence. The great and ex-
clusive Whitmonby, who had dined once at Lady Wathin's
table, and vowed never more to repeat that offence to
his patience, lamented bitterly to Henry Wilmers that
the sole woman worthy of sitting at a little Sunday
evening dinner with the cream of the choicest men of
the time was away wasting herself in that insane modern
chase of the picturesque ! He called her a perverted
Célimène.

Redworth had less to regret than the rest of her male
friends, as he was receiving at intervals pleasant descriptive letters, besides manuscript sheets of ANTONIA's new
piece of composition, to correct the proofs for the press,

N

and he read them critically, he thought.    He read them
with a watchful eye to guard them from the critics.    AN-
TONIA, whatever her faults as a writer, was not one of the
order whose Muse is the Public Taste.    She did at least
draw her inspiration from herself, and there was much to
be feared in her work, if a sale was the object.    Otherwise
Redworth's highly critical perusal led him flatly to admire.    This was like her, and that was like her, and here
and there a phrase gave him the very play of her mouth,
the flash of her eyes.    Could he possibly wish, or bear, to
have anything altered ?    But she had reason to desire an
extended sale of the work.    Her aim, in the teeth of her
independent style, was at the means of independence—
a feminine method of attempting to conciliate contraries ;
and after despatching the last sheets to the printer, he
meditated upon the several ways which might serve to
assist her ; the main way running thus in his mind :—We
have a work of genius.    Genius is good for the public.
What is good for the public should be recommended by
the critics.    It should be.    How then to come at them to
get it done ?    As he was not a member of the honourable
literary craft, and regarded its arcana altogether externally, it may be confessed of him that he deemed the
Incorruptible corruptible ;—not, of course, with filthy
coin slid into sticky palms.    Critics are human, and exceedingly, beyond the common lot, when touched ; and
they are excited by mysterious hints of loftiness in
authorship ; by rumours of veiled loveliness ; whispers
of a general anticipation ; and also Editors can jog them.
Redworth was rising to be a Railway King of a period
soon to glitter with rails, iron in the concrete, golden in
the visionary.    He had already his Court, much against
his will.    The powerful magnetic attractions of those
who can help the world to fortune, was exercised by him
in spite of his disgust of sycophants.    He dropped words

to right and left of a coming work by ANTONIA.  And
who was ANTONIA ?—Ah ! there hung the riddle.—An
exalted personage ?—So much so that he dared not name
her even in confidence to ladies ;  he named the publishers.
To men he said he was at liberty to speak of her only as
the most beautiful woman of her time.  His courtiers
of both sexes were recommended to read the new story,
THE PRINCESS EGERIA.

Oddly, one great lady of his Court had heard a forth-
coming work of this title spoken of by Percy Dacier, not
a man to read silly fiction, unless there was meaning
behind the lines : that is, rich scandal of the aristocracy,
diversified by stinging epigrams to the address of dis-
cernible personages.  She talked of THE PRINCESS
EGERIA : nay, laid her finger on the identical Princess.
Others followed her.  Dozens were soon flying with the
torch : a new work immediately to be published from
the pen of the Duchess of Stars !—And the Princess who
lends her title to the book is a living portrait of the
Princess of Highest Eminence, the Hope of all Civilization.—Orders for copies of THE PRINCESS EGERIA reached
the astonished publishers before the book was advertized.

Speaking to editors, Redworth complimented them with
friendly intimations of the real authorship of the remarkable work appearing.  He used a certain penetrative mildness of tone in saying that ' he hoped the book would
succeed ' : it deserved to ;  it was original ;  but the
originality might tell against it.  All would depend upon
a favourable launching of such a book.  ' Mrs. Warwick ?
Mrs. Warwick ? ' said the most influential of editors,
Mr. Marcus Tonans ;  ' what ! that singularly handsome
woman ? . . . The  Dannisburgh  affair ? . . . She 's
Whitmonby's heroine.  If she writes as cleverly as she
talks, her work is worth trumpeting.'  He promised to
see that it went into good hands for the review, and a

prompt review—an essential point; none of your long
digestions of the contents.

Diana's indefatigable friend had fair assurances that her
book would be noticed before it dropped dead to the public
appetite for novelty. He was anxious next, notwithstanding his admiration of the originality of the conception and the cleverness of the writing, lest the Literary
Reviews should fail ' to do it justice ' : he used the term ;
for if they wounded her, they would take the pleasure
out of success ; and he had always present to him that
picture of the beloved woman kneeling at the fire-grate
at The Crossways, which made the thought of her suffering any wound his personal anguish, so crucially sweet
and saintly had her image then been stamped on him.
He bethought him, in consequence, while sitting in the
House of Commons, engaged upon the affairs of the
nation, and honestly engaged, for he was a vigilant
worker—that the Irish Secretary, Charles Rainer, with
whom he stood in amicable relations, had an interest, to
the extent of reputed ownership, in the chief of the
Literary Reviews. He saw Rainer on the benches, and
marked him to speak to him. Looking for him shortly
afterward, the man was gone. ' Off to the Opera, if he 's
not too late for the drop,' a neighbour said, smiling queerly,
as though he ought to know ; and then Redworth recollected current stories of Rainer's fantastical devotion
to the popular prima donna of the angelical voice. He
hurried to the Opera and met the vomit, and heard in the
crush-room how divine she had been that night. A
fellow member of the House, tolerably intimate with
Rainer, informed him, between frightful stomachic
roulades of her final aria, of the likeliest place where
Rainer might be found when the Opera was over : not
at his Club, nor at his chambers : on one of the bridges—
Westminster, he fancied.

There was no need for Redworth to run hunting the
man at so late an hour, but he was drawn on by the similarity in dissimilarity of this devotee of a woman, who
could worship her at a distance, and talk of her to everybody. Not till he beheld Rainer's tall figure cutting the
bridge-parapet, with a star over his shoulder, did he reflect on the views the other might entertain of the
nocturnal solicitation to see ' justice done ' to a lady's
new book in a particular Review, and the absurd
outside of the request was immediately smothered by
the natural simplicity and pressing necessity of its
inside.

He crossed the road and said, ' Ah ? ' in recognition.
' Were you at the Opera this evening ? '

' Oh, just at the end,' said Rainer, pacing forward.
' It 's a fine night. Did you hear her ? '

' No ; too late.'

Rainer pressed ahead, to meditate by himself, as was
his wont. Finding Redworth beside him, he mono-
loguized in his depths : ' They 'll kill her. She puts her
soul into it, gives her blood. There 's no failing of the
voice. You see how it wears her. She 's doomed. Half
a year's rest on Como . . . somewhere . . . she might
be saved ! She won't *refuse* to work.'

' Have you spoken to her ? ' said Redworth.

' And next to Berlin ! Vienna ! A horse would be——
I ? I don't know her,' Rainer replied. ' Some of their
women stand it. She 's delicately built. You can't
treat a lute like a drum without destroying the instrument. We look on at a murder ! '

The haggard prospect from that step of the climax
checked his delivery.

Redworth knew him to be a sober man in office, a man
with a head for statecraft : he had made a weighty
speech in the House a couple of hours back. This Opera

cantatrice, no beauty, though gentle, thrilling, winning, was his corner of romance.

' Do you come here often ? ' he asked.

' Yes, I can't sleep.'

' London at night, from the bridge, looks fine. By the way . . .'

' It 's lonely here, that 's the advantage,' said Rainer ; ' I keep silver in my pocket for poor girls going to their homes, and I 'm left in peace. An hour later, there 's the dawn down yonder.'

' By the way,' Redworth interposed, and was told that after these nights of her singing she never slept till morning. He swallowed the fact, sympathized, and resumed : ' I want a small favour.'

' No business here, please ! '

' Not a bit of it. You know Mrs. Warwick. . . . You know of her. She 's publishing a book. I want you to use your influence to get it noticed quickly, if you can.'

' Warwick ? Oh, yes, a handsome woman. Ah, yes ; the Dannisburgh affair, yes. What did I hear !— They say she 's thick with Percy Dacier at present. Who was talking of her ! Yes, old Lady Dacier. So she 's a friend of yours ? '

' She 's an old friend,' said Redworth, composing himself ; for the dose he had taken was not of the sweetest, and no protestations could be uttered by a man of the world to repel a charge of tattlers. ' The truth is, her book is clever. I have read the proofs. She *must* have an income, and she won't apply to her husband, and literature should help her, if she 's fairly treated. She 's Irish by descent ; Merion's daughter, witty as her father. It 's odd you haven't met her. The mere writing of the book is extraordinarily good. If it 's put into capable hands for review ! that 's all it requires. And full of life . . . bright dialogue . . . capital sketches. The

book 's a piece of literature.  Only it must have com-
petent critics ! '

So he talked while Rainer ejaculated :  ' Warwick ?
Warwick ? ' in the irritating tone of dozens of others.
' What did I hear of her husband ?  He has a post. . . .
Yes, yes.  Some one said the verdict in that case knocked
him over—heart disease, or something.'

He glanced at the dark Thames water.  ' Take my
word for it, the groves of Academe won't compare with
one of our bridges at night, if you seek philosophy.  You
see the London above and the London below : round us
the sleepy city, and the stars in the water looking like
souls of suicides.  I caught a girl with a bad fit on her
once.  I had to lecture her !  It 's when we become
parsons we find out our cousinship with these poor peri-
patetics, whose " last philosophy " is a jump across the
parapet.  The bridge at night is a bath for a public man.
But choose another ;  leave me mine.'

Redworth took the hint.  He stated the title of Mrs.
Warwick's book, and imagined from the thoughtful cast
of Rainer's head, that he was impressing THE PRINCESS
EGERIA on his memory.

Rainer burst out, with clenched fists :  ' He beats her !
The fellow lives on her and beats her ;  strikes that
woman !  He drags her about to every Capital in Europe
to make money for him, and the scoundrel pays her with
blows.'

In the course of a heavy tirade against the scoundrel,
Redworth apprehended that it was the cantatrice's
husband.  He expressed his horror and regret ;  paused,
and named THE PRINCESS EGERIA and a certain Critical
Review.  Another outburst seemed to be in preparation.
Nothing further was to be done for the book at that hour.
So, with a blunt ' Good night,' he left Charles Rainer
pacing, and thought on his walk home of the strange

effects wrought by women unwittingly upon men (Englishmen); those women, or some of them, as little knowing it as the moon her traditional influence upon the tides. He thought of Percy Dacier too. In his bed he could have wished himself peregrinating a bridge.

THE PRINCESS EGERIA appeared, with the reviews at her heels, a pack of clappers, causing her to fly over editions clean as a doe the gates and hedges—to quote Mr. Sullivan Smith, who knew not a sentence of the work save what he gathered of it from Redworth, at their chance meeting on Piccadilly pavement, and then immediately he knew enough to blow his huntsman's horn in honour of the sale. His hallali rang high. ' Here 's another Irish girl to win their laurels ! 'Tis one of the blazing successes. A most enthralling work, beautifully composed. And where is she now, Mr. Redworth, since she broke away from that husband of hers, that wears the clothes of the worst tailor ever begotten by a thread on a needle, as I tell every soul of 'em in my part of the country ? '

' You have seen him ? ' said Redworth.

' Why, sir, wasn't he on show at the Court he applied to for relief and damages ? as we heard when we were watching the case daily, scarce drawing our breath for fear the innocent—and one of our own blood, would be crushed. Sure, there he stood ; ay, and looking the very donkey for a woman to flip off her fingers, like the dust from my great uncle's prise of snuff ! She 's a glory to the old country. And better you than another, I 'd say, since it wasn't an Irishman to have her : but what induced the dear lady to take *him*, is the question we 're all of us asking ! And it 's mournful to think that somehow you contrive to get the pick of us in the girls ! If ever we 're united, 'twill be by a trick of circumvention of that sort, pretty sure. There 's a turn in the market when they shut their eyes and drop to the handiest : and London 's

a vortex that poor dear dull old Dublin can't compete
with.   I 'll beg you for the address of the lady her friend,
Lady Dunstane.'

Mr. Sullivan Smith walked with Redworth through the
park to the House of Commons, discoursing of Rails and
his excellent old friend's rise to the top rung of the ladder
and Beanstalk land, so elevated that one had to look up
at him with watery eyes, as if one had flung a ball at the
meridian sun.   Arrived at famed St. Stephen's, he sent in
his compliments to the noble patriot and accepted an
invitation to dinner.

'And mind you read THE PRINCESS EGERIA,' said
Redworth.

'Again and again, my friend.   The book is bought.'
Sullivan Smith slapped his breastpocket.

'There 's a bit of Erin in it.'

'It sprouts from Erin.'

'Trumpet it.'

'Loud as cavalry to the charge ! '

Once with the title stamped on his memory, the zealous
Irishman might be trusted to become an ambulant adver-
tizer.   Others, personal friends, adherents, courtiers of
Redworth's, were active.   Lady Pennon and Henry
Wilmers, in the upper circle ; Whitmonby and Westlake,
in the literary ; spread the fever for this new book.   The
chief interpreter of public opinion caught the way of the
wind and headed the gale.

Editions of the book did really run like fires in summer
furze ; and to such an extent that a simple literary performance grew to be respected in Great Britain, as representing Money.

## CHAPTER XVIII

### THE AUTHORESS

THE effect of a great success upon Diana, at her second literary venture, was shown in the transparent sedateness of a letter she wrote to Emma Dunstane, as much as in her immediate and complacent acceptance of the magical change of her fortunes. She spoke one thing and acted another, but did both with a lofty calm that deceived the admiring friend who clearly saw the authoress behind her mask, and feared lest she should be too confidently trusting to the powers of her pen to support an establishment.

' If the public were a perfect instrument to strike on, I should be tempted to take the wonderful success of my PRINCESS at her first appearance for a proof of natural aptitude in composition, and might think myself the genius. I know it to be as little a Stradivarius as I am a Paganini. It is an eccentric machine, in tune with me for the moment, because I happen to have hit it in the ringing spot. The book is a *new face* appealing to a mirror of the common surface emotions ; and the kitchen rather than the dairy offers an analogy for the real value of that " top-skim." I have not seen what I consider good in the book once mentioned among the laudatory notices— except by your dear hand, my Emmy. Be sure I will stand on guard against the " vaporous generalizations," and other " tricks " you fear. Now that you are studying Latin for an occupation—how good and wise it was of Mr. Redworth to propose it !—I look upon you with awe as a classic authority and critic. I wish I had leisure to study with you. What I do is nothing like so solid and durable.

' THE PRINCESS EGERIA originally (I must have written word of it to you—I remember the evening off Palermo !) was conceived as a sketch ; by gradations she grew into a sort of semi-Scudéry romance, and swelled to her present portliness. That was done by a great deal of piecing, not to say puffing, of her frame. She would be healthier and have a chance of living longer if she were reduced by a reversal of the processes. But how would the judicious clippings and prickings affect our "pensive public " ? Now that I have furnished a house and have a fixed address, under the paws of creditors, I feel I am in the wizard-circle of my popularity and subscribe to its laws or waken to incubus and the desert. Have I been rash ? You do not pronounce. If I have bound myself to pipe as others please, it need not be *entirely* ; and I can promise you it shall not be ; but still I am sensible when I lift my "little quill " of having forced the note of a woodland wren into the popular nightingale's—which may end in the daw's, from straining ; or worse, a toy-whistle.

' That is, in the field of literature. Otherwise, within me deep, I am not aware of any transmutation of the celestial into coined gold. I sound myself, and ring clear. Incessant writing is my refuge, my solace—escape out of the personal net. I delight in it, as in my early morning walks at Lugano, when I went threading the streets and by the lake away to " the heavenly mount," like a dim idea worming upward in a sleepy head to bright wakefulness.

' My anonymous critic, of whom I told you, is intoxicating with eulogy. The signature " Apollonius " appears to be of literary-middle indication. He marks passages approved by you. I have also had a complimentary letter from Mr. Dacier.

' For an instance of this delight I have in writing, so strong is it that I can read pages I have written, and tear

the stuff to strips (I did yesterday), and resume, as if
nothing had happened. The waves within are ready for
any displacement. That must be a good sign. I do
not doubt of excelling my PRINCESS ; and if *she* received
compliments, the next may hope for more. Consider, too,
the novel pleasure of earning money by the labour we
delight in. It is an answer to your question whether I
am happy. Yes, as the savage islander before the ship
entered the bay with the fire-water. My blood is wine,
and I have the slumbers of an infant. I dream, wake,
forget my dream, barely dress before the pen is galloping ;
barely breakfast ; no toilette till noon. A savage in good
sooth ! You see, my Emmy, I could not house with the
" companionable person " you hint at. The poles can
never come together till the earth is crushed. She would
find my habits intolerable, and I hers contemptible,
though we might both be companionable persons. My
dear, I could not even live with *myself*. My blessed little
quill, which helps me divinely to live out of myself, is
and must continue to be my one companion. It is my
mountain height, morning light, wings, cup from the
springs, my horse, my goal, my lancet and replenisher,
my key of communication with the highest, grandest,
holiest between earth and heaven—the vital air con-
necting them.

' In justice let me add that I have not been troubled by
hearing of any of the mysterious legal claims, et caetera.
I am sorry to hear bad reports of health. I wish him
entire felicity—no step taken to bridge division ! The
thought of it makes me tigrish.

' A new pianist playing his own pieces (at Lady Singleby's concert) has given me exquisite pleasure and set
me composing songs—not to his music, which could be
rendered only by sylphs moving to " soft recorders " in
the humour of wildness, languor, bewitching caprices,

giving a new sense to melody. How I wish you had been with me to hear him ! It was the most Æolian thing ever caught from a night-breeze by the soul of a poet.

'But do not suppose me having headlong tendencies to the melting mood. (The above, by the way, is a Pole settled in Paris, and he is to be introduced to me at Lady Pennon's.)—What do you say to my being invited by Mr. Whitmonby to aid him in writing leading articles for the paper he is going to conduct ! " write as you talk and it will do," he says. I am choosing my themes. To write —of politics—as I talk, seems to me like an effort to jump away from my shadow. The black dog of consciousness declines to be shaken off. If some one commanded me to *talk as I write* ! I suspect it would be a way of winding me up to a sharp critical pitch rapidly.

'Not good news of Lord D. I have had messages. Mr. Dacier conceals his alarm. The PRINCESS gave *great gratification*. She did me her best service there. Is it not cruel that the interdict of the censor should force me to depend for information upon such scraps as I get from a gentleman passing my habitation on his way to the House ? And he is not, he never has been, sympathetic in that direction. He sees my grief, and assumes an undertakerly air, with some notion of acting in concert, one supposes—little imagining how I revolt from that crape-hatband formalism of sorrow !

'One word of her we call our inner I. I am not drawing upon her resources for my daily needs ; not wasting her at all, I trust ; certainly not walling her up, to deafen her voice. It would be to fall away from you. She bids me sign myself, my beloved, ever, ever your Tony.'

The letter had every outward show of sincereness in expression, and was endowed to wear that appearance by the writer's impulse to protest with so resolute a vigour as to delude herself. Lady Dunstane heard of Mr. Dacier's

novel attendance at concerts.   The world made a note of
it ;  for the gentleman was notoriously without ear for
music.

Diana's comparison of her hours of incessant writing to
her walks under the dawn at Lugano, her boast of the
similarity of her delight in both, deluded her uncorrupted
conscience to believe that she was now spiritually as free
as in that fair season of the new spring in her veins.   She
was not an investigating physician, nor was Lady Dunstane, otherwise they would have examined the material
points of her conduct—indicators of the spiritual secret
always.   What are the patient's acts ?   The patient's
mind was projected too far beyond them to see the fore-
finger they stretched at her ;  and the friend's was not
that of a prying doctor on the look out for betraying
symptoms.   Lady Dunstane did ask herself why Tony
should have incurred the burden of a costly household—
a very costly : Sir Lukin had been at one of Tony's little
dinners :—but her wish to meet the world on equal terms,
after a long dependency, accounted for it in seeming to
excuse.   The guests on the occasion were Lady Pennon,
Lady Singleby, Mr. Whitmonby, Mr. Percy Dacier,
Mr. Tonans ;—' Some other woman,' Sir Lukin said, and
himself.   He reported the cookery as matching the
conversation, and that was princely ;  the wines not less :
an extraordinary fact to note of a woman.   But to hear
Whitmonby and Diana Warwick !   How he told a story,
neat as a postman's knock, and she tipped it with a remark
and ran to a second, drawing in Lady Pennon, and then
Dacier, ' and me ! ' cried Sir Lukin ;  ' she made us all
toss the ball from hand to hand, and all talk up to the
mark ;  and none of us noticed that we all went together
to the drawing-room, where we talked for another hour,
and broke up fresher than we began.'

' That break between the men and the women after

dinner was Tony's aversion, and I am glad she has instituted a change,' said Lady Dunstane.

She heard also from Redworth of the unexampled concert of the guests at Mrs. Warwick's dinner parties. He had met on one occasion the Esquarts, the Pettigrews, Mr. Percy Dacier, and a Miss Paynham. Redworth had not a word to say of the expensive household. Whatever Mrs. Warwick did was evidently good to him. On another evening the party was composed of Lady Pennon, Lord Larrian, Miss Paynham, a clever Mrs. Wollasley, Mr. Henry Wilmers, and again Mr. Percy Dacier.

When Diana came to Copsley, Lady Dunstane remarked on the recurrence of the name of Miss Paynham in the list of her guests.

'And Mr. Percy Dacier's too,' said Diana, smiling. 'They are invited each for specific reasons. It pleases Lord Dannisburgh to hear that a way has been found to enliven his nephew ; and my little dinners are effective, I think. He wakes. Yesterday evening he capped flying jests with Mr. Sullivan Smith. But you speak of Miss Paynham.' Diana lowered her voice on half a dozen syllables, till the half-tones dropped into her steady look. 'You approve, Emmy ? '

The answer was : ' I do—true or not.'

' Between us two, dear, I fear ! . . . In either case, she has been badly used. Society is big engine enough to protect itself. I incline with British juries to do rough justice to the victims. She has neither father nor brother. I have had no confidences : but it wears the look of a cowardly business. With two words in his ear, I could arm an Irishman to do some work of chastisement :—he would select the rascal's necktie for a cause of quarrel : and lords have to stand their ground as well as commoners. They measure the same number of feet when stretched their length. However, vengeance with the heavens !

though they seem tardy. Lady Pennon has been very
kind about it; and the Esquarts invite her to
Lockton. Shoulder to shoulder, the tide may be
stemmed.'

'She would have gone under, but for you, dear Tony!'
said Emma, folding arms round her darling's neck and
kissing her. 'Bring her here some day.'

Diana did not promise it. She had her vision of Sir
Lukin in his fit of lunacy.

'I am too weak for London now,' Emma resumed. 'I
should like to be useful. Is she pleasant?'

'Sprightly by nature. She has worn herself with
fretting.'

'Then bring her to stay with me, if I cannot keep you.
She will talk of you to me.'

'I will bring her for a couple of days,' Diana said. 'I
am too busy to remain longer. She paints portraits to
amuse herself. She ought to be pushed, wherever she is
received about London, while the season is warm. One
season will suffice to establish her. She is pretty, near
upon six and twenty: foolish, of course: she pays for
having had a romantic head. Heavy payment, Emmy!
I drive at laws, but hers is an instance of the creatures
wanting simple human kindness.'

'The good law will come with a better civilization; but
before society can be civilized it has to be debarbarized,'
Emma remarked, and Diana sighed over the task and the
truism.

'I should have said in younger days, because it will not
look plainly on our nature and try to reconcile it with our
conditions. But now I see that the sin is cowardice.
The more I know of the world the more clearly I perceive
that its top and bottom sin is cowardice, physically and
morally alike. Lord Larrian owns to there being few
heroes in an army. We must fawn in society. What

is the meaning of that dread of one example of tolerance ?
O my dear ! let us give it the right name. Society is
the best thing we have, but it is a crazy vessel worked by
a crew that formerly practised piracy, and now, in expiation, professes piety, fearful of a discovered Omni-
potence, which is in the image of themselves and captain.
Their old habits are not quite abandoned, and their new
one is used as a lash to whip the exposed of us for a propitiation of the capricious potentate whom they worship
in the place of the true God.'

Lady Dunstane sniffed. ' I smell the leading article.'

Diana joined with her smile, ' No, the style is rather
different.'

' Have you not got into a trick of composing in speaking, at times ? '

Diana confessed, ' I think I have at times. Perhaps
the daily writing of all kinds and the nightly talking . . .
I may be getting strained.'

' No, Tony ; but longer visits in the country to me
would refresh you. I miss your lighter touches. London
is a school, but, you know it, not a school for comedy nor
for philosophy ; that is gathered on my hills, with London
distantly in view, and then occasional descents on it well
digested.'

' I wonder whether it is affecting me ! ' said Diana,
musing. ' A metropolitan hack ! and while thinking
myself free, thrice harnessed ; and all my fun gone. Am
I really as dull as a tract, my dear ? I must be, or I
should be proving the contrary instead of asking. My
pitfall is to fancy I have powers equal to the first look-out
of the eyes of the morning. Enough of me. We talked
of Mary Paynham. If only some right good man would
marry her ! '

Lady Dunstane guessed at the right good man in Diana's
mind. ' Do you bring them together ? '

Diana nodded, and then shook doleful negatives to signify no hope.

'None whatever—if we mean the same person,' said Lady Dunstane, bethinking her, in the spirit of wrath she felt at such a scheme being planned by Diana to snare the right good man, that instead of her own true lover Red- worth, it might be only Percy Dacier. So filmy of mere sensations are these little ideas as they flit in converse, that she did not reflect on her friend's ignorance of Red- worth's love of her, or on the unlikely choice of one in Dacier's high station to reinstate a damsel.

They did not name the person.

'Passing the instance, which is cruel, I will be just to society thus far,' said Diana. 'I was in a boat at Rich- mond last week, and Leander was revelling along the mud-banks, and took it into his head to swim out to me, and I was moved to take him on board. The ladies in the boat objected, for he was not only wet but very muddy. I was forced to own that their objections were reasonable. My sentimental humaneness had no argument against muslin dresses, though my dear dog's eyes appealed pathetically, and he would keep swimming after us. The analogy excuses the world for protecting itself in extreme cases ; nothing, nothing excuses its insensibility to cases which may be pleaded. You see the pirate crew turned pious—ferocious in sanctity.' She added, half laughing : 'I am reminded by the boat, I have unveiled my anony- mous critic, and had a woeful disappointment. He wrote like a veteran ; he is not much more than a boy. I re- ceived a volume of verse, and a few lines begging my acceptance. I fancied I knew the writing, and wrote asking him whether I had not to thank him, and inviting him to call. He seems a nice lad of about two and twenty, mad for literature ; and he must have talent. Arthur Rhodes by name. I may have a chance of helping

him. He was an articled clerk of Mr. Braddock's, the
same who valiantly came to my rescue once. He was
with us in the boat.'

'Bring him to me some day,' said Lady Dunstane.

Miss Paynham's visit to Copsley was arranged, and it
turned out a failure. The poor young lady came in a
flutter, thinking that the friend of Mrs. Warwick would
expect her to discourse cleverly. She attempted it, to
Diana's amazement. Lady Dunstane's opposingly corresponding stillness provoked Miss Paynham to expatiate,
for she had sprightliness and some mental reserves of the
common order. Clearly, Lady Dunstane mused while
listening amiably, Tony never could have designed this
gabbler for the mate of Thomas Redworth!

Percy Dacier seemed to her the more likely one, in that
light, and she thought so still, after Sir Lukin had introduced him at Copsley for a couple of days of the hunting
season. Tony's manner with him suggested it ; she had
a dash of leadership. They were not intimate in look or
tongue.

But Percy Dacier also was too good for Miss Paynham,
if that was Tony's plan for him, Lady Dunstane thought,
with the relentlessness of an invalid and recluse's distaste.
An aspect of penitence she had not demanded, but the
silly gabbler under a stigma she could not pardon.

Her opinion of Miss Paynham was diffused in her
silence.

Speaking of Mr. Dacier, she remarked, ' As you say of
him, Tony, he can brighten, and when you give him a
chance he is entertaining. He has fine gifts. If I were a
member of his family I should beat about for a match for
him. He strikes me as one of the young men who would
do better married.'

' He is doing very well, but the wonder is that he doesn't
marry,' said Diana. ' He ought to be engaged. Lady

Esquart told me that he was. A Miss Asper—great heiress ; and the Daciers want money. However, there it is.'

Not many weeks later Diana could not have spoken of Mr. Percy Dacier with this air of indifference without corruption of her inward guide.


## CHAPTER XIX

### A DRIVE IN SUNLIGHT AND A DRIVE IN MOONLIGHT

THE fatal time to come for her was in the Summer of that year.

Emma had written her a letter of unwonted bright spirits, contrasting strangely with an inexplicable oppression of her own that led her to imagine her recent placid life the pause before thunder, and to share the mood of her solitary friend she flew to Copsley, finding Sir Lukin absent, as usual. They drove out immediately after breakfast, on one of those high mornings of the bared bosom of June when distances are given to our eyes, and a soft air fondles leaf and grassblade, and beauty and peace are overhead, reflected, if we will. Rain had fallen in the night. Here and there hung a milkwhite cloud with folded sail. The South-west left it in its bay of blue, and breathed below. At moments the fresh scent of herb and mould swung richly in warmth. The young beech-leaves glittered, pools of rain-water made the roadways laugh, the grass-banks under hedges rolled their interwoven weeds in cascades of many-shaded green to right and left of the pair of dappled ponies, and a squirrel crossed ahead, a lark went up a little way to ease his heart, closing his wings when the burst was over ; startled black-birds, darting with a clamour like a broken cock-crow, looped the wayside woods from hazel to oak-scrub ; short flights, quick spirts everywhere, steady sunshine above.

Diana held the reins. The whip was an ornament, as the plume of feathers to the general officer. Lady Dunstane's ponies were a present from Redworth, who always chose the pick of the land for his gifts. They joyed in their trot, and were the very love-birds of the breed for their pleasure of going together, so like that Diana called them the Dromios. Through an old gravel-cutting a gateway led to the turf of the down, springy turf bordered on a long line, clear as a racecourse, by golden gorse covers, and leftward over the gorse the dark ridge of the fir and heath country ran companionably to the South-west, the valley between, with undulations of wood and meadow sunned or shaded, clumps, mounds, promontories, away to broad spaces of tillage banked by wooded hills, and dimmer beyond and farther, the faintest shadowiness of heights, as a veil to the illimitable. Yews, junipers, radiant beeches, and gleams of the service-tree or the white-beam spotted the semicircle of swelling green Down black and silver. The sun in the valley sharpened his beams on squares of buttercups, and made a pond a diamond.

'You see, Tony,' Emma said, for a comment on the scene, 'I could envy Italy for having you, more than you for being in Italy.'

'Feature and colour !' said Diana. 'You have them here, and on a scale that one can embrace. I should like to build a hut on this point, and wait for such a day to return. It brings me to life.' She lifted her eyelids on her friend's worn sweet face, and knowing her this friend up to death, past it in her hopes, she said bravely, 'It is the Emma of days and scenes to me ! It helps me to

forget myself, as I do when I think of you, dearest ; but
the subject has latterly been haunting me, I don't know
why, and ominously, as if my nature were about to
horrify my soul. But I am not sentimentalizing, you are
really this day and scene in my heart.'

Emma smiled confidingly. She spoke her reflection :
' The heart must be troubled a little to have the thought.
The flower I gather here tells me that we may be happy in
privation and suffering if simply we can accept beauty. I
won't say expel the passions, but keep passion sober, a
trotter in harness.'

Diana caressed the ponies' heads with the droop of her
whip : ' I don't think I know him ! ' she said.

Between sincerity and a suspicion so cloaked and dull
that she did not feel it to be the opposite of candour, she
fancied she was passionless because she could accept the
visible beauty, which was Emma's prescription and test ;
and she forced herself to make much of it, cling to it,
devour it ; with envy of Emma's contemplative happiness,
through whose grave mind she tried to get to the peace in
it, imagining that she succeeded. The cloaked and dull
suspicion weighed within her nevertheless. She took it for
a mania to speculate on herself. There are states of the
crimson blood when the keenest wits are childish, notably
in great-hearted women aiming at the majesty of their sex
and fearful of confounding it by the look direct and the
downright word. Yet her nature compelled her inwardly
to phrase the sentence : ' Emma is a wife ! ' The character of her husband was not considered, nor was the
meaning of the exclamation pursued.

They drove through the gorse into wild land of heath
and flowering hawthorn, and along by tracts of yew and
juniper to another point, jutting on a furzy sand-mound,
rich with the mild splendour of English scenery, which
Emma stamped on her friend's mind by saying : ' A

cripple has little to envy in you who can fly when she has
feasts like these at her doors.'

They had an inclination to boast on the drive home of
the solitude they had enjoyed ; and just then, as the
road in the wood wound under great beeches, they beheld
a London hat.   The hat was plucked from its head.   A
clear-faced youth, rather flushed, dusty at the legs,
addressed Diana.

' Mr. Rhodes ! ' she said, not discouragingly.

She was petitioned to excuse him ;  he thought she
would wish to hear the news in town last night as early as
possible ;  he hesitated and murmured it.

Diana turned to Emma :  ' Lord Dannisburgh ! '—her
paleness told the rest.

Hearing from Mr. Rhodes that he had walked the distance from town, and had been to Copsley, Lady Dunstane
invited him to follow the pony-carriage thither, where he
was fed and refreshed by a tea-breakfast, as he preferred
walking on tea, he said.   ' I took the liberty to call at
Mrs. Warwick's house,' he informed her ;  ' the footman
said she was at Copsley.   I found it on the map—I knew
the direction—and started about two in the morning.   I
wanted a walk.'

It was evident to her that he was one of the young
squires bewitched whom beautiful women are constantly
enlisting.   There was no concealment of it, though he
stirred a sad enviousness in the invalid lady by descanting
on the raptures of a walk out of London in the youngest
light of day, and on the common objects he had noticed
along the roadside, and through the woods, more sustaining, closer with nature than her compulsory feeding on the
cream of things.

' You are not fatigued ? ' she inquired, hoping for that
confession at least ;  but she pardoned his boyish vaunting to walk the distance back without any fatigue at all.

He had a sweeter reward for his pains ; and if the business of the chronicler allowed him to become attached to pure throbbing felicity wherever it is encountered, he might be diverted by the blissful unexpectedness of good fortune befalling Mr. Arthur Rhodes in having the honour to conduct Mrs. Warwick to town. No imagined happiness, even in the heart of a young man of two and twenty, could have matched it. He was by her side, hearing and seeing her, not less than four hours. To add to his happiness, Lady Dunstane said she would be glad to welcome him again. She thought him a pleasant specimen of the self-vowed squire.

Diana was sure that there would be a communication for her of some sort at her house in London ; perhaps a message of farewell from the dying lord, now dead. Mr. Rhodes had only the news of the evening journals, to the effect that Lord Dannisburgh had expired at his residence, the Priory, Hallowmere, in Hampshire. A message of farewell from him, she hoped for : knowing him as she did, it seemed a certainty ; and she hungered for that last gleam of life in her friend. She had no anticipation of the burden of the message awaiting her.

A consultation as to the despatching of the message, had taken place among the members of Lord Dannisburgh's family present at his death. Percy Dacier was one of them, and he settled the disputed point, after some time had been spent in persuading his father to take the plain view of obligation in the matter, and in opposing the dowager countess, his grandmother, by stating that he had already sent a special messenger to London. Lord Dannisburgh on his death-bed had expressed a wish that Mrs. Warwick would sit with him for an hour one night before the nails were knocked in his coffin. He spoke of it twice, putting it the second time to Percy as a formal request to be made to her, and Percy had promised him

that Mrs. Warwick should have the message.  He had
done his best to keep his pledge, aware of the disrelish of
the whole family for the lady's name, to say nothing of
her presence.

'She won't come,' said the earl.

'She 'll come,' said old Lady Dacier.

'If the woman respects herself she 'll hold off it,' the
earl insisted because of his desire that way.  He signified
in mutterings that the thing was improper and absurd, a
piece of sentiment, sickly senility, unlike Lord Dannisburgh.  Also that Percy had been guilty of excessive
folly.

To which Lady Dacier nodded her assent, remarking :
'The woman is on her mettle.  From what I 've heard
of her, she 's not a woman to stick at trifles.  She 'll take
it as a sort of ordeal by touch, and she 'll come.'

They joined in abusing Percy, who had driven away to
another part of the country.  Lord Creedmore, the heir of
the house, was absent, hunting in America, or he might
temporarily have been taken into favour by contrast.
Ultimately they agreed that the woman must be allowed
to enter the house, but could not be received.  The earl
was a widower ;  his mother managed the family, and
being hard to convince, she customarily carried her point,
save when it involved Percy's freedom of action.  She was
one of the veterans of her sex that age to toughness ;  and
the 'hysterical fuss ' she apprehended in the visit of this
woman to Lord Dannisburgh's death-bed and body, did
not alarm her.  For the sake of the household she determined to remain, shut up in her room.  Before night the
house was empty of any members of the family excepting
old Lady Dacier and the outstretched figure on the bed.

Dacier fled to escape the hearing of the numberless
ejaculations re-awakened in the family by his uncle's
extraordinary dying request.  They were an outrage to

the lady, of whom he could now speak as a privileged
champion ; and the request itself had an air of proving
her stainless, a white soul and efficacious advocate at the
celestial gates (reading the mind of the dying man).   So
he thought at one moment : he had thought so when
charged with the message to her ; had even thought it a
natural wish that she should look once on the face she
would see no more, and say farewell to it, considering that
in life it could not be requested.   But the susceptibility
to sentimental emotion beside a death-bed, with a dying
man's voice in the ear, requires fortification if it is to be
maintained ; and the review of his uncle's character did
not tend to make this very singular request a proof that
the lady's innocence was honoured in it.   His epicurean
uncle had no profound esteem for the kind of innocence.
He had always talked of Mrs. Warwick with warm respect for her : Dacier knew that he had bequeathed her a
sum of money.   The inferences were either way.   Lord
Dannisburgh never spoke evilly of any woman, and he
was perhaps bound to indemnify her materially as well as
he could for what she had suffered.—On the other hand,
how easy it was to be the dupe of a woman so handsome
and clever.—Unlikely too that his uncle would consent to
sit at the Platonic banquet with her.—Judging by himself, Dacier deemed it possible for man.   He was not
quick to kindle, and had lately seen much of her, had
found her a Lady Egeria, helpful in counsel, prompting,
inspiriting, reviving as well-waters, and as temperately
cool : not one sign of native slipperiness.   Nor did she
stir the mud in him upon which proud man is built.   The
shadow of the scandal had checked a few shifty sensations
rising now and then of their own accord, and had laid
them, with the lady's benign connivance.   This was good
proof in her favour, seeing that she must have perceived
of late the besetting thirst he had for her company ; and

alone or in the medley equally.   To see her, hear, exchange ideas with her ; and to talk of new books, try to
listen to music at the opera and at concerts, and admire
her playing of hostess, were novel pleasures, giving him
fresh notions of life, and strengthening rather than disturbing the course of his life's business.

At any rate, she was capable of friendship.   Why not
resolutely believe that she had been his uncle's true and
simple friend !   He adopted the resolution, thanking her
for one recognized fact :—he hated marriage, and would
by this time have been in the yoke, but for the agreeable
deviation of his path to her society.   Since his visit to
Copsley, moreover, Lady Dunstane's idolizing of her
friend had influenced him.   Reflecting on it, he recovered
from the shock which his uncle's request had caused.

Certain positive calculations were running side by side
with the speculations in vapour.   His messenger would
reach her house at about four of the afternoon.   If then at
home, would she decide to start immediately ?—Would
she come ?   That was a question he did not delay to
answer.   Would she defer the visit ?   Death replied to
that.   She would not delay it.

She would be sure to come at once.   And what of the
welcome she would meet ?   Leaving the station in London
at six in the evening, she might arrive at the Priory, all
impediments counted, between ten and eleven at night.
Thence, coldly greeted, or not greeted, to the chamber of
death.

A pitiable and cruel reception for a woman upon such a
mission !

His mingled calculations and meditations reached that
exclamatory terminus in feeling, and settled on the
picture of Diana, about as clear as light to blinking eyes,
but enough for him to realize her being there and alone,
woefully alone.   The supposition of an absolute loneliness

was most possible. He had intended to drive back
the next day, when the domestic storm would be over,
and take the chances of her coming. It seemed now a
piece of duty to return at night, a traverse of twenty
rough up and down miles from Itchenford to the heath-
land rolling on the chalk wave of the Surrey borders,
easily done after the remonstrances of his host were
stopped.

Dacier sat in an open carriage, facing a slip of bright
moon. Poetical impressions, emotions, any stirrings of
his mind by the sensational stamp on it, were new to him,
and while he swam in them, both lulled and pricked by
his novel accessibility to nature's lyrical touch, he asked
himself whether, if he were near the throes of death, the
thought of having Diana Warwick to sit beside his vacant
semblance for an hour at night would be comforting.
And why had his uncle specified an hour of the night ?
It was a sentiment, like the request : curious in a man so
little sentimental. Yonder crescent running the shadowy
round of the hoop roused comparisons. Would one really
wish to have her beside one in death ? In life—ah !
But suppose her denied to us in life. Then the desire for
her companionship appears passingly comprehensible.
Enter into the sentiment, you see that the hour of darkness is naturally chosen. And would even a grand old
Pagan crave the presence beside his dead body for an
hour of the night of a woman he did not esteem ? Dacier
answered no. The negative was not echoed in his mind.
He repeated it, and to the same deadness.

He became aware that he had spoken for himself, and
he had a fit of sourness. For who can say he is not a fool
before he has been tried by a woman ! Dacier's wretched
tendency under vexation to conceive grotesque analogies,
anti-poetic, not to say cockney similes, which had slightly
chilled Diana at Rovio, set him looking at yonder crescent

with the hoop, as at the shape of a white cat climbing a wheel. Men of the northern blood will sometimes lend their assent to poetical images, even to those that do not stun the mind like bludgeons and imperatively, by much repetition, command their assent ; and it is for a solid exchange and interest in usury with soft poetical creatures when they are so condescending ; but they are seized by the grotesque. In spite of efforts to efface or supplant it, he saw the white cat, nothing else, even to thinking that she had jumped cleverly to catch the wheel. He was a true descendant of practical hard-grained fighting Northerners, of gnarled dwarf imaginations, chivalrous though they were, and heroes to have serviceable and valiant gentlemen for issue. Without at all tracing back to its origin his detestable image of the white cat on the dead circle, he kicked at the links between his uncle and Diana Warwick, whatever they had been ; particularly at the present revival of them. Old Lady Dacier's blunt speech, and his father's fixed opinion, hissed in his head.

They were ignorant of his autumnal visit to the Italian Lakes, after the winter's Nile-boat expedition ; and also of the degree of his recent intimacy with Mrs. Warwick ; or else, as he knew, he would have heard more hissing things. Her patronage of Miss Paynham exposed her to attacks where she was deemed vulnerable ; Lady Dacier muttered old saws as to the flocking of birds ; he did not accurately understand it, thought it indiscreet, at best. But in regard to his experience, he could tell himself that a woman more guileless of luring never drew breath. On the contrary, candour said it had always been he who had schemed and pressed for the meeting. He was at liberty to do it, not being bound in honour elsewhere. Besides, despite his acknowledgement of her beauty, Mrs. Warwick was not quite his ideal of the perfectly beautiful woman.

Constance Asper came nearer to it.  He had the English
taste for red and white, and for cold outlines : he secretly
admired a statuesque demeanour with a statue's eyes.
The national approbation of a reserved haughtiness in
woman, a tempered disdain in her slightly lifted small
upperlip and drooped eyelids, was shared by him ; and
Constance Asper, if not exactly aristocratic by birth,
stood well for that aristocratic insular type, which seems
to promise the husband of it a casket of all the trusty
virtues, as well as the security of frigidity in the casket.
Such was Dacier's native taste ; consequently the attractions of Diana Warwick for him were, he thought,
chiefly mental, those of a Lady Egeria.  She might or
might not be good, in the vulgar sense.  She was an
agreeable woman, an amusing companion, very suggestive,
inciting, animating ; and her past history must be left as
her own.  Did it matter to him ?  What he saw was
bright, a silver crescent on the side of the shadowy ring.
Were it a question of marrying her !—That was out
of the possibilities.  He remembered, moreover, having
heard from a man, who professed to know, that Mrs.
Warwick had started in married life by treating her
husband cavalierly to an intolerable degree : ' Such as no
Englishman could stand,' the portly old informant
thundered, describing it and her in racy vernacular.  She
might be a devil of a wife.  She was a pleasant friend ;
just the soft bit sweeter than male friends which gave the
flavour of sex without the artful seductions.  He required
them strong to move him.

He looked at last on the green walls of the Priory,
scarcely supposing a fair watcher to be within ; for the
contrasting pale colours of dawn had ceased to quicken
the brilliancy of the crescent, and summer daylight
drowned it to fainter than a silver coin in water.  It lay
dispieced like a pulled rag.  Eastward, over Surrey, stood

the full rose of morning. The Priory clock struck four.
When the summons of the bell had gained him admittance,
and he heard that Mrs. Warwick had come in the night, he
looked back through the doorway at the rosy colour, and
congratulated himself to think that her hour of watching
was at an end. A sleepy footman was his informant.
Women were in my lord's dressing-room, he said. Upstairs, at the death-chamber, Dacier paused. No sound
came to him. He hurried to his own room, paced about,
and returned. Expecting to see no one but the dead, he
turned the handle, and the two circles of a shaded lamp,
on ceiling and on table, met his gaze.

## CHAPTER XX

### DIANA'S NIGHT-WATCH IN THE CHAMBER OF DEATH

HE stepped into the room, and thrilled to hear the quiet
voice beside the bed : ' Who is it ? '

Apologies and excuses were on his tongue. The vibration of those grave tones checked them.

' It is you,' she said.

She sat in shadow, her hands joined on her lap. An
unopened book was under the lamp.

He spoke in an underbreath : ' I have just come. I
was not sure I should find you here. Pardon.'

' There is a chair.'

He murmured thanks and entered into the stillness,
observing her.

' You have been watching. . . . You must be tired.'

' No.'

' An hour was asked, only one.'

' I could not leave him.'

' Watchers are at hand to relieve you.'

' It is better for him to have me.'

The chord of her voice told him of the gulfs she had sunk in during the night. The thought of her endurance became a burden.

He let fall his breath for patience, and tapped the floor with his foot.

He feared to discompose her by speaking. The silence grew more fearful, as the very speech of Death between them.

' You came. I thought it right to let you know instantly. I hoped you would come to-morrow.'

' I could not delay.'

' You have been sitting alone here since eleven ! '

' I have not found it long.'

' You must want some refreshment . . . tea ? '

' I need nothing.'

' It can be made ready in a few minutes.'

' I could not eat or drink.'

He tried to brush away the impression of the tomb in the heavily-curtained chamber by thinking of the summer-morn outside ; he spoke of it, the rosy sky, the dewy grass, the piping birds. She listened, as one hearing of a quitted sphere.

Their breathing in common was just heard if either drew a deeper breath. At moments his eyes wandered and shut. Alternately in his mind Death had vaster meanings and doubtfuller ; Life cowered under the shadow or out-shone it. He glanced from her to the figure in the bed, and she seemed swallowed.

He said : ' It is time for you to have rest. You know your room. I will stay till the servants are up.'

She replied : ' No, let this night with him be mine.'

' I am not intruding . . . ? '

' If you wish to remain . . .'

No traces of weeping were on her face. The lamp-shade revealed it colourless, and lustreless her eyes. She was robed in black. She held her hands clasped.

' You have not suffered ? '

' Oh, no.'

She said it without sighing : nor was her speech mournful, only brief.

' You have seen death before ? '

' I sat by my father four nights. I was a girl then. I cried till I had no more tears.'

He felt a burning pressure behind his eyeballs.

' Death is natural,' he said.

' It is natural to the aged. When they die honoured . . .' She looked where the dead man lay. ' To sit beside the young, cut off from their dear opening life . . . ! ' A little shudder swept over her. ' Oh ! that ! '

' You were very good to come. We must all thank you for fulfilling his wish.'

' He knew it would be my wish.'

Her hands pressed together.

' He lies peacefully ! '

' I have raised the lamp on him, and wondered each time. So changeless he lies. But so like a sleep that will wake. We never see peace but in the features of the dead. Will you look ? They are beautiful. They have a heavenly sweetness.'

The desire to look was evidently recurrent with her. Dacier rose.

Their eyes fell together on the dead man, as thoughtfully as Death allows to the creatures of sensation.

' And after ? ' he said in low tones.

' I trust to my Maker,' she replied. ' Do you see a change since he breathed his last ? '

' Not any.'

' You were with him ? '

P

' Not in the room.   Two minutes later.'

' Who . . . ? '

' My father.   His niece, Lady Cathairn.'

' If our lives are lengthened we outlive most of those we would have to close our eyes.   He had a dear sister.'

' She died some years back.'

' I helped to comfort him for that loss.'

' He told me you did.'

The lamp was replaced on the table.

' For a moment, when I withdraw the light from him, I feel sadness.   As if the light we lend to anything were of value to him now ! '

She bowed her head deeply.   Dacier left her meditation undisturbed.   The birds on the walls outside were audible, tweeting, chirping.

He went to the window-curtains and tried the shutter-bars.   It seemed to him that daylight would be cheer-fuller for her.   He had a thirst to behold her standing bathed in daylight.

' Shall I open them ? ' he asked her.

' I would rather the lamp,' she said.

They sat silently until she drew her watch from her girdle.   ' My train starts at half-past six.   It is a walk of thirty-five minutes to the station.   I did it last night in that time.'

' You walked here in the dark alone ? '

' There was no fly to be had.   The station-master sent one of his porters with me.   We had a talk on the road. I like those men.'

Dacier read the hour by the mantelpiece clock.   ' If you must really go by the early train, I will drive you.'

' No, I will walk ;  I prefer it.'

' I will order your breakfast at once.'

He turned on his heel.   She stopped him.   ' No, I have no taste for eating or drinking.'

'Pray . . .' said he, in visible distress.

She shook her head. 'I could not. I have twenty minutes longer. I can find my way to the station; it is almost a straight road out of the park-gates.'

His heart swelled with anger at the household for the treatment she had been subjected to, judging by her resolve not to break bread in the house.

They resumed their silent sitting. The intervals for a word to pass between them were long, and the ticking of the time-piece fronting the death-bed ruled the chamber, scarcely varied.

The lamp was raised for the final look, the leave-taking.

Dacier buried his face, thinking many things—the common multitude in insurrection.

'A servant should be told to come now,' she said. 'I have only to put on my bonnet and I am ready.'

'You will take no . . . ? '

'Nothing.'

'It is not too late for a carriage to be ordered.'

'No—the walk ! '

They separated.

He roused the two women in the dressing-room, asleep with heads against the wall. Thence he sped to his own room for hat and overcoat, and a sprinkle of cold water. Descending the stairs, he beheld his companion issuing from the chamber of death. Her lips were shut, her eyelids nervously tremulous.

They were soon in the warm sweet open air, and they walked without an interchange of a syllable through the park into the white hawthorn lane, glad to breathe. Her nostrils took long draughts of air, but of the change of scene she appeared scarcely sensible.

At the park-gates, she said : 'There is no necessity for your coming.'

His answer was : 'I think of myself. I gain something every step I walk with you.'

'To-day is Thursday,' said she. 'The funeral is . . .?'

'Monday has been fixed. According to his directions, he will lie in the churchyard of his village—not in the family vault.'

'I know,' she said hastily. 'They are privileged who follow him and see the coffin lowered. He spoke of this quiet little resting-place.'

'Yes, it's a good end. I do not wonder at his wish for the honour you have done him. I could wish it too. But more living than dead—that is a natural wish.'

'It is not to be called an honour.'

'I should feel it so—an honour to me.'

'It is a friend's duty. The word is too harsh ;—it was his friend's desire. He did not ask it so much as he sanctioned it. For to him what has my sitting beside him been ! '

'He had the prospective happiness.'

'He knew well that my soul would be with him—as it was last night. But he knew it would be my poor human happiness to see him with my eyes, touch him with my hand, before he passed from our sight.'

Dacier exclaimed : 'How you can love ! '

'Is the village church to be seen ? ' she asked.

'To the right of those elms ; that is the spire. The black spot below is a yew. You love with the whole heart when you love.'

'I love my friends,' she replied.

'You tempt me to envy those who are numbered among them.'

'They are not many.'

'They should be grateful.'

'You have some acquaintance with them all.'

And an enemy ? Had you ever one ? Do you know of one ? '

' Direct and personal designedly ? I think not. We give that title to those who are disinclined to us and add a dash of darker colour to our errors. Foxes have enemies in the dogs ; heroines of melodramas have their persecuting villains. I suppose that conditions of life exist where one meets the original complexities. The bad are in every rank. The inveterately malignant I have not found. Circumstances may combine to make a whisper as deadly as a blow, though not of such evil design. Perhaps if we lived at a Court of a magnificent despot we should learn that we are less highly civilized than we imagine ourselves ; but that is a fire to the passions, and the extreme is not the perfect test. Our civilization counts positive gains— unless you take the melodrama for the truer picture of us. It is always the most popular with the English.—And look, what a month June is ! Yesterday morning I was with Lady Dunstane on her heights, and I feel double the age. He was fond of this wild country. We think it a desert, a blank, whither he has gone, because we will strain to see in the utter dark, and nothing can come of that but the bursting of the eyeballs.'

Dacier assented : ' There 's no use in peering beyond the limits.'

' No,' said she ; ' the effect is like the explaining of things to a dull head—the finishing stroke to the understanding ! Better continue to brood. We get to some unravelment if we are left to our own efforts. I quarrel with no priest of any denomination. That they should quarrel among themselves is comprehensible in their wisdom, for each has the specific. But they show us *their* way of solving the great problem, and we ought to thank them, though one or the other abominate us. You are advised to talk with Lady Dunstane on these themes,

She is perpetually in the antechamber of death, and her soul is perennially sunshine.—See the pretty cottage under the laburnum curls !   Who lives there ? '

' His gamekeeper, Simon Rofe.'

' And what a playground for the children, that bit of common by their garden-palings ! and the pond, and the blue hills over the furzes.  I hope those people will not be turned out.'

Dacier could not tell.  He promised to do his best for them.

' But,' said she, ' you are the lord here now.'

' Not likely to be the tenant.  Incomes are wanted to support even small estates.'

' The reason is good for courting the income.'

He disliked the remark ;  and when she said presently : ' Those windmills make the landscape homely,' he rejoined :  ' They remind one of our wheeling London gamins round the cab from the station.'

' They remind you,' said she, and smiled at the chance discordant trick he had, remembering occasions when it had crossed her.

' This is homelier than Rovio,' she said ;  ' quite as nice in its way.'

' You do not gather flowers here.'

' Because my friend has these at her feet.'

' May one petition without a rival, then, for a souvenir ? '

' Certainly, if you care to have a common buttercup.'

They reached the station, five minutes in advance of the train.  His coming manœuvre was early detected, and she drew from her pocket the little book he had seen lying unopened on the table, and said :  ' I shall have two good hours for reading.'

' You will not object ? . . . I must accompany you to town.  Permit it, I beg.  You shall not be worried to talk.'

'No ; I came alone and return alone.'

'Fasting and unprotected ! Are you determined to take away the worst impression of us ? Do not refuse me this favour.'

'As to fasting, I could not eat : and unprotected no woman is in England if she is a third-class traveller. That is my experience of the class ; and I shall return among my natural protectors—the most unselfishly chivalrous to women in the whole world.'

He had set his heart on going with her, and he attempted eloquence in pleading, but that exposed him to her humour ; he was tripped.

'It is not denied that you belong to the knightly class,' she said ; 'and it is not necessary that you should wear armour and plumes to proclaim it ; and your appearance would be ample protection from the drunken sailors travelling, you say, on this line ; and I may be deplorably mistaken in imagining that I could tame them. But your knightliness is due elsewhere ; and I commit myself to the fortune of war. It is a battle for women everywhere ; under the most favourable conditions among my dear common English. I have not my maid with me, or else I should not dare.'

She paid for a third-class ticket, amused by Dacier's look of entreaty and trouble.

'Of course I obey,' he murmured.

'I have the habit of exacting it in matters concerning my independence,' she said ; and it arrested some rumbling notions in his head as to a piece of audacity on the starting of the train. They walked up and down the platform till the bell rang and the train came rounding beneath an arch.

'Oh, by the way, may I ask ? '—he said : ' was it your article in Whitmonby's journal on a speech of mine last week ? '

' The guilty writer is confessed.'

' Let me thank you.'

' Don't.    But try to believe it written on public grounds —if the task is not too great.'

' I may call ? '

' You will be welcome.'

' To tell you of the funeral—the last of him ! '

' Do not fail to come.'

She could have laughed to see him jumping on the steps of the third-class carriages one after another to choose her company for her.   In those pre-democratic blissful days before the miry Deluge, the opinion of the requirements of poor English travellers entertained by the Seigneur Directors of the class above them, was that they differed from cattle in stipulating for seats.   With the exception of that provision to suit their weakness, the accommodation extended to them resembled pens, and the seats were emphatically seats of penitence, intended to grind the sitter for his mean pittance payment and absence of aspiration to a higher state.   Hard angular wood, a low roof, a shabby square of window aloof, demanding of him to quit the seat he insisted on having, if he would indulge in views of the passing scenery, —such was the furniture of dens where a refinement of castigation was practised on villain poverty by denying leathers to the windows, or else buttons to the leathers, so that the windows had either to be up or down, but refused to shelter and freshen simultaneously.

Dacier selected a compartment occupied by two old women, a mother and babe and little maid, and a labouring man.   There he installed her, with an eager look that she would not notice.

' You will want the window down,' he said.

She applied to her fellow-travellers for the permission ; and struggling to get the window down, he was irritated

to animadvert on ' these carriages ' of the benevolent
railway Company.

' Do not forget that the wealthy are well treated, or
you may be unjust,' said she, to pacify him.

His mouth sharpened its line while he tried arts and
energies on the refractory window. She told him to leave
it. ' You can't breathe this atmosphere ! ' he cried, and
called to a porter, who did the work, remarking that it was
rather stiff.

The door was banged and fastened. Dacier had to
hang on the step to see her in the farewell. From the
platform he saw the top of her bonnet ; and why she
should have been guilty of this freak of riding in an un-
wholesome carriage, tasked his power of guessing. He
was too English even to have taken the explanation, for
he detested the distinguishing of the races in his country,
and could not therefore have comprehended her peculiar
tenacity of the sense of injury as long as enthusiasm did
not arise to obliterate it. He required a course of lessons
in Irish.

Sauntering down the lane, he called at Simon Rofe's
cottage, and spoke very kindly to the gamekeeper's wife.
That might please Diana. It was all he could do at
present.

## CHAPTER XXI

### ' THE YOUNG MINISTER OF STATE '

DESCRIPTIONS in the newspapers of the rural funeral of
Lord Dannisburgh had the effect of rousing flights of
tattlers with a twittering of the disused name of Warwick ;
our social Gods renewed their combat, and the verdict
of the jury was again overhauled, to be attacked and

maintained, the carpers replying to the champions that they
held to their view of it : as heads of bull-dogs are expected
to do when they have got a grip of one.   It is a point of
muscular honour with them never to relax their hold.
They will tell you why :—they formed that opinion from
the first.   And but for the swearing of a particular
witness, upon whom the plaintiff had been taught to rely,
the verdict would have been different—to prove their
soundness of judgement.   They could speak from private
positive information of certain damnatory circumstances,
derived from authentic sources.   Visits of a gentleman
to the house of a married lady in the absence of the
husband ?   Oh !—The British Lucretia was very properly
not legally at home to the masculine world of that day.
She plied her distaff in pure seclusion, meditating on her
absent lord ; or else a fair proportion of the masculine
world, which had not yet, has not yet, ' doubled Cape
Turk,' approved her condemnation to the sack.

There was talk in the feminine world, at Lady Wathin's
assemblies.   The elevation of her husband had extended
and deepened her influence on the levels where it reigned
before, but without, strange as we may think it now,
assisting to her own elevation, much aspired for, to the
smooth and lively upper pavement of Society, above its
tumbled strata.   She was near that distinguished surface,
not on it.   Her circle was practically the same as it was
previous to the coveted nominal rank enabling her to
trample on those beneath it.   And women like that Mrs.
Warwick, a woman of no birth, no money, not even honest
character, enjoyed the entry undisputed, circulated among
the highest :—because people took her rattle for wit !
—and because also our nobility, Lady Wathin feared,
had no due regard for morality.   Our aristocracy,
brilliant and ancient though it was, merited rebuke.
She grew severe upon aristocratic scandals, whereof were

plenty among the frolicsome host just overhead, as vexatious as the drawing-room party to the lodger in the floor
below, who has not received an invitation to partake of
the festivities, and is required to digest the noise. But
if ambition is oversensitive, moral indignation is ever
consolatory, for it plants us on the Judgement Seat.
There indeed we may, sitting with the very Highest,
forget our personal disappointments in dispensing re-
probation for misconduct, however eminent the offenders.

She was Lady Wathin, and once on an afternoon's call
to see poor Lady Dunstane at her town-house, she had
been introduced to Lady Pennon, a patroness of Mrs.
Warwick, and had met a snub—an icy check-bow of the
aristocratic head from the top of the spinal column, and
not a word, not a look ;—the half-turn of a head devoid of
mouth and eyes ! She practised that forbidding check-
bow herself to perfection, so the endurance of it was
horrible. A noli me tangere, her husband termed it, in
his ridiculous equanimity ; and he might term it what he
pleased—it was insulting. The solace she had was in
hearing that hideous Radical Revolutionary things were
openly spoken at Mrs. Warwick's evenings with her
friends :—impudently named ' the elect of London.'
Pleasing to reflect upon Mrs. Warwick as undermining
her supporters, to bring them some day down with a
crash ! Her ' elect of London ' were a queer gathering,
by report of them ! And Mr. Whitmonby too, no doubt
a celebrity, was the right-hand man at these dinner-parties
of Mrs. Warwick. Where will not men go to be flattered
by a pretty woman ! He had declined repeated, succes-
sive invitations to Lady Wathin's table. But there of
course he would not have had ' the freedom ' : that is,
she rejoiced in thinking defensively and offensively, a
moral wall enclosed *her* topics. The Hon. Percy Dacier
had been brought to her Thursday afternoon by Mr.

Quintin Manx, and he had one day dined with her ; and
he knew Mrs. Warwick—a little, he said.  The opportunity was not lost to convey to him, entirely in the
interest of sweet Constance Asper, that the moral world
entertained a settled view of the very clever woman Mrs.
Warwick certainly was.—He had asked Diana, on their
morning walk to the station, whether she had an enemy :
so prone are men, educated by the Drama and Fiction
in the belief that the garden of civilized life must be at
the mercy of the old wild devourers, to fancy ' villain
whispers ' an indication of direct animosity.  Lady
Wathin had no sentiment of the kind.

But she had become acquainted with the other side of
the famous Dannisburgh case—the unfortunate plaintiff ;
and compassion as well as morality moved her to put on a
speaking air when Mr. Warwick's name was mentioned.
She pictured him to the ladies of her circle as ' one of our
true gentlemen in his deportment and his feelings.'  He
was, she would venture to say, her *ideal* of an English
gentleman.  ' But now,' she added commiseratingly,
' ruined ; ruined in his health and in his prospects.'  A
lady inquired if it was the verdict that had thus affected
him.  Lady Wathin's answer was reported over moral,
or substratum, London :  ' He is the victim of a fatal
passion for his wife ; and would take her back to-morrow
were she to solicit his forgiveness.'  Morality had something to say against this active marital charity, attribut-
able, it was to be feared, to weakness of character on the
part of the husband.  Still Mrs. Warwick undoubtedly
was one of those women (of Satanic construction) who
have the art of enslaving the men unhappy enough to
cross their path.  The nature of the art was hinted, with
the delicacy of dainty feet which have to tread in mire
to get to safety.  Men, alas ! are snared in this way.
Instances too numerous for the good repute of the swinish

sex, were cited, and the question of how Morality was
defensible from their grossness passed without a tactical
reply. There is no defence. Those women come like
the Cholera Morbus—and owing to similar causes. They
will prevail until the ideas of men regarding women are
purified. Nevertheless the husband who could forgive,
even propose to forgive, was deemed by consent generous,
however weak. Though she might not have been wholly
guilty, she had bitterly offended. And he despatched
an emissary to her ?—The theme, one may, in their
language, ' fear,' was relished as a sugared acid. It was
renewed in the late Autumn of the year, when ANTONIA
published her new book, entitled THE YOUNG MINISTER
OF STATE. The signature of the authoress was now
known ; and from this resurgence of her name in public,
suddenly a radiation of tongues from the circle of Lady
Wathin declared that the repentant Mrs. Warwick *had*
gone back to her husband's bosom and forgiveness !
The rumour spread in spite of sturdy denials at odd
corners, counting the red-hot proposal of Mr. Sullivan
Smith to eat his head and boots for breakfast if it was
proved correct. It filled a yawn of the Clubs for the
afternoon. Soon this wanton rumour was met and
stifled by another of more morbific density, heavily
charged as that which led the sad Eliza to her pyre.

ANTONIA'S hero was easily identified. THE YOUNG
MINISTER OF STATE could be he only who was now at all
her parties, always meeting her ; had been spied walking
with her daily in the park near her house, on his march
down to Westminster during the session ; and who
positively went to concerts and sat under fiddlers to be
near her. It accounted moreover for his treatment of
Constance Asper. What effrontery of the authoress, to
placard herself with him in a book ! The likeness of the
hero to Percy Dacier once established became striking to

glaringness—a proof of her ability, and more of her
audacity ; still more of her intention to flatter him up to
his perdition. By the things written of him, one would
imagine the conversations going on behind the scenes.
She had the wiles of a Cleopatra, not without some of the
Nilene's experiences. A youthful Antony-Dacier would
be little likely to escape her toils. And so promising a
young man ! The sigh, the tear for weeping over his
destruction, almost fell, such vivid realizing of the
prophesy appeared in its pathetic pronouncement.

This low rumour, or malaria, began blowing in the
winter, and did not travel fast ; for strangely, there was
hardly a breath of it in the atmosphere of Dacier, none in
Diana's. It rose from groups not so rapidly and largely
mixing, and less quick to kindle ; whose crazy sincereness
battened on the smallest morsel of fact and collected the
fictitious by slow absorption. But as guardians of
morality, often doing good duty in their office, they are
persistent. When Parliament assembled, Mr. Quintin
Manx, a punctual member of the House, if nothing else,
arrived in town. He was invited to dine with Lady
Wathin. After dinner she spoke to him of the absent
Constance, and heard of her being well, and expressed a
great rejoicing at that. Whereupon the burly old ship-
owner frowned and puffed. Constance, he said, had
plunged into these new spangle, candle and high singing
services ; was all for symbols, harps, effigies, what not.
Lady Wathin's countenance froze in hearing of it. She
led Mr. Quintin to a wall-sofa, and said : ' Surely the dear
child must have had a disappointment, for her to have
taken to those foolish displays of religion ! It is generally a sign.'

' Well, ma'am—my lady—I let girls go their ways in
such things. I don't interfere. But it 's that fellow, or
nobody, with her. She has fixed her girl's mind on him,

and if she can't columbine as a bride, she will as a nun.
Young people must be at some harlequinade.'

' But it is very shocking. And he ? '

' He plays fast and loose, warm and cold. I 'm ready
to settle twenty times a nobleman's dowry on my niece :
and she 's a fine girl, a handsome girl, educated up to the
brim, fit to queen it in any drawing-room. He holds her
by some arts that don't hold him, it seems. He 's all for
politics.'

' Constance can scarcely be his dupe so far, I should
think.'

' How do you mean ? '

' Everything points to one secret of his conduct.'

' A woman ? '

Lady Wathin's head shook for her sex's pained affirmative.

Mr. Quintin in the same fashion signified the downright
negative. ' The fellow 's as cold as a fish.'

' Flattery will do anything. There is, I fear, one.'

' Widow ? wife ? maid ? '

' Married, I regret to say.'

' Well, if he 'd get over with it,' said Quintin, in whose
notions the seductiveness of a married woman could be
only temporary, for all the reasons pertaining to her state.
At the same time his view of Percy Dacier was changed in
thinking it possible that a woman could divert him from
his political and social interests. He looked incredulous.

' You have heard of a Mrs. Warwick ? ' said Lady
Wathin.

' Warwick ! I have. I 've never seen her. At my
broker's in the City yesterday I saw the name on a
Memorandum of purchase of Shares in a concern promising ten per cent., and not likely to carry the per annum
into the plural. He told me she was a grand kind of
woman, past advising.'

'For what amount ? '

'Some thousands, I think it was.'

'She has *no* money': Lady Wathin corrected her
emphasis : ' or *ought* to have none.'

'She can't have got it from *him*.'

'Did you notice her Christian name ? '

'I don't recollect it, if I did. I thought the woman a
donkey.'

'Would you consider me a busybody were I to try to
mitigate this woman's evil influence ? I love dear Constance, and should be happy to serve her.'

'I want my girl married,' said old Quintin. 'He 's
one of my Parliamentary chiefs, with first-rate prospects ;
good family, good sober fellow—at least I thought so ; by
nature, I mean ; barring your incantations. He suits me,
she liking him.'

'She admires him, I am sure.'

'She 's dead on end for the fellow ! '

Lady Wathin felt herself empowered by Quintin Manx
to undertake the release of sweet Constance Asper's knight
from the toils of his enchantress. For this purpose she
had first an interview with Mr. Warwick, and next she
hurried to Lady Dunstane at Copsley. There, after
jumbling Mr. Warwick's connubial dispositions and Mrs.
Warwick's last book, and Mr. Percy Dacier's engagement
to the great heiress in a gossipy hotch-potch, she contrived to gather a few items of fact, as that THE YOUNG
MINISTER was probably modelled upon Mr. Percy Dacier.
Lady Dunstane made no concealment of it as soon as she
grew sensible of the angling. But she refused her help
to any reconciliation between Mr. and Mrs. Warwick.
She declined to listen to Lady Wathin's entreaties. She
declined to give her reasons.—These bookworm women,
whose pride it is to fancy that they can think for themselves, have a great deal of the heathen in them, as

morality discovers when it wears the enlistment ribands
and applies to them to win recruits for a service under
the direct blessing of Providence.

Lady Wathin left some darts behind her, in the form of
moral exclamations ; and really intended morally. For
though she did not like Mrs. Warwick, she had no wish
to wound, other than by stopping her further studies of
the Young Minister, and conducting him to the young
lady loving him, besides restoring a bereft husband to
his own. How sadly pale and worn poor Mr. Warwick
appeared ! The portrayal of his withered visage to
Lady Dunstane had quite failed to gain a show of sympathy. And so it is ever with your book-worm women
pretending to be philosophical ! You sound them vainly
for a manifestation of the commonest human sensibilities.
They turn over the leaves of a Latin book on their laps
while you are supplicating them to assist in a work of
charity !

Lady Wathin's interjectory notes haunted Emma's
ear. Yet she had seen nothing in Tony to let her suppose
that there was trouble of her heart below the surface ;
and her Tony when she came to Copsley shone in the mood
of the day of Lord Dannisburgh's drive down from
London with her. She was running on a fresh work ;
talked of composition as a trifle.

' I suppose the YOUNG MINISTER *is* Mr. Percy Dacier ? '
said Emma.

' Between ourselves he is,' Diana replied, smiling at a
secret guessed. ' You know my model and can judge of
the likeness.'

' You write admiringly of him, Tony.'

' And I do admire him. So would you, Emmy, if you
knew him as well as I do now. He pairs with Mr. Redworth ; he also is the friend of women. But he lifts us to
rather a higher level of intellectual friendship. When the

ice has melted—and it is thick at first—he pours forth
all his ideas without reserve; and they are deep and
noble. Ever since Lord Dannisburgh's death and our
sitting together, we have been warm friends—intimate,
I would say, if it could be said of one so self-contained.
In that respect, no young man was ever comparable with
him. And I am encouraged to flatter myself that he un-
bends to me more than to others.'

'He is engaged, or partly, I hear; why does he not
marry?'

'I wish he would!' Diana said, with a most brilliant
candour of aspect.

Emma read in it, that it would complete her happiness,
possibly by fortifying her sense of security; and that
seemed right. Her own meditations, illumined by the
beautiful face in her presence, referred to the security of
Mr. Dacier.

'So, then, life is going smoothly,' said Emma.

'Yes, at a good pace and smoothly: not a torrent—
Thames-like, "without o'erflowing full." It is not
Lugano and the Salvatore. Perhaps it is better: as
action is better than musing.'

'No troubles whatever?'

'None. Well, except an "adorer" at times. I have
to take him as my portion. An impassioned Caledonian
has a little bothered me. I met him at Lady Pennon's,
and have been meeting him, as soon as I put foot out of
my house, ever since. If I could impress and impound
him to marry Mary Paynham, I should be glad. By the
way, I have consented to let her try at a portrait of me.
No, I have no troubles. I have friends, the choicest of
the nation; I have health, a field for labour, fairish success with it; a mind alive, such as it is. I feel like that
midsummer morning of our last drive out together, the
sun high, clearish, clouded enough to be cool. And still

I envy Emmy on her sofa, mastering Latin, biting at
Greek. What a wise recommendation that was of Mr.
Redworth's ! He works well in the House. He spoke
excellently the other night.'

' He runs over to Ireland this Easter.'

' He sees for himself, and speaks with authority. He
sees and feels. Englishmen mean well, but they require
an extremity of misery to waken their feelings.'

' It is coming, he says ; and absit omen ! '

' Mr. Dacier says he is the one Englishman who may
always be sure of an Irish hearing ; and he does not cajole
them, you know. But the English defect is really not
want of feeling so much as want of foresight. They will
not look ahead. A famine ceasing, a rebellion crushed,
they jog on as before, with their Dobbin trot and blinker
confidence in " Saxon energy." They should study the
Irish. I think it was Mr. Redworth who compared the
governing of the Irish to the management of a horse : the
rider should not grow restive when the steed begins to
kick : calmer ; firm, calm, persuasive.'

' Does Mr. Dacier agree ? '

' Not always. He has the inveterate national belief
that Celtic blood is childish, and the consequently illogical
disregard of its hold of impressions. The Irish—for I
have them in my heart, though I have not been among
them for long at a time—must love you to serve you, and
will hate you if you have done them injury and they have
not wiped it out—they with a treble revenge, or you with
cordial benefits. I have told him so again and again :
ventured to suggest measures.'

' He listens to you, Tony ? '

' He says I have brains. It ends in a compliment.'

' You have inspired Mr. Redworth.'

' If I have, I have lived for some good.'

Altogether her Tony's conversation proved to Emma

that her perusal of the model of THE YOUNG MINISTER OF
STATE was an artist's, free, open, and not discoloured by
the personal tincture.   Her heart plainly was free and
undisturbed.   She had the same girl's love of her walks
where wildflowers grew ; if possible, a keener pleasure.
She hummed of her happiness in being at Copsley, singing
her Planxty Kelly and The Puritani by turns.   She stood
on land : she was not on the seas.   Emma thought so
with good reason.

She stood on land, it was true, but she stood on a cliff
of the land, the seas below and about her ;  and she was
enabled to hoodwink her friend because the assured sensation of her firm footing deceived her own soul, even
while it took short flights to the troubled waters.   Of her
firm footing she was exultingly proud.   She stood high,
close to danger, without giddiness.   If at intervals her
soul flew out like lightning from the rift (a mere shot of
involuntary fancy, it seemed to her), the suspicion of in-
stability made her draw on her treasury of impressions of
the mornings at Lugano—her loftiest, purest, dearest ;
and these reinforced her.   She did not ask herself why
she should have to seek them for aid.   In other respects
her mind was alert and held no sly covers, as the fiction
of a perfect ignorant innocence combined with common
intelligence would have us to suppose that the minds of
women can do.   She was honest as long as she was not
directly questioned, pierced to the innermost and sanctum
of the bosom.   She could honestly summon bright light
to her eyes in wishing the man were married.   She did
not ask herself why she called it up.   The remorseless
progressive interrogations of a Jesuit Father in pursuit
of the bosom's verity might have transfixed it and shown
her to herself even then a tossing vessel as to the spirit,
far away from that firm land she trod so bravely.

Descending  from  the  woody  heights  upon  London,

Diana would have said that her only anxiety concerned young Mr. Arthur Rhodes, whose position she considered precarious, and who had recently taken a drubbing for venturing to show a peep of his head, like an early crocus, in the literary market. Her ANTONIA'S last book had been reviewed obediently to smart taps from the then commanding bâton of Mr. Tonans, and Mr. Whitmonby's choice picking of specimens down three columns of his paper. A Literary Review (Charles Rainer's property) had suggested that perhaps ‘ the talented authoress might be writing too rapidly ’ ; and another, actuated by the public taste of the period for our ‘ vigorous homely Saxon ’ in one and two syllable words, had complained of a ‘ tendency to polysyllabic phraseology.’ The remainder, a full majority, had sounded eulogy with all their band-instruments, drum, trumpet, fife, trombone. Her foregoing work had raised her to Fame, which is the Court of a Queen when the lady has beauty and social influence, and critics are her dedicated courtiers, gaping for the royal mouth to be opened, and reserving the kicks of their independent manhood for infamous outsiders, whom they hoist in the style and particular service of pitch-forks. They had fallen upon a little volume of verse, ‘ like a body of barn-door hens on a stranger chick,’ Diana complained ; and she chid herself angrily for letting it escape her forethought to propitiate them on the author's behalf. Young Rhodes was left with scarce a feather ; and what remained to him appeared a preposterous ornament for the decoration of a shivering and welted poet. He laughed, or tried the mouth of laughter. ANTONIA'S literary conscience was vexed at the different treatment she had met and so imperatively needed that the reverse of it would have threatened the smooth sailing of her costly household. A merry-go-round of creditors required a corresponding whirligig of receipts.

She felt mercenary, debased by comparison with the well-scourged verse-mason, Orpheus of the untenanted city, who had done his publishing ingenuously for glory : a good instance of the comic-pathetic. She wrote to Emma, begging her to take him in at Copsley for a few days :—
' I told you I had no troubles. I am really troubled about this poor boy. He has very little money and has embarked on literature. I cannot induce any of my friends to lend him a hand. Mr. Redworth gruffly insists on his going back to his law-clerk's office and stool, and Mr. Dacier says that no place is vacant. The reality of Lord Dannisburgh's death is brought before me by my helplessness. He would have made him an assistant private Secretary, pending a Government appointment, rather than let me plead in vain.'

Mr. Rhodes with his travelling bag was packed off to Copsley, to enjoy a change of scene after his run of the gauntlet. He was very heartily welcomed by Lady Dunstane, both for her Tony's sake and his own modest worship of that luminary, which could permit of being transparent ; but chiefly she welcomed him as the living proof of Tony's disengagement from anxiety, since he was her one spot of trouble, and could easily be comforted by reading with her, and wandering through the Spring woods along the heights. He had a happy time, midway in air between his accomplished hostess and his protecting Goddess. His bruises were soon healed. Each day was radiant to him, whether it rained or shone ; and by his looks and what he said of himself Lady Dunstane understood that he was in the highest temper of the human creature tuned to thrilling accord with nature. It was her generous Tony's work. She blessed it, and liked the youth the better.

During the stay of Mr. Arthur Rhodes at Copsley, Sir Lukin came on a visit to his wife. He mentioned reports

in the scandal-papers : one, that Mr. P. D. would shortly
lead to the altar the lovely heiress Miss A., Percy Dacier
and Constance Asper :—another, that a reconciliation was
to be expected between the beautiful authoress Mrs. W.
and her husband.   ' Perhaps it 's the best thing she can
do,' Sir Lukin added.

Lady Dunstane pronounced a woman's unforgiving :
' Never.'   The revolt of her own sensations assured her
of Tony's unconquerable repugnance.   In conversation
subsequently with Arthur Rhodes, she heard that he knew
the son of Mr. Warwick's attorney, a Mr. Fenn ; and he
had gathered from him some information of Mr. Warwick's
condition of health.   It had been alarming ; young Fenn
said it was confirmed heart-disease.   His father frequently
saw Mr. Warwick, and said he was fretting himself to
death.

It seemed just a possibility that Tony's natural com-
passionateness had wrought on her to immolate herself
and nurse to his end the man who had wrecked her life.
Lady Dunstane waited for news.   At last she wrote,
touching the report incidentally.   There was no reply.
The silence ensuing after such a question responded
forcibly.


## CHAPTER XXII

### BETWEEN DIANA AND DACIER : THE WIND EAST OVER
### BLEAK LAND

ON the third day of the Easter recess Percy Dacier landed
from the Havre steamer at Caen and drove straightway
for the sandy coast, past fields of colza to brine-blown
meadows of coarse grass, and then to the low dunes and
long stretching sands of the ebb in semicircle : a desolate

place at that season ; with a dwarf fishing-village by the
shore ; an East wind driving landward in streamers every
object that had a scrap to fly.   He made head to the inn,
where the first person he encountered in the passage was
Diana's maid Danvers, who relaxed from the dramatic
exaggeration of her surprise at the sight of a real English
gentleman in these woebegone regions, to inform him that
her mistress might be found walking somewhere along the
sea-shore, and had her dog to protect her.   They were to
stay here a whole week, Danvers added, for a conveyance
of her private sentiments.   Second thoughts however
whispered to her shrewdness that his arrival could only
be by appointment.   She had been anticipating something
of the sort for some time.

Dacier butted against the stringing wind, that kept him
at a rocking incline to his left for a mile.   He then discerned in what had seemed a dredger's dot on the sands,
a lady's figure, unmistakably she, without the corrobor-
ating testimony of Leander paw-deep in the low-tide
water.   She was out at a distance on the ebb-sands,
hurtled, gyred, beaten to all shapes, in rolls, twists,
volumes, like a blown banner-flag, by the pressing wind.
A kerchief tied her bonnet under her chin.   Bonnet and
breast-ribands rattled rapidly as drummer-sticks.   She
stood near the little running ripple of the flat sea-water,
as it hurried from a long streaked back to a tiny imitation
of spray.   When she turned to the shore she saw him advancing, but did not recognize ; when they met she merely
looked with wide parted lips.   This was no appointment.

' I had to see you,' Dacier said.

She coloured to a deeper red than the rose-conjuring
wind had whipped in her cheeks.   Her quick intuition of
the reason of his coming barred a mental evasion, and she
had no thought of asking either him or herself what special
urgency had brought him.

' I have been here four days.'

' Lady Esquart spoke of the place.'

' Lady Esquart should not have betrayed me.'

' She did it inadvertently, without an idea of my profiting by it.'

Diana indicated the scene in a glance. ' Dreary country, do you think ? '

' Anywhere ! '—said he.

They walked up the sand-heap. The roaring Easter with its shrieks and whistles at her ribands was not favourable to speech. His ' Anywhere ! ' had a penetrating significance, the fuller for the break that left it vague.

Speech between them was commanded ; he could not be suffered to remain. She descended upon a sheltered pathway running along a ditch, the border of pastures where cattle cropped, raised heads, and resumed their one comforting occupation.

Diana gazed on them, smarting from the buffets of the wind she had met.

' No play of their tails to-day '; she said, as she slackened her steps. ' You left Lady Esquart well ? '

' Lady Esquart . . . I think was well. I had to see you. I thought you would be with her in Berkshire. She told me of a little sea-side place close to Caen.'

' You had to see me ? '

' I miss you now if it 's a day ! '

' I heard a story in London . . .'

' In London there are many stories. I heard one. Is there a foundation for it ? '

' No.'

He breathed relieved. ' I wanted to see you once before . . . if it was true. It would have made a change in my life—a gap.'

' You do me the honour to like my Sunday evenings ? '

' Beyond everything London can offer.'

' A letter would have reached me.'

' I should have had to wait for the answer. There is no truth in it ? '

Her choice was to treat the direct assailant frankly or imperil her defence by the ordinary feminine evolutions, which might be taken for inviting : poor pranks always.

' There have been overtures,' she said.

' Forgive me ; I have scarcely the right to ask . . . speak of it.'

' My friends may use their right to take an interest in my fortunes.'

' I thought I might, on my way to Paris, turn aside . . . coming by this route.'

' If you determined not to lose much of your time.'

The coolness of her fencing disconcerted a gentleman conscious of his madness. She took instant advantage of any circuitous move ; she gave him no practicable point. He was little skilled in the arts of attack, and felt that she checked his impetuousness ; respected her for it, chafed at it, writhed with the fervours precipitating him here, and relapsed on his pleasure in seeing her face, hearing her voice.

' Your happiness, I hope, is the chief thought in such a case,' he said.

' I am sure you would consider it.'

' I can't quite forget my own.'

' You compliment an ambitious hostess.'

Dacier glanced across the pastures, ' What was it that tempted you to this place ? '

' A poet would say it looks like a figure in the shroud. It has no features ; it has a sort of grandeur belonging to death. I heard of it as the place where I might be certain of not meeting an acquaintance.'

' And I am the intruder.'

'An hour or two will not give you that title.'

'Am I to count the minutes by my watch ? '

'By the sun.    We will supply you  an omelette and piquette, and send you back sobered and friarly to Caen for Paris at sunset.'

'Let the fare be Spartan,   I could take my black broth with philosophy every day of the year under your auspices.    What I should miss . . .'

'You bring no news of the world or the House ? '

'None.    You know as much as I know.    The Irish agitation is chronic.    The Corn-law threatens to be the same.'

'And your Chief—in personal colloquy ? '

'He keeps a calm front.    I may tell you :—there is nothing I would not confide to you : he has let fall some dubious words in private.    I don't know what to think of them.'

'But if he should waver ? '

'It 's not wavering.    It 's the openness of his mind.'

'Ah ! the mind.    We imagine it free.    The House and the country are the sentient frame governing the mind of the politician more than his ideas.    He cannot think independently of them :—nor I of my natural anatomy.    You will test the truth of that after your omelette and piquette, and marvel at the quitting of your line of route for Paris. As soon as the mind attempts to think independently, it is like a kite with the cord cut, and performs a series of darts and frisks, that have the look of wildest liberty till you see it fall flat to earth.    The openness of his mind is most honourable to him.'

'Ominous for his party.'

'Likely to be good for his country.'

'That is the question.'

'Prepare to encounter it.    In politics I am with the active  minority  on  behalf  of  the  inert  but  suffering

majority. That is my rule. It leads, unless you have
a despotism, to the conquering side. It is always the
noblest. I won't say, listen to me ; only do believe my
words have some weight. This is a question of bread.'

' It involves many other questions.'

' And how clearly those leaders put their case ! They
are admirable debaters. If I were asked to write against
them, I should have but to quote them to confound my
argument. I tried it once, and wasted a couple of my
precious hours.'

' They are cogent debaters,' Dacier assented. ' They
make me wince now and then, without convincing me :—
I own it to you. The confession is not agreeable, though
it 's a small matter.'

' One's pride may feel a touch with the foils as keenly
as the point of a rapier,' said Diana.

The remark drew a sharp look of pleasure from
him.

' Does the Princess Egeria propose to dismiss the individual she inspires, when he is growing most sensible of
her wisdom ? '

' A young Minister of State should be gleaning at large
when holiday is granted him.'

Dacier coloured. ' May I presume on what is currently
reported ? '

' Parts, parts ; a bit here, a bit there,' she rejoined.
' Authors find their models where they can, and generally
hit on the nearest.'

' Happy the nearest ! '

' If you run to interjections I shall cite you a sentence
from your latest speech in the House.'

He asked for it, and to school him she consented to
flatter with her recollection of his commonest words :
' " Dealing with subjects of this nature emotionally does
not advance us a calculable inch." '

' I must have said that in relation to hard matter of business.'

' It applies.  There is my hostelry, and the spectral form of Danvers, utterly *dépaysée*.  Have you spoken to the poor soul ?  I can never discover the links of her attachment to my service.'

' She knows a good mistress.—I have but a few minutes, if you are relentless.  May I . . ., shall I ever be privileged to speak your Christian name ? '

' My Christian name !  It is Pagan.  In one sphere I am Hecate.  Remember that.'

' I am not among the people who so regard you.'

' The time may come.'

' Diana ! '

' Constance ! '

' I break no tie.  I owe no allegiance whatever to the name.'

' Keep to the formal title with me.  We are Mrs. Warwick and Mr. Dacier.  I think I am two years younger than you ; socially therefore ten in seniority ; and I know how this flower of friendship is nourished and may be withered.  You see already what you have done ?  You have cast me on the discretion of my maid.  I suppose her trusty, but I am at her mercy, and a breath from her to the people beholding me as Hecate queen of Witches ! . . . I have a sensation of the scirocco it would blow.'

' In that event, the least I can offer is my whole life.'

' We will not conjecture the event.'

' The best I could hope for ! '

' I see I shall have to revise the next edition of THE YOUNG MINISTER, and make an emotional curate of him.  Observe Danvers.  The woman is wretched ; and now she sees me coming she pretends to be using her wits in studying the things about her, as I have directed.  She is a riddle. I have the idea that any morning she may explode ; and yet I trust her and sleep soundly. I must be free, though I vex the world's watchdogs.—So, Danvers, you are noticing how thoroughly Frenchwomen do their work.'

Danvers replied with a slight mincing : ' They may, ma'am ; but they chatter chatter so.'

' The result proves that it is not a waste of energy. They manage their fowls too.'

' They 've no such thing as mutton, ma'am.'

Dacier patriotically laughed.

' She strikes the apology for wealthy and leisurely land-lords,' Diana said.

Danvers remarked that the poor fed meagrely in France. She was not convinced of its being good for them by hear-ing that they could work on it sixteen hours out of the four and twenty.

Mr. Percy Dacier's repast was furnished to him half an hour later. At sunset Diana, taking Danvers beside her, walked with him to the line of the country road bearing on Caen. The wind had sunk. A large brown disk paused rayless on the western hills.

' A Dacier ought to feel at home in Normandy ; and you may have sprung from this neighbourhood,' said she, simply to chat. ' Here the land is poorish, and a mile inland rich enough to bear repeated crops of colza, which tries the soil, I hear. As for beauty, those blue hills you see, enfold charming valleys. I meditate an expedition to Harcourt before I return. An English professor of his native tongue at the Lycée at Caen told me on my way here that for twenty shillings a week you may live in royal ease round about Harcourt. So we have our bed and board in prospect if fortune fails us, Danvers.'

' I would rather die in England, ma'am,' was the maid's reply.

Dacier set foot on his carriage-step. He drew a long breath to say a short farewell, and he and Diana parted.

They parted as the plainest of sincere good friends, each at heart respecting the other for the repression of that which their hearts craved ; any word of which might have carried them headlong, bound together on a Mazeppa-race, with scandal for the hounding wolves, and social ruin for the rocks and torrents.

Dacier was the thankfuller, the most admiring of the two ; at the same time the least satisfied. He saw the abyss she had aided him in escaping ; and it was refreshful to look abroad after his desperate impulse. Prominent as he stood before the world, he could not think without a shudder of behaving like a young frenetic of the passion. Those whose aim is at the leadership of the English people know, that however truly based the charges of hypocrisy, soundness of moral fibre runs throughout the country and is the national integrity, which may condone old sins for present service, but will not have present sins to flout it. He was in tune with the English character. The passion was in him nevertheless, and the stronger for a slow growth that confirmed its union of the mind and heart. Her counsel fortified him, her suggestions opened springs ; her phrases were golden-lettered in his memory ; and more, she had worked an extraordinary change in his views of life and aptitude for social converse : he acknowledged it with genial candour. Through her he was encouraged, led, excited to sparkle with the witty, feel new gifts, or a greater breadth of nature ; and thanking her, he became thirstily susceptible to her dark beauty ; he claimed to have found the key of her, and he prized it. She was not passionless : the blood flowed warm. Proud, chaste, she was nobly spirited ; having an intellectual refuge from the besiegings of the blood ; a rock-fortress. The ' wife

no wife' appeared to him, striking the higher elements
of the man, the commonly masculine also.—Would he
espouse her, had he the chance?—to-morrow! this
instant! With her to back him, he would be doubled
in manhood, doubled in brain and heart-energy. To call
her wife, spring from her and return, a man might accept
his fate to fight Trojan or Greek, sure of his mark on the
enemy.

But if, after all, this imputed Helen of a decayed Paris
passed, submissive to the legitimate solicitor, back to her
husband?

The thought shot Dacier on his legs for a look at the
blank behind him. He vowed she had promised it should
not be. Could it ever be, after the ruin the meanly suspicious fellow had brought upon her?—Diana voluntarily
reunited to the treacherous cur?

He sat, resolving sombrely that if the debate arose he
would try what force he had to save her from such an
ignominy, and dedicate his life to her, let the world wag
its tongue. So the knot would be cut.

Men unaccustomed to a knot in their system find the
prospect of cutting it an extreme relief, even when they
know that the cut has an edge to wound mortally as well
as pacify. The wound was not heavy payment for the
rapture of having so incomparable a woman his own. He
reflected wonderingly on the husband, as he had previously done, and came again to the conclusion that it was
a poor creature, abjectly jealous of a wife he could neither
master, nor equal, nor attract. And thinking of jealousy,
Dacier felt none; none of individuals, only of facts: her
marriage, her bondage. Her condemnation to perpetual
widowhood angered him, as at an unrighteous decree.
The sharp sweet bloom of her beauty, fresh in swarthi-
ness, under the whipping Easter, cried out against that
loathed inhumanity. Or he made it cry.

Being a stranger to the jealousy of men, he took the soft
assurance that he was preferred above them all.  Com-
petitors were numerous : not any won her eyes as he did.
She revealed nothing of the same pleasures in the shining
of the others touched by her magical wand.  Would she
have pardoned one of them the ' Diana ! ' bursting from
his mouth ?

She was not a woman for trifling, still less for secresy.
He was as little the kind of lover.  Both would be ready
to take up their burden, if the burden was laid on them.
—Diana had thus far impressed him.

Meanwhile he faced the cathedral towers of the ancient
Norman city, standing up in the smoky hues of the West ;
and a sentence out of her book seemed fitting to the scene
and what he felt.  He rolled it over luxuriously as the
next of delights to having her beside him.—She wrote of ;
' *Thoughts that are bare dark outlines, coloured by some old
passion of the soul, like towers of a distant city seen in the
funeral waste of day.*'—His bluff English anti-poetic
training would have caused him to shrug at the stuff coming from another pen : he might condescendingly have
criticized it, with a sneer embalmed in humour.  The
words were hers ; she had written them ; almost by a sort
of anticipation, he imagined ; for he at once fell into the
mood they suggested, and had a full crop of the ' bare
dark outlines ' of thoughts coloured by his particular
form of passion.

Diana had impressed him powerfully when she set him
swallowing and assimilating a sentence ethereally thin in
substance, of mere sentimental significance, that he would
antecedently have read aloud in a drawing-room, picking
up the book by hazard, as your modern specimen of
romantic vapouring.  Mr. Dacier however was at the
time in observation of the towers of Caen, fresh from her
presence, animated to some conception of her spirit.  He

R

drove into the streets, desiring, half determining, to risk
a drive back on the morrow.

The cold light of the morrow combined with his fear of
distressing her to restrain him. Perhaps he thought it
well not to risk his gains. He was a northerner in blood.
He may have thought it well not further to run the personal risk immediately.


# CHAPTER XXIII

### RECORDS A VISIT TO DIANA FROM ONE OF THE WORLD'S GOOD WOMEN

PURE disengagement of contemplativeness had selected
Percy Dacier as the model of her YOUNG MINISTER OF
STATE, Diana supposed. Could she otherwise have dared
to sketch him ? She certainly would not have done it
now.

That was a reflection similar to what is entertained by
one who has dropped from a precipice to the midway
ledge over the abyss, where caution of the whole sensitive
being is required for simple self-preservation. How could
she have been induced to study and portray him ! It
seemed a form of dementia.

She thought this while imagining the world to be interrogating her. When she interrogated herself, she flew
to Lugano and her celestial Salvatore, that she might be
defended from a charge of the dreadful weakness of her
sex. Surely she there had proof of her capacity for pure
disengagement. Even in recollection the springs of
spiritual happiness renewed the bubbling crystal play.
She believed that a divineness had wakened in her there,
to strengthen her to the end, ward her from any complicity in her sex's culprit blushing.

Dacier's cry of her name was the cause, she chose to think, of the excessive circumspection she must henceforth practise ; precariously footing, embracing hardest earth, the plainest rules, to get back to safety. Not that she was personally endangered, or at least not spiritually ; she could always fly in soul to her heights. But she had now to be on guard, constantly in the fencing attitude. And watchful of herself as well. That was admitted with a ready frankness, to save it from being a necessitated and painful confession : for the voluntary acquiescence, if it involved her in her sex, claimed an individual exemption. ' Women are women, and I am a woman : but I am I, and unlike them : I see we are weak, and weakness tempts : in owning the prudence of guarded steps, I am armed. It is by dissembling, feigning immunity, that we are imperilled.' She would have phrased it so, with some anger at her feminine nature as well as at the subjection forced on her by circumstances.

Besides, her position and Percy Dacier's threw the fancied danger into remoteness. The world was her stepmother, vigilant to become her judge ; and the world was his taskmaster, hopeful of him, yet able to strike him down for an offence. She saw their situation as he did. The course of folly must be bravely taken, if taken at all. Disguise degraded her to the reptiles.

This was faced. Consequently there was no fear of it.

She had very easily proved that she had skill and self-possession to keep him rational, and therefore they could continue to meet. A little outburst of frenzy to a reputably handsome woman could be treated as the froth of a passing wave. Men have the trick, infants their fevers.

Diana's days were spent in reasoning. Her nights were not so tuneable to the superior mind. When asleep she was the sport of elves that danced her into tangles too

deliciously unravelled, and left new problems for the wise-
eyed and anxious morning. She solved them with the
thought that in sleep it was the mere ordinary woman
who fell a prey to her tormentors ; awake, she dispersed
the swarm, her sky was clear. Gradually the persecution
ceased, thanks to her active pen.

A letter from her legal adviser, old Mr. Braddock, informed her that no grounds existed for apprehending
marital annoyance, and late in May her household had
resumed its customary round.

She examined her accounts. The Debit and Credit sides
presented much of the appearance of male and female in
our jog-trot civilization. They matched middling well ;
with rather too marked a tendency to strain the leash and
run frolic on the part of friend Debit (the wanton male),
which deepened the blush of the comparison. Her father
had noticed the same funny thing in his effort to balance
his tugging accounts : ' Now then for a look at Man and
Wife ' : except that he made Debit stand for the portly
frisky female, Credit the decorous and contracted other
half, a prim gentleman of a constitutionally lean habit of
body, remonstrating with her. ' You seem to forget that
we are married, my dear, and must walk in step or bundle
into the Bench,' Dan Merion used to say.

Diana had not so much to rebuke in Mr. Debit ; or not
at the first reckoning. But his ways were curious. She
grew distrustful of him, after dismissing him with a quiet
admonition and discovering a series of ambush bills,
which he must have been aware of when he was allowed
to pass as an honourable citizen. His answer to her reproaches pleaded the necessitousness of his purchases
and expenditure : a capital plea ; and Mrs. Credit was
requested by him, in a courteous manner, to drive her pen
the faster, so that she might wax to a corresponding size
and satisfy the world's idea of fitness in couples. She

would have costly furniture, because it pleased her taste ;
and a French cook, for a like reason, in justice to her
guests ; and trained servants ; and her tribe of pensioners ; flowers she would have profuse and fresh at her
windows and over the rooms ; and the pictures and en-
gravings on the walls were (always for the good reason
mentioned) choice ones ; and she had a love of old lace,
she loved colours as she loved cheerfulness, and silks, and
satin hangings, Indian ivory carvings, countless mirrors,
Oriental woods, chairs and desks with some feature or a
flourish in them, delicate tables with antelope legs, of
approved workmanship in the chronology of European
upholstery, and marble clocks of cunning device to symbol Time, mantelpiece decorations, illustrated 'editions
of her favourite authors ; her bed-chambers, too, gave
the nest for sleep a dainty cosiness in aërial draperies.
Hence, more or less directly, the peccant bills. Credit
was reduced to reckon to a nicety the amount she could
rely on positively : her fixed income from her investments
and the letting of The Crossways : the days of half-
yearly payments that would magnify her to some pro-
portions beside the alarming growth of her partner, who
was proud of it, and referred her to the treasures she
could summon with her pen, at a murmur of dissatis-
faction. His compliments were sincere ; they were
seductive. He assured her that she had struck a rich
vein in an inexhaustible mine ; by writing only a very
little faster she could double her income ; counting a
broader popularity, treble it ; and so on a tide of success
down the widening river to a sea sheer golden. Behold
how it sparkles ! Are we then to stint our winged hours
of youth for want of courage to realize the riches we can
command ? Debit was eloquent, he was unanswerable.

Another calculator, an accustomed and lamentably-
scrupulous arithmetician, had been at work for some

time upon a speculative summing of the outlay of Diana's
establishment, as to its chances of swamping the income.
Redworth could guess pretty closely the cost of a household, if his care for the holder set him venturing on aver-
ages. He knew nothing of her ten per cent. investment
and considered her fixed income a beggarly regiment to
marshal against the invader. He fancied however, in
his ignorance of literary profits, that a popular writer,
selling several editions, had come to an El Dorado. There
was the mine. It required a diligent working. Diana
was often struck by hearing Redworth ask her *when* her
next book might be expected. He appeared to have an
eagerness in hurrying her to produce, and she had to say
that she was not a nimble writer. His flattering impatience was vexatious. He admired her work, yet he did
his utmost to render it little admirable. His literary taste
was not that of young Arthur Rhodes, to whom she could
read her chapters, appearing to take counsel upon them
while drinking the eulogies : she suspected him of prosaic-
ally wishing her to make money, and though her ex-
chequer was beginning to know the need of it, the author's
lofty mind disdained such sordidness :—to be excused,
possibly, for a failing productive energy. She encountered obstacles to imaginative composition. With the
pen in her hand, she would fall into heavy musings ;
break a sentence to muse, and not on the subject. She
slept unevenly at night, was drowsy by day, unless the
open air was about her, or animating friends. Redworth's
urgency to get her to publish was particularly annoying
when she felt how greatly THE YOUNG MINISTER OF
STATE would have been improved had she retained the
work to brood over it, polish, re-write passages, perfect
it. Her musings embraced long dialogues of that work,
never printed ; they sprang up, they passed from
memory ; leaving a distaste for her present work : THE

CANTATRICE : far more poetical than the preceding, in
the opinion of Arthur Rhodes ; and the story was more
romantic ; modelled on a Prima Donna she had met at
the musical parties of Henry Wilmers, after hearing
Redworth tell of Charles Rainer's quaint passion for the
woman, or the idea of the woman. Diana had courted
her, studied and liked her. The picture she was drawing
of the amiable and gifted Italian, of her villain Roumanian
husband, and of the eccentric, high-minded, devoted
Englishman, was good in a fashion ; but considering the
theme, she had reasonable apprehension that her CANTA-
TRICE would not repay her for the time and labour bestowed on it. No clever transcripts of the dialogue of the
day occurred ; no hair-breadth 'scapes, perils by sea and
land, heroisms of the hero, fine shrieks of the heroine ; no
set scenes of catching pathos and humour ; no distinguishable points of social satire—equivalent to a smacking of
the public on the chaps, which excites it to grin with keen
discernment of the author's intention. She did not
appeal to the senses nor to a superficial discernment. So
she had the anticipatory sense of its failure ; and she
wrote her best, in perverseness ; of course she wrote
slowly ; she wrote more and more realistically of the
characters and the downright human emotions, less of
the wooden supernumeraries of her story, labelled for
broad guffaw or deluge tears—the grappling natural links
between our public and an author. Her feelings were
aloof. They flowed at a hint of a scene of THE YOUNG
MINISTER. She could not put them into THE CANTATRICE.
And Arthur Rhodes pronounced this work poetical
beyond its predecessors, for the reason that the chief characters were alive and the reader felt their pulses. He
meant to say, they were poetical inasmuch as they were
creations.

The slow progress of a work not driven by the author's

feelings necessitated frequent consultations between Debit
and Credit, resulting in altercations, recriminations, discord of the yoked and divergent couple.  To restore them
to their proper trot in harness, Diana reluctantly went to
her publisher for an advance item of the sum she was to
receive, and the act increased her distaste.  An idea came
that she would soon cease to be able to write at all.  What
then ?  Perhaps by selling her invested money, and
ultimately The Crossways, she would have enough for
her term upon earth.  Necessarily she had to think that
short, in order to reckon it as nearly enough.  ' I am sure,'
she said to herself, ' I shall not trouble the world very long.'
A strange languor beset her ; scarcely melancholy, for
she conceived the cheerfulness of life and added to it in
company ; but a nervelessness, as though she had been
left by the stream on the banks, and saw beauty and
pleasure sweep along and away, while the sun that primed
them dried her veins.  At this time she was gaining her
widest reputation for brilliancy of wit.  Only to welcome
guests were her evenings ever spent at home.  She had
no intimate understanding of the deadly wrestle of the
conventional woman with her nature which she was
undergoing below the surface.  Perplexities she acknowledged, and the prudence of guardedness.  ' But as I am
sure not to live very long, we may as well meet.'  Her
meetings with Percy Dacier were therefore hardly shunned,
and his behaviour did not warn her to discountenance
them.  It would have been cruel to exclude him from
her select little dinners of eight.  Whitmonby, Westlake,
Henry Wilmers and the rest, she perhaps aiding, schooled
him in the conversational art.  She heard it said of him,
that the courted discarder of the sex, hitherto a mere
politician, was wonderfully humanized.  Lady Pennon
fell to talking of him hopefully.  She declared him to be
one of the men who unfold tardily, and only await the

mastering passion. If the passion had come, it was controlled. His command of himself melted Diana. How could she forbid his entry to the houses she frequented ? She was glad to see him. He showed his pleasure in seeing her. Remembering his tentative indiscretion on those foreign sands, she reflected that he had been easily checked : and the like was not to be said of some others. Beautiful women in her position provoke an intemperateness that contrasts touchingly with the self-restraint of a particular admirer. Her ' impassioned Caledonian ' was one of a host, to speak of whom and their fits of lunacy even to her friend Emma, was repulsive. She bore with them, foiled them, passed them, and recovered her equanimity ; but the contrast called to her to dwell on it, the self-restraint whispered of a depth of passion. . . .

She was shocked at herself for a singular tremble she experienced, without any beating of the heart, on hearing one day that the marriage of Percy Dacier and Miss Asper was at last definitely fixed. Mary Paynham brought her the news. She had it from a lady who had come across Miss Asper at Lady Wathin's assemblies, and considered the great heiress extraordinarily handsome.

' A golden miracle,' Diana gave her words to say. ' Good looks and gold together are rather superhuman. The report may be this time true.'

Next afternoon the card of Lady Wathin requested Mrs. Warwick to grant her a private interview.

Lady Wathin, as one of the order of women who can do anything in a holy cause, advanced toward Mrs. Warwick, unabashed by the burden of her mission, and spinally prepared, behind benevolent smilings, to repay dignity of mien with a similar erectness of dignity. They touched fingers and sat. The preliminaries to the matter of the interview were brief between ladies physically sensible of antagonism and mutually too scornful of subterfuges in one another's presence to beat the bush.

Lady Wathin began. ' I am, you are aware, Mrs. Warwick, a cousin of your friend Lady Dunstane.'

' You come to me on business ? ' Diana said.

' It may be so termed. I have no personal interest in it. I come to lay certain facts before you which I think you should know. We think it better that an acquaintance, and one of your sex, should state the case to you, instead of having recourse to formal intermediaries, lawyers . . .'

' Lawyers ? '

' Well, my husband is a lawyer, it is true. In the course of his professional vocations he became acquainted with Mr. Warwick. We have latterly seen a good deal of him. He is, I regret to say, seriously unwell.'

' I have heard of it.'

' He has no female relations, it appears. He needs more care than he can receive from hirelings.'

' Are you empowered by him, Lady Wathin ? '

' I am, Mrs. Warwick. We will not waste time in apologies. He is most anxious for a reconciliation. It seems to Sir Cramborne and to me the most desireable thing for all parties concerned, if you can be induced to regard it in that light. Mr. Warwick may or may not live ; but the estrangement is quite undoubtedly the cause of his illness. I touch on nothing connected with it. I simply wish that you should not be in ignorance of his proposal and his condition.'

Diana bowed calmly. ' I grieve at his condition. His proposal has already been made and replied to.'

' Oh, but, Mrs. Warwick, an immediate and decisive refusal of a proposal so fraught with consequences . . . ! '

' Ah, but, Lady Wathin, you are now outstepping the limits prescribed by the office you have undertaken.'

' You will not lend ear to an intercession ? '

' I will not.'

' Of course, Mrs. Warwick, it is not for me to hint at things that lawyers could say on the subject.'

' Your forbearance is creditable, Lady Wathin.'

' Believe me, Mrs. Warwick, the step is—I speak in my husband's name as well as my own—strongly to be advised.'

' If I hear one word more of it, I leave the country.'

' I should be sorry indeed at any piece of rashness depriving your numerous friends of your society. We have recently become acquainted with Mr. Redworth, and I know the loss you would be to them. I have not attempted an appeal to your feelings, Mrs. Warwick.'

' I thank you warmly, Lady Wathin, for what you have not done.'

The aristocratic airs of Mrs. Warwick were annoying to Lady Wathin when she considered that they were borrowed, and that a pattern morality could regard the woman as ostracized : nor was it agreeable to be looked at through eyelashes under partially lifted brows. She had come to appeal to the feelings of the wife ; at any rate, to discover if she had some and was better than a wild adventuress.

' Our life below is short ! ' she said. To which Diana tacitly assented.

' We have our little term, Mrs. Warwick. It is soon over.'

' On the other hand, the platitudes concerning it are eternal.'

Lady Wathin closed her eyes, that the like effect might be produced on her ears. ' Ah ! they are the truths. But it is not my business to preach. Permit me to say that I feel deeply for your husband.'

' I am glad of Mr. Warwick's having friends ; and they are many, I hope.'

'They cannot behold him perishing, without an effort on his behalf.'

A chasm of silence intervened. Wifely pity was not sounded in it.

'He will question me, Mrs. Warwick.'

'You can report to him the heads of our conversation, Lady Wathin.'

'Would you—it is your husband's most earnest wish; and our house is open to his wife and to him for the purpose; and it seems to us that . . . indeed it might avert a catastrophe you would necessarily deplore :—would you consent to meet him at my house ? '

'It has already been asked, Lady Wathin, and refused.'

'But at my house—under our auspices ! '

Diana glanced at the clock. 'Nowhere.'

'Is it not—pardon me—a wife's duty, Mrs. Warwick, at least to listen ? '

'Lady Wathin, I have listened to you.'

'In the case of his extreme generosity so putting it, for the present, Mrs. Warwick, that he asks only to be heard personally by his wife ! It may preclude so much.'

Diana felt a hot wind across her skin.

She smiled and said : 'Let me thank you for bringing to an end a mission that must have been unpleasant to you.'

'But you will meditate on it, Mrs. Warwick, will you not ? Give me that assurance ! '

'I shall not forget it,' said Diana.

Again the ladies touched fingers, with an interchange of the social grimace of cordiality. A few words of compassion for poor Lady Dunstane's invalided state covered Lady Wathin's retreat.

She left, it struck her ruffled sentiments, an icy libertine, whom any husband caring for his dignity and comfort was well rid of ; and if only she could have contrived allusively

to bring in the name of Mr. Percy Dacier, just to show
these arrant coquettes, or worse, that they were not quite
so privileged to pursue their intrigues obscurely as they
imagined, it would have soothed her exasperation.

She left a woman the prey of panic.

Diana thought of Emma and Redworth, and of their
foolish interposition to save her character and keep her
bound. She might now have been free ! The struggle
with her manacles reduced her to a state of rebelliousness,
from which issued vivid illuminations of the one means
of certain escape : an abhorrent hissing cavern, that led to
a place named Liberty, her refuge, but a hectic place.

Unable to write, hating the house which held her a fixed
mark for these attacks, she had an idea of flying straight
to her beloved Lugano lake, and there hiding, abandoning
her friends, casting off the slave's name she bore, and
living free in spirit.   She went so far as to reckon the cost
of a small household there, and justify the violent step
by an exposition of retrenchment upon her large London
expenditure.   She had but to say farewell to Emma, no
other tie to cut !   One morning on the Salvatore heights
would wash her clear of the webs defacing and entangling
her.

## CHAPTER XXIV

### INDICATES A SOUL PREPARED FOR DESPERATION

THE month was August, four days before the closing of
Parliament, and Diana fancied it good for Arthur Rhodes
to run down with her to Copsley.   He came to her invitation joyfully, reminding her of Lady Dunstane's wish to
hear some chapters of THE CANTATRICE, and the MS. was
packed.   They started, taking rail and fly, and winding up

the distance on foot. August is the month of sober maturity and majestic foliage, songless, but a crowned and royal-robed queenly month ; and the youngster's appreciation of the homely scenery refreshed Diana ; his delight in being with her was also pleasant. She had no wish to exchange him for another ; and that was a strengthening thought.

At Copsley the arrival of their luggage had prepared the welcome. Warm though it was, Diana perceived a change in Emma, an unwonted reserve, a doubtfulness of her eyes, in spite of tenderness ; and thus thrown back on herself, thinking that if she had followed her own counsel (as she called her impulse) in old days, there would have been no such present misery, she at once, and unconsciously, assumed a guarded look. Based on her knowledge of her honest footing, it was a little defiant. Secretly in her bosom it was sharpened to a slight hostility by the knowledge that her mind had been straying. The guilt and the innocence combined to clothe her in mail, the innocence being positive, the guilt so vapoury. But she was armed only if necessary, and there was no requirement for armour. Emma did not question at all. She saw the alteration in her Tony : she was too full of the tragic apprehensiveness overmastering her to speak of trifles. She had never confided to Tony the exact nature and the growth of her malady, thinking it mortal, and fearing to alarm her dearest.

A portion of the manuscript was read out by Arthur Rhodes in the evening ; the remainder next morning. Redworth perceptibly was the model of the English hero ; and as to his person, no friend could complain of the sketch ; his clear-eyed heartiness, manliness, wholesomeness—a word of Lady Dunstane's regarding him,—and his handsome braced figure, were well painted. Emma forgave the insistance on a certain bluntness of the nose, in consideration of the fond limning of his honest and expressive eyes,

and the 'light on his temples,' which they had noticed
together. She could not so easily forgive the realistic
picture of the man : an exaggeration, she thought, of
small foibles, that even if they existed, should not have
been stressed. The turn for 'calculating' was shown up
ridiculously ; Mr. Cuthbert Dering was calculating in his
impassioned moods as well as in his cold. His head was a
long division of ciphers. He had statistics for spectacles,
and beheld the world through them, and the mistress he
worshipped.

'I see,' said Emma, during a pause ; 'he is a Saxon.
You still affect to have the race *en grippe*, Tony.'

'I give him every credit for what he is,' Diana replied.
'I admire the finer qualities of the race as much as any
one. You want to have them presented to you in
enamel, Emmy.'

But the worst was an indication that the mania for calculating in and out of season would lead to the catastrophe
destructive of his happiness. Emma could not bear that.
Without asking herself whether it could be possible that
Tony knew the secret, or whether she would have laid it
bare, her sympathy for Redworth revolted at the exposure.
She was chilled. She let it pass ; she merely said : 'I
like the writing.'

Diana understood that her story was condemned.

She put on her robes of philosophy to cloak discourage-
ment. 'I am glad the writing pleases you.'

'The characters are as true as life ! ' cried Arthur
Rhodes. 'The Cantatrice drinking porter from the
pewter at the slips after harrowing the hearts of her
audience, is dearer to me than if she had tottered to a sofa
declining sustenance ; and because her creatrix has infused
such blood of life into her that you accept naturally whatever she does. She was exhausted, and required the
porter, like a labourer in the cornfield.'

Emma looked at him, and perceived the poet swamped by the admirer. Taken in conjunction with Mr. Cuthbert Dering's frenzy for calculating, she disliked the incident of the porter and the pewter.

' While the Cantatrice swallowed her draught, I suppose Mr. Dering counted the cost ? ' she said.

' It really might be hinted,' said Diana.

The discussion closed with the accustomed pro and con upon the wart of Cromwell's nose, Realism rejoicing in it, Idealism objecting.

Arthur Rhodes was bidden to stretch his legs on a walk along the heights in the afternoon, and Emma was further vexed by hearing Tony complain of Redworth's treatment of the lad, whom he would not assist to any of the snug little posts he was notoriously able to dispense.

' He has talked of Mr. Rhodes to me,' said Emma. ' He thinks the profession of literature a delusion, and doubts the wisdom of having poets for clerks.'

' John-Bullish ! ' Diana exclaimed. ' He speaks contemptuously of the poor boy.'

' Only inasmuch as the foolishness of the young man in throwing up the Law provokes his practical mind to speak.'

' He might take my word for the " young man's " ability. I want him to have the means of living, that he may write. He has genius.'

' He may have it. I like him, and have said so. If he were to go back to his law-stool, I have no doubt that Redworth would manage to help him.'

' And make a worthy ancient Braddock of a youth of splendid promise ! Have I sketched him too Saxon ? '

' It is the lens, and not the tribe, Tony.'

THE CANTATRICE was not alluded to any more ; but Emma's disapproval blocked the current of composition, already subject to chokings in the brain of the author. Diana stayed three days at Copsley, one longer than she

had intended, so that Arthur Rhodes might have his fill of
country air.

'I would keep him, but I should be no companion for
him,' Emma said.

'I suspect the gallant squire is only to be satisfied by
landing me safely,' said Diana, and that small remark
grated, though Emma saw the simple meaning. When
they parted, she kissed her Tony many times. Tears were
in her eyes. It seemed to Diana that she was anxious to
make amends for the fit of alienation, and she was kissed
in return warmly, quite forgiven, notwithstanding the
deadly blank she had caused in the imagination of the
writer for pay, distracted by the squabbles of Debit and
Credit.

Diana chatted spiritedly to young Rhodes on their drive
to the train. She was profoundly discouraged by Emma's
disapproval of her work. It wanted but that one drop to
make a recurrence to the work impossible. There it must
lie ! And what of the aspects of her household ?—Perhaps, after all, the Redworths of the world are right, and
Literature as a profession is a delusive pursuit. She did
not assent to it without hostility to the world's Redworths.
—'They have no sensitiveness, we have too much. We
are made of bubbles that a wind will burst, and as the
wind is always blowing, your practical Redworths have
their crow of us.'

She suggested advice to Arthur Rhodes upon the
prudence of his resuming the yoke of the Law.

He laughed at such a notion, saying that he had some
expectations of money to come.

'But I fear,' said he, ' that Lady Dunstane is very very
ill. She begged me to keep her informed of your address.'

Diana told him he was one of those who should know it
whithersoever she went. She spoke impulsively, her sentiments of friendliness for the youth being temporarily

s

brightened by the strangeness of Emma's conduct in deputing it to him to fulfil a duty she had never omitted. ' What can she think I am going to do ! '

On her table at home lay a letter from Mr. Warwick. She read it hastily in the presence of Arthur Rhodes, having at a glance at the handwriting anticipated the proposal it contained and the official phrasing.

Her gallant squire was invited to dine with her that evening, costume excused.

They conversed of Literature as a profession, of poets dead and living, of politics, which he abhorred and shied at, and of his prospects. He wrote many rejected pages, enjoyed an income of eighty pounds per annum, and eked out a subsistence upon the modest sum his pen procured him ; a sum extremely insignificant ; but great Nature was his own, the world was tributary to him, the future his bejewelled and expectant bride. Diana envied his youthfulness. Nothing is more enviable, nothing richer to the mind, than the aspect of a cheerful poverty. How much nobler it was, contrasted with Redworth's amassing of wealth !

When alone, she went to her bedroom and tried to write, tried to sleep. Mr. Warwick's letter was looked at. It seemed to indicate a threat ; but for the moment it did not disturb her so much as the review of her moral prostration. She wrote some lines to her lawyers, quoting one of Mr. Warwick's sentences. That done, his letter was dismissed. Her intolerable languor became alternately a defeating drowsiness and a fever. She succeeded in the effort to smother the absolute cause : it was not suffered to show a front ; at the cost of her knowledge of a practised self-deception. ' I wonder whether the world is as bad as a certain class of writers tell us ! ' she sighed in weariness, and mused on their soundings and probings of poor humanity, which the world accepts for the very bottom-

truth if their dredge brings up sheer refuse of the abomin-
able.  The world imagines those to be at our nature's
depths who are impudent enough to expose its muddy
shallows.  She was in the mood for such a kind of writing :
she could have started on it at once but that the theme was
wanting ; and it may count on popularity, a great repute
for penetration.  It is true of its kind, though the dredging
of nature is the miry form of art.  When it flourishes we
may be assured we have been overenamelling the higher
forms.  She felt, and shuddered to feel, that she could
draw from dark stores.  Hitherto in her works it had been
a triumph of the good.  They revealed a gaping deficiency
of the subtle insight she now possessed.  ' Exhibit
humanity as it is, wallowing, sensual, wicked, behind the
mask,' a voice called to her ; she was allured by the contemplation of the wide-mouthed old dragon Ego, whose
portrait, decently painted, establishes an instant touch of
exchange between author and public, the latter detected
and confessing.  Next to the pantomime of Humour and
Pathos, a cynical surgical knife at the human bosom
seems the surest talisman for this agreeable exchange ; and
she could cut.  She gave herself a taste of her powers.
She cut at herself mercilessly, and had to bandage the
wound in a hurry to keep in life.

Metaphors were her refuge.  Metaphorically she could
allow her mind to distinguish the struggle she was undergoing, sinking under it.  The banished of Eden had to put
on metaphors, and the common use of them has helped
largely to civilize us.  The sluggish in intellect detest
them, but our civilization is not much indebted to that
major faction.  Especially are they needed by the
pedestalled woman in her conflict with the natural.
Diana saw herself through the haze she conjured up.
' Am I worse than other women ? ' was a piercing twi-
thought.  Worse, would be hideous isolation.  The not

worse, abased her sex. She could afford to say that the world was bad : not that women were.

Sinking deeper, an anguish of humiliation smote her to a sense of drowning. For what if the poetic ecstasy on her Salvatore heights had not been of origin divine ? had sprung from other than spiritual founts ? had sprung from the reddened sources she was compelled to conceal ? Could it be ? She would not believe it. But there was matter to clip her wings, quench her light, in the doubt.

She fell asleep like the wrecked flung ashore.

Danvers entered her room at an early hour for London to inform her that Mr. Percy Dacier was below, and begged permission to wait.

Diana gave orders for breakfast to be proposed to him. She lay staring at the wall until it became too visibly a reflection of her mind.


## CHAPTER XXV

### ONCE MORE THE CROSSWAYS AND A CHANGE OF TURNINGS

THE suspicion of his having come to impart the news of his proximate marriage ultimately endowed her with sovereign calmness. She had need to think it, and she did. Tea was brought to her while she dressed ; she descended the stairs revolving phrases of happy congratulation and the world's ordinary epigrams upon the marriage-tie, neatly mixed.

They read in one another's faces a different meaning from the empty words of excuse and welcome. Dacier's expressed the buckling of a strong set purpose ; but, grieved by the look of her eyes, he wasted a moment to say : ' You have not slept. You have heard . . . ? '

' What ? ' said she, trying to speculate ; and that was a sufficient answer.

' I hadn't the courage to call last night ; I passed the windows. Give me your hand, I beg.'

She gave her hand in wonderment, and more wonderingly felt it squeezed. Her heart began the hammerthump. She spoke an unintelligible something ; saw herself melting away to utter weakness—pride, reserve, simple prudence, all going ; crumbled ruins where had stood a fortress imposing to men. Was it love ? Her heart thumped shiveringly.

He kept her hand, indifferent to the gentle tension.

' This is the point : I cannot live without you. I have gone on . . . Who was here last night ? Forgive me.'

' You know Arthur Rhodes.'

' I saw him leave the door at eleven. Why do you torture me ? There 's no time to lose now. You will be claimed. Come, and let us two cut the knot. It is the best thing in the world for me—the only thing. Be brave ! I have your hand. Give it for good, and for heaven's sake don't play the sex. Be yourself. Dear soul of a woman ! I never saw the soul in one but in you. I have waited : nothing but the dread of losing you sets me speaking now. And for you to be sacrificed a second time to that——! Oh, no ! You know you can trust me. On my honour, I take breath from you. You are my better in everything— guide, goddess, dearest heart ! Trust me ; make me master of your fate.'

' But my friend ! ' the murmur hung in her throat. He was marvellously transformed ; he allowed no space for the arts of defence and evasion.

' I wish I had the trick of courting. There 's not time ; and I 'm a simpleton at the game. We can start this evening. Once away, we leave it to them to settle the matter, and then you are free, and mine to the death.'

'But speak, speak! What is it?' Diana said.

'That if we delay, I'm in danger of losing you altogether.'

Her eyes lightened: 'You mean that you have heard he has determined . . . ?'

'There's a process of the law. But stop it. Just this one step, and it ends. Whether intended or not, it hangs over you, and you will be perpetually tormented. Why waste your whole youth?—and mine as well! For I am bound to you as much as if we had stood at the altar—where we will stand together the instant you are free.'

'But where have you heard . . . ?'

'From an intimate friend. I will tell you—sufficiently intimate—from Lady Wathin. Nothing of a friend, but I see this woman at times. She chose to speak of it to me—it doesn't matter why. She is in his confidence, and pitched me a whimpering tale. Let those people chatter. But it's exactly for those people that you are hanging in chains, all your youth shrivelling. Let them shout their worst! It's the bark of a day; and you won't hear it; half a year, and it will be over, and I shall bring you back—the husband of the noblest bride in Christendom! You don't mistrust me?'

'It is not that,' said she. 'But now drop my hand. I am imprisoned.'

'It's asking too much. I've lost you too many times. I have the hand and I keep it. I take nothing but the hand. It's the hand I want. I give you mine. I love you. Now I know what love is!—and the word carries nothing of its weight. Tell me you do not doubt my honour.'

'Not at all. But be rational. I must think, and I cannot while you keep my hand.'

He kissed it. 'I keep my own against the world.'

A cry of rebuke swelled to her lips at his conqueror's

tone. It was not uttered, for directness was in his character and his wooing loyal—save for bitter circumstances,
delicious to hear ; and so narrow was the ring he had
wound about her senses, that her loathing of the circumstances pushed her to acknowledge within her bell of a
heart her love for him.

He was luckless enough to say : ' Diana ! '

It rang horridly of her husband. She drew her hand to
loosen it, with repulsing brows. ' Not that name ! '

Dacier was too full of his honest advocacy of the passionate lover to take a rebuff. There lay his unconscious
mastery, where the common arts of attack would have
tripped him with a quick-witted woman, and where a man
of passion, not allowing her to succumb in dignity, would
have alarmed her to the breaking loose from him.

' Lady Dunstane calls you Tony.'

' She is my dearest and oldest friend.'

' You and I don't count by years. You are the dearest
to me on earth, Tony ! '

She debated as to forbidding that name.

The moment's pause wrapped her in a mental hurricane,
out of which she came with a heart stopped, her olive
cheeks ashen-hued. She had seen that the step was
possible.

' Oh ! Percy, Percy, are we mad ? '

' Not mad. We take what is ours. Tell me, have I
ever, ever disrespected you ? You were sacred to me ;
and you are, though now the change has come. Look back
on it—it is time lost, years that are dust. But look forward, and you cannot imagine our separation. What I
propose is plain sense for us two. Since Rovio, I have
been at your feet. Have I not some just claim for recompense ? Tell me ! Tony ! '

The sweetness of the secret name, the privileged name,
in his mouth stole through her blood, melting resistance.

She had consented. The swarthy flaming of her face avowed it even more than the surrender of her hand. He gained much by claiming little : he respected her, gave her no touches of fright and shame ; and it was her glory to fall with pride. An attempt at a caress would have awakened her view of the whitherward : but she was treated as a sovereign lady rationally advised.

' Is it since Rovio, Percy ? '

' Since the morning when you refused me one little flower.'

' If I had given it, you might have been saved ! '

' I fancy I was doomed from the beginning.'

' I was worth a thought ? '

' Worth a life ! worth ten thousand ! '

' You have reckoned it all like a sane man :—family, position, the world, the scandal ? '

' All. I have long known that you were the mate for me. You have to weather a gale, Tony. It won't last. My dearest ! it won't last many months. I regret the trial for you, but I shall be with you, burning for the day to reinstate you and show you the queen you are.'

' Yes, we two can have no covert dealings, Percy,' said Diana. They would be hateful—baseness ! Rejecting any baseness, it seemed to her that she stood in some brightness. The light was of a lurid sort. She called on her heart to glory in it as the light of tried love, the love that defied the world. Her heart rose. She and he would at a single step give proof of their love for one another : and this kingdom of love—how different from her recent craven languors !—this kingdom awaited her, was hers for one word ; and beset with the oceans of enemies, it was unassailable. If only they were true to the love they vowed, no human force could subvert it : and she doubted him as little as of herself. This new kingdom of love,

never entered by her, acclaiming her, was well-nigh unimaginable, in spite of the many hooded messengers it had
despatched to her of late.  She could hardly believe that
it had come.

' But see me as I am,' she said ;  she faltered it through
her direct gaze on him.

' With chains to strike off ?  Certainly ;  it is done,'
he replied.

' Rather heavier than those of the slave-market !  I am
the deadest of burdens.  It means that your enemies, personal—if you have any, and political—you have numbers,
will raise a cry. . . . Realize it.  You may still be my
friend.  I forgive the bit of wildness.'

She provoked a renewed kissing of her hand ;  for magnanimity in love is an overflowing danger ;  and when he
said : ' The burden you have to bear outweighs mine out
of all comparison.  What is it to a man—a public man or
not !  The woman is always the victim.  That 's why I
have held myself in so long ' :—her strung frame softened.
She half yielded to the tug on her arm.

' Is there no talking for us without foolishness ? ' she
murmured.  The foolishness had wafted her to sea, far
from sight of land.  ' Now sit, and speak soberly.  Discuss
the matter.—Yes, my hand, but I must have my wits.
Leave me free to use them till we choose our path.  Let it
be the brains between us, as far as it can.  You ask me to
join my fate to yours.  It signifies a sharp battle for you,
dear friend ;  perhaps the blighting of the most promising
life in England.  One question is, can I countervail the
burden I shall be, by such help to you as I can afford ?
Burden, is no word—I rake up a buried fever.  I have
partially lived it down, and instantly I am covered with
spots.  The old false charges and this plain offence make a
monster of me.'

' And meanwhile you are at the disposal of the man who

falsely charged you and armed the world against you,' said
Dacier.

'I can fly. The world is wide.'

'Time slips. Your youth is wasted. If you escape the
man, he will have triumphed in keeping you from me.
And I thirst for you ; I look to you for aid and counsel ; I
want my mate. You have not to be told how you inspire
me ? I am really less than half myself without you. If
I am to do anything in the world, it must be with your aid,
you beside me. Our hands are joined : one leap ! Do
you not see that after . . . well, it cannot be friendship.
It imposes rather more on me than I can bear. You are
not the woman to trifle ; nor I, Tony, the man for it with a
woman like you. You are my spring of wisdom. You
interdict me altogether—can you ?—or we unite our fates,
like these hands now. Try to get yours away ! '

Her effort ended in a pressure. Resistance, nay, to hesitate at the joining of her life with his after her submission
to what was a scorching fire in memory, though it was less
than an embrace, accused her of worse than foolishness.

'Well, then,' said she, ' wait three days. Deliberate.
Oh ! try to know yourself, for your clear reason to guide
you. Let us be something better than the crowd abusing
us, not simple creatures of impulse—as we choose to call
the animal. What if we had to confess that we took to
our heels the moment the idea struck us ! Three days.
We may then pretend to a philosophical resolve. Then
come to me : or write to me.'

'How long is it since the old Rovio morning, Tony ? '

'An age.'

'Date my deliberations from that day.'

The thought of hers having to be dated possibly from an
earlier day, robbed her of her summit of feminine isolation,
and she trembled, chilled and flushed ; she lost all anchor-
age.

'So it must be to-morrow,' said he, reading her closely, 'not later. Better at once. But women are not to be hurried.'

'Oh! don't class me, Percy, pray! I think of you, not of myself.'

'You suppose that in a day or two I might vary?'

She fixed her eyes on him, expressing certainty of his unalterable stedfastness. The look allured. It changed: her head shook. She held away and said: 'No, leave me; leave me, dear, dear friend. Percy, my dearest! I will not "play the sex." I am yours if . . . if it is your wish. It may as well be to-morrow. Here I am useless; I cannot write, not screw a thought from my head. I dread that "process of the Law" a second time. To-morrow, if it must be. But no impulses. Fortune is blind; she may be kind to us. The blindness of Fortune is her one merit, and fools accuse her of it, and they profit by it! I fear we all of us have our turn of folly: we throw the stake for good luck. I hope my sin is not very great. I know my position is desperate. I feel a culprit. But I am sure I have courage, perhaps brains to help. At any rate, I may say this: I bring no burden to my lover that he does not know of.'

Dacier pressed her hand. 'Money we shall have enough. My uncle has left me fairly supplied.'

'What would he think?' said Diana, half in a glimpse of meditation.

'Think me the luckiest of the breeched. I fancy I hear him thanking you for "making a man" of me.'

She blushed. Some such phrase might have been spoken by Lord Dannisburgh.

'I have but a poor sum of money,' she said. 'I may be able to write abroad. Here I cannot—if I am to be persecuted.'

'You shall write, with a new pen!' said Dacier. 'You

shall live, my darling Tony. You have been held too long
in this miserable suspension, neither maid nor wife, neither
woman nor stockfish. Ah! shameful. But we 'll right it.
The step, for us, is the most reasonable that could be considered. You shake your head. But the circumstances
make it so. Courage, and we come to happiness ! And
that, for you and me, means work. Look at the case of
Lord and Lady Dulac. It 's identical, except that she is
no match beside you : and I do not compare her antecedents with yours. But she braved the leap, and forced the
world to swallow it, and now, you see, she 's perfectly
honoured. I know a place on a peak of the Maritime Alps,
exquisite in summer, cool, perfectly solitary, no English,
snow round us, pastures at our feet, and the Mediterranean below. There ! my Tony. To-morrow night we
start. You will meet me—shall I call here ?—well, then
at the railway station, the South-Eastern, for Paris : say,
twenty minutes to eight. I have your pledge ? You
will come ? '

She sighed it, then said it firmly, to be worthy of him.
Kind Fortune, peeping under the edge of her bandaged
eyes, appeared willing to bestow the beginning of happiness upon one who thought she had a claim to a small taste
of it before she died. It seemed distinguishingly done, to
give a bite of happiness to the starving !

' I fancied when you were announced that you came for
congratulations upon your approaching marriage, Percy.'

' I shall expect to hear them from you to-morrow evening at the station, dear Tony,' said he.

The time was again stated, the pledge repeated. He
forbore entreaties for privileges, and won her gratitude.

They named once more the place of meeting and the
hour : more significant to them than phrases of intensest
love and passion. Pressing hands sharply for pledge of
good faith, they sundered.

She still had him in her eyes when he had gone. Her old world lay shattered ; her new world was up without a dawn, with but one figure, the sun of it, to light the swinging strangeness.

Was ever man more marvellously transformed ? or woman more wildly swept from earth into the clouds ? So she mused in the hum of her tempest of heart and brain, forgetful of the years and the conditions preparing both of them for this explosion.

She had much to do : the arrangements to dismiss her servants, write to house-agents and her lawyer, and write fully to Emma, write the enigmatic farewell to the Esquarts and Lady Pennon, Mary Paynham, Arthur Rhodes, Whitmonby (stanch in friendship, but requiring friendly touches), Henry Wilmers, and Redworth. He was reserved to the last, for very enigmatical adieux : he would hear the whole story from Emma ; must be left to think as he liked.

The vague letters were excellently well composed : she was going abroad, and knew not when she would return ; bade her friends think the best they could of her in the meantime. Whitmonby was favoured with an anecdote, to be read as an apologue by the light of subsequent events. But the letter to Emma tasked Diana. Intending to write fully, her pen committed the briefest sentences : the tenderness she felt for Emma wakening her heart to sing that she was loved, loved, and knew love at last ; and Emma's foreseen antagonism to the love and the step it involved rendered her pleadings in exculpation a stammered confession of guiltiness, ignominious, unworthy of the pride she felt in her lover. ' I am like a cartridge rammed into a gun, to be discharged at a certain hour tomorrow,' she wrote ; and she sealed a letter so frigid that she could not decide to post it. All day she imagined hearing a distant cannonade. The light of the day following was not like earthly light.  Danvers assured her there was no fog in London.

'London is insupportable ;  I am going to Paris, and shall send for you in a week or two,' said Diana.

'Allow me to say, ma'am, that you had better take me with you,' said Danvers.

'Are you afraid of travelling by yourself, you foolish creature ? '

'No, ma'am, but I don't like any hands to undress and dress my mistress but my own.'

'I have not lost the art,' said Diana, chafing for a magic spell to extinguish the woman, to whom, immediately pitying her, she said :  'You are a good faithful soul.  I think you have never kissed me.  Kiss me on the forehead.'

Danvers put her lips to her mistress's forehead, and was asked :  'You still consider yourself attached to my fortunes ? '

'I do, ma'am, at home or abroad ;  and if you will take me with you . . .'

'Not for a week or so.'

'I shall not be in the way, ma'am.'

They played at shutting eyes.  The petition of Danvers was declined ;  which taught her the more ;  and she was emboldened to say :  'Wherever my mistress goes, she ought to have her attendant with her.'  There was no answer to it but the refusal.

The hours crumbled slowly, each with a blow at the passages of retreat.  Diana thought of herself as another person, whom she observed, not counselling her, because it was a creature visibly pushed by the Fates.  In her own mind she could not perceive a stone of solidity anywhere, nor a face that had the appearance of our common life. She heard the cannon at intervals.  The things she said set Danvers laughing, and she wondered at the woman's mingled mirth and stiffness. Five o'clock struck. Her letters were sent to the post. Her boxes were piled from stairs to door. She read the labels, for her good-bye to the hated name of Warwick :—why ever adopted ! Emma might well have questioned why ! Women are guilty of such unreasoning acts ! But this was the close to that chapter. The hour of six went by. Between six and seven came a sound of knocker and bell at the street-door. Danvers rushed into the sitting-room to announce that it was Mr. Redworth. Before a word could be mustered, Redworth was in the room. He said : ' You must come with me at once ! '

## CHAPTER XXVI

### IN WHICH A DISAPPOINTED LOVER RECEIVES A MULTITUDE OF LESSONS

DACIER waited at the station, a good figure of a sentinel over his luggage and a spy for one among the inpouring passengers. Tickets had been confidently taken, the private division of the carriages happily secured. On board the boat she would be veiled. Landed on French soil, they threw off disguises, breasted the facts. And those ? They lightened. He smarted with his eagerness.

He had come well in advance of the appointed time, for he would not have had her hang about there one minute alone.

Strange as this adventure was to a man of prominent station before the world, and electrical as the turning-point of a destiny that he was given to weigh deliberately and far-sightedly, Diana's image strung him to the pitch of it. He looked nowhere but ahead, like an archer putting hand for his arrow.

Presently he compared his watch and the terminus clock.
She should now be arriving.   He went out to meet her and
do service.   Many cabs and carriages were peered into,
couples inspected, ladies and their maids, wives and their
husbands—an August exodus to the Continent.   Nowhere
the starry she.   But he had a fund of patience.   She was
now in some block of the streets.   He was sure of her, sure
of her courage.   Tony and recreancy could not go together.
Now that he called her Tony, she was his close comrade,
known ;   the name was a caress and a promise, breathing
of her, as the rose of sweetest earth.   He counted it to be
a month ere his family would have wind of the altered
position of his affairs, possibly a year to the day of his
making the dear woman his own in the eyes of the world.
She was dear past computation, womanly, yet quite unlike
the womanish women, unlike the semi-males courteously
called dashing, unlike the sentimental.   His present
passion for her lineaments declared her surpassingly
beautiful, though his critical taste was rather for the white
statue that gave no warmth.   She had brains and ardour,
she had grace and sweetness, a playful petulancy enlivening our atmosphere, and withal a refinement, a distinction,
not to be classed ;   and justly might she dislike the being
classed.   Her humour was a perennial refreshment, a
running well, that caught all the colours of light ;   her wit
studded the heavens of the recollection of her.   In his
heart he felt that it was a stepping down for the brilliant
woman to give him her hand ;   a condescension and an act
of valour.   She who always led or prompted when they
conversed, had now in her generosity abandoned the lead
and herself to him, and she deserved his utmost honouring.
But where was she ?   He looked at his watch, looked
at the clock.   They said the same : ten minutes to the
moment of the train's departure.
A man may still afford to dwell on the charms and merits

of his heart's mistress while he has ten minutes to spare. The dropping minutes, however, detract one by one from her individuality and threaten to sink her in her sex entirely. It is the inexorable clock that says she is as other women. Dacier began to chafe. He was unaccustomed to the part he was performing :—and if she failed him ? She would not. She would be late, though. No, she was in time ! His long legs crossed the platform to overtake a tall lady veiled and dressed in black. He lifted his hat ; he heard an alarmed little cry and retired. The clock said, Five minutes : a secret chiromancy in addition indicating on its face the word Fool. An odd word to be cast at him ! It rocked the icy pillar of pride in the background of his nature. Certainly standing solus at the hour of eight P.M., he would stand for a fool. Hitherto he had never allowed a woman the chance to posture him in that character. He strode out, returned, scanned every lady's shape, and for a distraction watched the veiled lady whom he had accosted. Her figure suggested pleasant features. Either she was disappointed or she was an adept. At the shutting of the gates she glided through, not without a fearful look around and at him. She disappeared. Dacier shrugged. His novel assimilation to the rat-rabble of amatory intriguers tapped him on the shoulder unpleasantly. A luckless member of the fraternity too ! The bell, the clock and the train gave him his title. ' And I was ready to fling down everything for the woman ! ' The trial of a superb London gentleman's resources in the love-passion could not have been much keener. No sign of her.

He who stands ready to defy the world, and is baffled by the absence of his fair assistant, is the fool doubled, so completely the fool that he heads the universal shout ; he does not spare himself. The sole consolation he has is to revile the sex. Women ! women ! Whom have they not made a fool of ! His uncle as much as any—and professing

T

to know them.  Him also! the man proud of escaping
their wiles.  'For this woman . . . ! ' he went on saying
after he had lost sight of her in her sex's trickeries.  The
nearest he could get to her was to conceive that the arrant
coquette was now laughing at her utter subjugation and
befooling of the man popularly supposed invincible.  If it
were known of him !  The idea of his being a puppet fixed
for derision was madly distempering.  He had only to ask
the affirmative of Constance Asper to-morrow !  A vision
of his determining to do it, somewhat comforted him.

Dacier walked up and down the platform, passing his
pile of luggage, solitary and eloquent on the barrow.
Never in his life having been made to look a fool, he felt
the red heat of the thing, as a man who has not blessedly
become acquainted with the swish in boyhood finds his
untempered blood turn to poison at a blow ; he cannot
healthily take a licking.  But then it had been so splendid
an insanity when he urged Diana to fly with him.  Any
one but a woman would have appreciated the sacrifice.

His luggage had to be removed.  He dropped his porter
a lordly fee and drove home.  From that astonished solitude he strolled to his Club.  Curiosity mastering the
wrath it was mixed with, he left his Club and crossed the
park southward in the direction of Diana's house, abusing
her for her inveterate attachment to the regions of Westminster.  There she used to receive Lord Dannisburgh ;
innocently, no doubt—assuredly quite innocently ; and
her husband had quitted the district.  Still it was rather
childish for a woman to be always haunting the seats of
Parliament.  Her disposition to imagine that she was
able to inspire statesmen came in for a share of ridicule ;
for when we know ourselves to be ridiculous, a retort in
kind, unjust upon consideration, is balm.  The woman
dragged him down to the level of common men ; that was
the peculiar injury, and it swept her undistinguished into

the stream of women.   In appearance, as he had proved
to the fellows at his Club, he was perfectly self-possessed,
mentally distracted and bitter, hating himself for it,
snapping at the cause of it.   She had not merely disappointed, she had slashed his high conceit of himself,
curbed him at the first animal dash forward, and he
champed the bit with the fury of a thwarted racer.

Twice he passed her house.   Of course no light was
shown at her windows.   They were scanned malignly.

He held it due to her to call and inquire whether there
was any truth in the report of Mrs. Warwick's illness.
Mrs. Warwick !   She meant to keep the name.

A maid-servant came to the door with a candle in her
hand revealing red eyelids.   She was not aware that her
mistress was unwell.   Her mistress had left home some
time after six o'clock with a gentleman.   She was unable
to tell him the gentleman's name.   William, the footman,
had opened the door to him.   Her mistress's maid Mrs.
Danvers had gone to the Play—with William.   She
thought that Mrs. Danvers might know who the gentleman was.   The girl's eyelids blinked, and she turned
aside.   Dacier consoled her with a piece of gold, saying
he would come and see Mrs. Danvers in the morning.

His wrath was partially quieted by the new speculations
offered up to it.   He could not .conjure a suspicion of
treachery in Diana Warwick ; and a treachery so foully
cynical !   She had gone with a gentleman.   He guessed on
all sides ;  he struck at walls, as in complete obscurity.

The mystery of her conduct troubling his wits for the
many hours was explained by Danvers.   With a sympathy
that she was at pains to show, she informed him that her
mistress was not at all unwell, and related of how Mr. Redworth had arrived just when her mistress was on the point
of starting for Paris and the Continent ; because poor Lady
Dunstane was this very day to undergo an operation under

the surgeons at Copsley, and she did not wish her mistress to be present, but Mr. Redworth thought her mistress ought to be there, and he had gone down thinking she was there, and then came back in hot haste to fetch her, and was just in time, as it happened, by two or three minutes.

Dacier rewarded the sympathetic woman for her intelligence, which appeared to him to have shot so far as to require a bribe. Gratitude to the person soothing his unwontedly ruffled temper was the cause of the indiscretion in the amount he gave.

It appeared to him that he ought to proceed to Copsley for tidings of Lady Dunstane. Thither he sped by the handy railway and a timely train. He reached the park-gates at three in the afternoon, telling his flyman to wait. As he advanced by short cuts over the grass, he studied the look of the rows of windows. She was within, and strangely to his clouded senses she was no longer Tony, no longer the deceptive woman he could in justice abuse. He and she, so close to union, were divided. A hand resembling the palpable interposition of Fate had swept them asunder. Having the poorest right—not any—to reproach her, he was disarmed, he felt himself a miserable intruder ; he summoned his passion to excuse him, and gained some unsatisfied repose of mind by contemplating its devoted sincerity ; which roused an effort to feel for the sufferer—Diana Warwick's friend. With the pair of surgeons named, the most eminent of their day, in attendance, the case must be serious. To vindicate the breaker of her pledge, his present plight likewise assured him of that, and nearing the house he adopted instinctively the funeral step and mood, just sensible of a novel smallness. For the fortifying testimony of his passion had to be put aside, he was obliged to disavow it for a simpler motive if he applied at the door. He stressed the motive, produced the sentiment, and passed thus naturally into

hypocrisy, as lovers precipitated by their blood among the
crises of human conditions are often forced to do.    He had
come to inquire after Lady Dunstane.    He remembered
that it had struck him as a duty, on hearing of her dangerous illness.

The door opened before he touched the bell.    Sir Lukin
knocked against him and stared.

' Ah !—who ?—you ? ' he said, and took him by the
arm and pressed him on along the gravel.    ' Dacier, are
you ?    Redworth 's in there.    Come on a step, come !
It 's the time for us to pray.    Good God !    There 's
mercy for sinners.    If ever there was a man ! . . . But,
oh, good God ! she 's in their hands this minute.    My
saint is under the knife.'

Dacier was hurried forward by a powerful hand.    ' They
say it lasts about five minutes, four and a half—or more !
My God !    When they turned me out of her room, she
smiled to keep me calm.    She said : " Dear husband " :—
the veriest wretch and brutallest husband ever poor
woman . . . and a saint ! a saint on earth !    Emmy ! '
Tears burst from him.

He pulled forth his watch and asked Dacier for the
time.

' A minute 's gone in a minute.    It 's three minutes and
a half.    Come faster.    They 're at their work !    It 's life
or death.    I 've had death about me.    But for a woman !
and your wife ! and that brave soul !    She bears it so.
Women *are* the bravest creatures afloat.    If they make
her shriek, it 'll be only if she thinks I 'm out of hearing.
No : I see her.    She bears it !—They mayn't have begun
yet.    It may all be over !    Come into the wood.    I must
pray.    I must go on my knees.'

Two or three steps in the wood, at the mossed roots of
a beech, he fell kneeling, muttering, exclaiming.

The tempest of penitence closed with a blind look at his

watch, which he left dangling. He had to talk to drug his thoughts.

' And mind you,' said he, when he had rejoined Dacier and was pushing his arm again, rounding beneath the trees to a view of the house, ' for a man steeped in damnable iniquity ! She bears it all for me, because I begged her, for the chance of her living. It 's my doing—this knife ! Macpherson swears there *is* a chance. Thomson backs him. But they 're at her, cutting ! . . . The pain must be awful—the mere pain ! The gentlest creature ever drew breath ! And women fear blood—and her own !— And a head ! She ought to have married the best man alive, not a——! I can't remember her once complaining of me—not once. A common donkey compared to her ! All I can do is to pray. And she knows the beast I am, and has forgiven me. There isn't a blessed text of Scripture that doesn't cry out in praise of her. And they cut and hack . . . ! ' He dropped his head. The vehement big man heaved, shuddering. His lips worked fast.

' She is not alone with them, unsupported.? ' said Dacier.

Sir Lukin moaned for relief. He caught his watch swinging and stared at it. ' What a good fellow you were to come ! Now 's the time to know your friends. There 's Diana Warwick, true as steel. Redworth came on her tip-toe for the Continent ; he had only to mention . . . Emmy wanted to spare her. She would not have sent— wanted to spare her the sight. I offered to stand by . . . Chased me out. Diana Warwick 's there :—worth fifty of me ! Dacier, I 've had my sword-blade tried by Indian horsemen, and I know what true as steel means. She 's there. And I know she shrinks from the sight of blood. My oath on it, she won't quiver a muscle ! Next to my wife, you may take my word for it, Dacier, Diana Warwick is the pick of living women. I could prove it. They go

together. I could prove it over and over. She's the
loyallest woman anywhere. Her one error was that
marriage of hers, and how she ever pitched herself into it,
none of us can guess.' After a while, he said : ' Look at
your watch.'

' Nearly twenty minutes gone.'

' Are they afraid to send out word ? It's that window ! '
He covered his eyes, and muttered, sighed. He became
abruptly composed in appearance. ' The worst of a black
sheep like me is, I'm such an infernal sinner, that Providence ! . . . But both surgeons gave me their word of
honour that there *was* a chance. A chance ! But it's
the end of me if Emmy—— Good God ! no ! the knife's
enough ; don't let her be killed ! It would be murder.
Here am I talking ! I ought to be praying. I should
have sent for the parson to help me ; I can't get the proper
words—bellow like a rascal trooper strung up for the cat.
It must be twenty-five minutes now. Who's alive now ! '

Dacier thought of the Persian Queen crying for news of
the slaughtered, with her mind on her lord and husband :
' Who is *not* dead ? ' Diana exalted poets, and here was
an example of the truth of one to nature, and of the poor
husband's depth of feeling. They said not the same
thing, but it was the same cry de profundis.

He saw Redworth coming at a quick pace.

Redworth raised his hand. Sir Lukin stopped. ' He's
waving ! '

' It's good,' said Dacier.

' Speak ! are you sure ? '

' I judge by the look.'

Redworth stepped unfalteringly.

' It's over, all well,' he said. He brushed his forehead
and looked sharply cheerful.

' My dear fellow ! my dear fellow ! ' Sir Lukin grasped
his hand. ' It's more than I deserve. Over ? She has

borne it!  She would have gone to heaven and left me——!
Is she safe ? '
  ' Doing well.'
  ' Have you seen the surgeons ? '
  ' Mrs. Warwick.'
  ' What did she say ? '
  ' A nod of the head.'
  ' You saw her ? '
  ' She came to the stairs.'
  ' Diana Warwick never lies.    She wouldn't lie, not with
a nod !   They 've saved Emmy—do you think ? '
  ' It looks well.'
  ' My girl has passed the worst of it ? '
  ' That 's over.'
  Sir Lukin gazed glassily.   The necessity of his agony
was to lean to the belief, at a beckoning, that Providence
pardoned him, in tenderness for what would have been his
loss.   He realized it, and experienced a sudden calm :
testifying to the positive pardon.
  ' Now, look here, you two fellows, listen half a moment,'
he addressed Redworth and Dacier ;   ' I 've been the
biggest scoundrel of a husband unhung, and married to a
saint ;  and if she 's only saved to me, I 'll swear to serve
her faithfully, or may a thunderbolt knock me to perdition !  and thank God for his justice !  Prayers are
answered, mind you, though a fellow may be as black
as a sweep.   Take a warning from me.   I 've had my
lesson.'
  Dacier soon after talked of going.   The hope of seeing
Diana had abandoned him, the desire was almost extinct.
  Sir Lukin could not let him go.   He yearned to preach
to him or any one from his personal text of the sinner
honourably remorseful on account of and notwithstanding
the forgiveness of Providence, and he implored Dacier and
Redworth by turns to be careful when they married of

how they behaved to the sainted women their wives ;
never to lend ear to the devil, nor to believe, as he had done,
that there is no such thing as a devil, for he had been the
victim of him, and he knew. The devil, he loudly proclaimed, has a multiplicity of lures, and none more deadly
than when he baits with a petticoat. He had been hooked,
and had found the devil in person. He begged them
urgently to keep his example in memory. By following
this and that wildfire he had stuck himself in a bog—a
common result with those who would not see the devil at
work upon them ; and it required his dear suffering saint
to be at death's doors, cut to pieces and gasping, to open
his eyes. But, thank heaven, they were opened at last !
Now he saw the beast he was : a filthy beast ! unworthy
of tying his wife's shoestring. No confessions could expose to them the beast he was. But let them not fancy
there was no such thing as an active DEVIL about the
world.

Redworth divined that the simply sensational man
abased himself before Providence and heaped his gratitude
on the awful Power in order to render it difficult for the
promise of the safety of his wife to be withdrawn.

He said : ' There is good hope '; and drew an admonition upon himself.

' Ah ! my dear good Redworth,' Sir Lukin sighed from
his elevation of outspoken penitence : ' you will see as I
do some day. It *is* the devil, think as you like of it.
When you have pulled down all the Institutions of the
Country, what do you expect but ruins ? That Radicalism of yours has its day. You have to go through a
wrestle like mine to understand it. You say, the day is
fine, let 's have our game. Old England pays for it !
Then you 'll find how you love the old land of your birth
—the noblest ever called a nation !—with your Corn Law
Repeals !—eh, Dacier ?—You 'll own it was the devil

tempted you. I hear you apologizing. Pray God, it mayn't be too late ! '

He looked up at the windows. ' She may be sinking ! '

' Have no fears,' Redworth said ; ' Mrs. Warwick would send for you.'

' She would. Diana Warwick would be sure to send. Next to my wife, Diana Warwick 's . . . she 'd send, never fear. I dread that room. I 'd rather go through a regiment of sabres—though it 's over now. And Diana Warwick stood it. The worst is over, you told me. By heaven ! women are wonderful creatures. But she hasn't a peer for courage. I could trust her—most extraordinary thing, that marriage of hers !—not a soul has ever been able to explain it :—trust her to the death.'

Redworth left them, and Sir Lukin ejaculated on the merits of Diana Warwick to Dacier. He laughed scornfully : ' And that 's the woman the world attacks for want of virtue ! Why, a fellow hasn't a chance with her, not a chance. She comes out in blazing armour if you unmask a battery. I don't know how it might be if she were in love with a fellow. I doubt her thinking men worth the trouble. I never met the man. But if she *were* to take fire, Troy 'd be nothing to it. I wonder whether we might go in : I dread the house.'

Dacier spoke of departing.

' No, no, wait,' Sir Lukin begged him. ' I was talking about women. They *are* the devil—or he makes most use of them : and you must learn to see the cloven foot under their petticoats, if you 're to escape them. There 's no protection in being in love with your wife ; I married for love ; I am, I always have been, in love with her ; and I went to the deuce. The music struck up and away I waltzed. A woman like Diana Warwick might keep a fellow straight, because she 's all round you ; she 's man and woman in brains ; and legged like a deer, and breasted

like a swan, and a regular sheaf of arrows in her eyes.
Dark women—ah ! But she has a contempt for us, you
know. That 's the secret of her.—Redworth 's at the
door. Bad ? Is it bad ? I never was particularly fond
of that house—hated it. I love it now for Emmy's sake.
I couldn't live in another—though I should be haunted.
Rather her ghost than nothing—though I 'm an infernal
coward about the next world. But if you 're right with
religion you needn't fear. What I can't comprehend in
Redworth is his Radicalism, and getting richer and
richer.'

' It 's not a vow of poverty,' said Dacier.

' He 'll find they don't coalesce, or his children will.
Once the masses are uppermost ! It 's a bad day, Dacier,
when we 've no more gentlemen in the land. Emmy
backs him, so I hold my tongue. To-morrow 's a Sunday.
I wish you were staying here ; I 'd take you to church
with me—we shirk it when we haven't a care. It couldn't
do you harm. I 've heard capital sermons. I 've always
had the good habit of going to church, Dacier. Now 's
the time for remembering them. Ah, my dear fellow, I 'm
not a parson. It would have been better for me if I had
been.'

And for you too ! his look added plainly. He longed to
preach ; he was impelled to chatter.

Redworth reported the patient perfectly quiet, breathing calmly.

' Laudanum ? ' asked Sir Lukin. ' Now there 's a
poison we 've got to bless ! And we set up in our wisdom
for knowing what is good for us ! '

He had talked his hearers into a stupefied assent to
anything he uttered.

' Mrs. Warwick would like to see you in two or three
minutes ; she will come down,' Redworth said to Dacier.

' That looks well, eh ? That looks bravely,' Sir Lukin

cried. ' Diana Warwick wouldn't leave the room without a certainty. I dread the look of those men ; I shall have to shake their hands ! And so I do, with all my heart : only— But God bless them ! But we must go in, if she 's coming down.'

They entered the house, and sat in the drawing-room, where Sir Lukin took up from the table one of his wife's Latin books, a Persius, bearing her marginal notes. He dropped his head on it, with sobs.

The voice of Diana recalled him to the present. She counselled him to control himself ; in that case he might for one moment go to the chamber-door and assure himself by the silence that his wife was resting. She brought permission from the surgeons and doctor, on his promise to be still.

Redworth supported Sir Lukin tottering out.

Dacier had risen. He was petrified by Diana's face, and thought of her as whirled from him in a storm, bearing the marks of it. Her underlip hung for short breaths ; the big drops of her recent anguish still gathered on her brows ; her eyes were tearless, lustreless ; she looked ancient in youth, and distant by a century, like a tall woman of the vaults, issuing white-ringed, not of our light.

She shut her mouth for strength to speak to him.

He said : ' You are not ill ? You are strong ? '

' I ? Oh, strong. I will sit. I cannot be absent longer than two minutes. The trial of her strength is to come. If it were courage, we might be sure. The day is fine ? '

' A perfect August day.'

' I held her through it. I am thankful to heaven it was no other hand than mine. She wished to spare me. She was glad of her Tony when the time came. I thought I was a coward—I could have changed with her to save her ;

I am a strong woman, fit to submit to that work. I should not have borne it as she did. She expected to sink under it. All her dispositions were made for death—bequests to servants and to . . . to friends : every secret liking they had, thought of ! '

Diana clenched her hands.

' I hope ! ' Dacier said.

' You shall hear regularly. Call at Sir William's house to-morrow. He sleeps here to-night. The suspense must last for days. It is a question of vital power to bear the shock. She has a mind so like a flying spirit that, just before the moment, she made Mr. Lanyan Thomson smile by quoting some saying of her Tony's.'

' Try by-and-by to recollect it,' said Dacier.

' And you were with that poor man ! How did he pass the terrible time ? I pitied him.'

' He suffered ; he prayed.'

' It was the best he could do. Mr. Redworth was as he always is at the trial, a pillar. Happy the friend who knows him for one ! He never thinks of himself in a crisis. He is sheer strength to comfort and aid. They will drive you to the station with Mr. Thomson. He returns to relieve Sir William to-morrow. I have learnt to admire the men of the knife ! No profession equals theirs in self-command and beneficence. Dr. Bridgenorth is permanent here.'

' I have a fly, and go back immediately,' said Dacier.

' She shall hear of your coming. Adieu.'

Diana gave him her hand. It was gently pressed.

A wonderment at the utter change of circumstances took Dacier passingly at the sight of her vanishing figure.

He left the house, feeling he dared have no personal wishes. It had ceased to be the lover's hypocrisy with him.

The crisis of mortal peril in that house enveloped its inmates, and so wrought in him as to enshroud the stripped outcrying husband, of whom he had no clear recollection, save of the man's agony. The two women, striving against death, devoted in friendship, were the sole living images he brought away ; they were a new vision of the world and our life.

He hoped with Diana, bled with her. She rose above him high, beyond his transient human claims. He envied Redworth the common friendly right to be near her. In reflection, long after, her simplicity of speech, washed pure of the blood-emotions, for token of her great nature, during those two minutes of their sitting together, was dearer, sweeter to the lover than if she had shown by touch or word that a faint allusion to their severance was in her mind ; and this despite a certain vacancy it created.

He received formal information of Lady Dunstane's progress to convalescence. By degrees the simply official tone of Diana's letters combined with the ceasing of them and the absence of her personal charm to make a gentleman not remarkable for violence in the passion so calmly reasonable as to think the dangerous presence best avoided for a time. Subject to fits of the passion, he certainly was, but his position in the world was a counselling spouse, jealous of his good name. He did not regret his proposal to take the leap ; he would not have regretted it if taken. On the safe side of the abyss, however, it wore a gruesome look to his cool blood.

## CHAPTER XXVII

### CONTAINS MATTER FOR SUBSEQUENT EXPLOSION

AMONG the various letters inundating Sir Lukin Dunstane upon the report of the triumph of surgical skill achieved by Sir William Macpherson and Mr. Lanyan

Thomson, was one from Lady Wathin, dated Adlands, an estate of Mr. Quintin Manx's in Warwickshire, petitioning for the shortest line of reassurance as to the condition of her dear cousin, and an intimation of the period when it might be deemed possible for a relative to call and offer her sincere congratulations : a letter deserving a personal reply, one would suppose. She received the following, in a succinct female hand corresponding to its terseness ; every *t* righteously crossed, every *i* punctiliously dotted, as she remarked to Constance Asper, to whom the communication was transferred for perusal :—

'DEAR LADY WATHIN,—Lady Dunstane is gaining strength. The measure of her pulse indicates favourably. She shall be informed in good time of your solicitude for her recovery. The day cannot yet be named for visits of any kind. You will receive information as soon as the house is open.

' I have undertaken the task of correspondence, and beg you to believe me,

'Very truly yours,

'D. A. WARWICK.'

Miss Asper speculated on the handwriting of her rival. She obtained permission to keep the letter, with the intention of transmitting it per post to an advertising interpreter of character in caligraphy.

Such was the character of the fair young heiress, exhibited by her performances much more patently than the run of a quill would reveal it.

She said, ' It is rather a pretty hand, I think.'

' Mrs. Warwick is a practised writer,' said Lady Wathin. ' Writing is her profession, if she has any. She goes to nurse my cousin. Her husband says she is an excellent nurse. He says what he can for her. But you must be in the last extremity, or she is ice. His appeal to her

has been totally disregarded. Until he drops down in
the street, as his doctor expects him to do some day,
she will continue her course; and even then . . .'
An adventuress desiring her freedom! Lady Wathin
looked. She was too devout a woman to say what she
thought. But she knew the world to be very wicked. Of
Mrs. Warwick, her opinion was formed.. She would not
have charged the individual creature with a criminal
design; all she did was to stuff the person her virtue
abhorred with the wickedness of the world, and that is a
common process in antipathy.

She sympathized, moreover, with the beautiful devotedness of the wealthy heiress to her ideal of man. It had
led her to make the acquaintance of old Lady Dacier, at
the house in town, where Constance Asper had first met
Percy; Mrs. Grafton Winstanley's house, representing
neutral territory or debateable land for the occasional
intercourse of the upper class and the climbing in the
professions or in commerce; Mrs. Grafton Winstanley
being on the edge of aristocracy by birth, her husband,
like Mr. Quintin Manx, a lord of fleets. Old Lady Dacier's
bluntness in speaking of her grandson would have shocked
Lady Wathin as much as it astonished, had she been less
of an ardent absorber of aristocratic manners. Percy was
plainly called a donkey, for hanging off and on with a
handsome girl of such expectations as Miss Asper. 'But
what you can't do with a horse, you can't hope to do with
a donkey.' She added that she had come for the purpose of seeing the heiress, of whose points of person she
delivered a judgement critically appreciative as a horse-
fancier's on the racing turf. 'If a girl like that holds to
it, she's pretty sure to get him at last. It's no use to
pull his neck down to the water.'

Lady Wathin delicately alluded to rumours of an
entanglement, an admiration he had, ahem.

' A married woman,' the veteran nodded. ' I thought
that was off ? She must be a clever intriguer to keep him
so long.'

' She is undoubtedly clever,' said Lady Wathin, and it
was mumbled in her hearing : ' The woman seems to have
a taste for our family.'

They agreed that they could see nothing to be done.
The young lady must wither, Mrs. Warwick have
her day. The veteran confided her experienced why
to Lady Wathin : ' All the tales you tell of a
woman of that sort are sharp sauce to the palates of
men.'

They might be, to the men of the dreadful gilded idle
class !

Mrs. Warwick's day appeared indefinitely prolonged,
judging by Percy Dacier's behaviour to Miss Asper.
Lady Wathin watched them narrowly when she had the
chance, a little ashamed of her sex, or indignant rather at
his display of courtliness in exchange for her open betrayal of her preference. It was almost to be wished that
she would punish him by sacrificing herself to one of her
many brilliant proposals of marriage. But such are
women !—precisely because of his holding back he
tightened the cord attaching him to her tenacious heart.
This was the truth. For the rest, he was gracefully
courteous ; an observer could perceive the charm he
exercised. He talked with a ready affability, latterly with
greater social ease ; evidently not acting the indifferent
conqueror, or so consummately acting it as to mask the
air. And yet he was ambitious, and he was not rich.
Notoriously was he ambitious, and with wealth to back
him, a great entertaining house, troops of adherents, he
would gather influence, be propelled to leadership. The
vexation of a constant itch to speak to him on the subject,
and the recognition that he knew it all as well as she,

tormented Lady Wathin.  He gave her comforting news
of her dear cousin in the Winter.

' You have heard from Mrs. Warwick ? ' she said.

He replied, ' I had the latest from Mr. Redworth.'

' Mrs. Warwick has relinquished her post ? '

' When she does, you may be sure that Lady Dunstane
is perfectly re-established.'

' She is an excellent nurse.'

' The best, I believe.'

' It is a good quality in sickness.'

' Proof of good all through.'

' Her husband might have the advantage of it.  His
state is really pathetic.  If she has feeling, and could
only be made aware, she might perhaps be persuaded to
pass from the friendly to the wifely duty.'

Mr. Dacier bent his head to listen, and he bowed.

He was fast in the toils ; and though we have assurance
that evil cannot triumph in perpetuity, the aspect of it
throning provokes a kind of despair.  How strange if
ultimately the lawyers once busy about the uncle were
to take up the case of the nephew, and this time reverse
the issue, by proving it !  For poor Mr. Warwick was
emphatic on the question of his honour.  It excited him
dangerously.  He was long-suffering, but with the slightest clue terrible.  The unknotting of the entanglement
might thus happen :—and Constance Asper would welcome her hero still.

Meanwhile there was actually nothing to be done : a
deplorable absence of motive villainy ; apparently an
absence of the beneficent Power directing events to their
proper termination.  Lady Wathin heard of her cousin's
having been removed to Cowes in May, for light Solent
and Channel voyages on board Lord Esquart's yacht.
She heard also of heavy failures and convulsions in the
City of London, quite unconscious that the Fates, or

agents of the Providence she invoked to precipitate the catastrophe, were then beginning cavernously their performance of the part of villain in Diana's history.

Diana and Emma enjoyed happy quiet sailings under May breezes on the many-coloured South-western waters, heart in heart again ; the physical weakness of the one, the moral weakness of the other, creating that mutual dependency which makes friendship a pulsating tie. Diana's confession had come of her letter to Emma. When the latter was able to examine her correspondence, Diana brought her the heap for perusal, her own sealed scribble, throbbing with all the fatal might-have-been, under her eyes. She could have concealed and destroyed it. She sat beside her friend, awaiting her turn, hearing her say at the superscription : ' Your writing, Tony ? ' and she nodded. She was asked : ' Shall I read it ? ' She answered : ' Read.' They were soon locked in an embrace. Emma had no perception of coldness through those brief dry lines ; her thought was of the matter.

' The danger is over now ? ' she said.

' Yes, that danger is over now.'

' You have weathered it ? '

' I love him.'

Emma dropped a heavy sigh in pity of her, remotely in compassion for Redworth, the loving and unbeloved. She was too humane and wise of our nature to chide her Tony for having her sex's heart. She had charity to bestow on women ; in defence of them against men and the world, it was a charity armed with the weapons of battle. The wife madly stripped before the world by a jealous husband, and left chained to the rock, her youth wasting, her blood arrested, her sensibilities chilled and assailing her under their multitudinous disguises, and for whom the world is merciless, called forth Emma's tenderest commiseration ; and that wife being Tony, and stricken with the curse of love, in other circumstances the blessing, Emma bled for her.

'But nothing desperate ? ' she said.

'No ; you have saved me.'

'I would knock at death's doors again, and pass them, to be sure of that.'

'Kiss me ; you may be sure. I would not put my lips to your cheek if there were danger of my faltering.'

'But you love him.'

'I do : and because I love him I will not let him be fettered to me.'

'You will see him.'

'Do not imagine that his persuasions undermined your Tony. I am subject to panics.'

'Was it your husband ? '

'I had a visit from Lady Wathin. She knows him. She came as peacemaker. She managed to hint at his authority. Then came a letter from him—of supplication, interpenetrated with the hint : a suffused atmosphere. Upon that, unexpected by me, my—let me call him so once, forgive me !—lover came. Oh ! he loves me, or did then. Percy ! He had been told that I should be claimed. I felt myself the creature I am—a wreck of marriage. But I fancied I could serve him :—I saw golden. My vanity was the chief traitor. Cowardice of course played a part. In few things that we do, where self is concerned, will cowardice not be found. And the hallucination colours it to seem a lovely heroism. That was the second time Mr. Redworth arrived. I am always at crossways, and he rescues me ; on this occasion unknowingly.'

'There 's a divinity . . .' said Emma. 'When I think of it I perceive that Patience is our beneficent fairy godmother, who brings us our harvest in the long result.'

' My dear, does she bring us our labourers' rations, to sustain us for the day ? ' said Diana.

' Poor fare, but enough.'

' I fear I was born godmotherless.'

' You have stores of patience, Tony ; only now and then fits of desperation.'

' My nature's frailty, the gap in it : we will give it no fine names—they cover our pitfalls. I am open to be carried on a tide of unreasonableness when the coward cries out. But I can say, dear, that after one rescue, a similar temptation is unlikely to master me. I do not subscribe to the world's decrees for love of the monster, though I am beginning to understand the dues of allegiance. We have ceased to write letters. You may have faith in me.'

' I have, with my whole soul,' said Emma.

So the confession closed ; and in the present instance there were not any forgotten chambers to be unlocked and ransacked for addenda confessions.

The subjects discoursed of by the two endeared the hours to them. They were aware that the English of the period would have laughed a couple of women to scorn for venturing on them, and they were not a little hostile in consequence, and shot their epigrams profusely, applauding the keener that appeared to score the giant bulk of their intolerant enemy, who holds the day, but not the morrow. Us too he holds for the day, to punish us if we have temporal cravings. He scatters his gifts to the abject ; tossing to us rebels bare dog-biscuit. But the life of the spirit is beyond his region ; we have our morrow in his day when we crave nought of him. Diana and Emma delighted to discover that they were each the rebel of their earlier and less experienced years, each a member of the malcontent minor faction, the salt of earth, to whom their salt must serve for nourishment, as they admitted, relishing it determinedly, not without gratification.

Sir Lukin was busy upon his estate in Scotland. They summoned young Arthur Rhodes to the island, that he might have a taste of the new scenes. Diana was always wishing for his instruction and refreshment; and Redworth came to spend a Saturday and Sunday with them, and showed his disgust of the idle boy, as usual, at the same time consulting them on the topic of furniture for the Berkshire mansion he had recently bought, rather vaunting the Spanish pictures his commissioner in Madrid was transmitting. The pair of rebels, vexed by his treatment of the respectful junior, took him for an incarnation of their enemy, and pecked and worried the man astonishingly. He submitted to it like the placable giant. Yes, he was a Liberal, and furnishing and decorating the house in the stability of which he trusted. Why not? We must accept the world as it is, try to improve it by degrees.—Not so : humanity will not wait for you, the victims are shrieking beneath the bricks of your enormous edifice, behind the canvas of your pictures. ' But you may really say that luxurious yachting is an odd kind of insurgency,' avowed Diana. ' It 's the tangle we are in.'

' It 's the coat we have to wear ; and why fret at it for being comfortable ? '

' I don't half enough, when I think of my shivering neighbours.'

' Money is of course a rough test of virtue,' said Redworth. ' We have no other general test.'

Money ! The ladies proclaimed it a mere material test ; Diana, gazing on sunny sea, with an especial disdain. And name us your sort of virtue. There is more virtue in poverty. He denied that. Inflexibly British, he declared money, and also the art of getting money, to be

hereditary virtues, deserving of their reward. The reward a superior wealth and its fruits ? Yes, the power
to enjoy and spread enjoyment : and let idleness envy
both ! He abused idleness, and by implication the
dilettante insurgency fostering it. However, he was
compensatingly heterodox in his view of the Law's persecution of women ; their pertinacious harpings on the theme
had brought him to that ; and in consideration of the
fact, as they looked from yacht to shore, of their being
rebels participating largely in the pleasures of the tyrant's
court, they allowed him to silence them, and forgave him.

Thoughts upon money and idleness were in confusion
with Diana. She had a household to support in London,
and she was not working ; she could not touch THE
CANTATRICE while Emma was near. Possibly, she again
ejaculated, the Redworths of the world were right : the
fruitful labours were with the mattock and hoe, or the
mind directing them. It was a crushing invasion of mate-
rialism, so she proposed a sail to the coast of France, and
thither they flew, touching Cherbourg, Alderney, Sark,
Guernsey, and sighting the low Brittany rocks. Memorable days to Arthur Rhodes. He saw perpetually the
one golden centre in new scenes. He heard her voice, he
treasured her sayings ; her gestures, her play of lip and
eyelid, her lift of head, lightest movements, were imprinted
on him, surely as the heavens are mirrored in the quiet
seas, firmly and richly as earth answers to the sprinkled
grain. For he was blissfully athirst, untroubled by a
hope. She gave him more than she knew of : a present
that kept its beating heart into the future ; a height of
sky, a belief in nobility, permanent through manhood
down to age. She was his foam-born Goddess of those
leaping waters ; differently hued, crescented, a different
influence. He had a happy week, and it charmed Diana
to hear him tell her so. In spite of Redworth, she had

faith in the fruit-bearing powers of a time of simple happiness, and shared the youth's in reflecting it.   Only the happiness must be simple, that of the glass to the lovely face : no straining of arms to retain, no heaving of the bosom in vacancy.

His poverty and capacity for pure enjoyment led her to think of him almost clingingly when hard news reached her from the quaint old City of London, which despises poverty and authorcraft and all mean adventurers, and bows to the lordly merchant, the mighty financier, Redworth's incarnation of the virtues.   Happy days on board the yacht Clarissa !   Diana had to recall them with effort. They who sow their money for a promising high percentage have built their habitations on the sides of the most eruptive mountain in Europe.   Ætna supplies more certain harvests, wrecks fewer vineyards and peaceful dwellings.   The greed of gain is our volcano.   Her wonder leapt up at the slight inducement she had received to embark her money in this Company : a South-American mine, collapsed almost within hearing of the trumpets of prospectus, after two punctual payments of the half-yearly interest.   A Mrs. Ferdinand Cherson, an elder sister of the pretty Mrs. Fryar-Gunnett, had talked to her of the cost of things one afternoon at Lady Singleby's garden-party, and spoken of the City as the place to help to swell an income, if only you have an acquaintance with some of the chief City men.   The great mine was named, and the rush for allotments.   She knew a couple of the Directors.   They vowed to her that ten per cent. was a trifle ; the fortune to be expected out of the mine was already clearly estimable at forties and fifties.   For their part they anticipated cent. per cent.   Mrs. Cherson said she wanted money, and had therefore invested in the mine.   It seemed so consequent, the cost of things being enormous !   She and her sister Mrs. Fryar-Gunnett

owned husbands who did their bidding, because of their
having the brains, it might be understood. Thus five
thousand pounds invested would speedily bring five
thousand pounds per annum. Diana had often dreamed
of the City of London as the seat of magic ; and taking
the City's contempt for authorcraft and the intangible as,
from its point of view, justly founded, she had mixed her
dream strangely with an ancient notion of the City's
probity. Her broker's shaking head did not damp her
ardour for shares to the full amount of her ability to
purchase. She remembered her satisfaction at the allot-
ment ; the golden castle shot up from this fountain mine.
She had a frenzy for mines and fished in some English
with smaller sums. 'I am now a miner,' she had exclaimed, between dismay at her audacity and the pride of
it. Why had she not consulted Redworth ? He would
peremptorily have stopped the frenzy in its first intoxicating effervescence. She, like Mrs. Cherson, like all
women who have plunged upon the cost of things, wanted
money. She naturally went to the mine. Address him
for counsel in the person of dupe, she could not ; shame
was a barrier. Could she tell him that the prattle of a
woman, spendthrift as Mrs. Cherson, had induced her to
risk her money ? Latterly the reports of Mrs. Fryar-
Gunnett were not of the flavour to make association of
their names agreeable to his hearing.

She had to sit down in the buzz of her self-reproaches
and amazement at the behaviour of that reputable City,
shrug, and recommence the labour of her pen. Material
misfortune had this one advantage ; it kept her from
speculative thoughts of her lover, and the meaning of his
absence and silence.

Diana's perusal of the incomplete CANTATRICE was done
with the cold critical eye interpreting for the public. She
was forced to write on nevertheless, and exactly in the

ruts of the foregoing matter. It propelled her. No
longer perversely, of necessity she wrote her best, convinced that the work was doomed to unpopularity, resolved that it should be at least a victory in style.  A fit
of angry cynicism now and then set her composing phrases
as baits for the critics to quote, condemnatory of the
attractiveness of the work.  Her mood was bad.  In
addition, she found Whitmonby cool ; he complained of
the coolness of her letter of adieu ; complained of her
leaving London so long.  How could she expect to be
his Queen of the London Salon if she lost touch of the
topics ?  He made no other allusion.  They were soon on
amicable terms, at the expense of flattering arts that she
had not hitherto practised.  But Westlake revealed unimagined marvels of the odd corners of the masculine
bosom.  He was the man of her circle the neatest in
epigram, the widest of survey, an Oriental traveller, a
distinguished writer, and if not personally bewitching,
remarkably a gentleman of the world.  He was wounded ;
he said as much.  It came to this : admitting that he
had no claims, he declared it to be unbearable for him to
see another preferred.  The happier was unmentioned, and
Diana scraped his wound by rallying him.  He repeated
that he asked only to stand on equal terms with the
others ; her preference of one was past his tolerance.
She told him that since leaving Lady Dunstane she had
seen but Whitmonby, Wilmers, and him.  He smiled
sarcastically, saying he had never had a letter from her,
except the formal one of invitation.

'Powers of blarney, have you forsaken a daughter of
Erin ? ' cried Diana.  'Here is a friend who has a craving for you, and I talk sense to him.  I have written to
none of my set since I last left London.'

She pacified him by doses of cajolery new to her tongue.
She liked him, abhorred the thought of losing any of her

friends, so the cajoling sentences ran until Westlake betrayed an inflammable composition, and had to be put out, and smoked sullenly. Her resources were tried in restoring him to reason. The months of absence from London appeared to have transformed her world. Tonans was moderate. The great editor rebuked her for her prolonged absence from London, not so much because it discrowned her as Queen of the Salon, but candidly for its rendering her service less to him. Everything she knew of men and affairs was to him stale.

' How do you get to the secrets ? ' she asked.

' By sticking to the centre of them,' he said.

' But how do you manage to be in advance and act the prophet ? '

' Because I will have them at any price, and that is known.'

She hinted at the peccant City Company.

' I think I have checked the mining mania, as I did the railway,' said he ; ' and so far it was a public service. There 's no checking of maniacs.'

She took her whipping within and without. ' On another occasion I shall apply to you, Mr. Tonans.'

' Ah, there was a time when you could have been a treasure to me,' he rejoined ; alluding of course to the Dannisburgh days.

In dejection, as she mused on those days, and on her foolish ambition to have a London house where her light might burn, she advised herself, with Redworth's voice, to quit the house, arrest expenditure, and try for happiness by burning and shining in the spirit : devoting herself, as Arthur Rhodes did, purely to literature. It became almost a decision.

Percy she had still neither written to nor heard from, and she dared not hope to meet him. She fancied a wish to have tidings of his marriage : it would be peace, if in

desolation.  Now that she had confessed and given her
pledge to Emma, she had so far broken with him as to
render the holding him chained a cruelty, and his reserve
whispered of a rational acceptance of the end between
them.  She thanked him for it ; an act whereby she was
instantly melted to such softness that a dread of him
haunted her.  Coward, take up your burden for armour !
she called to her poor dungeoned self wailing to have
common nourishment.  She knew how prodigiously it
waxed on crumbs ; nay, on the imagination of small
morsels.  By way of chastizing it, she reviewed her life,
her behaviour to her husband, until she sank backward
to a depth deprived of air and light.  That life with her
husband was a dungeon to her nature deeper than any
imposed by present conditions.  She was then a revolutionary to reach to the breath of day.  She had now to be
only not a coward, and she could breathe as others did.
' Women who sap the moral laws pull down the pillars of
the temple on their sex,' Emma had said.  Diana perceived something of her personal debt to civilization.  Her
struggles passed into the doomed CANTATRICE occupying
days and nights under pressure for immediate payment ;
the silencing of friend Debit, ridiculously calling himself
Credit, in contempt of sex and conduct, on the ground
that he was he solely by virtue of being she.  He had got
a trick of singing operatic solos in the form and style of
the delightful tenor Tellio, and they were touching in
absurdity, most real in unreality.  Exquisitely trilled,
after Tellio's manner,

> ' The tradesmen all beseech ye,
>     The landlord, cook and maid,
> Complete THE CANTATRICE,
>     That they may soon be paid,'

provoked her to laughter in pathos.  He approached,

posturing himself operatically, with perpetual new verses, rhymes to Danvers, rhymes to Madame Sybille, the cook. Seeing Tellio at one of Henry Wilmers' private concerts, Diana's lips twitched to dimples at the likeness her familiar had assumed. She had to compose her countenance to talk to him ; but the moment of song was the trial. Lady Singleby sat beside her, and remarked : ' You have always fun going on in you ! ' She partook of the general impression that Diana Warwick was too humorous to nurse a downright passion.

Before leaving, she engaged Diana to her annual garden-party of the closing season, and there the meeting with Percy occurred, not unobserved. Had they been over-heard, very little to implicate them would have been gathered. He walked in full view across the lawn to her, and they presented mask to mask.

' The beauty of the day tempts you at last, Mrs. Warwick.'

' I have been finishing a piece of work.'

Lovely weather, beautiful dresses : agreed. Diana wore a yellow robe with a black bonnet, and he commented on the becoming hues ; for the first time, he noticed her dress ! Lovely women ? Dacier hesitated. One he saw. But surely he must admire Mrs. Fryar-Gunnett ? And who steps beside her, transparently fascinated, with visage at three-quarters to the rays within her bonnet ? Can it be Sir Lukin Dunstane ? and beholding none but his charmer !

Dacier withdrew his eyes thoughtfully from the spectacle, and moved to woo Diana to a stroll. She could not restrain her feet ; she was out of the ring of her courtiers for the moment. He had seized his opportunity.

' It is nearly a year ! ' he said.

' I have been nursing nearly all the time, doing the work I do best.'

' Unaltered ? '

' A year must leave its marks.'

' Tony ! '

' You speak of a madwoman, a good eleven months dead. Let her rest. Those are the conditions.'

' Accepted, if I may see her.'

' Honestly accepted ? '

' Imposed fatally, I have to own. I have felt with you : you are the wiser. But, admitting that, surely we can meet. I may see you ? '

' My house has not been shut.'

' I respected the house. I distrusted myself.'

' What restores your confidence ? '

' The strength I draw from you.'

One of the Beauties at a garden-party is lucky to get as many minutes as had passed in quietness. Diana was met and captured. But those last words of Percy's renewed her pride in him by suddenly building a firm faith in herself. Noblest of lovers ! she thought, and brooded on the little that had been spoken, the much conveyed, for a proof of perfect truthfulness.

The world had watched them. It pronounced them discreet if culpable ; probably cold to the passion both. Of Dacier's coldness it had no doubt, and Diana's was presumed from her comical flights of speech. She was given to him because of the known failure of her other adorers. He in the front rank of politicians attracted her with the lustre of his ambition ; she him with her mingling of talent and beauty. An astute world ; right in the main, owing to perceptions based upon brute nature ; utterly astray in particulars, for the reason that it takes no count of the soul of man or woman. Hence its glee at a catastrophe ; its poor stock of mercy. And when no catastrophe follows, the prophet, for the honour of the profession, must decry her as cunning beyond aught yet revealed of a serpent sex.

Save for a word or two, the watchman might have over-heard and trumpeted his report of their interview at Diana's house. After the first pained breathing, when they found themselves alone in that room where they had plighted their fortunes, they talked allusively to define the terms imposed on them by Reason. The thwarted step was unmentioned ; it was a past madness. But Wisdom being recognized, they could meet. It would be hard if that were denied ! They talked very little of their position ; both understood the mutual acceptance of it ; and now that he had seen her and was again under the spell, Dacier's rational mind, together with his delight in her presence, compelled him honourably to bow to the terms. Only, as these were severe upon lovers, the innocence of their meetings demanded indemnification in frequency.

'Come whenever you think I can be useful,' said Diana.

They pressed hands at parting, firmly and briefly, not for the ordinary dactylology of lovers, but in sign of the treaty of amity.

She soon learnt that she had tied herself to her costly household.

## CHAPTER XXVIII

### DIALOGUE ROUND THE SUBJECT OF A PORTRAIT, WITH SOME INDICATIONS OF THE TASK FOR DIANA

An enamoured Egeria who is not a princess in her worldly state nor a goddess by origin has to play one of those parts which strain the woman's faculties past naturalness. She must never expose her feelings to her lover ; she must make her counsel weighty ; otherwise she is little his

nymph of the pure wells, and what she soon may be, the
world will say.  She has also, most imperatively, to
dazzle him without the betrayal of artifice, where simple
spontaneousness is beyond conjuring.  But feelings that
are constrained becloud the judgement besides arresting
the fine jet of delivery wherewith the mastered lover is
taught through his ears to think himself prompted, and
submit to be controlled, by a creature super-feminine.
She must make her counsel so weighty in poignant praises
as to repress impulses that would rouse her own ;  and her
betraying impulsiveness was a subject of reflection to
Diana after she had given Percy Dacier, metaphorically,
the key of her house.  Only as his true Egeria could she
receive him.  She was therefore grateful, she thanked and
venerated this noblest of lovers for his not pressing to the
word of love, and so strengthening her to point his mind,
freshen his moral energies and inspirit him.  His chivalrous acceptance of the conditions of their renewed intimacy was a radiant knightliness to Diana, elevating her
with a living image for worship :—he so near once to being
the absolute lord of her destinies !  How to reward him,
was her sole dangerous thought.  She prayed and strove
that she might give him of her best, to practically help
him ;  and she had reason to suppose she could do it, from
the visible effect of her phrases.  He glistened in repeating them ;  he had fallen into the habit ;  before witnesses
too ;  in the presence of Miss Paynham, who had taken
earnestly to the art of painting, and obtained her dear
Mrs. Warwick's promise of a few sittings for the sketch of
a portrait, near the close of the season.  'A very daring
thing to attempt,' Miss Paynham said, when he was
comparing her first outlines and the beautiful breathing
features.  'Even if one gets the face, the lips will seem
speechless, to those who know her.'

'If they have no recollection,' said Dacier.

' I mean, the endeavour should be to represent them at the moment of speaking.'

' Put it into the eyes.'   He looked at the eyes.

She looked at the mouth.   ' But it is the mouth, more than the eyes.'

He looked at the face.   ' Where there is character, you have only to study it to be sure of a likeness.'

' That is the task, with one who utters jewels, Mr. Dacier.'

' Bright wit, I fear, is above the powers of your art.'

' Still I feel it could be done.   See—now—that ! '

Diana's lips had opened to say : ' Confess me a model model : I am dissected while I sit for portrayal.   I must be for a moment like the frog of the two countrymen who were disputing as to the manner of his death, when he stretched to yawn, upon which they agreed that he had defeated the truth for both of them.   I am not quite inanimate.'

' Irish countrymen,' said Dacier.

' The story adds, that blows were arrested ;  so confer the nationality as you please.'

Diana had often to divert him from a too intent perusal of her features with sparkles and stories current or invented to serve the immediate purpose.

Miss Paynham was Mrs. Warwick's guest for a fortnight, and observed them together.   She sometimes charitably laid down her pencil and left them, having forgotten this or that.   They were conversing of general matters with their usual crisp precision on her return, and she was rather like the two countrymen, in debating whether it was excess of coolness or discreetness ;  though she was convinced of their inclinations, and expected love some day to be leaping up.   Diana noticed that she had no reminder for leaving the room when it was Mr. Redworth present.   These two had become very friendly, according to her hopes; and Miss Paynham was extremely solicitous to draw suggestions from Mr. Redworth and win his approval.

'Do I appear likely to catch the mouth now, do you think, Mr. Redworth?'

He remarked, smiling at Diana's expressive dimple, that the mouth was difficult to catch. He did not gaze intently. Mr. Redworth was the genius of friendship, 'the friend of women,' Mrs. Warwick had said of him. Miss Paynham discovered it, as regarded herself. The portrait was his commission to her, kindly proposed, secretly of course, to give her occupation and the chance of winning a vogue with the face of a famous Beauty. So many, however, were Mrs. Warwick's visitors, and so lively the chatter she directed, that accurate sketching was difficult to an amateurish hand. Whitmonby, Sullivan Smith, Westlake, Henry Wilmers, Arthur Rhodes, and other gentlemen, literary and military, were almost daily visitors when it became known that the tedium of the beautiful sitter required beguiling and there was a certainty of finding her at home. On Mrs. Warwick's Wednesday numerous ladies decorated the group. Then was heard such a rillet of dialogue without scandal or politics, as nowhere else in Britain; all vowed it subsequently; for to the remembrance it seemed magical. Not a breath of scandal, and yet the liveliest flow. Lady Pennon came attended by a Mr. Alexander Hepburn, a handsome Scot, at whom Dacier shot one of his instinctive keen glances, before seeing that the hostess had mounted a transient colour. Mr. Hepburn, in settling himself on his chair rather too briskly, contrived the next minute to break a precious bit of China standing by his elbow; and Lady Pennon cried out, with sympathetic anguish: 'Oh, my dear, what a trial for you!'

'Brittle is foredoomed,' said Diana, unruffled.

She deserved compliments, and would have had them if she had not wounded the most jealous and petulant of her courtiers.

' Then the Turk is a sapient custodian ! ' said Westlake, vexed with her flush at the entrance of the Scot.

Diana sedately took his challenge. ' *We*, Mr. Westlake, have the philosophy of ownership.'

Mr. Hepburn penitentially knelt to pick up the fragments, and Westlake murmured over his head : ' As long as it is we who are the cracked.'

' Did we not start from China ? '

' We were consequently precipitated to Stamboul.'

' You try to elude the lesson.'

' I remember my first paedagogue telling me so when he rapped the book on my cranium.'

' The mark of the book is not a disfigurement.'

It was gently worded, and the shrewder for it. The mark of the book, if not a disfigurement, was a characteristic of Westlake's fashion of speech. Whitmonby nodded twice, for signification of a palpable hit in that bout ; and he noted within him the foolishness of obtruding the remotest allusion to our personality when crossing the foils with a woman. She is down on it like the lightning, quick as she is in her contracted circle ; politeness guarding her from a riposte.

Mr. Hepburn apologized very humbly, after regaining his chair. Diana smiled and said : ' Incidents in a drawing-room are prize-shots at Dulness.'

' And in a dining-room too,' added Sullivan Smith. ' I was one day at a dinner-party, apparently of undertakers hired to mourn over the joints and the birds in the dishes, when the ceiling came down, and we all sprang up merry as crickets. It led to a pretty encounter and a real prize-shot.'

' Does that signify a duel ? ' asked Lady Pennon.

' 'Twould be the vulgar title, to bring it into discredit with the populace, my lady.'

' Rank me one of the populace then ! I hate duelling and rejoice that it is discountenanced.'

' The citizens, and not the populace, I think Mr. Sullivan Smith means,' Diana said. ' The citizen is generally right in morals. My father also was against the practice, when it raged at its " prettiest." I have heard him relate a story of a poor friend of his, who had to march out for a trifle, and said, as he accepted the invitation, " It 's all nonsense ! " and walking to the measured length, " It 's all nonsense, you know ! " and when lying on the ground, at his last gasp, " I told you it was all nonsense ! " '

Sullivan Smith leaned over to Whitmonby and Dacier amid the ejaculations, and whispered : ' A lady's way of telling the story !—and excuseable to her :—she had to *Jonah* the adjective. What the poor fellow said was . . .' he murmured the sixty-pounder adjective, as in the belly of the whale, to rightly emphasize his noun.

Whitmonby nodded to the superior relish imparted by the vigour of masculine veracity in narration. ' A story for its native sauce piquante,' he said.

' Nothing without it ! '

They had each a dissolving grain of contempt for women compelled by their delicacy to spoil that kind of story which demands the piquant accompaniment to flavour it racily and make it passable. For to see in-sipid mildness complacently swallowed as an excellent thing, knowing the rich smack of savour proper to the story, is your anecdotal gentleman's annoyance. But if the anecdote had supported him, Sullivan Smith would have let the expletive rest.

Major Carew Mahoney capped Mrs. Warwick's tale of the unfortunate duellist with another, that confessed the

practice absurd, though he approved of it ; and he cited
Lord Larrian's opinion : ' It keeps men braced to civil
conduct.'

' I would not differ with the dear old lord ; but no ! the
pistol is the sceptre of the bully,' said Diana.

Mr. Hepburn, with the widest of eyes on her in perpetuity, warmly agreed ; and the man was notorious among
men for his contrary action.

' Most righteously our Princess Egeria distinguishes her
reign by prohibiting it,' said Lady Singleby.

' And how,' Sullivan Smith sighed heavily, ' how, I 'd
ask, are ladies to be protected from the bully ? '

He was beset : ' So it was all for us ? all in consideration for our benefit ? '

He mournfully exclaimed : ' Why, surely ! '

' That is the funeral apology of the Rod, at the close of
every barbarous chapter,' said Diana.

' Too fine in mind, too fat in body ; that is a consequence with men, dear madam. The conqueror stands
to his weapons, or he loses his possessions.'

' Mr. Sullivan Smith jumps at his pleasure from the
special to the general, and will be back, if we follow him,
Lady Pennon. It is the trick men charge to women,
showing that they can resemble us.'

Lady Pennon thumped her knee. ' Not a bit. There 's
no resemblance, and they know nothing of us.'

' Women are a blank to them, I believe,' said Whitmonby, treacherously bowing ; and Westlake said :
' Traces of a singular scrawl have been observed when
they were held in close proximity to the fire.'

' Once, on the top of a coach,' Whitmonby resumed, ' I
heard a comely dame of the period when summers are
ceasing threatened by her husband with a divorce, for
omitting to put sandwiches in their luncheon-basket. She
made him the inscrutable answer : ' Ah, poor man ! you

will go down ignorant to your grave ! " We laughed,
and to this day I cannot tell you why.'

' That laugh was from a basket lacking provision ;—
and I think we could trace our separation to it,' Diana
said to Lady Pennon, who replied : ' They expose themselves ; they get no nearer to the riddle.'

Miss Courtney, a rising young actress, encouraged by a
smile from Mrs. Warwick, remarked : ' On the stage, we
have each our parts equally.'

' And speaking parts ; not personæ mutæ.'

' The stage has advanced in verisimilitude,' Henry
Wilmers added slyly ; and Diana rejoined : ' You recognize a verisimilitude of the mirror when it is in advance
of reality. Flatter the sketch, Miss Paynham, for a likeness to be seen. Probably there are still Old Conservatives who would prefer the personation of us by boys.'

' I don't know,' Westlake affected dubiousness. ' I
have heard that a step to the riddle is gained by a serious
contemplation of boys.'

' Serious ? '

' That is the doubt.'

' The doubt throws its light on the step ! '

' I advise them not to take any leap from their step,'
said Lady Pennon.

' It would be a way of learning that we are no wiser
than our sires ; but perhaps too painful a way,' Whitmonby observed. ' Poor Mountford Wilts boasted of
knowing women ; and he married. To jump into the
mouth of the enigma, is not to read it.'

' You are figures of conceit when you speculate on us,
Mr. Whitmonby.'

' An occupation of our leisure, my lady, for your
amusement.'

' The leisure of the humming-top, a thousand to the
minute, with the pretence that it sleeps ! ' Diana said.

'The sacrilegious hand to strip you of your mystery is withered as it stretches,' exclaimed Westlake. 'The sage and the devout are in accord for once.'

'And whichever of the two I may be, I 'm one of them, happy to do my homage blindfold!' Sullivan Smith waved the sign of it.

Diana sent her eyes over him and Mr. Hepburn, seeing Dacier. 'That rosy mediævalism seems the utmost we can expect.' An instant she saddened, foreboding her words to be ominous, because of suddenly thirsting for a modern cry from him, the silent. She quitted her woman's fit of earnestness, and took to the humour that pleased him. 'Aslauga's knight, at his blind man's buff of devotion, catches the hem of the tapestry and is found by his lady kissing it in a trance of homage five hours long! Sir Hilary of Agincourt, returned from the wars to his castle at midnight, hears that the châtellaine is away dancing, and remains with all his men mounted in the courtyard till the grey morn brings her back! Adorable! We had a flag flying in those days. Since men began to fret the riddle, they have hauled it down half-mast. Soon we shall behold a bare pole and hats on around it. That is their solution.'

A smile circled at the hearing of Lady Singleby say: 'Well! I am all for our own times, however literal the men.'

'We are two different species!' thumped Lady Pennon, swimming on the theme. 'I am sure, I read what they write of women! And their heroines!'

Lady Esquart acquiesced: 'We are utter fools or horrid knaves.'

'Nature's original hieroglyphs—which have that appearance to the peruser,' Westlake assented.

'And when they would decipher us, and they hit on one of our "arts," the literary pirouette they perform is

memorable.' Diana looked invitingly at Dacier. ' But
I for one discern a possible relationship and a likeness.'
  ' I think it exists—behind a curtain,' Dacier replied.
  ' Before the era of the Nursery. Liberty to grow ;
independence is the key of the secret.'
  ' And what comes after the independence ? ' he inquired.
  Whitmonby, musing that some distraction of an earnest
incentive spoilt Mrs. Warwick's wit, informed him : ' The
two different species then break their shallow armistice
and join the shock of battle for possession of the earth,
and we are outnumbered and exterminated, to a certainty.
So I am against independence.'
  ' Socially a Mussulman, subject to explosions ! ' Diana
said. ' So the eternal duel between us is maintained, and
men will protest that they are for civilization.   Dear me,
I should like to write a sketch of the women of the future
—don't be afraid !—the far future.   What a different
earth you will see ! '
  And very different creatures ! the gentlemen unanimously surmised.   Westlake described the fairer portion,
no longer the weaker ; frightful hosts.
  Diana promised him a sweeter picture, if ever she
brought her hand to paint it.
  ' You would be offered up to the English national hang-
man, Jehoiachim Sneer,' interposed Arthur Rhodes, evidently firing a gun too big for him, of premeditated
charging, as his patroness perceived ; but she knew him to
be smarting under recent applications of the swish of Mr.
Sneer, and that he rushed to support her.   She covered
him by saying : ' If he has to be encountered, he kills
none but the cripple,' wherewith the dead pause ensuing
from a dose of outlandish speech in good company was
bridged, though the youth heard Westlake mutter unpleasantly : ' Jehoiachim,' and had to endure a stare of

Dacier's, who did not conceal his want of comprehension of the place he occupied in Mrs. Warwick's gatherings.

'They know nothing of us whatever!' Lady Pennon harped on her dictum.

'They put us in a case and profoundly study the captive creature,' said Diana : 'but would any *man* understand this . . . ?' She dropped her voice and drew in the heads of Lady Pennon, Lady Singleby, Lady Esquart and Miss Courtney : ' Real woman's nature speaks. A maid of mine had a " follower." She was a good girl ; I was anxious about her and asked her if she could trust him. " Oh, yes, ma'am," she replied, " I can ; he 's quite like a female." I longed to see the young man, to tell him he had received the highest of eulogies.'

The ladies appreciatingly declared that such a tale was beyond the understandings of men. Miss Paynham primmed her mouth, admitting to herself her inability to repeat such a tale : an act that she deemed not ' quite like a lady.' She had previously come to the conclusion that Mrs. Warwick, with all her generous qualities, was deficient in delicate sentiment—owing perhaps to her coldness of temperament. Like Dacier also, she failed to comprehend the patronage of Mr. Rhodes : it led to suppositions ; indefinite truly, and not calumnious at all ; but a young poet, rather good-looking and well built, is not the same kind of wing-chick as a young actress, like Miss Courtney—Mrs. Warwick's latest shieldling : he is hardly enrolled for the reason that was assumed to sanction Mrs. Warwick's maid in the encouragement of her follower. Miss Paynham sketched on, with her thoughts in her bosom : a damsel castigatingly pursued by the idea of sex as the direct motive of every act of every person surrounding her ; deductively therefore that a certain form of the impelling passion, mild or terrible, or capricious, or it might be less pardonable, was unceasingly at work among the human couples up to decrepitude. And she too frequently hit the fact to doubt her gift of reading into them. Mr. Dacier was plain, and the state of young Mr. Rhodes ; and the Scottish gentleman was at least a vehement admirer. But she penetrated the breast of Mr. Thomas Redworth as well, mentally tore his mask of friendship to shreds. He was kind indeed in commissioning her to do the portrait. His desire for it, and his urgency to have the features exactly given, besides the infrequency of his visits of late, when a favoured gentleman was present, were the betraying signs. Deductively, moreover, the lady who inspired the passion in numbers of gentlemen and set herself to win their admiration with her lively play of dialogue, must be coquettish ; she could hold them only by coldness. Anecdotes, epigrams, drolleries, do not bubble to the lips of a woman who is under an emotional spell : rather they prove that she has the spell for casting. It suited Mr. Dacier, Miss Paynham thought : it was cruel to Mr. Redworth ; at whom, of all her circle, the beautiful woman looked, when speaking to him, sometimes tenderly.

' Beware the silent one of an assembly ! ' Diana had written. She did not think of her words while Miss Paynham continued mutely sketching. The silent ones, with much conversation around them, have their heads at work, critically perforce ; the faster if their hands are occupied ; and the point they lean to do is the pivot of their thoughts. Miss Paynham felt for Mr. Redworth.

Diana was unaware of any other critic present than him she sought to enliven, not unsuccessfully, notwithstanding his English objection to the pitch of the converse she led, and a suspicion of effort to support it :—just a doubt, with all her easy voluble run, of the possibility of naturalness

in a continuous cleverness.  But he signified pleasure,
and in pleasing him she was happy : in the knowledge
that she dazzled, was her sense of safety.  Percy hated
scandal ; he heard none.  He wanted stirring, cheering ;
in her house he had it.  He came daily, and as it was her
wish that new themes, new flights of converse, should
delight him and show her exhaustless, to preserve her
ascendancy, she welcomed him without consulting the
world.  He was witness of Mr. Hepburn's presentation
of a costly China vase, to repair the breach in her array
of ornaments, and excuse a visit.  Judging by the absence
of any blow within, he saw not a sign of coquettry.  Some
such visit had been anticipated by the prescient woman,
so there was no reddening.  She brought about an exchange of sentences between him and her furious admirer,
sparing either of them a glimpse of which was the sacrifice
to the other, amusing them both.  Dacier could allow
Mr. Hepburn to outsit him ; and he left them, proud of
his absolute confidence in her.

She was mistaken in imagining that her social vivacity,
mixed with comradeship of the active intellect, was the
charm which kept Mr. Percy Dacier temperate when he
well knew her to distinguish him above her courtiers.
Her powers of dazzling kept him tame ; they did not
stamp her mark on him.  He was one of the order of
highly polished men, ignorant of women, who are impressed for long terms by temporary flashes, that hold
them bound until a fresh impression comes, to confirm
or obliterate the preceding.  Affairs of the world he could
treat competently ;  he had a head for high politics and
the management of men ;  the feminine half of the world
was a confusion and a vexation to his intelligence, char-
acterless ;  and one woman at last appearing decipher-
able, he fancied it must be owing to her possession of
character, a thing prized the more in women because of

his latent doubt of its existence. Character, that was
the mark he aimed at ; that moved him to homage as
neither sparkling wit nor incomparable beauty, nor the
unusual combination, did. To be distinguished by a
woman of character (beauty and wit for jewellery), was
his minor ambition in life, and if Fortune now gratified
it, he owned to the flattery. It really seemed by every
test that she had the quality. Since the day when he
beheld her by the bedside of his dead uncle, and that one
on the French sea-sands, and again at Copsley, ghostly
white out of her wrestle with death, bleeding holy sweat
of brow for her friend, the print of her features had been
on him as an index of depth of character, imposing
respect and admiration—a sentiment imperilled by her
consent to fly with him. Her subsequent reserve until
they met—by an accident that the lady at any rate was
not responsible for, proved the quality positively. And
the nature of her character, at first suspected, vanquished
him more, by comparison, than her vivid intellect, which
he originally, and still lingeringly, appreciated in condescension, as a singular accomplishment, thrilling at times,
now and then assailably feminine. But, after her consent
to a proposal that caused him retrospective worldly
shudders, and her composed recognition of the madness, a
character capable of holding him in some awe was real
majesty, and it rose to the clear heights, with her mental
attributes for satellites. His tendency to despise women
was wholesomely checked by the experience to justify
him in saying, Here is a worthy one ! She was health
to him, as well as trusty counsel. Furthermore, where
he respected, he was a governed man, free of the common
masculine craze to scale fortresses for the sake of lowering
flags. Whilst under his impression of her character, he
submitted honourably to the ascendancy of a lady whose
conduct suited him and whose preference flattered ;

whose presence was very refreshing ; whose letters were
a stimulant.   Her letters were really running well-waters,
not a lover's delusion of the luminous mind of his lady.
They sparkled in review and preserved their integrity
under critical analysis.   The reading of them hurried
him in pursuit of her from house to house during the
autumn ;   and as she did not hint at the shadow his
coming cast on her, his conscience was easy.   Regarding
their future, his political anxieties were a mountainous
defile, curtaining the outlook.   They met at Lockton,
where he arrived after a recent consultation with his
Chief, of whom, and the murmurs of the Cabinet, he
spoke to Diana openly, in some dejection.

'They might see he has been breaking with his party
for the last four years,' she said.   'The plunge to be taken
is tremendous.'

'But will he ?   He appears too despondent for a
header.'

'We cannot dance on a quaking floor.'

'No ;   it 's exactly that quake of the floor which gives
" much qualms," to me as well,' said Dacier.

'A treble Neptune's power ! ' she rejoined, for his
particular delectation.   'Enough if he hesitates.   I
forgive him his nausea.   He awaits the impetus, and it
will reach him, and soon.   He will not wait for the mob
at his heels, I am certain.   A Minister who does that, is
a post, and goes down with the first bursting of the dam.
He has tried compromise and discovered that it does not
appease the Fates ;   is not even a makeshift-mending at
this hour.   He is a man of nerves, very sensitively built ;
as quick—quicker than a woman, I could almost say,
to feel the tremble of the air—forerunner of imperative
changes.'

Dacier brightened fondly.   'You positively describe
him ;   paint him to the life, without knowing him ! '

'I have seen him; and if I paint, whose are the colours ? '

'Sometimes I repeat you to him, and I get all the credit,' said Dacier.

'I glow with pride to think of speaking anything that you repeat,' said Diana, and her eyes were proudly lustreful.

Their love was nourished on these mutual flatteries. Thin food for passion ! The innocence of it sanctioned the meetings and the appointments to meet. When separated they were interchanging letters, formally worded in the apostrophe and the termination, but throbbingly full : or Diana thought so of Percy's letters, with grateful justice ; for his manner of opening his heart in amatory correspondence was to confide important secret matters, up to which mark she sprang to reply in counsel. He proved his affection by trusting her ; his respect by his tempered style :—' A Greenland style of writing,' she had said of an unhappy gentleman's episto-lary compositions resembling it ; and now the same official baldness was to her mind Italianly rich ; it called forth such volumes.

Flatteries that were thin food for passion appeared the simplest exchanges of courtesy, and her meetings with her lover, judging by the nature of the discourse they held, so consequent to their joint interest in the great crisis antici-pated, as to rouse her indignant surprise and a turn for downright rebellion when the Argus world signified the fact of its having one eye, or more, wide open.

Debit and Credit, too, her buzzing familiars, insisted on an audience at each ear, and at the house-door, on her return to London.

## CHAPTER XXIX

### SHOWS THE APPROACHES OF THE POLITICAL AND THE DOMESTIC CRISIS IN COMPANY

THERE was not much talk of Diana between Lady Dunstane and her customary visitor Tom Redworth now. She was shy in speaking of the love-stricken woman, and more was in his mind for thought than for speech. She sometimes wondered how much he might know, ending with the reflection that little passing around was unknown to him. He had to shut his mind against thought, against all meditation upon Mrs. Warwick ; it was based scientifically when speculating and calculating, on the material element—a talisman. Men and women crossing the high seas of life he had found most readable under that illuminating inquiry, as to their means. An inspector of seaworthy ships proceeds in like manner. Whence would the money come ? He could not help the bent of his mind ; but he could avoid subjecting her to the talismanic touch. The girl at the Dublin Ball, the woman at the fire-grate of The Crossways, both in one were his Diana. Now and then, hearing an ugly whisper, his manful sympathy with the mere woman in her imprisoned liberty, defended her desperately from charges not distinctly formulated within him :—' She 's not made of stone.' That was a height of self-abnegation to shake the poor fellow to his roots ; but, then, he had no hopes of his own ; and he stuck to it. Her choice of a man like Dacier, too, of whom Redworth judged highly, showed nobility. She irradiated the man ; but no baseness could be in such an alliance. If allied, they were bound together for good. The tie—supposing a villain

world not wrong—was only not the sacred tie because of
impediments. The tie !—he deliberated, and said stoutly
No. Men of Redworth's nature go through sharp contests, though the duration of them is short, and the tussle
of his worship of this woman with the materialistic turn
of his mind was closed by the complete shutting up of
the latter under lock and bar ; so that a man, very little
of an idealist, was able to sustain her in the pure imagination—where she did almost belong to him. She
was his, in a sense, because she might have been his—but
for an incredible extreme of folly. The dark ring of the
eclipse cast by some amazing foolishness round the shining
crescent perpetually in secret claimed the whole sphere of
her, by what might have been, while admitting her lost
to him in fact. To Thomas Redworth's mind the lack
of perfect sanity in his conduct at any period of manhood,
was so entirely past belief that he flew at the circumstances confirming the charge, and had wrestles with the
angel of reality, who did but set him dreaming backward,
after flinging him.

He heard at Lady Wathin's that Mrs. Warwick was in
town for the winter. ' Mr. Dacier is also in town,' Lady
Wathin said, with an acid indication of the needless
mention of it. ' We have not seen him.' She invited
Redworth to meet a few friends at dinner. ' I think you
admire Miss Asper : in my idea a very saint among young
women ;—and you know what the young women of our
day are. She will be present. She is, you are aware,
England's greatest heiress. Only yesterday, hearing of
that poor man Mr. Warwick's desperate attack of illness—
heart !—and of his having no relative or friend to soothe
his pillow,—he is lying in absolute loneliness,—she offered
to go and nurse him ! Of course it could not be done. It
is not her place. The beauty of the character of a dear
innocent young girl, with every gratification at command,

who could make the offer, strikes me as unparalleled.  She
was perfectly sincere—she *is* sincerity.  She asked at
once, Where is he ?  She wished me to accompany her
on a first visit.  I saw a tear.'

Redworth had called at Lady Wathin's for information
of the state of Mr. Warwick, concerning which a rumour
was abroad.  No stranger to the vagrant compassionate-
ness of sentimentalists ;—rich, idle, conscience-pricked or
praise-catching ;—he was unmoved by the tale that Miss
Asper had proposed to go to Mr. Warwick's sick-bed in the
uniform of a Sister of Charity :—' Speaking French ! '
Lady Wathin exclaimed ; and his head rocked, as he said :
' An Englishman would not be likely to know better.'

' She speaks exquisite French—all European lan-
guages, Mr. Redworth.  She does not pretend to *wit*.
To my thinking, depth of sentiment is a far more feminine
accomplishment.  It assuredly will be found a greater
treasure.'

The modest man (modest in such matters) was led by
degrees to fancy himself sounded regarding Miss Asper :
a piece of sculpture glacially decorative of the domestic
mansion in person, to his thinking ; and as to the nature
of it—not a Diana, with all her faults !

If Diana had any faults, in a world and a position so
heavily against her !  He laughed to himself, when alone,
at the neatly implied bitter reproach cast on the wife by
the forsaken young lady, who proposed to nurse the abandoned husband of the woman bereaving her of the man
she loved.  Sentimentalists enjoy these tricks, the con-
ceiving or the doing of them—the former mainly, which
are cheaper, and equally effective.  Miss Asper might be
deficient in wit ; this was a form of practical wit, occasionally exhibited by creatures acting on their instincts.
Warwick he pitied, and he put compulsion on himself to
go and see the poor fellow, the subject of so sublime a

Y

generosity. Mr. Warwick sat in an arm-chair, his legs out straight on the heels, his jaw dragging hollow cheeks, his hands loosely joined ; improving in health, he said. A demure woman of middle age was in attendance. He did not speak of his wife. Three times he said disconnectedly, ' I hear reports,' and his eyelids worked. Redworth talked of general affairs, without those consolatory efforts, useless between men, which are neither medicine nor good honest water :—he judged by personal feelings. In consequence, he left an invalid the sourer for his visit.

Next day he received a briefly-worded summons from Mrs. Warwick.

Crossing the park on the line to Diana's house, he met Miss Paynham, who grieved to say that Mrs. Warwick could not give her a sitting ; and in a still mournfuller tone, imagined he would find her at home, and alone by this time. ' I left no one but Mr. Dacier there,' she observed.

' Mrs. Warwick will be disengaged to-morrow, no doubt,' he said consolingly.

Her head performed the negative. ' They talk politics, and she becomes animated, loses her pose. I will persevere, though I fear I have undertaken a task too much for me.'

' I am deeply indebted to you for the attempt.' Redworth bowed to her and set his face to the Abbey-towers, which wore a different aspect in the smoked grey light since his two minutes of colloquy. He had previously noticed that meetings with Miss Paynham produced a similar effect on him, a not so very impressionable man. And how was it done ? She told him nothing he did not know or guess.

Diana was alone. Her manner, after the greeting, seemed feverish. She had not to excuse herself for abruptness when he heard the nature of the subject. Her counsellor and friend was informed, in feminine style, that she had requested him to call, for the purpose of consulting him with regard to a matter she had decided upon ; and it was, the sale of The Crossways. She said that it would have gone to her heart once ; she supposed she had lost her affection for the place, or had got the better of her superstitions. She spoke lamely as well as bluntly. The place was hers, she said ; her own property. Her husband could not interdict a sale.

Redworth addressed himself to her smothered antagonism. ' Even if he had rights, as they are termed . . . I think you might count on their not being pressed.'

' I have been told of illness.' She tapped her foot on the floor.

' His present state of health is unequal to his ordinary duties.'

' Emma Dunstane is fully supplied with the latest intelligence, Mr. Redworth. You know the source.'

' I mention it simply . . .'

' Yes, yes. What I have to protest is, that in this respect I am free. The Law has me fast, but leaves me its legal view of my small property. I have no authority over me. I can do as I please in this, without a collision, or the dread of one. It is the married woman's perpetual dread when she ventures a step. Your Law originally presumed her a China-footed animal. And more, I have a claim for maintenance.'

She crimsoned angrily.

Redworth showed a look of pleasure, hard to understand. ' The application would be sufficient, I fancy,' he said.

' It should have been offered.'

' Did you not decline it ? '

' I declined to apply for it. I thought— But Mr.

Redworth, another thing, concerning us all : I want very
much to hear your ideas of the prospects of the League ;
because I know you have ideas.  The leaders are terrible
men ; they fascinate me.  They appear to move with an
army of facts.  They are certainly carrying the country.
I am obliged to think them sincere.  Common agitators
would not hold together, as they do.  They gather
strength each year.  If their statistics are not illusory—
an army of phantoms instead of one of facts ;—and they
knock at my head without admission, I have to confess ;—
they must win.'

'Ultimately, it is quite calculable that they will win,'
said Redworth ; and he was led to discourse of rates and
duties and prohibitive tariffs to a woman surprisingly
athirst, curious for every scrap of intelligence relating to
the power, organization, and schemes of the League.
'Common sense is the secret of every successful civil
agitation,' he said.  'Rap it unremittingly on crowds of
the thickest of human heads, and the response comes at
last to sweep all before it.  You may reckon that the
country will beat the landlords—for that is our question.
Is it one of your political themes ? '

'I am not presumptuous to such a degree :—a poor
scholar,' Diana replied.  'Women striving to lift their
heads among men deserve the sarcasm.'

He denied that any sarcasm was intended, and the
lesson continued.  When she had shaped in her mind
some portion of his knowledge of the subject, she reverted
casually to her practical business.  Would he undertake
to try to obtain a purchaser of The Crossways, at the price
he might deem reasonable ?  She left the price entirely to
his judgement.  And now she had determined to part with
the old place, the sooner the better !  She said that smiling ;  and Redworth smiled, outwardly and inwardly.
Her talk of her affairs was clearer to him than her curiosity

for the mysteries of the League.   He gained kind looks
besides warm thanks by the promise to seek a purchaser ;
especially by his avoidance of prying queries.   She
wanted just this excellent automaton fac-totum ;  and she
referred him to Mr. Braddock for the title-deeds, et caetera
—the chirping phrase of ladies happily washing their
hands of the mean details of business.

' How of your last work ? ' he asked her.

Serenest equanimity rejoined :  ' As I anticipated, it is
not popular.   The critics are of one mind with the public.
You may have noticed, they rarely flower above that
rocky surface.   THE CANTATRICE sings them a false note.
My next will probably please them less.'

Her mobile lips and brows shot the faint upper-wreath
of a smile hovering.   It was designed to display her
philosophy.

' And what is the name of your next ? ' said he.

' I name it THE MAN OF TWO MINDS, if you can allow
that to be in nature.'

' Contra-distinguished from the woman ? '

' Oh ! you must first believe the woman to have one.'

' You are working on it ? '

' By fits.   And I forgot, Mr. Redworth : I have mislaid
my receipts, and must ask you for the address of your wine-
merchant ;—or, will you ?   Several dozen of the same
wines.   I can trust him to be in awe of you, and the good
repute of my table depends on his honesty.'

Redworth took the definite order for a large supply of
wine.

She gave him her hand : a lost hand, dear to hold, need-
ing to be guided, he feared.   For him, it was merely a hand,
cut off from the wrist ;  and he had performed that executive part !   A wiser man would now have been the lord of
it. . . . So he felt, with his burning wish to protect and
cherish the beloved woman, while saying :  ' If we find a

speedy bidder for The Crossways, you will have to thank
our railways.'

' You ! ' said Diana, confident in his ability to do everything of the practical kind.

Her ingenuousness tickled him. He missed her comic
touches upon men and things, but the fever shown by her
manner accounted for it.

As soon as he left her, she was writing to the lover who
had an hour previously been hearing her voice ; the note
of her theme being Party ; and how to serve it, when to
sacrifice it to the Country. She wrote, carolling bars of
the Puritani marches ; and such will passion do, that her
choice of music was quite in harmony with her theme.
The martially-amorous melodies of Italian Opera in those
days fostered a passion challenged to intrepidity from the
heart of softness ; gilding at the same time, and putting
warm blood even into dull arithmetical figures which
might be important to her lover, her hero fronting battle.
She condensed Redworth's information skilfully, heartily
giving it and whatever she had imbibed, as her own, down
to the remark : ' Common sense in questions of justice, is
a weapon that makes way into human heads and wins
the certain majority, if we strike with it incessantly.'
Whether anything she wrote was her own, mattered little :
the savour of Percy's praise, which none could share with
her, made it instantly all her own. Besides she wrote to
strengthen him ; she naturally laid her friends and the
world under contribution ; and no other sort of writing
was possible. Percy had not a common interest in fiction ;
still less for high comedy. He liked the broad laugh when
he deigned to open books of that sort ; puns and strong
flavours and harlequin surprises ; and her work would not
admit of them, however great her willingness to force her
hand for his amusement : consequently her inventiveness
deadened. She had to cease whipping it. ' My poor old

London cabhorse of a pen shall go to grass ! ' she sighed,
looking to the sale of The Crossways for money ; looking
no farther.

Those marshalled battalions of Debit and Credit were in
hostile order, the weaker simply devoted to fighting for
delay, when a winged messenger bearing the form of old
Mr. Braddock descended to her with the reconciling news
that a hermit bachelor, an acquaintance of Mr. Redworth's
—both of whom wore a gloomy hue in her mind immediately—had offered a sum for the purchase of The Crossways.   Considering the out-of-the-way district, Mr. Braddock thought it an excellent price to get.   She thought the
reverse, but confessed that double the sum would not have
altered her opinion.   Double the sum scarcely counted for
the service she required of it for much more than a year.
The money was paid shortly after into her Bank, and
then she enjoyed the contemptuous felicity of tossing
meat to her lions, tigers, wolves, and jackals, who, but for
the fortunate intervention, would have been feeding on
her.   These menagerie beasts of prey were the lady's
tradesmen, Debit's hungry brood.   She had a rapid
glimpse of a false position in regarding that legitimate
band so scornfully : another glimpse likewise of a day to
come when they might not be stopped at the door.   She
was running a race with something ;—with what ?   It
was unnamed ; it ran in a shroud.

At times she surprised her heart violently beating when
there had not been a thought to set it in motion.   She
traced it once to the words, ' next year,' incidentally mentioned.   ' Free,' was a word that checked her throbs, as
at a question of life or death.   Her solitude, excepting
the hours of sleep, if then, was a time of irregular breathing.
The something unnamed, running beside her, became a
dreadful familiar ; the race between them past contemplation for ghastliness.   ' But this is your Law ! ' she

cried to the world, while blinding her eyes against a peep
of the shrouded features.

Singularly, she had but to abandon hope, and the
shadowy figure vanished, the tragic race was ended.   How
to live and think, and not to hope : the slave of passion
had this problem before her.

Other tasks were supportable, though one seemed hard
at moments and was not passive ;  it attacked her.   The
men and women of her circle derisively, unanimously,
disbelieved in an innocence that forfeited reputation.
Women were complimentarily assumed to be not such
gaping idiots.   And as the weeks advanced, a change
came over Percy.   The gentleman had grown restless at
covert congratulations, hollow to his knowledge, however
much caressing vanity, and therefore secretly a wound to
it.   One day, after sitting silent, he bluntly proposed to
break ' this foolish trifling ' ;  just in his old manner,
though not so honourably ;   not very definitely either.
Her hand was taken.

' I feared that dumbness ! ' Diana said, letting her hand
go, but keeping her composure.   ' My friend Percy, I am
not a lion-tamer, and if you are of those animals, we
break the chapter.   Plainly you think that where there
appears to be a choice of fools, the woman is distinctly
designed for the person.   Drop my hand, or I shall repeat the fable of the Goose with the Golden Eggs.'

' Fables are applicable only in the school-room,' said he ;
and he ventured on ' Tony ! '

' I vowed an oath to my dear Emma—as good as to the
heavens ! and that of itself would stay me from being insane again.'   She released herself.   ' Signor Percy, you
teach me to suspect you of having an idle wish to pluck
your plaything to pieces :—to boast of it ?   Ah ! my
friend, I fancied I was of more value to you.   You must
come less often ;  even to not at all, if you are one of those

idols with feet of clay which leave the print of their steps
in a room ; or fall and crush the silly idolizer.'

'But surely you know . . .' said he. 'We can't have
to wait long.' He looked full of hopeful meanings.

'A reason . . . !' She kept down her breath. A long-
drawn sigh followed, through parted lips. She had a
sensation of horror. 'And I cannot propose to nurse
him—Emma will not hear of it,' she said. 'I dare not.
Hypocrite to that extreme ? Oh, no ! But I must hear
nothing. As it is, I am haunted. Now let this pass.
Tony me no Tonies ; I am *atony* to such whimpering
business now we are in the van of the struggle. All
round us it sounds like war. Last night I had Mr.
Tonans dining here ; he wished to meet you ; and you
must have a private meeting with Mr. Whitmonby : he
will be useful ; others as well. You are wrong in affecting
contempt of the Press. It perches you on a rock ; but
the swimmer in politics knows what draws the tides.
Your own people, your set, your class, are a drag to you,
like inherited superstitions to the wakening brain. The
greater the glory ! For you see the lead you take ? You
are saving your class. They should lead, and will, if they
prove worthy in the crisis. Their curious error is to
believe in the stability of a monumental position.'

'Perfectly true !' cried Dacier ; and the next minute,
heated by approbation, was begging for her hand earnestly.
She refused it.

'But you say things that catch me !' he pleaded.
'Remember, it was nearly mine. It soon will be mine.
I heard yesterday from Lady Wathin . . . well, if it
pains you !'

'Speak on,' said Diana, resigned to her thirsty ears.

'He is not expected to last through the autumn.'

'The calculation is hers ? '

'Not exactly :—judging from the symptoms.'

Diana flashed a fiery eye into Dacier's, and rose. She was past danger of melting, with her imagination darkened by the funeral image ; but she craved solitude, and had to act the callous, to dismiss him.

' Good. Enough for the day. Now leave me, if you please. When we meet again, stifle that raven's croak. I am not a " Sister of Charity," but neither am I a vulture hovering for the horse in the desert to die. A poor simile !—when it is my own and not another's breath that I want. Nothing in nature, only gruesome German stories will fetch comparisons for the yoke of this Law of yours. It seems the nightmare dream following an ogre's supper.'

She was not acting the shiver of her frame.

To-morrow was open to him, and prospect of better fortune, so he departed, after squeezing the hand she ceremoniously extended.

But her woman's intuition warned her that she had not maintained the sovereign impression which was her security. And hope had become a flame in her bosom that would no longer take the common extinguisher. The race she ran was with a shrouded figure no more, but with the figure of the shroud ; she had to summon paroxysms of a pity hard to feel, images of sickness, helplessness, the vaults, the last human silence—for the stilling of her passionate heart. And when this was partly effected, the question, Am I going to live ? renewed her tragical struggle. Who was it under the vaults, in the shroud, between the planks ? and with human sensibility to swell the horror ! Passion whispered of a vaster sorrow needed for herself ; and the hope conjuring those frightful complexities was needed to soothe her. She pitied the man, but she was an enamoured woman. Often of late she had been sharply stung, relaxed as well, by the obser-vations of Danvers assisting at her toilette. Had she

beauty and charm, beauty and rich health in the young
summer blooming of her days ?—and all doomed to
waste ?  No insurgency of words arose in denunciation
of the wrong done to her nature.  An undefined heavy
feeling of wrong there was, just perceptive enough to let
her know, without gravely shaming, that one or another
must be slain for peace to come ; for it is the case in which
the world of the Laws overloading her is pitiless to women,
deaf past ear-trumpets, past intercession ; detesting
and reviling them for a feeble human cry, and for one
apparent step of revolt piling the pelted stones on them.
It will not discriminate shades of hue, it massacres all the
shadowed.  They are honoured, after a fashion, at a
certain elevation.  Descending from it, and purely to
breathe common air (thus in her mind), they are scourged
and outcast.  And alas !  the very pleading for them
excites a sort of ridicule in their advocate.  How ?  She
was utterly, even desperately, nay personally, earnest,
and her humour closed her lips ; though comical views
of the scourged and outcast coming from the opposite
party—the huge bully world—she would not have tolerated.  Diana raged at a prevailing strength on the part
of that huge bully world, which seemed really to embrace
the atmosphere.  Emma had said : ' The rules of Christian
Society are a blessed Government for us women.  We
owe it so much that there is not a brick of the fabric we
should not prop.'  Emma's talk of obedience to the Laws,
being Laws, was repeated by the rebel, with an involuntary unphrased comparison of the vessel in dock and the
vessel at sea.

When Dacier next called to see Mrs. Warwick, he heard
that she had gone to Copsley for a couple of weeks.  The
lesson was emphasized by her not writing :—and was it
the tricky sex, or the splendid character of the woman,
which dealt him this punishment ?  Knowing how much

Diana forfeited for him, he was moved to some enthusiasm, despite his inclination to be hurt.

She, on her return to London, gained a considerable increase of knowledge as to her position in the eye of the world ; and unlike the result of her meditations derived from the clamouring tradesmen, whom she could excuse, she was neither illuminated nor cautioned by that dubious look ; she conscientiously revolted. Lady Pennon hinted a word for her Government. ' A good deal of what you so capitally call " Green tea talk " is going on, my dear.' Diana replied, without pretending to misunderstand : ' Gossip is a beast of prey that does not wait for the death of the creature it devours. They are welcome to my shadow, if the liberty I claim casts one, and it feeds them.' To which the old lady rejoined : ' Oh ! I am with you through thick and thin. I presented you at Court, and I stand by you. Only, walk carefully. Women have to walk with a train. You are too famous not to have your troops of watchers.'

' But I mean to prove,' said Diana, ' that a woman can walk with her train independent of the common reserves and artifices.'

' Not on highways, my dear ! '

Diana, praising the speaker, referred the whole truth in that to the material element of her metaphor.

She was more astonished by Whitmonby's candid chiding ; but with him she could fence, and men are easily diverted. She had sent for him, to bring him and Percy Dacier together to a conference. Unaware of the project, he took the opportunity of their privacy to speak of the great station open to her in London being imperilled ; and he spoke of ' tongues,' and ahem ! A very little would have induced him to fill that empty vocable with a name.

She had to pardon the critic in him for an unpleasant

review of her hapless CANTATRICE ; and as a means of
evasion, she mentioned the poor book and her slaughter
of the heroine, that he had complained of.

' I killed her ; I could not let her live.  You were unjust in accusing the authoress of heartlessness.'

' If I did, I retract,' said he.  ' She steers too evidently from the centre of the vessel.  She has the organ
in excess.'

' Proof that it is not squandered.'

' The point concerns direction.'

' Have I made so bad a choice of my friends ? '

' It is the common error of the sprightly to suppose that
in parrying a thrust they blind our eyes.'

' The world sees always what it desires to see, Mr.
Whitmonby.'

' The world, my dear Mrs. Warwick, is a blundering
machine upon its own affairs, but a cruel sleuth-hound to
rouse in pursuit.'

' So now you have me chased by sight and scent.  And
if I take wing ? '

' Shots !  volleys !—You are lawful game.  The choice
you have made of your friends, should oblige you to think
of them.'

' I imagine I do.  Have I offended any, or one ? '

' I will not say that.  You know the commotion in a
French kitchen when the guests of the house declined a
particular dish furnished them by command.  The cook
and his crew were loyal to their master, but, for the love
of their Art, they sent him notice.  It is ill serving a mad
sovereign.'

Diana bowed to the compact little apologue.

' I will tell you another story, traditional in our family
from my great-grandmother, a Spanish woman,' she said.
' A cavalier serenaded his mistress, and rascal mercenaries
fell upon him before he could draw sword.  He battered

his guitar on their pates till the lattice opened with a cry, and startled them to flight. " Thrice blessed and beloved ! " he called to her above, in reference to the noise, " it was merely a diversion of the accompaniment." Now there was loyal service to a sovereign ! '

' You are certainly an angel ! ' exclaimed Whitmonby. ' I swallow the story, and leave it to digestion to discover the appositeness. Whatever tuneful instrument one of your friends possesses shall solace your slumbers or batter the pate of your enemy. But discourage the habitual serenader.'

' The musician you must mean is due here now, by appointment to meet you,' said Diana, and set him momentarily agape with the name of Mr. Percy Dacier.

That was the origin of the alliance between the young statesman and a newspaper editor. Whitmonby, accepting proposals which suited him, quitted the house, after an hour of political talk, no longer inclined to hint at the ' habitual serenader,' but very ready to fall foul of those who did, as he proved when the numbers buzzed openly. Times were masculine ; the excitement on the eve of so great a crisis, and Diana's comprehension of it and fine heading cry, put that weak matter aside. Moreover, he was taught to suppose himself as welcome a guest as Dacier ; and the cook could stand criticism ; the wines— wonderful to say of a lady's table—were trusty ; the talk, on the political evenings and the social and anecdotal supper-nights, ran always in perfect accord with his ideal of the conversational orchestra : an improvized harmony, unmatched elsewhere. She did not, he considered, so perfectly assort her dinner-guests ; that was her one fault. She had therefore to strain her adroitness to cover their deficiencies and fuse them. But what other woman could have done it ! She led superbly. If an Irishman was present, she kept him from overflooding, managed to

extract just the flavour of him, the smack of salt. She
did even, at Whitmonby's table, on a red-letter Sunday
evening, in concert with him and the Dean, bring down
that cataract, the Bodleian, to the levels of interchanging
dialogue by seasonable touches, inimitably done, and
never done before. Sullivan Smith, unbridled in the
middle of dinner, was docile to her. ' Irishmen,' she said,
pleading on their behalf to Whitmonby, who pronounced
the race too raw for an Olympian feast, ' are invaluable if
you hang them up to smoke and cure ' ; and the master
of social converse could not deny that they were responsive to her magic. The supper-nights were mainly devoted to Percy's friends. He brought as many as he
pleased, and as often as it pleased him ; and it was her
pride to provide Cleopatra banquets for the lover whose
anxieties were soothed by them, and to whom she sacrificed her name willingly in return for a generosity that
certain chance whispers of her heart elevated to the pitch
of measureless.

So they wore through the Session and the Autumn,
clouds heavier, the League drumming, the cry of Ireland
' ominously Banshee,' as she wrote to Emma.


## CHAPTER XXX

### IN WHICH THERE IS A TASTE OF A LITTLE DINNER AND AN AFTERTASTE

' But Tony lives ! ' Emma Dunstane cried, on her solitary
height, with the full accent of envy marking the verb ;
and when she wrote enviously to her friend of the life
among bright intelligences, and of talk worth hearing, it
was a happy signification that health, frail though it might

be, had grown importunate for some of the play of life. Diana sent her word to name her day, and she would have her choicest to meet her dearest. They were in the early days of December, not the best of times for improvized gatherings. Emma wanted, however, to taste them as they cropped ; she was also, owing to her long isolation, timid at a notion of encountering the pick of the London world, prepared by Tony to behold ' a wonder more than worthy of them,' as her friend unadvisedly wrote. That was why she came unexpectedly, and for a mixture of reasons, went to an hotel. Fatality designed it so. She was reproached, but she said : ' You have to write or you entertain at night ; I should be a clog and fret you. My hotel is Maitland's ; excellent ; I believe I am to lie on the pillow where a crowned head reposed ! You will perceive that I am proud as well as comfortable. And I would rather meet your usual set of guests.'

' The reason why I have been entertaining at night is, that Percy is harassed and requires enlivening,' said Diana. ' He brings his friends. My house is open to them, if it amuses him. What the world says, is past a thought. I owe him too much.'

Emma murmured that the world would soon be pacified.

Diana shook her head. ' The poor man is better ; able to go about his affairs ; and I am honestly relieved. It lays a spectre. As for me, I do not look ahead. I serve as a kind of secretary to Percy. I labour at making abstracts by day, and at night preside at my supper-table. You would think it monotonous ; no incident varies the course we run. I have not time to ask whether it is happiness. It seems to bear a resemblance.'

Emma replied : ' He may be everything you tell me. He should not have chosen the last night of the Opera to go to your box and sit beside you till the fall of the curtain. The presence at the Opera of a man notoriously indifferent to music was enough in itself.'

Diana smiled with languor. 'You heard of that? But the Opera was The Puritani, my favourite. And he saw me sitting in Lady Pennon's box alone. We were compromised neck-deep already. I can kiss you, my own Emmy, till I die; but what the world says, is what the wind says. Besides he has his hopes. . . . If I am blackened ever so thickly, he can make me white. Dear me! if the world knew that he comes here almost nightly! It will; and does it matter? I am his in soul; the rest is waste-paper—a half-printed sheet.'

'Provided he is worthy of such devotion!'

'He is absolute worthiness. He is the prince of men:— I dread to say, mine! for fear. But Emmy will not judge him to-morrow by contrast with more voluble talkers.—I can do anything but read poetry now. That kills me!— See him through me. In nature, character, intellect, he has no rival. Whenever I despond—and it comes now and then—I rebuke myself with this one admonition: Simply to have known him! Admit that for a woman to find one who is worthy among the opposite creatures, is a happy termination of her quest, and in some sort dismisses her to the Shades, an uncomplaining ferry-bird. If my end were at hand I should have no cause to lament it. We women miss life only when we have to confess we have never met the man to reverence.'

Emma had to hear a very great deal of Mr. Percy. Diana's comparison of herself to 'the busy bee at a window-pane,' was more in her old manner; and her friend would have hearkened to the marvels of the gentleman less unrefreshed, had it not appeared to her that her Tony gave in excess for what was given in return. She hinted her view.

'It is expected of our sex,' Diana said.

z

The work of busy bee at a window-pane had at any rate
not spoilt her beauty, though she had voluntarily, profit-
lessly, become this man's drudge, and her sprightly fancy,
her ready humour and darting look all round in discussion,
were rather deadened.

But the loss was not perceptible in the circle of her
guests.  Present at a dinner little indicating the last, were
Whitmonby, in lively trim for shuffling, dealing, cutting,
trumping or drawing trumps ;  Westlake, polishing epigrams under his eyelids ;  Henry Wilmers, who timed an
anecdote to strike as the passing hour without freezing the
current ;  Sullivan Smith, smoked, cured and ready to
flavour ;  Percy Dacier, pleasant listener, measured
speaker ;  and young Arthur Rhodes, the neophyte of the
hostess's training ;  of whom she had said to Emma, ' The
dear boy very kindly serves to frank an unlicenced widow ' ;
and whom she prompted and made her utmost of, with her
natural tact.  These she mixed and leavened.  The talk
was on high levels and low ;  an enchantment to Emma
Dunstane :  now a story ;  a question opening new routes ;
sharp sketches of known personages ;  a paradox shot by
laughter as soon as uttered ;  and all so smoothly ;  not a
shadow of the dominant holder-forth or a momentary
prospect of dead flats ;  the mellow ring of appositeness
being the concordant note of deliveries running linked as
they flashed, and a tolerant philosophy of the sage in the
world recurrently the keynote.

Once only had Diana to protect her nurseling.  He cited
a funny line from a recent popular volume of verse, in
perfect à propos, looking at Sullivan Smith ;  who replied,
that the poets had become too many for him, and he read
none now.  Diana said :  ' There are many Alexanders,
but Alexander of Macedon is not dwarfed by the number.'
She gave him an opening for a smarter reply, but he lost
it in a comment—against Whitmonby's cardinal rule :

' The neatest turn of the wrist that ever swung a hero to
crack a crown ! ' and he bowed to young Rhodes : ' I 'll
read your versicler to-morrow morning early.' The latter
expressed a fear that the hour was too critical for poetry.

' I have taken the dose at a very early hour,' said
Whitmonby, to bring conversation to the flow again,
' and it effaced the critical mind completely.'

' But did not silence the critical nose,' observed Westlake.

Wilmers named the owner of the longest nose in Europe.

' Potentially, indeed a critic ! ' said Diana.

' Nights beside it must be fearful, and good matter for
a divorce, if the poor dear lady could hale it to the doors
of the Vatican ! ' Sullivan Smith exclaimed. ' But there 's
character in noses.'

' Calculable by inches ? ' Dacier asked.

' More than in any other feature,' said Lady Dunstane.
' The Riffords are all prodigiously gifted and amusing :
*suspendens omnia naso.* It should be prayed for in
families.'

' Totum ut te faciant, Fabulle, nasum,' rejoíned Whitmonby. ' Lady Isabella was reading the tale of the
German princess, who had a sentinel stationed some hundred yards away to whisk off the flies, and she owned to
me that her hand instinctively travelled upward.'

' Candour is the best concealment, when one has to carry
a saddle of absurdity,' said Diana. Touchstone's " poor
thing, but mine own," is godlike in its enveloping fold.'

' The most comforting sermon ever delivered on property in poverty,' said Arthur Rhodes.

Westlake assented. ' His choice of Audrey strikes me
as an exhibition of the sure instinct for pasture of the
philosophical jester in a forest.'

' With nature's woman, if he can find her, the urban
seems equally at home,' said Lady Dunstane.

'Baron Pawle is an example,' added Whitmonby.   'His
cook is a pattern wife to him.   I heard him say at table
that she was responsible for all except the wines.   "I
wouldn't have them on my conscience, with a Judge!"
my lady retorted.'

'When poor Madame de Jacquières was dying,' said
Wilmers, 'her confessor sat by her bedside, prepared for
his ministrations.   "*Pour commencer, mon ami, jamais je
n'ai fait rien hors nature.*"'

Lord Wadaster had uttered something tolerably similar : 'I am a sinner, and in good society.'   Sir Abraham
Hartiston, a minor satellite of the Regent, diversified
this : 'I am a sinner, and go to good society.'   Madame
la Comtesse de la Roche-Aigle, the cause of many deaths,
declared it unwomanly to fear anything save '*les reve-
nants.*'   Yet the countess could say the pretty thing :
'Foot on a flower, then think of me!'

'Sentimentality puts up infant hands for absolution,'
said Diana.

'But tell me,' Lady Dunstane inquired generally, 'why
men are so much happier than women in laughing at their
spouses?'

They are humaner, was one dictum ; they are more
frivolous, ironically another.

'It warrants them for blowing the bugle-horn of masculine superiority night and morning from the castle-walls,'
Diana said.

'I should imagine it is for joy of heart that they still
have cause to laugh!' said Westlake.

On the other hand, are women really pained by having
to laugh at their lords?   Curious little speeches flying
about the great world, affirmed the contrary.   But the
fair speakers were chartered libertines, and their laugh
admittedly had a biting acid.   The parasite is concerned
in the majesty of the tree.

' We have entered Botany Bay,' Diana said to Emma ; who answered : ' A metaphor is the Deus ex machinâ of an argument '; and Whitmonby, to lighten a shadow of heaviness, related allusively an anecdote of the Law-Courts. Sullivan Smith begged permission to ' black cap ' it with Judge FitzGerald's sentence upon a convicted criminal : ' Your plot was perfect but for One above.' Dacier cited an execrable impromptu line of the Chief of the Opposition in Parliament. The Premier, it was remarked, played him like an angler his fish on the hook ; or say, Mr. Serjeant Rufus his witness in the box.

' Or a French journalist an English missionary,' said Westlake ; and as the instance was recent it was relished.

The talk of Premiers offered Whitmonby occasion for a flight to the Court of Vienna and Kaunitz. Wilmers told a droll story of Lord Busby's missing the Embassy there. Westlake furnished a sample of the tranquil sententiousness of Busby's brother Robert during a stormy debate in the House of Commons.

' I remember,' Dacier was reminded, ' hearing him say, when the House resembled a Chartist riot, " Let us stand aside and meditate on Life. If Youth could know, in the season of its reaping of the Pleasures, that it is but sowing Doctor's bills ! " '

Latterly a malady had supervened, and Bob Busby had retired from the universal to the special ;—his mysterious case.

' Assure him, that is endemic. He may be cured of his desire for the exposition of it,' said Lady Dunstane.

Westlake chimed with her : ' Yes, the charm in discoursing of one's case is over when the individual appears no longer at odds with Providence.'

' But then we lose our Tragedy,' said Whitmonby.

' Our Comedy too,' added Diana. ' We must consent to be Busbied for the sake of the instructive recreations.'

'A curious idea, though,' said Sullivan Smith, 'that
some of the grand instructive figures were in their day
colossal bores ! '

'So you see the marvel of the poet's craft at last ? '
Diana smiled on him, and he vowed : ' I 'll read nothing
else for a month ! ' Young Rhodes bade him beware of a
deluge in proclaiming it.

They rose from table at ten, with the satisfaction of
knowing that they had not argued, had not wrangled, had
never stagnated, and were digestingly refreshed ; as it
should be among grown members of the civilized world,
who mean to practise philosophy, making the hour of the
feast a balanced recreation and a regeneration of body and
mind.

'Evenings like these are worth a pilgrimage,' Emma
said, embracing Tony outside the drawing-room door. ' I
am so glad I came : and if I am strong enough, invite me
again in the Spring. To-morrow early I start for Copsley,
to escape this London air. I shall hope to have you there
soon.'

She was pleased by hearing Tony ask her whether she
did not think that Arthur Rhodes had borne himself well ;
for it breathed of her simply friendly soul.

The gentlemen followed Lady Dunstane in a troop,
Dacier yielding perforce the last adieu to young Rhodes.

Five minutes later Diana was in her dressing-room,
where she wrote at night, on the rare occasions now when
she was left free for composition. Beginning to dwell on
THE MAN OF TWO MINDS, she glanced at the woman likewise divided, if not similarly ; and she sat brooding. She
did not accuse her marriage of being the first fatal step :
her error was the step into Society without the wherewithal to support her position there. Girls of her kind,
airing their wings above the sphere of their birth, are cryingly adventuresses. As adventuresses they are treated.

Vain to be shrewish with the world ! Rather let us turn and scold our nature for irreflectively rushing to the cream and honey ! Had she subsisted on her small income in a country cottage, this task of writing would have been holiday. Or better, if, as she preached to Mary Paynham, she had apprenticed herself to some productive craft. The simplicity of the life of labour looked beautiful. What will not look beautiful contrasted with the fly in the web ? She had chosen to be one of the flies of life.

Instead of running to composition, her mind was eloquent with a sermon to Arthur Rhodes, in Redworth's vein ; more sympathetically, of course. ' For I am not one of the lecturing Mammonites ! ' she could say.

She was far from that. Penitentially, in the thick of her disdain of the arrogant money-getters, she pulled out a drawer where her bank-book lay, and observed it contemplatively ; jotting down a reflection before the dread book of facts was opened : ' Gaze on the moral path you should have taken, you are asked for courage to commit a sanctioned suicide, by walking back to it stripped—a skeleton self.' She sighed forth : ' But I have no courage : I never had ! '

The book revealed its tale in a small pencilled computation of the bank-clerk's, on the peccant side. Credit presented many pages blanks. She seemed to have withdrawn from the struggle with such a partner.

It signified an immediate appeal to the usurers, unless the publisher could be persuaded, with three parts of the book in his hands, to come to the rescue. Work ! roared old Debit, the sinner turned slavedriver.

Diana smoothed her wrists, compressing her lips not to laugh at the simulation of an attitude of combat. She took up her pen.

And strange to think, she could have flowed away at once on the stuff that Danvers delighted to read !—wicked

princes, rogue noblemen, titled wantons, daisy and lily
innocents, traitorous marriages, murders, a gallows dangling a corpse dotted by a moon, and a woman bowed beneath.   She could have written, with the certainty that in
the upper and the middle as well as in the lower classes
of the country, there would be a multitude to read that
stuff, so cordially, despite the gaps between them, are
they one in their literary tastes.   And why should they
not read it ?   Her present mood was a craving for excitement ; for incident, wild action, the primitive machinery
of our species ; any amount of theatrical heroics, pathos,
and clown-gabble.   A panorama of scenes came sweeping
round her.

She was, however, harnessed to a different kind of
vehicle, and had to drag it.   The sound of the house-door
shutting, imagined perhaps, was a fugitive distraction.
Now to animate The Man of Two Minds !

He is courting, but he is burdened with the task of
tasks.   He has an ideal of womanhood and of the union
of couples : a delicacy extreme as his attachment : and he
must induce the lady to school herself to his ideal, not
allowing her to suspect him less devoted to her person ;
while she, an exacting idol, will drink any quantity of
idealization as long as he starts it from a full acceptance
of her acknowledged qualities.   Diana could once have
tripped the scene along airily.   She stared at the opening
sentence, a heavy bit of moralized manufacture, fit to yoke
beside that on her view of her bank-book.

' It has come to this—I have no head,' she cried.

And is our public likely to muster the slightest taste for
comic analysis that does not tumble to farce ?   The doubt
reduced her whole MS. to a leaden weight, composed for
sinking.   Percy's addiction to burlesque was a further
hindrance, for she did not perceive how her comedy could
be strained to gratify it.

There was a knock, and Danvers entered.

' You have apparently a liking for late hours,' observed her mistress. ' I told you to go to bed.'

' It is Mr. Dacier,' said Danvers.

' He wishes to see me ? '

' Yes, ma'am. He apologized for disturbing you.'

' He must have some good reason.'

What could it be ! Diana's glass approved her appearance. She pressed the black swell of hair above her temples, rather amazed, curious, inclined to a beating of the heart.


## CHAPTER XXXI

### A CHAPTER CONTAINING GREAT POLITICAL NEWS AND THEREWITH AN INTRUSION OF THE LOVE-GOD

DACIER was pacing about the drawing-room, as in a place too narrow for him.

Diana stood at the door. ' Have you forgotten to tell me anything I ought to know ? '

He came up to her and shut the door softly behind her, holding her hand. ' You are near it. I returned . . . But tell me first :—You were slightly under a shadow this evening, dejected.'

' Did I show it ? '

She was growing a little suspicious, but this cunning touch of lover-like interest dispersed the shade.

' To me you did.'

' It was unpardonable to let it be seen.'

' No one else could have observed it.'

Her woman's heart was thrilled ; for she had concealed the dejection from Emma.

' It was nothing,' she said ; ' a knot in the book I am

writing. We poor authors are worried now and then. But you ? '

His face rippled by degrees brightly, to excite a reflection in hers.

' Shall I tune you with good news ?  I think it will excuse me for coming back.'

' Very good news ? '

' Brave news, as far as it goes.'

' Then it concerns you ! '

' Me, you, the country.'

' Oh ! do I guess ? ' cried Diana.  ' But speak, pray ;  I burn.'

What am I to have for telling it ? '

' Put no price. You know my heart. I guess—or fancy.  It relates to your Chief ? '

Dacier smiled in a way to show the lock without the key ;  and she was insensibly drawn nearer to him, speculating on the smile.

' Try again,' said he, keenly appreciating the blindness to his motive of her studious dark eyes, and her open-lipped breathing.

' Percy !  I must be right.'

' Well, you are.  He has decided ! '

' Oh !  that is the bravest possible.  When did you hear ? '

' He informed me of his final decision this afternoon.'

' And you were charged with the secret all the evening, and betrayed not a sign !  I compliment the diplomatic statesman.  But when will it be public ? '

' He calls Parliament together the first week of next month.'

' The proposal is— ?  No more compromises ! '

' Total ! '

Diana clapped hands ;  and her aspect of enthusiasm was intoxicating.  ' He is a wise man and a gallant

Minister ! And while you were reading me through, I was blind to you,' she added meltingly.

'I have not made too much of it ? ' said he.

'Indeed you have not.'

She was radiant with her dark lightnings, yet visibly subject to him under the spell of the news he had artfully lengthened out to excite and overbalance her :—and her enthusiasm was all pointed to his share in the altered situation, as he well knew and was flattered in knowing.

'So Tony is no longer dejected ? I thought I could freshen you and get my excuse.'

'Oh ! a high wind will make a dead leaf fly like a bird. I soar. Now I do feel proud. I have longed for it—to have you leading the country : not tugged at like a waggon with a treble team uphill. We two are a month in advance of all England. You stand by him ?—only to hear it, for I am sure of it ! '

'We stand or fall together.'

Her glowing look doated on the faithful lieutenant.

'And if the henchman is my hero, I am but a waiting-woman. But I must admire his leader.'

'Tony ! '

'Ah ! no,' she joined her hands, wondering whither her armed majesty had fled ; 'no softness ! no payments ! Flatter me by letting me think you came to a head—not a silly woman's heart, with one name on it, as it has not to betray. I have been frank ; you need no proofs . . .'

The supplicating hands left her figure an easy prey to the storm, and were crushed in a knot on her bosom. She could only shrink. 'Ah ! Percy . . . you undo my praise of you—my pride in receiving you.'

They were speechless perforce.

'You see, Tony, my dearest, I am flesh and blood after all.'

'You drive me to be ice and door-bolts ! '

Her eyes broke over him reproachfully.

' It is not so much to grant,' he murmured.

' It changes everything between us.'

' Not me.   It binds me the faster.'

' It makes me a loathsome hypocrite.'

' But, Tony ! is it so much ? '

' Not if you value it low.'

' But how long do you keep me in this rag-puppet's state of suspension ? '

' Patience.'

' Dangling and swinging day and night ! '

' The rag-puppet shall be animated and repaid if I have life.   I wish to respect my hero.   Have a little mercy.   Our day will come : perhaps as wonderfully as this wonderful news.   My friend, drop your hands. Have you forgotten who I am ?   I want to think, Percy ! '

' But you are mine.'

' You are abasing your own.'

' No, by heaven ! '

' Worse, dear friend ;   you are lowering yourself to the woman who loves you.'

' You must imagine me superhuman.'

' I worship you—or did.'

' Be reasonable, Tony.   What harm !   Surely a trifle of recompense ?   Just to let me feel I live !   You own you love me.   Then I am your lover.'

' My dear friend Percy, when I have consented to be your paramour, this kind of treatment of me will not want apologies.'

The plain speaking from the wound he dealt her was effective with a gentleman who would never have enjoyed his privileges had he been of a nature unsusceptible to her distinct wish and meaning.

He sighed.   ' You know how my family bother me.

The woman I want, the only woman I could marry, I can't have.'

' You have her in soul.'

' Body and soul, it must be ! I believe you were made without fire.'

' Perhaps. The element is omitted with some of us : happily, some think. Now we can converse. There seems to be a measurement of distances required before men and women have a chance with their brains :—or before a man will understand that he can be advised and seconded. When will the Cabinet be consulted ? '

' Oh, a few days. Promise me . . .'

' Any honourable promise ! '

' You will not keep me waiting longer than the end of the Session ? '

' Probably there will be an appeal to the country.'

' In any case, promise me : have some compassion.'

' Ah, the compassion ! You do not choose your words, Percy, or forget who is the speaker.'

' It is Tony who forgets the time she has kept her lover dangling. Promise, and I will wait.'

' You hurt my hand, sir.'

' I could crack the knuckles. Promise ! '

' Come to me to-morrow.'

' To-morrow you are in your armour—triple brass ! All creation cries out for now. We are mounted on barbs and you talk of ambling.'

' Arthur Rhodes might have spoken that.'

' Rhodes ! ' he shook off the name in disgust. ' Pet him as much as you like ; don't . . .' he was unable to phrase his objection.

She cooled him further with eulogies of the chevaleresque manner of speaking which young Mr. Rhodes could assume ; till for very wrath of blood—not jealousy : he had none of any man, with her ; and not passion ; the little he had was a fitful gust—he punished her coldness by taking what hastily could be gathered.

Her shape was a pained submission ; and she thought : Where is the woman who ever knows a man !—as women do think when one of their artifices of evasion with a lover, or the trick of imposingness, has apparently been subduing him. But the pain was less than previously, for she was now mistress of herself, fearing no abysses.

Dacier released her quickly, saying : ' If I come to-morrow, shall I have the promise ? '

She answered : ' Be sure I shall not lie.'

' Why not let me have it before I go ? '

' My friend, to tell you the truth, you have utterly distracted me.'

' Forgive me if I did hurt your hand.'

' The hand ? You might strike it off.'

' I can't be other than a mortal lover, Tony. There 's the fact.'

' No ; the fault is mine when I am degraded. I trust you : there 's the error.'

The trial for Dacier was the sight of her quick-lifting bosom under the mask of cold language : an attraction and repulsion in union ; a delirium to any lover impelled to trample on weak defences. But the evident pain he inflicted moved his pity, which helped to restore his conception of the beauty of her character. She stood so nobly meek. And she was never prudish, only self-respecting. Although the great news he imparted had roused an ardent thirst for holiday and a dash out of harness, and he could hardly check it, he yielded her the lead.

' Trust me you may,' he said. ' But you know we are one. The world has given you to me, me to you. Why should we be asunder ? There 's no reason in it.'

She replied : ' But still I wish to burn a little incense in honour of myself, or else I cannot live. It is the truth. You make Death my truer friend, and at this moment I would willingly go out. You would respect me more dead than alive. I could better pardon you too.'

He pleaded for the red mouth's pardon, remotely irritated by the suspicion that she swayed him overmuch : and he had deserved the small benevolences and donations of love, crumbs and heavenly dews !

' Not a word of pardon,' said Diana. ' I shall never count an iota against you " in the dark backward and abysm of Time." This news is great, and I have sunk beneath it. Come to-morrow. Then we will speak upon whatever you can prove rational. The hour is getting late.'

Dacier took a draught of her dark beauty with the crimson he had kindled over the cheeks. Her lips were firmly closed, her eyes grave ; dry, but seeming to waver tearfully in their heavy fulness. He could not doubt her love of him ; and although chafing at the idea that she swayed him absurdly—beyond the credible in his world of wag-tongues—he resumed his natural soberness, as a garment, not very uneasily fitting : whence it ensued—for so are we influenced by the garb we put on us—that his manly sentiment of revolt in being condemned to play second, was repressed by the refreshment breathed on him from her lofty character, the pure jewel proffered to his inward ownership.

' Adieu for the night,' he said, and she smiled. He pressed for a pressure of her hand. She brightened her smile instead, and said only : ' Good night, Percy.'

## CHAPTER XXXII

WHEREIN WE BEHOLD A GIDDY TURN AT THE SPECTRAL
CROSSWAYS

DANVERS accompanied Mr. Dacier to the house-door.
Climbing the stairs, she found her mistress in the drawing-
room still.

' You must be cold, ma'am,' she said, glancing at the
fire-grate.

' Is it a frost ? ' said Diana.

' It 's midnight and midwinter, ma'am.'

' Has it struck midnight ? '

The mantel-piece clock said five minutes past.

' You had better go to bed, Danvers, or you will lose
your bloom. Stop ; you are a faithful soul. Great
things are happening and I am agitated. Mr. Dacier
has told me news. He came back purposely.'

' Yes, ma'am,' said Danvers. ' He had a great deal to
tell ? '

' Well, he had.' Diana coloured at the first tentative
impertinence she had heard from her maid. ' What is
the secret of you, Danvers ? What attaches you to me ? '

' I 'm sure I don't know, ma'am. I 'm romantic.'

' And you think me a romantic object ? '

' I 'm sure I can't say, ma'am. I 'd rather serve you
than any other lady ; and I wish you was happy.'

' Do you suppose I am unhappy ? '

' I 'm sure—but if I may speak, ma'am : so handsome
and clever a lady ! and young ! I can't bear to see it.'

' Tush, you silly woman. You read your melting tales,
and imagine. I must go and write for money : it is my
profession. And I haven't an idea in my head. This

news disturbs me. Ruin if I don't write ; so I must.—I can't ! '

Diana beheld the ruin. She clasped the great news for succour. Great indeed : and known but to her of all the outer world. She was ahead of all—ahead of Mr. Tonans ! 

The visionary figure of Mr. Tonans petrified by the great news, drinking it, and confessing her ahead of him in the race for secrets, arose toweringly. She had not ever seen the Editor in his den at midnight. With the rumble of his machinery about him, and fresh matter arriving and flying into the printing-press, it must be like being in the very furnace-hissing of Events : an Olympian Council held in Vulcan's smithy. Consider the bringing to the Jove there news of such magnitude as to stupefy him ! He, too, who had admonished her rather sneeringly for staleness in her information. But this news, great though it was, and throbbing like a heart plucked out of a breathing body, throbbed but for a brief term, a day or two ; after which, great though it was, immense, it relapsed into a common organ, a possession of the multitude, merely historically curious.

' You are not afraid of the streets at night ? ' Diana said to her maid, as they were going upstairs.

' Not when we 're driving, ma'am,' was the answer.

THE MAN OF TWO MINDS faced his creatrix in the dressing-room, still delivering that most ponderous of sentences—a smothering pillow !

I have mistaken my vocation, thought Diana : I am certainly the flattest proser who ever penned a line.

She sent Danvers into the bedroom on a trifling errand, unable to bear the woman's proximity, and oddly unwilling to dismiss her.

She pressed her hands on her eyelids. Would Percy have humiliated her so if he had respected her ? He took advantage of the sudden loss of her habitual queenly

initiative at the wonderful news to debase and stain their
intimacy.  The lover's behaviour was judged by her
sensations :  she felt humiliated, plucked violently from
the throne where she had long been sitting securely, very
proudly.  That was at an end.  If she was to be better
than the loathsomest of hypocrites, she must deny him
his admission to the house.  And then what was her life !

Something that was pressing her low, she knew not how,
and left it unquestioned, incited her to exaggerate the
indignity her pride had suffered.  She was a dethroned
woman.  Deeper within, an unmasked actress, she said.
Oh, she forgave him !  But clearly he took her for the
same as other women consenting to receive a privileged
visitor.  And sounding herself to the soul, was she so
magnificently better ?  Her face flamed.  She hugged
her arms at her breast to quiet the beating, and dropped
them when she surprised herself embracing the memory.
He had brought political news, and treated her as—name
the thing !  Not designedly, it might be :  her position
invited it.  'The world had given her to him.'  The
world is always a prophet of the mire ; but the world
is no longer an utterly mistaken world.  She shook before
it.

She asked herself why Percy or the world should think
highly of an adventuress, who was a denounced wife, a
wretched author, and on the verge of bankruptcy.  She
was an adventuress.  When she held The Crossways she
had at least a bit of solid footing :  now gone.  An
adventuress without an idea in her head :  witness her
dullard, The Man of Two Minds, at his work of sermonizing
his mistress.

The tremendous pressure upon our consciousness of the
material cause, when we find ourselves cast among the
breakers of moral difficulties and endeavour to elude that
mud-visaged monster, chiefly by feigning unconsciousness,

was an experience of Diana's, in the crisis to which she was wrought. Her wits were too acute, her nature too direct, to permit of a lengthened confusion. She laid the scourge on her flesh smartly.—I gave him these privileges because I am weak as the weakest, base as my enemies proclaim me. I covered my woman's vile weakness with an air of intellectual serenity that he, choosing his moment, tore away, exposing me to myself, as well as to him, the most ordinary of reptiles. I kept up a costly household for the sole purpose of seeing him and having him near me. Hence this bitter need of money!—Either it must be money or disgrace. Money would assist her quietly to amend and complete her work. Yes, and this want of money, in a review of the last two years, was the material cause of her recklessness. It was, her revived and uprising pudency declared, the principal, the only cause. Mere want of money.

And she had a secret worth thousands! The secret of a day, no more : anybody's secret after some four and twenty hours.

She smiled at the fancied elongation and stare of the features of Mr. Tonans in his editorial midnight den.

What if he knew it and could cap it with something novel and stranger ? Hardly. But it was an inciting suggestion.

She began to tremble as a lightning-flash made visible her fortunes recovered, disgrace averted, hours of peace for composition stretching before her : a summer afternoon's vista.

It seemed a duel between herself and Mr. Tonans, and she sure of her triumph—Diana victrix !

' Danvers ! ' she called.

' Is it to undress, ma'am ? ' said the maid, entering to her.

' You are not afraid of the streets, you tell me. I have

to go down to the City, I think.  It is urgent.  Yes, I must go.  If I were to impart the news to you, your head would be a tolling bell for a month.'

'You will take a cab, ma'am.'

'We must walk out to find one.  I must go, though I should have to go on foot.  Quick with bonnet and shawl ; muffle up warmly.  We have never been out so late : but does it matter ?  You 're a brave soul, I 'm sure, and you shall have your fee.'

'I don't care for money, ma'am.'

'When we get home you shall kiss me.'

Danvers clothed her mistress in furs and rich wrappings : Not paid for !  was Diana's desperate thought, and a wrong one ; but she had to seem the precipitated bankrupt and succeeded.  She was near being it.  The boiling of her secret carried her through the streets rapidly and unobservantly except of such small things as the glow of the lights on the pavements and the hushed cognizance of the houses, in silence to a thoroughfare where a willing cabman was met.  The destination named, he nodded alertly : he had driven gentlemen there at night from the House of Commons, he said.

'*Our* Parliament is now sitting, and you drive ladies,' Diana replied.

'I hope I know one, never mind the hour,' said he of the capes.

He was bidden to drive rapidly.

'Complexion a tulip : you do not often see a pale cabman,' she remarked to Danvers, who began laughing, as she always expected to do on an excursion with her mistress.

'Do you remember, ma'am, the cabman taking us to the coach, when you thought of going to the continent ? '

'And I went to The Crossways ?  I have forgotten him.'

'He declared you was so beautiful a lady he would drive you to the end of England for nothing.'

'It must have been when I was paying him. Put it out of your mind, Danvers, that there are individual cabmen. They are the painted flowers of our metropolitan thoroughfares, and we gather them in rows.'

'They have their feelings, ma'am.'

'Brandied feelings are not pathetic to me.'

'I like to think kindly of them,' Danvers remarked, in reproof of her inhumanity ; adding : 'They may overturn us ! ' at which Diana laughed.

Her eyes were drawn to a brawl of women and men in the street. 'Ah ! that miserable sight ! ' she cried. 'It is the everlasting nightmare of London.'

Danvers humped, femininely injured by the notice of it. She wondered her mistress should deign to.

Rolling on between the blind and darkened houses, Diana transferred her sensations to them, and in a fit of the nerves imagined them beholding a funeral convoy without followers.

They came in view of the domed cathedral, hearing, in a pause of the wheels, the bell of the hour. 'Faster ! faster ! my dear man,' Diana murmured, and they entered a small still square of many lighted windows.

'This must be where the morrow is manufactured,' she said. 'Tell the man to wait.—Or rather it's the mirror of yesterday : we have to look backward to see forward in life.'

She talked her cool philosophy to mask her excitement from herself.

Her card, marked : '*Imperative—two minutes*,' was taken up to Mr. Tonans. They ascended to the editorial ante-room. Doors opened and shut, hasty feet traversed the corridors, a dull hum in dumbness told of mighty business at work. Diana received the summons to the mighty head of the establishment. Danvers was left to speculate. She heard the voice of Mr. Tonans : ' Not more than two ! ' This was not a place for compliments. Men passed her, hither and yonder, cursorily noticing the presence of a woman. She lost, very strangely to her, the sense of her sex and became an object—a disregarded object. Things of more importance were about. Her feminine self-esteem was troubled ; all idea of attractiveness expired. Here was manifestly a spot where women had dropped from the secondary to the cancelled stage of their extraordinary career in a world either blowing them aloft like soap-bubbles or quietly shelving them as supernumeraries. A gentleman—sweet vision !—shot by to the editor's door, without even looking cursorily. He knocked. Mr. Tonans appeared and took him by the arm, dictating at a great rate ; perceived Danvers, frowned at the female, and requested him to wait in the room, which the gentleman did, not once casting eye upon a woman. At last her mistress returned to her, escorted so far by Mr. Tonans, and he refreshingly bent his back to bow over her hand : so we have the satisfaction of knowing that we are not such poor creatures after all ! Suffering in person, Danvers was revived by the little show of homage to her sex.

They descended the stairs.

' You are not an Editor of a paper, but you may boast that you have been near the nest of one,' Diana said, when they resumed their seats in the cab. She breathed deeply from time to time, as if under a weight, or relieved of it, but she seemed animated, and she dropped now and again a funny observation of the kind that tickled Danvers and caused the maid to boast of her everywhere as better than a Play.

At home, Danvers busied her hands to supply her mistress a cup of refreshing tea and a plate of biscuits.

Diana had stunned herself with the strange weight of the expedition, and had not a thought. In spite of tea at that hour, she slept soundly through the remainder of the night, dreamlessly till late into the morning.

## CHAPTER XXXIII

### EXHIBITS THE SPRINGING OF A MINE IN A NEWSPAPER ARTICLE

THE powers of harmony would seem to be tried to their shrewdest pitch when Politics and Love are planted together in a human breast. This apparently opposite couple can nevertheless chant a very sweet accord, as was shown by Dacier on his homeward walk from Diana's house. Let Love lead, the God will make music of any chamber-comrade. He was able to think of affairs of State while feeling the satisfied thirst of the lover whose pride, irritated by confidential wild eulogies of the beautiful woman, had recently clamoured for proofs of his commandership. The impression she stamped on him at Copsley remained, but it could not occupy the foreground for ever. He did not object to play second to her sprightly wits in converse, if he had some warm testimony to his mastery over her blood. For the world had given her to him, enthusiastic friends had congratulated him : she had exalted him for true knightliness ; and he considered the proofs well earned, though he did not value them low. They were little by comparison. They lighted, instead of staining, her unparalleled high character.

She loved him. Full surely did she love him, or such a woman would never have consented to brave the world ; once in their project of flight, and next, even more

endearingly when contemplated, in the sacrifice of her good
name ; not omitting that fervent memory of her pained
submission, but a palpitating submission, to his caress.
She was in his arms again at the thought of it.  He had
melted her, and won the confession of her senses by a
surprise, and he owned that never had woman been so
vigilantly self-guarded or so watchful to keep her lover
amused and aloof.  Such a woman deserved long service.
But then the long service deserved its time of harvest.
Her surging look of reproach in submission pointed to the
golden time, and as he was a man of honour, pledged to
her for life, he had no remorse, and no scruple in determining to exact her dated promise, on this occasion deliberately.  She was the woman to be his wife ; she was his
mind's mate : they had hung apart in deference to mere
scruples too long.  During the fierce battle of the Session
she would be his help, his fountain of counsel ; and she
would be the rosy gauze-veiled more than cold helper and
adviser, the being which would spur her womanly intelligence to acknowledge, on this occasion deliberately, the
wisdom of the step.  They had been so close to it !  She
might call it madness then : now it was wisdom.  Each
had complete experience of the other, and each vowed
the step must be taken.

As to the secret communicated, he exulted in the
pardonable cunning of the impulse turning him back to
her house after the guests had gone, and the dexterous
play of his bait on the line, tempting her to guess and quit
her queenly guard.  Though it had not been distinctly
schemed, the review of it in that light added to the enjoyment.  It had been dimly and richly conjectured as
a hoped result.  Small favours from her were really
worth, thrice worth, the utmost from other women.  They
tasted the sweeter for the winning of them artfully—an
honourable thing in love.  Nature, rewarding the lover's

ingenuity and enterprise, inspires him with old Greek notions of right and wrong : and love is indeed a fluid mercurial realm, continually shifting the principles of rectitude and larceny. As long as he means nobly, what is there to condemn him ? Not she in her heart. She was the presiding divinity.

And she, his Tony, that splendid Diana, was the woman the world abused ! Whom will it not abuse ?

The slough she would have to plunge in before he could make her his own with the world's consent, was already up to her throat. She must, and without further hesitation, be steeped, that he might drag her out, washed of the imputed defilement, and radiant, as she was in character. Reflection now said this ; not impulse.

Her words rang through him. At every meeting she said things to confound his estimate of the wits of women, or be remembered for some spirited ring they had :—*A high wind will make a dead leaf fly like a bird.* He murmured it and flew with her. She quickened a vein of imagination that gave him entrance to a strangely brilliant sphere, above his own, where, she sustaining, he too could soar ; and he did, scarce conscious of walking home, undressing, falling asleep.

The act of waking was an instantaneous recovery of his emotional rapture of the overnight ; nor was it a bar to graver considerations. His Chief had gone down to a house in the country ; his personal business was to see and sound the followers of their party—after another sight of his Tony. She would be sure to counsel sagaciously ; she always did. She had a marvellous intuition of the natures of the men he worked with, solely from his chance descriptions of them : it was as though he started the bird and she transfixed it. And she should not have matter to ruffle her smooth brows : that he swore to. She should sway him as she pleased, be respected after her prescribed

manner. The promise must be exacted; nothing besides the promise.—You see, Tony, you cannot be less
than Tony to me now, he addressed the gentle phantom
of her. Let me have your word, and I am your servant
till the Session ends.—Tony blushes her swarthy crimson:
Diana, fluttering, rebukes her; but Diana is the appeas-
able Goddess; Tony is the woman, and she loves him.
The glorious Goddess need not cut them adrift; they can
show her a book of honest pages.

Dacier could truthfully say he had worshipped, done
knightly service to the beloved woman, homage to the
aureole encircling her. Those friends of his, covertly
congratulating him on her preference, doubtless thought
him more privileged than he was; but they did not know
Diana; and they were welcome, if they would only believe,
to the knowledge that he was at the feet of this most
sovereign woman. He despised the particular Satyr-
world which, whatever the nature or station of the woman,
crowns the desecrator, and bestows the title of Fool on the
worshipper. He could have answered veraciously that
she had kept him from folly.

Nevertheless the term to service must come. In the
assurance of the approaching term he stood braced against
a blowing world; happy as men are when their muscles
are strung for a prize they pluck with the energy and aim
of their whole force.

Letters and morning papers were laid for him to peruse
in his dressing-room. He read his letters before the bath.
Not much public news was expected at the present season.
While dressing, he turned over the sheets of Whitmonby's
journal. Dull comments on stale tidings. Foreign news,
Home news, with the leaders on them, identically dull.
Behold the effect of Journalism: a witty man, sparkling
overnight, gets into his pulpit and proses; because he
must say something, and he really knows nothing.

Journalists have an excessive overestimate of their influence.  They cannot, as Diana said, comparing them with
men on the Parliamentary platform, cannot feel they are
aboard the big vessel ;  they can only strive to raise a
breeze, or find one to swell ;  and they cannot measure the
stoutness or the greatness of the good ship England.
Dacier's personal ambition was inferior to his desire to
extend and strengthen his England.  Parliament was the
field, Government the office.  How many conversations
had passed between him and Diana on that patriotic
dream !  She had often filled his drooping sails ;  he
owned it proudly :—and while the world, both the hoofed
and the rectilinear portions, were biting at her character !
Had he fretted her self-respect ?  He blamed himself,
but a devoted service must have its term.

The paper of Mr. Tonans was reserved for perusal at
breakfast.  He reserved it because Tonans was an opponent, tricksy and surprising now and then, amusing too ;
unlikely to afford him serious reflections.  The recent
endeavours of his journal to whip the Government-team
to a right-about-face were annoying, preposterous.
Dacier had admitted to Diana that Tonans merited the
thanks of the country during the discreditable Railway
mania, when his articles had a fine exhortative and prophetic twang, and had done marked good.  Otherwise, as
regarded the Ministry, the veering gusts of Tonans were
objectionable : he ' raised the breeze ' wantonly as well
as disagreeably.  Any one can whip up the populace if he
has the instruments ; and Tonans frequently intruded on
the Ministry's prerogative to govern.  The journalist was
bidding against the statesman.  But such is the condition
of a rapidly Radicalizing country !   We must take it as
it is.

With a complacent, What now, Dacier fixed his indifferent eyes on the first column of the leaders.

He read, and his eyes grew horny. He jerked back at each sentence, electrified, staring. The article was shorter than usual. Total Repeal was named; the precise date when the Minister intended calling Parliament together to propose it. The 'Total Repeal' might be guess-work— an Editor's bold stroke; but the details, the date, were significant of positive information. The Minister's definite and immediate instructions were exactly stated.

Where could the fellow have got hold of that? Dacier asked the blank ceiling.

He frowned at vacant corners of the room in an effort to conjure some speculation indicative of the source.

Had his Chief confided the secret to another and a traitor? Had they been overheard in his library when the project determined on was put in plain speech?

The answer was no, impossible, to each question.

He glanced at Diana. She? But it was past midnight when he left her. And she would never have betrayed him, never, never. To imagine it a moment was an injury to her.

Where else could he look? It had been specially mentioned in the communication as a secret by his Chief, who trusted him and no others. Up to the consultation with the Cabinet, it was a thing to be guarded like life itself. Not to a soul except Diana would Dacier have breathed syllable of any secret—and one of this weight!

He ran down the article again. There were the facts; undeniable facts; and they detonated with audible roaring and rounding echoes of them over England. How did they come there? As well inquire how man came on the face of the earth.

He had to wipe his forehead perpetually. Think as he would in exaltation of Diana to shelter himself, he was the accused. He might not be the guilty, but he had opened his mouth; and though it was to her only, and she, as

Dunstane had sworn, true as steel, he could not escape
condemnation.  He had virtually betrayed his master.
Diana would never betray her lover, but the thing was in
the air as soon as uttered : and off to the printing-press !
Dacier's grotesque fancy under annoyance pictured a
stream of small printer's devils in flight from his babbling
lips.

He consumed bits of breakfast, with a sour confession
that a newspaper-article had hit him at last, and stun-
ningly.

Hat and coat were called for.   The state of aimlessness
in hot perplexity demands a show of action.   Whither to
go first was as obscure as what to do.   Diana said of the
Englishman's hat and coat, that she supposed they were
to make him a walking presentment of the house he had
shut up behind him.   A shot of the eye at the glass confirmed the likeness, but with a ruefully wry-faced re-
pudiation of it internally :—Not so shut up ! the reverse
of that—a common babbler.

However, there was no doubt of Diana.   First he would
call on her.   The pleasantest dose in perturbations of the
kind is instinctively taken first.   She would console,
perhaps direct him to guess how the secret had leaked.—
But so suddenly, immediately !   It was inexplicable.

Sudden and immediate consequences were experienced.
On the steps of his house his way was blocked by the arrival of Mr. Quintin Manx, who jumped out of a cab,
bellowing interjections and interrogations in a breath.
Was there *anything* in that article ?   He had read it at
breakfast, and it had choked him.   Dacier was due at a
house and could not wait : he said, rather sharply, he was
not responsible for newspaper articles.   Quintin Manx,
a senior gentleman and junior landowner, vowed that no
Minister intending to sell the country should treat him as
a sheep.   The shepherd might go ; he would not carry his

flock with him. But was there a twinkle of probability
in the story ? . . . that article ! Dacier was unable to
inform him ; he was very hurried, had to keep an appointment.

'If I let you go, will you come and lunch with me at
two ?' said Quintin.

To get rid of him, Dacier nodded and agreed.

'Two o'clock, mind !' was bawled at his heels as he
walked off with his long stride, unceremoniously leaving
the pursy gentleman of sixty to settle with his cabman far
to the rear.

## CHAPTER XXXIV

### IN WHICH IT IS DARKLY SEEN HOW THE CRIMINAL'S JUDGE MAY BE LOVE'S CRIMINAL

WHEN we are losing balance on a precipice we do not
think much of the thing we have clutched for support.
Our balance is restored and we have not fallen ; that is
the comfortable reflection : we stand as others do, and
we will for the future be warned to avoid the dizzy stations
which cry for resources beyond a common equilibrium,
and where a slip precipitates us to ruin.

When, further, it is a woman planted in a burning blush,
having to idealize her feminine weakness, that she may not
rebuke herself for grovelling, the mean material acts by
which she sustains a tottering position are speedily swallowed in the one pervading flame. She sees but an ashen
curl of the path she has traversed to safety, if anything.

Knowing her lover was to come in the morning, Diana's
thoughts dwelt wholly upon the way to tell him, as
tenderly as possible without danger to herself, that her
time for entertaining was over until she had finished her

book ; indefinitely, therefore. The apprehension of his complaining pricked the memory that she had something to forgive. He had sunk her in her own esteem by compelling her to see her woman's softness. But how high above all other men her experience of him could place him notwithstanding ! He had bowed to the figure of herself, dearer than herself, that she set before him : and it was a true figure to the world ; a too fictitious to any but the most knightly of lovers. She forgave ; and a shudder seized her.—Snake ! she rebuked the delicious run of fire through her veins ; for she was not like the idol woman of imperishable type, who are never for a twinkle the prey of the blood : statues created by man's common desire to impress upon the sex his possessing pattern of them as domestic decorations.

When she entered the room to Dacier and they touched hands, she rejoiced in her coolness, without any other feeling or perception active. Not to be unkind, not too kind : this was her task. She waited for the passage of commonplaces.

' You slept well, Percy ? '

' Yes ; and you ? '

' I don't think I even dreamed.'

They sat. She noticed the cloud on him and waited for his allusion to it, anxious concerning him simply.

Dacier flung the hair off his temples. Words of Titanic formation were hurling in his head at journals and journalists. He muttered his disgust of them.

' Is there anything to annoy you in the papers to-day ? ' she asked, and thought how handsome his face was in anger.

The paper of Mr. Tonans was named by him. ' You have not seen it ? '

' I have not opened it yet.'

He sprang up. ' The truth is, those fellows can now

afford to buy right and left, corrupt every soul alive !
There must have been a spy at the keyhole.  I 'm pretty
certain—I could swear it was not breathed to any ear but
mine ; and there it is this morning in black and white.'

' *What* is ? ' cried Diana, turning to him on her chair.

' The thing I told you last night.'

Her lips worked, as if to spell the thing.   ' Printed, do
you say ? ' she rose.

' Printed.   In a leading article, loud as a trumpet ;  a
hue and cry running from end to end of the country.
And my Chief has already had the satisfaction of seeing
the secret he confided to me yesterday roared in all the
thoroughfares this morning.  They 've got the facts :
his decision to propose it, and the date—the whole of it !
But who could have betrayed it ? '

For the first time since her midnight expedition she felt
a sensation of the full weight of the deed.  She heard
thunder.

She tried to disperse the growing burden by an inward
summons to contempt of the journalistic profession, but
nothing would come.  She tried to minimize it, and her
brain succumbed.  Her views of the deed last night and
now throttled reason in two contending clutches.  The
enormity swelled its dimensions, taking shape, and pointing magnetically at her.  She stood absolutely, amazedly,
bare before it.

' Is it of such very great importance ? ' she said, like
one supplicating him to lessen it.

' A secret of State ?  If you ask whether it is of great
importance to me, relatively it is of course.  Nothing
greater.  Personally my conscience is clear.  I never
mentioned it—couldn't have mentioned it—to any one
but you.  I 'm not the man to blab secrets.  He spoke to
me because he knew he could trust me.  To tell you the
truth, I 'm brought to a dead stop.  I can't make a guess.

I 'm certain, from what he said, that he trusted me only with it : perfectly certain. I know him well. He was in his library, speaking in his usual conversational tone, deliberately, nor overloud. He stated that it was a secret between us.'

' Will it affect him ? '

' This article ? Why, naturally it will. You ask strange questions. A Minister coming to a determination like that ! It affects him vitally. The members of the Cabinet are not so devoted. . . . It affects us all—the whole Party ; may split it to pieces ! There 's no reckoning the upset right and left. If it were false, it could be refuted ; we could despise it as a trick of journalism. It 's true. There 's the mischief. Tonans did not happen to call here last night ?—absurd ! I left later than twelve.'

' No, but let me hear,' Diana said hurriedly, for the sake of uttering the veracious negative and to slur it over. ' Let me hear . . .' She could not muster an idea.

Her delicious thrilling voice was a comfort to him. He lifted his breast high and thumped it, trying to smile. ' After all, it 's pleasant being with you, Tony. Give me your hand—you may : I 'm bothered—confounded by this morning surprise. It was like walking against the muzzle of a loaded cannon suddenly unmasked. One can't fathom the mischief it will do. And I shall be suspected, and can't quite protest myself the spotless innocent. Not even to one's heart's mistress ! to the wife of the bosom ! I suppose I 'm no Roman. You won't give me your hand ? Tony, you might, seeing I am rather . . .'

A rush of scalding tears flooded her eyes.

' Don't touch me,' she said, and forced her sight to look straight at him through the fiery shower. ' I have done positive *mischief* ? '

' You, my dear Tony ? ' He doated on her face. ' I

don't blame you, I blame myself.   These things should
never be breathed.   Once in the air, the devil has hold of
them.   Don't take it so much to heart.   The thing 's bad
enough to bear as it is.   Tears !   Let me have the hand.
I came, on my honour, with the most honest intention to
submit to your orders : but if I see you weeping in sympathy ! '

' Oh ! for heaven's sake,' she caught her hands away
from him, ' don't be generous.   Whip me with scorpions.
And don't touch me,' cried Diana.   ' Do you understand ?
You did not name it as a secret.   I did not imagine it to
be a secret of immense, *immediate* importance.'

' But—*what* ? ' shouted Dacier, stiffening.

He wanted her positive meaning, as she perceived,
having hoped that it was generally taken and current, and
the shock to him over.

' I had . . . I had not a suspicion of doing harm,
Percy.'

' But what harm have you done ?   No riddles ! '

His features gave sign of the break in their common
ground, the widening gulf.

' I went . . . it was a curious giddiness : I can't
account for it.   I thought . . . '

' *Went ?*   You went where ? '

' Last night.   I would speak intelligibly : my mind has
gone.   Ah ! you look.   It is not so bad as my feeling.'

' But where did you go last night ?   What !—to
Tonans ? '

She drooped her head : she saw the track of her route
cleaving the darkness in a demoniacal zig-zag and herself
in demon's grip.

' Yes,' she confronted him.   ' I went to Mr. Tonans.'

' Why ? '

' I went to him——'

' You went alone ? '

'I took my maid.'

'Well ? '

'It was late when you left me . . .'

'Speak plainly ! '

'I am trying : I will tell you all.'

'At once, if you please.'

'I went to him—why ?   There is no accounting for it. He sneered constantly at any stale information.'

'You gave him constant information ? '

'No : in our ordinary talk.   He railed at me for being " out of it."   I must be childish : I went to show him— oh ! my vanity !   I think I must have been possessed.'

She watched the hardening of her lover's eyes.   They penetrated, and through them she read herself insufferably.

But it was with hesitation still that he said : 'Then you betrayed me ? '

'Percy !   I had not a suspicion of mischief.'

'You went straight to this man ? '

'Not thinking . . .'

'You sold me to a journalist ! '

'I thought it was a secret of a day.   I don't think you— no, you did not tell me to keep it secret.   A word from you would have been enough.   I was in extremity.'

Dacier threw his hands up and broke away.   He had an impulse to dash from the room, to get a breath of different air.   He stood at the window, observing tradesmen's carts, housemaids, blank doors, dogs, a beggar fifer.   Her last words recurred to him.   He turned : 'You were in extremity, you said.   What is the meaning of that ? What extremity ? '

Her large dark eyes flashed powerlessly ; her shape appeared to have narrowed ; her tongue, too, was a feeble penitent.

'You ask a creature to recall her acts of insanity.'

'There must be some signification in your words, I suppose.'

'I will tell you as clearly as I can.  You have the right to be my judge.  I was in extremity—that is, I saw no means . . . I could not write : it was ruin coming.'

'Ah ?—you took payment for playing spy ? '

'I fancied I could retrieve . . . Now I see the folly, the baseness.  I was blind.'

'Then you sold me to a journalist for money ? '

The intolerable scourge fetched a stifled scream from her and drove her pacing, but there was no escape ; she returned to meet it.

The room was a cage to both of them, and every word of either was a sting.

'Percy, I did not imagine he would use it—make use of it as he has done.'

'Not ?  And when he paid for it ? '

'I fancied it would be merely of general service—if any.'

'Distributed ; I see : not leading to the exposure of the communicant ! '

'You are harsh ; but I would not have you milder.'

The meekness of such a mischief-doer was revolting and called for the lash.

'Do me the favour to name the sum.  I am curious to learn what my imbecility was counted worth.'

'No sum was named.'

'Have I been bought for a song ? '

'It was a suggestion—no definite . . . nothing stipulated.'

'You were to receive money ! '

'Leave me a bit of veiling !  No, you shall behold me the thing I am.  Listen . . . I was poor . . .'

'You might have applied to me.'

'For money !  That I could not do.'

' Better than betraying me, believe me.'

' I had no thought of betraying. I hope I could have died rather than consciously betray.'

' Money ! My whole fortune was at your disposal.'

' I was beset with debts, unable to write, and, last night when you left me, abject. It seemed to me that you disrespected me . . .'

' Last night ! ' Dacier cried with lashing emphasis.

' It is evident to me that I have the reptile in me, Percy. Or else I am subject to lose my reason. I went . . . I went like a bullet : I cannot describe it ; I was mad. I need a strong arm, I want help. I am given to think that I do my best and can be independent ; I break down. I went blindly—now I see it—for the chance of recovering my position, as the gambler casts ; and he wins or loses. With me it is the soul that is lost. No exact sum was named ; thousands were hinted.'

' You are hardly practical on points of business.'

' I was insane.'

' I think you said you slept well after it,' Dacier remarked.

' I had so little the idea of having done evilly, that I slept without a dream.'

He shrugged :—the consciences of women are such smooth deeps, or running shallows.

' I have often wondered how your newspaper men got their information,' he said, and muttered : ' Money— women ! ' adding : ' Idiots to prime them ! And I one of the leaky vessels ! Well, we learn. I have been rather astonished at times of late at the scraps of secret knowledge displayed by Tonans. If he flourishes his thousands ! The wonder is, he doesn't corrupt the Ministers' wives. Perhaps he does. Marriage will become a dangersign to Parliamentary members. Foreign women do these tricks . . . women of a well-known stamp. It is now a full year, I think, since I began to speak to you of secret matters—and congratulated myself, I recollect, on your thirst for them.'

'Percy, if you suspect that I have uttered one word before last night, you are wrong. I cannot paint my temptation or my loss of sense last night. Previously I was blameless. I thirsted, yes ; but in the hope of helping you.'

He looked at her. She perceived how glitteringly loveless his eyes had grown. It was her punishment ; and though the enamoured woman's heart protested it excessive, she accepted it.

' I can never trust you again,' he said.

' I fear you will not,' she replied.

His coming back to her after the departure of the guests last night shone on him in splendid colours of single-minded loverlike devotion. ' I came to speak to my own heart. I thought it would give you pleasure ; thought I could trust you utterly. I had not the slightest conception I was imperilling my honour . . . ! '

He stopped. Her bloodless fixed features revealed an intensity of anguish that checked him. Only her mouth, a little open for the sharp breath, appeared dumbly beseeching. Her large eyes met his like steel to steel, as of one who would die fronting the weapon.

He strangled a loathsome inclination to admire.

' So good bye,' he said.

She moved her lips.

He said no more. In half a minute he was gone.

To her it was the plucking of life out of her breast.

She pressed her hands where heart had been. The pallor and cold of death took her body.

## CHAPTER XXXV

### REVEALS HOW THE TRUE HEROINE OF ROMANCE COMES FINALLY TO HER TIME OF TRIUMPH

THE shutting of her house-door closed for Dacier that woman's history in connection with himself. He set his mind on the consequences of the act of folly—the trusting a secret to a woman. All were possibly not so bad : none should be trusted.

The air of the street fanned him agreeably as he revolved the horrible project of confession to the man who had put faith in him. Particulars might be asked. She would be unnamed, but an imagination of the effect of naming her placarded a notorious woman in fresh paint : two members of the same family her victims !

And last night, no later than last night, he had swung round at this very corner of the street to give her the fullest proof of his affection. He beheld a dupe trotting into a carefully-laid pitfall. She had him by the generosity of his confidence in her. Moreover, the recollection of her recent feeble phrasing, when she stood convicted of the treachery, when a really clever woman would have developed her resources, led him to doubt her being so finely gifted. She was just clever enough to hoodwink. He attributed the dupery to a trick of imposing the idea of her virtue upon men. Attracted by her good looks and sparkle, they entered the circle of her charm, became delightfully intimate, suffered a rebuff, and were from that time prepared to serve her purpose. How many other wretched dupes had she dangling ? He spied at Westlake, spied at Redworth, at old Lord Larrian, at Lord Dannisburgh, at Arthur Rhodes, dozens. Old and young were alike to her if she saw an end to be gained by keeping them hooked. Tonans too, and Whitmonby. Newspaper editors were especially serviceable. Perhaps ' a young Minister of State ' held the foremost rank in that respect : if completely duped and squeezeable, he produced more substantial stuff.

The background of ice in Dacier's composition was brought to the front by his righteous contempt of her treachery. No explanation of it would have appeased him. She was guilty, and he condemned her. She stood condemned by all the evil likely to ensue from her misdeed. Scarcely had he left her house last night when she was away to betray him !—He shook her from him without a pang. Crediting her with the one merit she had— that of not imploring for mercy—he the more easily shook her off. Treacherous, she had not proved theatrical. So there was no fuss in putting out her light, and it was done. He was justified by the brute facts. Honourable, courteous, kindly gentleman, highly civilized, an excellent citizen and a patriot, he was icy at an outrage to his principles, and in the dominion of Love a sultan of the bow-string and chopper period, sovereignly endowed to stretch a finger for the scimitared Mesrour to make the erring woman head and trunk with one blow : and away with those remnants ! This internally he did. Enough that the brute facts justified him.

St. James's park was crossed, and the grass of the Green park, to avoid inquisitive friends. He was obliged to walk ; exercise, action of any sort, was imperative, and but for some engagement he would have gone to his fencing-rooms for a bout with the master. He remembered his engagement and grew doubly embittered. He had absurdly pledged himself to lunch with Quintin Manx ; that was, to pretend to eat while submitting to be questioned by a political dullard strong on his present right to overhaul and rail at his superiors. The house was one of a block along the North-Western line of Hyde park. He kicked at the subjection to go there, but a promise was binding, though he gave it when stunned. He could have silenced Mr. Manx with the posing interrogation : Why have I so long consented to put myself at the mercy of a bore ? For him, he could not answer it, though Manx, as leader of the Shipping interest, was influential. The man had to be endured, like other doses in politics.

Dacier did not once think of the great ship-owner's niece till Miss Constance Asper stepped into her drawing-room to welcome him. She was an image of repose to his mind. The calm pure outline of her white features refreshed him as the Alps the Londoner newly alighted at Berne ; smoke, wrangle, the wrestling city's wickedness, behind him.

' My uncle is very disturbed,' she said. ' Is the news—if I am not very indiscreet in inquiring ? '

' I have a practice of never paying attention to newspaper articles,' Dacier replied.

' I am only affected by living with one who does,' Miss Asper observed, and the lofty isolation of her head above politics gave her a moral attractiveness in addition to physical beauty. Her water-colour sketches were on her uncle's walls : the beautiful in nature claimed and absorbed her. She dressed with a pretty rigour, a lovely simplicity, picturesque of the nunnery. She looked indeed a high-born young lady-abbess.

' It 's a dusty game for ladies,' Dacier said, abhorring the women defiled by it.

And when one thinks of the desire of men to worship women, there is a pathos in a man's discovery of the fair young creature undefiled by any interest in public affairs, virginal amid her bower's environments.

The angelical beauty of a virgin mind and person capti-
vated him, by contrast.  His natural taste was to admire
it, shunning the lures and tangles of the women on high
seas, notably the married : who, by the way, contrive to
ensnare us through wonderment at a cleverness caught
from their traffic with the masculine world : often—if we
did but know !—a parrot-repetition of the last male
visitor's remarks.  But that which the fair maiden speaks,
though it may be simple, is her own.

She too is her own : or vowed but to one.  She is on all
sides impressive in purity.  The world worships her as its
perfect pearl : and we are brought refreshfully to acknowledge that the world is right.

By contrast, the white radiation of Innocence distinguished Constance Asper celestially.  As he was well
aware, she had long preferred him—the reserved among
many pleading pressing suitors.  Her steady faithfulness
had fed on the poorest crumbs.

He ventured to express the hope that she was well.

' Yes,' she answered, with eyelids lifted softly to thank
him for his concern in so humble a person.

' You look a little pale,' he said.

She coloured like a sea-water shell.  ' I am inclined to
paleness by nature.'

Her uncle disturbed them.  Lunch was ready.  He
apologized for the absence of Mrs. Markland, a maternal
aunt of Constance, who kept house for them.  Quintin
Manx fell upon the meats, and then upon the Minister.
Dacier found himself happily surprised by the accession
of an appetite.  He mentioned it, to escape from the
worrying of his host, as unusual with him at midday :
and Miss Asper, supporting him in that effort, said benevolently : ' Gentlemen should eat ; they have so many
fatigues and troubles.'  She herself did not like to be seen
eating in public.  Her lips opened to the morsels, as with

a bird's bill, though with none of the pecking eagerness
we complacently observe in poultry.

'But now, I say, positively, how about that article ? '
said Quintin.

Dacier visibly winced, and Constance immediately said :
' Oh ! spare us politics, dear uncle.'

Her intercession was without avail, but by contrast with
the woman implicated in the horrible article, it was a carol
of the seraphs.

' Come, you can say whether there 's anything in it,'
Dacier's host pushed him.

' I should not say it if I could,' he replied.

The mild sweetness of Miss Asper's look encouraged
him.

He was touched to the quick by hearing her say : ' You
ask for Cabinet secrets, uncle. All secrets are holy, but
secrets of State are under a seal next to divine.'

Next to divine ! She was the mouthpiece of his ruling
principle.

' I 'm not prying into secrets,' Quintin persisted ; ' all
I want to know is, whether there 's any foundation for that
article—all London 's boiling about it, I can tell you—or
it 's only newspaper's humbug.'

' Clearly the oracle for you is the Editor's office,'
rejoined Dacier.

' A pretty sort of answer I should get.'

' It would at least be complimentary.'

' How do you mean ? '

' The net was cast for you—and the sight of a fish in it ! '

Miss Asper almost laughed. ' Have you heard the
choir at St. Catherine's ? ' she asked.

Dacier had not. He repented of his worldliness, and
drinking persuasive claret, said he would go to hear it next
Sunday.

' Do,' she murmured.

'Well, you seem to be a pair against me,' her uncle grumbled. 'Anyhow I think it's important. People have been talking for some time, and I don't want to be taken unawares ; I won't be a yoked ox, mind you.'

'Have you been sketching lately ? ' Dacier asked Miss Asper.

She generally filled a book in the autumn, she said.

'May I see it ? '

'If you wish.'

They had a short tussle with her uncle and escaped. He was conducted to a room midway upstairs : an heiress's conception of a saintly little room ; and more impressive in purity, indeed it was, than a saint's, with the many crucifixes, gold and silver emblems, velvet prie-Dieu chairs, jewel-clasped sacred volumes : every invitation to meditate in luxury on an ascetic religiousness.

She depreciated her sketching powers. 'I am impatient with my imperfections. I am therefore doomed not to advance.'

'On the contrary, that is the state guaranteeing ultimate excellence,' he said, much disposed to drone about it.

She sighed : ' I fear not.'

He turned the leaves, comparing her modesty with the performance. The third of the leaves was a subject instantly recognized by him. It represented the place he had inherited from Lord Dannisburgh.

He named it.

She smiled : ' You are good enough to see a likeness ? My aunt and I were passing it last October, and I waited for a day, to sketch.'

'You have taken it from my favourite point of view.'

'I am glad.'

'How much I should like a copy ! '

'If you will accept that ? '

'I could not rob you.'

' I can make a duplicate.'

' The look of the place pleases you ? '

' Oh ! yes ; the pines behind it ; the sweet little village church ; even the appearance of the rustics ;—it is all impressively old English.   I suppose you are very seldom there ? '

' Does it look like a home to you ? '

' No place more ! '

' I feel the loneliness.'

' Where I live I feel no loneliness ! '

' You have heavenly messengers near you.'

' They do not always come.'

' Would you consent to make the place less lonely to me ? '

Her bosom rose.   In deference to her maidenly under-standing, she gazed inquiringly.

' If you love it ! ' said he.

' The place ? ' she said, looking soft at the possessor.

' Constance ! '

' Is it true ? '

' As you yourself.   Could it be other than true ?   This hand is mine ? '

' Oh ! Percy.'

Borrowing the world's poetry to describe them, the long prayed-for Summer enveloped the melting snows.

So the recollection of Diana's watch beside his uncle's death-bed was wiped out.   Ay, and the hissing of her treachery silenced.   This maidenly hand put him at peace with the world, instead of his defying it for a worthless woman—who could not do better than accept the shelter of her husband's house, as she ought to be told, if her friends wished her to save her reputation.

Dacier made his way downstairs to Quintin Manx, by whom he was hotly congratulated and informed of the extent of the young lady's fortune : on the strength of which it was expected that he would certainly speak a private word in elucidation of that newspaper article.

'I know nothing of it,' said Dacier, but promised to come and dine.

Alone in her happiness Constance Asper despatched various brief notes under her gold-symbolled crest to sisterly friends; one to Lady Wathin, containing the single line :

'Your prophesy is confirmed.'

Dacier was comfortably able to face his Club after the excitement of a proposal, with a bride on his hands. He was assaulted concerning the article, and he parried capitally. Say that her lips were rather cold : at any rate, they invigorated him. Her character was guaranteed—not the hazy idea of a dupe. And her fortune would be enormous : a speculation merely due to worldly prudence and prospective ambition.

At the dinner-table of four, in the evening, conversation would have seemed dull to him, by contrast, had it not been for the presiding grace of his bride, whose habitually eminent feminine air of superiority to the repast was throned by her appreciative receptiveness of his looks and utterances. Before leaving her, he won her consent to a very early marriage ; on the plea of a possibly approaching Session, and also that they had waited long. The consent, notwithstanding the hurry of preparations it involved, besides the annihilation of her desire to meditate on so solemn a change in her life and savour the congratulation of her friends and have the choir of St. Catherine's rigorously drilled in her favourite anthems, was beautifully yielded to the pressure of circumstances.

There lay on his table at night a letter ; a bulky letter. No need to tear it open for sight of the signature : the superscription was redolent of that betraying woman. He tossed it unopened into the fire.

As it was thick, it burned sullenly, discolouring his name on the address, as she had done, and still offering him a last chance of viewing the contents. She fought on the consuming fire to have her exculpation heard.

But was she not a shameless traitor ? She had caught him by his love of his country and hope to serve it. She had wound into his heart to bleed him of all he knew and sell the secrets for money. A wonderful sort of eloquence lay there, on those coals, no doubt. He felt a slight movement of curiosity to glance at two or three random sentences : very slight. And why read them now ? They were valueless to him, mere outcries. He judged her by the brute facts. She and her slowly-consuming letter were of a common blackness. Moreover, to read them when he was plighted to another woman would be senseless. In the discovery of her baseness, she had made a poor figure. Doubtless during the afternoon she had trimmed her intuitive Belial art of making ' the worse appear the better cause': queer to peruse, and instructive in an unprofitable department of knowledge—the tricks of the sex.

He said to himself, with little intuition of the popular taste : She wouldn't be a bad heroine of Romance ! He said it derisively of the Romantic. But the right worshipful heroine of Romance was the front-face female picture he had won for his walls. Poor Diana was the flecked heroine of Reality : not always the same ; not impeccable ; not an ignorant-innocent, nor a guileless : good under good leading ; devoted to the death in a grave crisis ; often wrestling with her terrestrial nature nobly ; and a growing soul ; but not one whose purity was carved in marble for the assurance to an Englishman that his possession of the changeless thing defies time and his fellows, is the pillar of his home and universally enviable. Your fair one of Romance cannot suffer a mishap without a plotting villain, perchance many of them, to wreak the dread iniquity : she cannot move without him ; she is the marble block, and if she is to have a feature, he is the sculptor ; she depends on him for life, and her human history at least is married to him far more than to the rescuing lover. No wonder, then, that men should find her thrice cherishable featureless, or with the most moderate possible indication of a countenance. Thousands of the excellent simple creatures do ; and every reader of her tale. On the contrary, the heroine of Reality is that woman whom you have met or heard of once in your course of years, and very probably despised for bearing in her composition the motive principle ; at best, you say, a singular mixture of good and bad ; anything but the feminine ideal of man. Feature to some excess, you think, distinguishes her. Yet she furnishes not any of the sweet sensual excitement pertaining to her spotless rival pursued by villany. She knocks at the doors of the mind, and the mind must open to be interested in her. Mind and heart must be wide open to excuse her sheer descent from the pure ideal of man.

Dacier's wandering reflections all came back in crowds to the judicial Bench of the Black Cap. He felt finely, apart from the treason, that her want of money degraded her : him too, by contact. Money she might have had to any extent : upon application for it, of course. How was he to imagine that she wanted money! Smilingly as she welcomed him and his friends, entertaining them royally, he was bound to think she had means. A decent propriety bound him not to think of the matter at all. He naturally supposed she was capable of conducting her affairs. And—money! It soiled his memory : though the hour at Rovio was rather pretty, and the scene at Copsley touching : other times also, short glimpses of the woman, were taking. The flood of her treachery effaced them. And why reflect ? Constance called to him to look her way.

Diana's letter died hard. The corners were burnt to black tissue, with an edge or two of discoloured paper. A small frayed central heap still resisted, and in kindness to the necessity for privacy, he impressed the fire-tongs to complete the execution. After which he went to his desk and worked, under the presidency of Constance.


## CHAPTER XXXVI

### IS CONCLUSIVE AS TO THE HEARTLESSNESS OF WOMEN WITH BRAINS

HYMENÆAL rumours are those which might be backed to run a victorious race with the tale of evil fortune ; and clearly for the reason that man's livelier half is ever alert to speed them. They travel with an astonishing celerity over the land, like flames of the dry beacon-faggots of old time in announcement of the invader or a conquest, gathering as they go : wherein, to say nothing of their vastly wider range, they surpass the electric wires. Man's nuptial half is kindlingly concerned in the launch of a new couple ; it is the business of the fair sex : and man himself (very strangely, but nature quickens him still) lends a not unfavouring eye to the preparations of the matrimonial vessel for its oily descent into the tides, where billows will soon be rising, captain and mate soon discussing the fateful question of who is commander. We consent, it appears, to hope again for mankind ; here is another chance ! Or else, assuming the happiness of the pair, that pomp of ceremonial, contrasted with the little wind-blown candle they carry between them, catches at our weaker fibres.

2 c

After so many ships have foundered, some keel up, like poisoned fish, at the first drink of water, it is a gallant spectacle, let us avow; and either the world perpetuating it is heroical or nature incorrigible in the species. Marriages are unceasing. Friends do it, and enemies; the unknown contractors of this engagement, or armistice, inspire an interest. It certainly is both exciting and comforting to hear that man and woman are ready to join in a mutual affirmative, say Yes together again. It sounds like the end of the war.

The proclamation of the proximate marriage of a young Minister of State and the greatest heiress of her day;— notoriously '*The* young Minister of State' of a famous book written by the beautiful, now writhing, woman madly enamoured of him—and the heiress whose dowry could purchase a Duchy; this was a note to make the gossips of England leap from their beds at the midnight hour and wag tongues in the market-place. It did away with the political hubbub over the Tonans article, and let it noise abroad like nonsense. The Hon. Percy Dacier espouses Miss Asper ; and she rescues him from the snares of a siren, he her from the toils of the Papists. She would have gone over to them, she was going when, luckily for the Protestant Faith, Percy Dacier intervened with his proposal. Town and country buzzed the news ; and while that dreary League trumpeted about the business of the nation, a people suddenly become Oriental chattered of nothing but the blissful union to be celebrated in princely state, with every musical accessory, short of Operatic.

Lady Wathin was an active agent in this excitement. The excellent woman enjoyed marriages of High Life : which, as there is presumably wealth to support them, are manifestly under *sanction* : and a marriage that she could consider one of her own contrivance, had a delicate flavour of a marriage in the family ; not quite equal to

the seeing a dear daughter of her numerous progeny conducted to the altar, but excelling it in the pomp that bids
the heavens open.  She and no other spread the tidings
of Miss Asper's debating upon the step to Rome at the
very instant of Percy Dacier's declaration of his love ;—
and it was a beautiful struggle, that of the half-dedicated
nun and her deep-rooted earthly passion, love prevailing !
She sent word to Lady Dunstane : ' You know the
interest I have always taken in dear Constance Asper,'
etc. ; inviting her to come on a visit a week before the
end of the month, that she might join in the ceremony of
a wedding ' likely to be the grandest of our time.'  Pitiful
though it was, to think of the bridal pair having but eight
or ten days at the outside, for a honeymoon, the beauty
of their ' mutual devotion to duty ' was urged by Lady
Wathin upon all hearers.

Lady Dunstane declined the invitation.  She waited to
hear from her friend, and the days went by ;  she could
only sorrow for her poor Tony, divining her state.  However little of wrong in the circumstances, they imposed a
silence on her decent mind, and no conceivable shape of
writing would transmit condolences.  She waited, with
a dull heartache : by no means grieving at Dacier's engagement to the heiress ; until Redworth animated her,
as the bearer of rather startling intelligence, indirectly
relating to the soul she loved.  An accident in the street
had befallen Mr. Warwick.  Redworth wanted to know
whether Diana should be told of it, though he had no
particulars to give ; and somewhat to his disappointment,
Lady Dunstane said she would write.  She delayed,
thinking the accident might not be serious ;  and the
information of it to Diana surely would be so.  Next day
at noon her visitor was Lady Wathin, evidently perturbed
and anxious to say more than she dared : but she received
no assistance.  After beating the air in every direction,

especially dwelling on the fond reciprocal affection of the two devoted lovers, to be united within three days' time, Lady Wathin said at last : ' And is it not shocking ! I talk of a marriage and am appalled by a death. That poor man died last night in the hospital. I mean poor Mr. Warwick. He was recovering, getting strong and well, and he was knocked down at a street-crossing and died last night. It is a warning to us ! '

' Mr. Redworth happened to hear of it at his Club, near which the accident occurred, and he called at the hospital. Mr. Warwick was then alive,' said Lady Dunstane ; adding : ' Well, if prevention is better than cure, as we hear ! Accidents are the specific for averting the maladies of age, which are a certain crop ! '

Lady Wathin's eyelids worked and her lips shut fast at the coldhearted remark void of meaning.

She sighed. ' So ends a life of misery, my dear ! '

' You are compassionate.'

' I hope so. But . . . Indeed I must speak, if you will let me. I think of the living.'

Lady Dunstane widened her eyes. ' Of Mrs. Warwick ? '

' She has now the freedom she desired. I think of others. Forgive me, but Constance Asper is to me as a daughter. I have perhaps no grounds for any apprehension. Love so ardent, so sincere, was never shown by bridegroom elect : and it is not extraordinary to those acquainted with dear Constance. But one may be a worshipped saint and experience defection. The terrible stories one hears of a power of fascination almost . . . ! ' Lady Wathin hung for the word.

' Infernal,' said Lady Dunstane, whose brows had been bent inquiringly. ' Have no fear. The freedom you allude to will not be used to interfere with any entertainment in prospect. It was *freedom* my friend desired. Now that her jewel is restored to her, she is not the person to throw it away, be sure. And pray, drop the subject.'

'One may rely . . . you think ? '

'Oh ! Oh ! '

'This release coming just before the wedding . . . ! '

'I should hardly suppose the man to be the puppet you depict, or indicate.'

'It is because men—so many—are not puppets that one is conscious of alarm.'

'Your previous remark,' said Lady Dunstane, ' sounded superstitious. Your present one has an antipodal basis. But, as for your alarm, check it : and spare me further. My friend has acknowledged powers. Considering that she does not use them, you should learn to respect her.'

Lady Wathin bowed stiffly. She refused to partake of lunch, having, she said, satisfied her conscience by the performance of a duty and arranged with her flyman to catch a train. Her cousin Lady Dunstane smiled loftily at everything she uttered, and she felt that if a woman like this Mrs. Warwick could put division between blood-relatives, she could do worse, and was to be dreaded up to the hour of the nuptials.

'I meant no harm in coming,' she said, at the shaking of hands.

'No, no ; I understand,' said her hostess : ' you are hen-hearted over your adopted brood. The situation is perceptible and your intention creditable.'

As one of the good women of the world, Lady Wathin in departing was indignant at the tone and dialect of a younger woman not modestly concealing her possession of the larger brain. Brains in women she both dreaded and detested ; she believed them to be devilish. Here were instances :—they had driven poor Sir Lukin to evil courses, and that poor Mr. Warwick straight under the wheels of a cab. Sir Lukin's name was trotting in public with a naughty Mrs. Fryar-Gunnett's : Mrs. Warwick might still trim her arts to baffle the marriage. Women with brains, moreover, are all heartless : they have no pity for distress, no horror of catastrophes, no joy in the happiness of the deserving. Brains in men advance a household to station ; but brains in women divide it and are the wrecking of society. Fortunately Lady Wathin knew she could rally a powerful moral contingent, the aptitude of which for a one-minded cohesion enabled it to crush those fractional daughters of mischief. She was a really good woman of the world, heading a multitude ; the same whom you are accustomed to hear exalted ; lucky in having had a guided girlhood, a thick-curtained prudence ; and in having stock in the moral funds, shares in the sentimental tramways. Wherever the world laid its hoards or ran its lines, she was found, and forcible enough to be eminent ; though at fixed hours of the day, even as she washed her hands, she abjured worldliness : a performance that cleansed her. If she did not make morality appear loveable to the objects of her dislike, it was owing to her want of brains to see the origin, nature and right ends of morality. But a world yet more deficient than she, esteemed her cordially for being a bulwark of the present edifice ; which looks a solid structure when the microscope is not applied to its components.

Supposing Percy Dacier a dishonourable tattler as well as an icy lover, and that Lady Wathin, through his bride, had become privy to the secret between him and Diana ? There is reason to think that she would have held it in terror over the baneful woman, but not have persecuted her : for she was by no means the active malignant of theatrical plots. No, she would have charged it upon the possession of brains by women, and have had a further motive for inciting the potent dignitary her husband to employ his authority to repress the sex's exercise of those fell weapons, hurtful alike to them and all coming near them.

So extreme was her dread of Mrs. Warwick, that she drove from the London railway station to see Constance and be reassured by her tranquil aspect.

Sweet Constance and her betrothed Percy were together, examining a missal.

Lady Dunstane despatched a few words of the facts to Diana. She hoped to hear from her ; rather hoped, for the moment, not to see her. No answer came. The great day of the nuptials came and passed. She counted on her husband's appearance the next morning, as the good gentleman made a point of visiting her, to entertain the wife he adored, whenever he had a wallet of gossip that would overlay the blank of his absence. He had been to the church of the wedding—he did not say with whom :— all the world was there ; and he rapturously described the ceremony, stating that it set women weeping and caused him to behave like a fool.

' You are impressionable,' said his wife.

He murmured something in praise of the institution of marriage—when celebrated impressively, it seemed.

' Tony calls the social world " the theatre of appetites," as we have it at present,' she said ; ' and the world at a wedding is, one may reckon, in the second act of the hungry tragi-comedy.'

' Yes, there 's the breakfast,' Sir Lukin assented. Mrs. Fryar-Gunnett was much more intelligible to him : in fact, quite so, as to her speech.

Emma's heart now yearned to her Tony. Consulting her strength, she thought she might journey to London, and on the third morning after the Dacier-Asper marriage, she started.

Diana's door was open to Arthur Rhodes when Emma reached it.

' Have you seen her ? ' she asked him.

His head shook dolefully. ' Mrs. Warwick is unwell ; she has been working too hard.'

' You also, I 'm afraid.'

' No.' He could deny that, whatever the look of him.

' Come to me at Copsley soon,' said she, entering to Danvers in the passage.

' My mistress is upstairs, my lady,' said Danvers. ' She is lying on her bed.'

' She is ill ? '

' She has been lying on her bed ever since.'

' Since what ? ' Lady Dunstane spoke sharply.

Danvers retrieved her indiscretion. ' Since she heard of the accident, my lady.'

' Take my name to her. Or no : I can venture.'

' I am not allowed to go in and speak to her. You will find the room quite dark, my lady, and very cold. It is her command. My mistress will not let me light the fire ; and she has not eaten or drunk of anything since. . . . She will die, if you do not persuade her to take nourishment : a little, for a beginning. It wants the beginning.'

Emma went upstairs, thinking of the enigmatical maid, that she must be a good soul after all. Diana's bedroom door was opened slowly.

' You will not be able to see at first, my lady,' Danvers whispered. ' The bed is to the left, and a chair. I would bring in a candle, but it hurts her eyes. She forbids it.'

Emma stepped in. The chill thick air of the unlighted London room was cavernous. She almost forgot the beloved of her heart in the thought that a living woman had been lying here more than two days and nights, fasting. The proof of an uttermost misery revived the circumstances within her to render her friend's presence in this desert of darkness credible. She found the bed by touch, silently, and distinguished a dark heap on the bed ; she heard no breathing. She sat and listened ; then she stretched her hand and met her Tony's. It lay open. It was the hand of a drowned woman.

Shutters and curtains and the fireless grate gave the room an appalling likeness to the vaults.

So like to the home of death it seemed, that in a few minutes the watcher had lost count of time and kept but a wormy memory of the daylight. She dared not speak, for some fear of startling ; for the worse fear of never getting answer. Tony's hand was lifeless. Her clasp of it struck no warmth.

She stung herself with bitter reproaches for having let common mundane sentiments, worthy of a Lady Wathin, bar her instant offer of her bosom to the beloved who suffered in this depth of mortal agony. Tony's love of a man, as she should have known, would be wrought of the elements of our being : when other women named Happiness, she said Life ; in division, Death. Her body lying still upon the bed here was a soul borne onward by the river of Death.

The darkness gave sight after a while, like a curtain lifting on a veil : the dead light of the underworld. Tony lay with her face up, her underlip dropped ; straight from head to feet. The outline of her face, without hue of it, could be seen : sign of the hapless women that have souls in love. Hateful love of men ! Emma thought, and was moved to feel at the wrist for her darling's pulse. He has killed her ! the thought flashed, as, with pangs chilling her frame, the pressure at the wrist continued insensible of the faintest beat. She clasped it, trembling, in pain to stop an outcry.

' It is Emmy,' said the voice.

Emma's heart sprang to heaven on a rush of thanks.

' My Tony,' she breathed softly.

She hung for a further proof of life in the motionless body. ' Tony ! ' she said.

The answer was at her hand, a thread-like return of her clasp.

' It is Emmy come to stay with you, never to leave you.'

The thin still answer was at her hand a moment ; the fingers fell away. A deep breath was taken twice to say : ' Don't talk to me.'

Emma retained the hand. She was warned not to press it by the deadness following its effort to reply.

But Tony lived ; she had given proof of life. Over this little wavering taper in the vaults Emma cowered, cherishing the hand, silently hoping for the voice.

It came : ' Winter.'

' It is a cold winter, Tony.'

' My dear will be cold.'

' I will light the fire.'

Emma lost no time in deciding to seek the match-box. The fire was lit and it flamed ; it seemed a revival in the room. Coming back to the bedside, she discerned her Tony's lack-lustre large dark eyes and her hollow cheeks : her mouth open to air as to the drawing-in of a sword ; rather as to the releaser than the sustainer. Her feet were on the rug her maid had placed to cover them. Emma leaned across the bed to put them to her breast, beneath her fur mantle, and held them there despite the half-animate tug of the limbs and the shaft of iciness they sent to her very heart. When she had restored them to some warmth, she threw aside her bonnet and lying beside Tony, took her in her arms, heaving now and then a deep sigh.

She kissed her cheek.

' It is Emmy.'

' Kiss her.'

' I have no strength.'

Emma laid her face on the lips. They were cold ; even the breath between them cold.

' Has Emmy been long . . . ? '

' Here, dear ? I think so. I am with my darling.'

Tony moaned. The warmth and the love were bringing back her anguish.

She said : ' I have been happy. It is not hard to go.'

Emma strained to her. ' Tony will wait for her soul's own soul to go, the two together.'

There was a faint convulsion in the body. ' If I cry, I shall go in pain.'

' You are in Emmy's arms, my beloved.'

Tony's eyes closed for forgetfulness under that sensation. A tear ran down from her, but the pain was lax and neighboured sleep, like the pleasure.

So passed the short winter day, little spoken.

Then Emma bethought her of a way of leading Tony to take food, and she said : ' I shall stay with you ; I shall send for clothes ; I am rather hungry. Don't stir, dear. I will be mistress of the house.'

She went below to the kitchen, where a few words in the ear of a Frenchwoman were sufficient to waken immediate comprehension of what was wanted, and smart service : within ten minutes an appetizing bouillon sent its odour over the bedroom. Tony, days back, had said her last to the act of eating ; but Emma sipping at the spoon and expressing satisfaction, was a pleasant picture. The bouillon smelt pleasantly.

' Your servants love you,' Emma said.

' Ah, poor good souls.'

' They crowded up to me to hear of you. Madame of course at the first word was off to her pots. And we English have the habit of calling ourselves the practical people !—This bouillon is consummate.—However, we

have the virtues of barbarians ; we can love and serve for
love.    I never tasted anything so good.    I could become
a glutton.'

' Do,' said Tony.

' I should be ashamed to " drain the bowl " all to myself : a solitary toper is a horrid creature, unless he makes
a song of it.'

' Emmy makes a song of it to me.'

' But " pledge me " is a noble saying, when you think of
humanity's original hunger for the whole.    It is there that
our civilizing commenced, and I am particularly fond of
hearing the call.    It is grandly historic.    So pledge me,
Tony.    We two can feed from one spoon ; it is a closer
bond than the loving cup.    I want you just to taste it and
excuse my gluttony.'

Tony murmured, ' No.'    The spoon was put to her
mouth.    She sighed to resist.    The stronger will compelled her to move her lips.    Emma fed her as a child, and
nature sucked for life.

The first effect was a gush of tears.

Emma lay with her that night, when the patient was
the better sleeper.    But during the night at intervals she
had the happiness of feeling Tony's hand travelling to
make sure of her.


## CHAPTER XXXVII

### AN EXHIBITION OF SOME CHAMPIONS OF THE STRICKEN LADY

CLOSE upon the hour of ten every morning the fortuitous
meeting of two gentlemen at Mrs. Warwick's housedoor
was a signal for punctiliously stately greetings, the saluta-
tion of the raised hat and a bow of the head from a position

of military erectness, followed by the remark : ' I trust
you are well, sir ' : to which the reply : ' I am very well,
sir, and trust you are the same,' was deemed a complimentary fulfilment of their mutual obligation in presence.   Mr.
Sullivan Smith's initiative imparted this exercise of formal
manners to Mr. Arthur Rhodes, whose renewed appearance, at the minute of his own arrival, he viewed, as he did
not conceal, with a disappointed and a reproving eye.   The
inquiry after the state of Mrs. Warwick's health having
received its tolerably comforting answer from the footman,
they left their cards in turn, then descended the doorsteps,
faced for the performance of the salute, and departed their
contrary ways.

The pleasing intelligence refreshed them one morning,
that they would be welcomed by Lady Dunstane.   There-
upon Mr. Sullivan Smith wheeled about to Mr. Arthur
Rhodes and observed to him : ' Sir, I might claim, by
right of seniority, to be the foremost of us two in offering
my respects to the lady, but the way is open to you.'

' Sir,' said Mr. Arthur Rhodes, ' permit me to defer to
your many superior titles to that distinction.'

' The honour, sir, lies rather in the bestowing than in
the taking.'

' I venture to think, sir, that though I cannot speak pure
Castilian, I require no lesson from a Grandee of Spain in
acknowledging the dues of my betters.'

' I will avow myself conquered, sir, by your overpower-
ing condescension,' said Mr. Sullivan Smith ;   ' and I
entreat you to ascribe my acceptance of your brief retirement to the urgent character of the business I have at
heart.'

He laid his fingers on the panting spot, and bowed.

Mr. Arthur Rhodes, likewise bowing, deferentially fell
to rearward.

' If I mistake not,' said the Irish gentleman, ' I am

indebted to Mr. Rhodes ; and we have been joint partici-
pators in the hospitality of Mrs. Warwick's table.'

The English gentleman replied : ' It was there that I
first had the pleasure of an acquaintance which is graven
on my memory, as the words of the wise king on tablets of
gold and silver.'

Mr. Sullivan Smith gravely smiled at the unwonted
match he had found in ceremonious humour, in Saxonland,
and saying : ' I shall not long detain you, Mr. Rhodes,'
he passed through the doorway.

Arthur waited for him, pacing up and down, for a quarter of an hour, when a totally different man reappeared in
the same person, and was the Sullivan Smith of the rosy
beaming features and princely heartiness. He was accosted : ' Now, my dear boy, it 's your turn to try if you
have a chance, and good luck go with ye. I 've said what
I could on your behalf, for you 're one of ten thousand in
this country, you are.'

Mr. Sullivan Smith had solemnified himself to proffer
a sober petition within the walls of the newly widowed
lady's house ; namely, for nothing less than that sweet
lady's now unfettered hand : and it had therefore been
perfectly natural to him, until his performance ended with
the destruction of his hopes, to deliver himself in the high
Castilian manner. Quite unexpected, however, was the
reciprocal loftiness of tone spontaneously adopted by the
young English squire, for whom, in consequence, he conceived a cordial relish ; and as he paced in the footsteps of
Arthur, anxious to quiet his curiosity by hearing how it
had fared with one whom he had to suppose the second
applicant, he kept ejaculating : ' Not a bit ! The fellow
can't be Saxon ! And she had a liking for him. She 's
nigh coming of the age when a woman takes to the chicks.
Better he than another, if it 's to be any one. For he 's
got fun in him ; he carries his own condiments, instead of

borrowing from the popular castors, as is their way over
here.   But I might have known there 's always sure to
be salt and savour in the man she covers with her wing.
Excepting, if you please, my dear lady, a bad shot you
made at a rascal cur, no more worthy of you than Beelze-
bub of Paradise.   No matter !   The daughters of Erin
must share the fate of their mother Isle, that their tears
may shine in the burst of sun to follow.   For personal and
patriotic motives, I would have cheered her and been like
a wild ass combed and groomed and tamed by the adorable
creature.   But her friend says there 's not a whisk of a
chance for me, and I must roam the desert, kicking up,
and worshipping the star I hail brightest.   They know me
not, who think I can't worship.   Why, what were I without my star ?   At best a pickled porker.'

Sullivan Smith became aware of a ravishing melodious-
ness in the soliloquy, as well as a clean resemblance in the
simile.   He would certainly have proceeded to improvize
impassioned verse, if he had not seen Arthur Rhodes on
the pavement.   ' So, here 's the boy.   Query, the face he
wears.'

' How kind of you to wait,' said Arthur.

' We 'll call it sympathy, for convenience,' rejoined
Sullivan Smith.   ' Well, and what next ? '

' You know as much as I do.   Thank heaven, she is
recovering.'

' Is that all ? '

' Why, what more ? '

Arthur was jealously inspected.

' You look open-hearted, my dear boy.'   Sullivan
Smith blew the sound of a reflective ahem.   ' Excuse me
for cornemusing in your company,' he said.   ' But seriously, there was only one thing to pardon your hurrying
to the lady's door at such a season, when the wind tells
tales to the world.   She 's down with a cold, you know.'

' An influenza,' said Arthur.

The simplicity of the acquiescence was vexatious to a champion desirous of hostilities, to vindicate the lady, in addition to his anxiety to cloak her sad plight.

' She caught it from contact with one of the inhabitants of this country.   'Tis the fate of us Irish, and we 're condemned to it for the sin of getting tired of our own.   I begin to sneeze when I land at Holyhead.   Unbutton a waistcoat here, in the hope of meeting a heart, and you 're lucky in escaping a pulmonary attack of no common severity, while the dog that infected you scampers off, to celebrate his honeymoon mayhap.   Ah, but call at her house in shoals, the world 'll soon be saying it 's worse than a coughing cold.   If you came to lead her out of it in triumph, the laugh 'd be with you, and the lady well covered.   D' ye understand ? '

The allusion to the dog's honeymoon had put Arthur Rhodes on the track of the darting cracker-metaphor.

' I think I do,' he said.   ' She will soon be at Copsley —Lady Dunstane's house, on the hills—and there we can see her.'

' And that 's next to the happiness of consoling—if only it had been granted !   She 's not an ordinary widow, to be caught when the tear of lamentation has opened a practicable path or water-way to the poor nightcapped jewel within.   So, and you 're a candid admirer, Mr. Rhodes !   Well, and I 'll be one with you ; for there 's not a star in the firmament more deserving of homage than that lady.'

' Let 's walk in the park and talk of her,' said Arthur.   ' There 's no sweeter subject to me.'

His boyish frankness rejoiced Sullivan Smith.   ' As long as you like !—nor to me ! ' he exclaimed.   ' And that ever since I first beheld her on the night of a Ball in Dublin : before I had listened to a word of her speaking : and she bore her father's Irish name :—none

of your Warwicks and your . . . But let the cur go barking. He can't tell what he 's lost ; perhaps he doesn't
care. And after inflicting his hydrophobia on her tender
fame ! Pooh, sir ; you call it a civilized country, where
you and I and dozens of others are ready to start up as
brothers of the lady, to defend her, and are paralyzed by
the Law. 'Tis a law they 've instituted for the protection
of dirty dogs—their majority ! '

' I owe more to Mrs. Warwick than to any soul I know,'
said Arthur.

' Let 's hear,' quoth Sullivan Smith ; proceeding :
' She 's the Arabian Nights in person, that 's sure ; and
Shakespeare's Plays, tragic and comuc ; and the Book
of Celtic History ; and Erin incarnate—down with a cold,
no matter where ; but we know where it was caught. So
there 's a pretty library for who 's to own her now she 's
enfranchized by circumstances ;—and a poetical figure
too ! '

He subsided for his companion to rhapsodize.

Arthur was overcharged with feeling, and could say
only : ' It would be another world to me if I lost her.'

' True ; but what of the lady ? '

' No praise of mine could do her justice.'

' That may be, but it 's negative of yourself, and not a
portrait of the object. Hasn't she the brain of Socrates
—or better, say Minerva, on the bust of Venus, and the
remainder of her finished off to an exact resemblance of
her patronymic Goddess of the bow and quiver ? '

' She has a wise head and is beautiful.'

' And chaste.'

Arthur reddened : he was prepared to maintain it,
could not speak it.

' She is to us in this London, what the run of water was
to Theocritus in Sicily : the nearest to the visibly divine,'
he said, and was applauded.

2 D

'Good, and on you go. Top me a few superlatives on that, and I 'm your echo, my friend. Isn't the seeing and listening to her like sitting under the silvery canopy of a fountain in high Summer ? '

'All the comparisons are yours,' Arthur said enviously.

'Mr. Rhodes, you are a poet, I believe, and all you require to loosen your tongue is a drop of Bacchus, so if you will do me the extreme honour to dine with me at my Club this evening, we 'll resume the toast that should never be uttered dry. You reprove me justly, my friend.'

Arthur laughed and accepted. The Club was named, and the hour, and some items of the little dinner : the birds and the year of the wines.

It surprised him to meet Mr. Redworth at the table of his host. A greater surprise was the partial thaw in Redworth's bearing toward him. But, as it was partial, and he a youth and poor, not even the genial influences of Bacchus could lift him to loosen his tongue under the repressing presence of the man he knew to be his censor, though Sullivan Smith encouraged him with praises and opportunities. He thought of the many occasions when Mrs. Warwick's art of management had produced a tacit harmony between them. She had no peer. The dinner failed of the pleasure he had expected from it. Redworth's bluntness killed the flying metaphors, and at the end of the entertainment he and Sullivan Smith were drumming upon politics.

'Fancies he has the key of the Irish difficulty ! ' said the latter, clapping hand on his shoulder, by way of blessing, as they parted at the Club-steps.

Redworth asked Arthur Rhodes the way he was going, and walked beside him.

'I suppose you take exercise ; don't get colds and that kind of thing,' he remarked in the old bullying fashion ;

and changed it abruptly. 'I am glad to have met you this evening. I hope you 'll dine with me one day next week. Have you seen Mrs. Warwick lately ? '

'She is unwell ; she has been working too hard,' said Arthur.

'Seriously unwell, do you mean ? '

'Lady Dunstane is at her house, and speaks of her recovering.'

'Ah. You 've not seen her ? '

'Not yet.'

'Well, good-night.'

Redworth left him, and only when moved by gratitude to the lad for his mention of Mrs. Warwick's 'working too hard,' as the cause of her illness, recollected the promised dinner and the need for having his address.

He had met Sullivan Smith accidentally in the morning and accepted the invitation to meet young Rhodes, because these two, of all men living, were for the moment dearest to him, as Diana Warwick's true and simple champions ; and he had intended a perfect cordiality toward them both ; the end being a semi-wrangle with the patriot, and a patronizing bluntness with the boy ; who, by the way, would hardly think him sincere in the offer of a seat at his table. He owned himself incomplete. He never could do the thing he meant, in the small matters not leading to fortune. But they led to happiness ! Redworth was guilty of a sigh : for now Diana Warwick stood free ; doubly free, he was reduced to reflect in a wavering dubiousness. Her more than inclination for Dacier, witnessed by him, and the shot of the world, flying randomly on the subject, had struck this cuirassier, making light of his armour, without causing any change of his habitual fresh countenance. As for the scandal, it had never shaken his faith in her nature. He thought of the passion. His heart struck at Diana's, and whatever might by chance be true in the scandal affected him little, if but her heart were at liberty. That was the prize he coveted, having long read the nature of the woman and wedded his spirit to it. She would complete him.

Of course, infatuated men argue likewise, and scandal does not move them. At a glance, the lower instincts and the higher spirit appear equally to have the philosophy of overlooking blemishes. The difference between appetite and love is shown when a man, after years of service, can hear and see, and admit the possible, and still desire in worship ; knowing that we of earth are begrimed and must be cleansed for presentation daily on our passage through the miry ways, but that our souls, if flame of a soul shall have come of the agony of flesh, are beyond the baser mischances : partaking of them indeed, but sub-limely. Now Redworth believed in the soul of Diana. For him it burned, and it was a celestial radiance about her, unquenched by her shifting fortunes, her wilful-nesses and, it might be, errors. She was a woman and weak ; that is, not trained for strength. She was a soul ; therefore perpetually pointing to growth in purification. He felt it, and even discerned it of her, if he could not have phrased it. The something sovereignly characteristic that aspired in Diana enchained him. With her, or rather with his thought of her soul, he understood the right union of women and men, from the roots to the flowering heights of that rare graft. She gave him comprehension of the meaning of love : a word in many mouths, not often ex-plained. With her, wound in his idea of her, he perceived it to signify a new start in our existence, a finer shoot of the tree stoutly planted in good gross earth ; the senses running their live sap, and the minds companioned, and the spirits made one by the whole-natured conjunction. In sooth, a happy prospect for the sons and daughters of Earth, divinely indicating more than happiness : the speeding of us, compact of what we are, between the ascetic rocks and the sensual whirlpools, to the creation of certain nobler races, now very dimly imagined.

Singularly enough, the man of these feelings was far from being a social rebel.  His Diana conjured them forth in relation to her, but was not on his bosom to enlighten him generally.  His notions of citizenship tolerated the female Pharisees, as ladies offering us an excellent social concrete where quicksands abound, and without quite justifying the Lady Wathins and Constance Aspers of the world, whose virtues he could set down to accident or to acid blood, he considered them supportable and estimable where the Mrs. Fryar-Gunnetts were innumerable, threatening to become a majority ;  as they will constantly do while the sisterhood of the chaste are wattled in formalism and throned in sourness.

Thoughts of Diana made phantoms of the reputable and their reverse alike.  He could not choose but think of her. She was free ;  and he too ;  and they were as distant as the horizon sail and the raft-floating castaway.  Her passion for Dacier might have burnt out her heart.  And at present he had no claim to visit her, dared not intrude. He would have nothing to say, if he went, save to answer questions upon points of business :  as to which, Lady Dunstane would certainly summon him when he was wanted.

Riding in the park on a frosty morning, he came upon Sir Lukin, who looked gloomy and inquired for news of Diana Warwick, saying that his wife had forbidden him to call at her house just yet.  ' She 's got a cold, you know,' said Sir Lukin ;  adding, ' confoundedly hard on women !—eh ?  Obliged to keep up a show.  And I 'd swear, by all that 's holy, Diana Warwick hasn't a spot, not a spot, to reproach herself with.  I fancy I ought to know women by this time.  And look here, Redworth, last night—that is, I mean yesterday evening, I broke with a woman—a lady of my acquaintance, you know, because she would go on scandal-mongering about Diana Warwick. I broke with her. I told her I 'd have out any man who abused Diana Warwick, and I broke with her. By Jove ! Redworth, those women can prove spitfires. They 've bags of venom under their tongues, barley-sugar though they look—and that 's her colour. But I broke with her for good. I doubt if I shall ever call on her again. And in point of fact, I won't.'

Mrs. Fryar-Gunnett was described in the colouring of the lady.

Sir Lukin, after some further remarks, rode on, and Redworth mused on a moral world that allows a woman of Mrs. Fryar-Gunnett's like to hang on to it, and to cast a stone at Diana ; forgetful, in his championship, that Diana was not disallowed a similar licence.

When he saw Emma Dunstane, some days later, she was in her carriage driving, as she said, to Lawyerland, for an interview with old Mr. Braddock, on her friend's affairs. He took a seat beside her. ' No, Tony is *not* well,' she replied to his question, under the veil of candour. ' She is recovering, but she—you can understand—suffered a shock. She is not able to attend to business, and certain things have to be done.'

' I used to be her man of business,' Redworth observed.

' She speaks of your kind services. This is mere matter for lawyers.'

' She is recovering ? '

' You may see her at Copsley next week. You can come down on Wednesdays or Saturdays ? '

' Any day. Tell her I want her opinion upon the state of things.'

' It will please her ; but you will have to describe the state of things.'

Emma feared she had said too much. She tried candour again for concealment. ' My poor Tony has been struck down low. I suppose it is like losing a diseased limb :—she has her freedom, at the cost of a blow to the system.'

' She may be trusted for having strength,' said Redworth.

' Yes.' Emma's mild monosyllable was presently followed by an exclamation : ' One has to experience the irony of Fate to comprehend how cruel it is ! ' Then she remembered that such language was peculiarly abhorrent to him.

' Irony of Fate ! ' he echoed her. ' I thought you were above that literary jargon.'

' And I thought I was : or thought it could be put in a dialect practically explicable,' she answered, smiling at the lion roused.

' Upon my word,' he burst out, ' I should like to write a book of Fables, showing how donkeys get into grinding harness, and dogs lose their bones, and fools have their sconces cracked, and all run jabbering of the irony of Fate, to escape the annoyance of tracing the causes. And what are they ? nine times out of ten, plain want of patience, or some debt for indulgence. There 's a subject :—let some one write, Fables in illustration of the irony of Fate : and I 'll undertake to tack-on my grandmother's maxims for a moral to each of 'em. We prate of that irony when we slink away from the lesson—the rod we conjure. And you to talk of Fate ! It 's the seed we sow, individually or collectively. I 'm bound-up in the prosperity of the country, and if the ship is wrecked, it ruins my fortune, but not me, unless I 'm bound-up in myself. At least I hope that 's my case.'

He apologized for intruding Mr. Thomas Redworth.

His hearer looked at him, thinking he required a more

finely pointed gift of speech for the ironical tongue, but relishing the tonic directness of his faculty of reason while she considered that the application of the phrase might be brought home to him so as to render ' my Grandmother's moral ' a conclusion less comfortingly, if quite intelligibly, summary. And then she thought of Tony's piteous instance ; and thinking with her heart, the tears insisted on that bitter irony of the heavens, which bestowed the long-withheld and coveted boon when it was empty of value or was but as a handful of spices to a shroud.

Perceiving the moisture in her look, Redworth understood that it was foolish to talk rationally. But on her return to her beloved, the real quality of the man had overcome her opposing state of sentiment, and she spoke of him with an iteration and throb in the voice that set a singular query whirring round Diana's ears. Her senses were too heavy for a suspicion.

## CHAPTER XXXVIII

### CONVALESCENCE OF A HEALTHY MIND DISTRAUGHT

FROM an abandonment that had the last pleasure of life in a willingness to yield it up, Diana rose with her friend's help in some state of fortitude, resembling the effort of her feet to bear the weight of her body. She plucked her courage out of the dust to which her heart had been scattered, and tasked herself to walk as the world does. But she was indisposed to compassionate herself in the manner of the burdened world. She lashed the creature who could not raise a head like others, and made the endurance of torture a support, such as the pride of being is to men. She would not have seen any similarity to pride in it ;

would have deemed it the reverse.  It was in fact the
painful gathering of the atoms composing pride.  For she
had not only suffered ; she had done wrongly : and when
that was acknowledged, by the light of her sufferings the
wrong-doing appeared gigantic, chorussing eulogies of the
man she had thought her lover : and who was her lover
once, before the crime against him.  In the opening of
her bosom to Emma, he was painted a noble figure ; one
of those that Romance delights to harass for the sake of
ultimately the more exquisitely rewarding.  He hated
treachery : she had been guilty of doing what he most
hated.  She glorified him for the incapacity to forgive ; it
was to her mind godlike.  And her excuses of herself ?

At the first confession, she said she had none, and sullenly maintained that there was none to exonerate.  Little
by little her story was related—her version of the story :
for not even as woman to woman, friend to great-hearted
friend, pure soul to soul, could Diana tell of the state of
shivering abjection in which Dacier had left her on the
fatal night ; of the many causes conducing to it, and of
the chief.  That was an unutterable secret, bound by all
the laws of feminine civilization not to be betrayed.  Her
excessive self-abasement and exaltation of him who had
struck her down, rendered it difficult to be understood ;
and not till Emma had revolved it and let it ripen in the
mind some days could she perceive with any clearness her
Tony's motives, or mania.  The very word Money thick-
ened the riddle : for Tony knew that her friend's purse
was her own to dip in at her pleasure ; yet she, to escape
so small an obligation, had committed the enormity for
which she held the man blameless in spurning her.

' You see what I am, Emmy,' Diana said.

' What I do not see, is that he had grounds for striking
so cruelly.'

' I proved myself unworthy of him.'

But does a man pretending to love a woman cut at one blow, for such a cause, the ties uniting her to him ? Unworthiness of that kind, is not commonly the capital offence in love.—Tony's deep prostration and her resplendent picture of her judge and executioner, kept Emma questioning within herself. Gradually she became enlightened enough to distinguish in the man a known, if not common, type of the externally soft and polished, internally hard and relentless, who are equal to the trials of love only as long as favouring circumstances and seemings nurse the fair object of their courtship.

Her thoughts recurred to the madness driving Tony to betray the secret ; and the ascent unhelped to get a survey of it and her and the conditions, was mountainous. She toiled up but to enter the regions of cloud ; sure nevertheless that the obscurity was penetrable and excuses to be discovered somewhere. Having never wanted money herself, she was unable perfectly to realize the urgency of the need : she began however to comprehend that the very eminent gentleman, before whom all human creatures were to bow in humility, had for an extended term considerably added to the expenses of Tony's household, by inciting her to give those little dinners to his political supporters, and bringing comrades perpetually to supper-parties, careless of how it might affect her character and her purse. Surely an honourable man was bound to her in honour ? Tony's remark : ' I have the reptile in me, dear,'—her exaggeration of the act, in her resigned despair,—was surely no justification for his breaking from her, even though he had discovered a vestige of the common ' reptile,' to leave her with a stain on her name ?—There would not have been a question about it if Tony had not exalted him so loftily, refusing, in visible pain, to hear him blamed.

Danvers had dressed a bed for Lady Dunstane in her

mistress's chamber, where often during the night Emma caught a sound of stifled weeping or the long falling breath of wakeful grief.  One night she asked whether Tony would like to have her by her side.

' No, dear,' was the answer in the dark ; ' but you know my old pensioners, the blind fifer and his wife ; I 've been thinking of them.'

' They were paid as they passed down the street yesterday, my love.'

' Yes, dear, I hope so.  But he flourishes his tune so absurdly.  I 've been thinking, that is the part I have played, instead of doing the female's duty of handing round the tin-cup for pennies.  I won't cry any more.'

She sighed and turned to sleep, leaving Emma to disburden her heart in tears.

For it seemed to her that Tony's intellect was weakened. She not merely abased herself and exalted Dacier preposterously, she had sunk her intelligence in her sensations : a state that she used to decry as the sin of mankind, the origin of error and blood.

Strangely too, the proposal came from her, or the suggestion of it, notwithstanding her subjectedness to the nerves, that she should show her face in public.  She said : ' I shall have to run about, Emmy, when I can fancy I am able to rattle up to the old mark.  At present, I feel like a wrestler who has had a fall.  As soon as the stiffness is over, it 's best to make an appearance, for the sake of one's backers, though I shall never be in the wrestling ring again.'

' That is a good decision—when you feel quite yourself, dear Tony,' Emma replied.

' I dare say I have disgraced my sex, but not as they suppose.  I feel my new self already, and can make the poor brute go through fire on behalf of the old.  What is the task ?—merely to drive a face ! '

' It is not known.'

' It will be known.'

' But this is a sealed secret.'

' Nothing is a secret that has been spoken. It 's in the air, and I have to breathe to live by it. And I would rather it were out. " She betrayed him." Rather that, than have them think—anything ! They will exclaim, How could she ! I have been unable to answer it to you—my own heart. How ? Oh ! our weakness is the swiftest dog to hunt us ; we cannot escape it. But I have the answer for them, that I trust with my whole soul none of them would have done the like.'

' None, my Tony, would have taken it to the soul as you do.'

' I talk, dear. If I took it honestly, I should be dumb, soon dust. The moment we begin to speak, the guilty creature is running for cover. She could not otherwise exist. I am sensible of evasion when I open my lips.'

' But Tony has told me all.'

' I think I have. But if you excuse my conduct, I am certain I have not.'

' Dear girl, accounting for it, is not the same as excusing.'

' Who can account for it ! I was caught in a whirl— Oh ! nothing supernatural : my weakness ; which it pleases me to call a madness—shift the ninety-ninth ! When I drove down that night to Mr. Tonans, I am certain I had my clear wits, but I felt like a bolt. I saw things, but at too swift a rate for the conscience of them. Ah ! let never Necessity draw the bow of our weakness : it is the soul that is winged to its perdition. I remember I was writing a story, named THE MAN OF TWO MINDS. I shall sign it, *By the Woman of Two Natures.* If ever it is finished. Capacity for thinking should precede the act of writing. It should ; I do not say that it does. Capacity for assimilating the public taste and reproducing it, is the commonest. The stuff is perishable, but it pays us for our labour, and in so doing saves us from becoming tricksters. Now I can see that Mr. Redworth had it in that big head of his—the authoress outliving her income!'

'He dared not speak.'

'Why did he not dare?'

'Would it have checked you?'

'I was a shot out of a gun, and I am glad he did not stand in my way. What power charged the gun, is another question. Dada used to say, that it is the devil's master-stroke to get us to accuse him. "So fare ye well, old Nickie Ben." My dear, I am a black sheep; a creature with a spotted reputation; I must wash and wash; and not with water—with sulphur-flames.' She sighed. 'I am down there where they burn. You should have let me lie and die. You were not kind. I was going quietly.'

'My love!' cried Emma, overborne by a despair that she traced to the woman's concealment of her bleeding heart,—'you live for me. Do set your mind on that. Think of what you are bearing, as your debt to Emma. Will you?'

Tony bowed her head mechanically.

'But I am in love with King Death, and must confess it,' she said. 'That hideous eating you forced on me, snatched me from him. And I feel that if I had gone, I should have been mercifully forgiven by everybody.'

'Except by me,' said Emma, embracing her. 'Tony would have left her friend for her last voyage in mourning. And my dearest will live to know happiness.'

'I have no more belief in it, Emmy.'

'The mistake of the world is to think happiness possible to the senses.'

'Yes; we distil that fine essence *through* the senses; and the act is called the pain of life. It is the death of

them. So much I understand of what our existence must
be. But I may grieve for having done so little.'

'That is the sound grief, with hope at the core—not in
love with itself and wretchedly mortal, as we find self is
under every shape it takes ; especially the chief one.'

'Name it.'

'It is best named Amor.'

There was a writhing in the frame of the hearer, for she
did want Love to be respected ; not shadowed by her misfortune. Her still-flushed senses protested on behalf of
the eternalness of the passion, and she was obliged to think
Emma's cold condemnatory intellect came of the no-
knowledge of it.

A letter from Mr. Tonans, containing an enclosure, was a
sharp trial of Diana's endurance of the irony of Fate. She
had spoken of the irony in allusion to her freedom. Now
that, according to a communication from her lawyers, she
was independent of the task of writing, the letter which
paid the price of her misery bruised her heavily.

'Read it and tear it all to strips,' she said in an abhor-
rence to Emma, who rejoined : 'Shall I go at once and see
him ? '

'Can it serve any end ? But throw it into the fire. Oh !
no simulation of virtue. There was not, I think, a stipulated return for what I did. But I perceive clearly—I can
read only by events—that there was an understanding.
You behold it. I went to him to sell it. He thanks me,
says I served the good cause well. I have not that consolation. If I had thought of the cause—of anything high,
it would have arrested me. On the fire with it ! '

The letter and square slip were consumed. Diana
watched the blackening papers.

'So they cease their sinning, Emmy ; and as long as I
am in torment, I may hope for grace. We talked of the
irony. It means, the pain of fire.'

' I spoke of the irony to Redworth,' said Emma ; ' incidentally, of course.'

' And he fumed ? '

' He is really not altogether the Mr. Cuthbert Dering of your caricature. He is never less than acceptably rational. I won't repeat his truisms ; but he said, or I deduced from what he said, that a grandmother's maxims would expound the enigma.'

' Probably the simple is the deep, in relation to the mysteries of life,' said Diana, whose wits had been pricked to a momentary activity by the letter. ' He behaves wisely ; so perhaps we are bound to take his words for wisdom. Much nonsense is talked and written, and he is one of the world's reserves, who need no more than enrolling, to make a sturdy phalanx of common sense. It 's a pity they are not enlisted and drilled to express themselves.' She relapsed. ' But neither he nor any of them could understand my case ! '

' He puts the idea of an irony down to the guilt of impatience, Tony.'

' Could there be a keener irony than that ? A friend of Dada's waited patiently for a small fortune, and when it arrived, he was a worn-out man, just assisted to go decently to his grave.'

' But he may have gained in spirit by his patient waiting.'

' Oh ! true. We are warmer if we travel on foot sunward, but it is a discovery that we are colder if we take to ballooning upward. The material good reverses its benefits the more nearly we clasp it. All life is a lesson that we live to enjoy but in the spirit. I will brood on your saying.'

' It is your own saying, silly Tony, as the only things worth saying always are ! ' exclaimed Emma, as she smiled happily to see her friend's mind reviving, though it was faintly and in the dark,

## CHAPTER XXXIX

### OF NATURE WITH ONE OF HER CULTIVATED DAUGHTERS AND A SHORT EXCURSION IN ANTI-CLIMAX

A MIND that after a long season of oblivion in pain returns to wakefulness without a keen edge for the world, is much in danger of souring permanently.   Diana's love of nature saved her from the dire mischance during a two months' residence at Copsley, by stupefying her senses to a state like the barely conscious breathing on the verge of sleep. February blew South-west for the pairing of the birds.   A broad warm wind rolled clouds of every ambiguity of form in magnitude over peeping azure, or skimming upon lakes of blue and lightest green, or piling the amphitheatre for majestic sunset.   Or sometimes those daughters of the wind flew linked and low, semi-purple, threatening the shower they retained and teaching gloom to rouse a song-ful nest in the bosom of the viewer.   Sometimes they were April, variable to soar with rain-skirts and sink with sun-shafts.   Or they drenched wood and field for a day and opened on the high South-western star.   Daughters of the wind, but shifty daughters of this wind of the dropping sun, they have to be watched to be loved in their trans-formations.

Diana had Arthur Rhodes and her faithful Leander for walking companions.   If Arthur said : ' Such a day would be considered melancholy by London people,' she thanked him in her heart, as a benefactor who had revealed to her things of the deepest.   The simplest were her food.   Thus does Nature restore us, by drugging the brain and making her creature confidingly animal for its new growth.   She imagined herself to have lost the power to think ; certainly

she had not the striving or the wish. Exercise of her
limbs to reach a point of prospect, and of her ears and eyes
to note what bird had piped, what flower was out on the
banks, and the leaf of what tree it was that lay beneath the
budding, satiated her daily desires. She gathered unknowingly a sheaf of landscapes, images, keys of dreamed
horizons, that opened a world to her at any chance breath
altering shape or hue : a different world from the one of
her old ambition. Her fall had brought her renovatingly
to earth, and the saving naturalness of the woman re-
created her childlike, with shrouded recollections of her
strange taste of life behind her ; with a tempered fresh
blood to enjoy aimlessly, and what would erewhile have
been a barrenness to her sensibilities.

In time the craving was evolved for positive knowledge,
and shells and stones and weeds were deposited on the
library-table at Copsley, botanical and geological books
comparingly examined, Emma Dunstane always eager to
assist ; for the samples wafted her into the heart of the
woods. Poor Sir Lukin tried three days of their society,
and was driven away headlong to Club-life. He sent down
Redworth, with whom the walks of the zealous inquirers
were profitable, though Diana, in acknowledging it to herself, reserved a decided preference for her foregone ethereal
mood, larger, and untroubled by the presence of a man.
The suspicion Emma had sown was not excited to an
alarming activity ; but she began to question : could the
best of men be simply a woman's friend ?—was not long
service rather less than a proof of friendship ? She could
be blind when her heart was on fire for another. Her
passion for her liberty, however, received no ominous
warning to look to the defences. He was the same blunt
speaker, and knotted his brows as queerly as ever at
Arthur, in a transparent calculation of how this fellow
meant to gain his livelihood. She wilfully put it to the

credit of Arthur's tact that his elder was amiable, without denying her debt to the good man for leaving her illness and her appearance unmentioned. He forbore even to scan her features. Diana's wan contemplativeness, in which the sparkle of meaning slowly rose to flash, as we see a bubble rising from the deeps of crystal waters, caught at his heart while he talked his matter-of-fact. But her instinct of a present safety was true. She and Arthur discovered—and it set her first meditating whether she did know the man so very accurately—that he had printed, for private circulation, when at Harrow School, a little book, a record of his observations in nature. Lady Dunstane was the casual betrayer. He shrugged at the nonsense of a boy's publishing ; anybody's publishing he held for a doubtful proof of sanity. His excuse was, that he had not published opinions. Let us observe, and assist in our small sphere ; not come mouthing to the footlights !

'We retire,' Diana said, for herself and Arthur.

'The wise thing, is to avoid the position that enforces publishing,' said he, to the discomposure of his raw junior.

In the fields he was genially helpful ; commending them to the study of the South-west wind, if they wanted to forecast the weather and understand the climate of our country. 'We have no Seasons, or only a shuffle of them. Old calendars give seven months of the year to the South-west, and that's about the average. Count on it, you may generally reckon what to expect. When you don't have the excess for a year or two, you are drenched the year following.' He knew every bird by its flight and its pipe, habits, tricks, hints of sagacity homely with the original human ; and his remarks on the sensitive life of trees and herbs were a spell to his thirsty hearers. Something of astronomy he knew ; but in relation to that science, he sank his voice, touchingly to Diana, who felt drawn to kinship with him when he had a pupil's tone. An allusion by Arthur to the poetical work of Aratus, led to a memorably pleasant evening's discourse upon the long reading of the stars by these our mortal eyes. Altogether the mind of the practical man became distinguishable to them as that of a plain brother of the poetic. Diana said of him to Arthur : ' He does not supply me with similes ; he points to the source of them.' Arthur, with envy of the man of positive knowledge, disguised an unstrung heart in agreeing.

Redworth alluded passingly to the condition of public affairs. Neither of them replied. Diana was wondering how one who perused the eternal of nature should lend a thought to the dusty temporary of the world. Subsequently she reflected that she was asking him to confine his great male appetite to the nibble of bread which nourished her immediate sense of life. Her reflections were thin as mist, coming and going like the mist, with no direction upon her brain, if they sprang from it. When he had gone, welcome though Arthur had seen him to be, she rebounded to a broader and cheerfuller liveliness. Arthur was flattered by an idea of her casting off incubus —a most worthy gentleman, and a not perfectly sympathetic associate. Her eyes had their lost light in them, her step was brisker ; she challenged him to former games of conversation, excursions in blank verse here and there, as the mood dictated. They amused themselves, and Emma too. She revelled in seeing Tony's younger face and hearing some of her natural outbursts. That Dacier never could have been the man for her, would have compressed and subjected her, and inflicted a further taste of bondage in marriage, she was assured. She hoped for the day when Tony would know it, and haply that another, whom she little comprehended, was her rightful mate.

March continued South-westerly and grew rainier, as
Redworth had foretold, bidding them look for gales and
storm, and then the change of wind.   It came, after wet-
tings of a couple scorning the refuge of dainty townsfolk
under umbrellas, and proud of their likeness to dripping
wayside wildflowers.   Arthur stayed at Copsley for a
week of the crisp North-easter ; and what was it, when he
had taken his leave, that brought Tony home from her
solitary walk in dejection ?   It could not be her seriously
regretting the absence of the youthful companion she had
parted with gaily, appointing a time for another meeting
on the heights, and recommending him to repair idle
hours with strenuous work.   The fit passed and was not
explained.   The winds are sharp with memory.   The hard
shrill wind crowed to her senses of an hour on the bleak
sands of the French coast : the beginning of the curtained
misery, inscribed as her happiness.   She was next day
prepared for her term in London with Emma, who promised her to make an expedition at the end of it by way
of holiday, to see The Crossways, which Mr. Redworth
said was not tenanted.

'You won't go through it like a captive ? ' said
Emma.

'I don't like it, dear,' Diana put up a comic mouth.
'The debts we owe ourselves are the hardest to pay.
That is the discovery of advancing age : and I used to
imagine it was quite the other way.   But they are the
debts of honour, imperative.   I shall go through it
grandly, you will see.   If I am stopped at my first recreancy and turned directly the contrary way, I think I
have courage.'

'You will not fear to meet . . . any one ? ' Emma
said.

'The world and all it contains !   I am robust, eager for
the fray, an Amazon, a brazen-faced hussy.   Fear and I

have parted. I shall not do you discredit. Besides you intend to have me back here with you ? And besides again, I burn to make a last brave appearance. I have not outraged the world, dear Emmy, whatever certain creatures in it may fancy.'

She had come out of her dejectedness with a shrewder view of Dacier ; equally painful, for it killed her romance, and changed the garden of their companionship in imagination to a waste. Her clearing intellect prompted it, whilst her nature protested, and reviled her to uplift him. He *had* loved her. ' I shall die knowing that a man did love me once,' she said to her widowed heart, and set herself blushing and blanching. But the thought grew inveterate : ' He could not bear much.' And in her quick brain it shot up a crop of similitudes for the quality of that man's love. She shuddered, as at a swift cleaving of cold steel. He had not given her a chance ; he had not replied to her letter written with the pen dipped in her heart's blood ; he must have gone straight away to the woman he married. This after almost justifying the scandalous world :—after . . . She realized her sensations of that night when the house-door had closed on him ; her feeling of lost sovereignty, degradation, feminine danger, friendlessness : and she was unaware, and never knew, nor did the world ever know, what cunning had inspired the frosty Cupid to return to her and be warmed by striking a bargain for his weighty secret. She knew too well that she was not of the snows which do not melt, however high her conceit of herself might place her. Happily she now stood out of the sun, in a bracing temperature, Polar ; and her compassion for women was deeply sisterly in tenderness and understanding. She spoke of it to Emma as her gain.

' I have not seen that you required to suffer to be considerate,' Emma said.

'It is on my conscience that I neglected Mary Paynham, among others—and because you did not take to her, Emmy.'

'The reading of it appears to me, that she has neglected you.'

'She was not in my confidence, and so I construe it as delicacy. One never loses by believing the best.'

'If one is not duped.'

'Expectations dupe us, not trust. The light of every soul burns upward. Of course, most of them are candles in the wind. Let us allow for atmospheric disturbance. Now I thank you, dear, for bringing me back to life. I see that I was really a selfish suicide, because I feel I have power to do some good, and belong to the army. When we are beginning to reflect, as I do now, on a recovered basis of pure health, we have the world at the dawn and know we are young in it, with great riches, great things gained and greater to achieve. Personally I behold a queer little wriggling worm for myself ; but as one of the active world I stand high and shapely ; and the very thought of doing work, is like a draught of the desert-springs to me. Instead of which, I have once more to go about presenting my face to vindicate my character. Mr. Redworth would admit no irony in that! At all events, it is anti-climax.'

'I forgot to tell you, Tony, you have been proposed for,' said Emma ; and there was a rush of savage colour over Tony's cheeks.

Her apparent apprehensions were relieved by hearing the name of Mr. Sullivan Smith.

'My poor dear countryman! And he thought me worthy, did he ? Some day, when we are past his repeating it, I 'll thank him.'

The fact of her smiling happily at the narration of Sullivan Smith's absurd proposal by mediatrix, proved to

Emma how much her nature thirsted for the smallest support in her self-esteem.

The second campaign of London was of bad augury at the commencement, owing to the ridiculous intervention of a street-organ, that ground its pipes in a sprawling roar of one of the Puritani marches, just as the carriage was landing them at the door of her house. The notes were harsh, dissonant, drunken, interlocked and horribly torn asunder, intolerable to ears not keen to extract the tune through dreadful memories. Diana sat startled and paralyzed. The melody crashed a revival of her days with Dacier, as in gibes ; and yet it reached to her heart. She imagined a Providence that was trying her on the threshold, striking at her feebleness. She had to lock herself in her room for an hour of deadly abandonment to misery, resembling the run of poison through her blood, before she could bear to lift eyes on her friend ; to whom subsequently she said : ' Emmy, there are wounds that cut sharp as the enchanter's sword, and we don't know we are in halves till some rough old intimate claps us on the back, merely to ask us how we are ! I have to join myself together again, as well as I can. It 's done, dear ; but don't notice the cement.'

' You will be brave,' Emma petitioned.

' I long to show you I will.'

The meeting with those who could guess a portion of her story, did not disconcert her. To Lady Pennon and Lady Singleby, she was the brilliant Diana of her nominal luminary issuing from cloud. Face and tongue, she was the same ; and once in the stream, she soon gathered its current topics and scattered her arrowy phrases. Lady Pennon ran about with them, declaring that the beautiful speaker, if ever down, was up, and up to her finest mark. Mrs. Fryar-Gunnett had then become the blazing regnant antisocial star ; a distresser of domesticity, the magnetic

attraction in the spirituous flames of that wild snap-
dragon bowl, called the Upper class ; and she was angeli-
cally blonde, a straw-coloured Beauty.   ' A lovely wheatsheaf, if the head were ripe,' Diana said of her.

' Threshed, says her fame, my dear,' Lady Pennon
replied, otherwise allusive.

' A wheatsheaf of contention for the bread of wind,'
said Diana, thinking of foolish Sir Lukin ; thoughtless of
talking to a gossip.

She would have shot a lighter dart, had she meant it to
fly and fix.

Proclaim, ye classics, what minor Goddess, or primal,
Iris or Ate, sped straight away on wing to the empty
wheatsheaf-ears of the golden-visaged Amabel Fryar-
Gunnett, daughter of Demeter in the field to behold, of
Aphrodite in her rosy incendiarism for the many of men ;
filling that pearly concave with a perversion of the uttered
speech, such as never lady could have repeated, nor man,
if less than a reaping harvester : which verily for women
to hear, is to stamp a substantial damnatory verification
upon the delivery of the saying :—

' Mrs. Warwick says of you, that you 're a bundle of
straws for everybody and bread for nobody.'

Or, stranger speculation, through what, and what
number of conduits, curious, and variously colouring, did
it reach the fair Amabel of the infant-in-cradle smile, in
that deformation of the original utterance !  To pursue
the thing, would be to enter the subtersensual perfumed
caverns of a Romance of Fashionable Life, with no hope
of coming back to light, other than by tail of lynx, like
the great Arabian seaman, at the last page of the final
chapter.  A prospectively popular narrative indeed !
and coin to reward it, and applause.  But I am reminded
that a story properly closed on the marriage of the heroine
Constance and her young Minister of State, has no time

for conjuring chemists' bouquet of aristocracy to lure the
native taste. When we have satisfied English sentiment,
our task is done, in every branch of art, I hear : and it
will account to posterity for the condition of the branches.
Those yet wakeful eccentrics interested in such a person
as Diana, to the extent of remaining attentive till the
curtain falls, demand of me to gather-up the threads
concerning her : which my gardener sweeping his pile
of dead leaves before the storm and night, advises me to
do speedily. But it happens that her resemblance to her
sex and species of a civilized period plants the main
threads in her bosom. Rogues and a policeman, or a
hurried change of front of all the actors, are not a part of
our slow machinery.

Nor is she to show herself to advantage. Only those
who read her woman's blood and character with the head,
will care for Diana of the Crossways now that the knot of
her history has been unravelled. Some little love they
must have for her likewise : and how it can be quickened
on behalf of a woman who never sentimentalizes publicly,
and has no dolly-dolly compliance, and muses on actual
life, and fatigues with the exercise of brains, and is in sooth
an alien : a princess of her kind and time, but a foreign
one, speaking a language distinct from the mercantile,
trafficking in ideas :—this is the problem. For to be true
to her, one cannot attempt at propitiation. She said
worse things of the world than that which was conveyed
to the boxed ears of Mrs. Fryar-Gunnett. Accepting the
war declared against her a second time, she performed the
common mental trick in adversity of setting her personally
known innocence to lessen her generally unknown error :
but anticipating that this might become known, and the
other not ; and feeling that the motives of the acknowledged error had served to guard her from being the culprit of the charge she writhed under, she rushed out of a

meditation compounded of mind and nerves, with derision
of the world's notion of innocence and estimate of error.
It was a mood lasting through her stay in London, and
longer, to the discomfort of one among her friends ; and
it was worthy of The Anti-climax Expedition, as she
called it.

For the rest, her demeanour to the old monster world
exacting the servility of her, in repayment for its tolerating
countenance, was faultless. Emma beheld the introduction to Mrs. Warwick of his bride, by Mr. Percy Dacier.
She had watched their approach up the Ball-room, thinking, how differently would Redworth and Tony have
looked. Differently, had it been Tony and Dacier : but
Emma could not persuade herself of a possible harmony
between them, save at the cost of Tony's expiation of the
sin of the greater heart in a performance equivalent to
Suttee. Perfectly an English gentleman of the higher
order, he seemed the effigy of a tombstone one, fixed upright, and civilly proud of his effigy bride. So far, Emma
considered them fitted. She perceived his quick eye on
her corner of the room ; necessarily, for a man of his breeding, without a change of expression. An emblem pertaining to her creed was on the heroine's neck ; also de-
pendant at her waist. She was white from head to foot ;
a symbol of purity. Her frail smile appeared deeply
studied in purity. Judging from her look and her reputation, Emma divined that the man was justly mated
with a devious filmy sentimentalist, likely to ' *fiddle harmonics on the sensual strings* ' for him at a mad rate in the
years to come. Such fiddling is indeed the peculiar diversion of the opulent of a fatly prosperous people ; who
take it, one may concede to them, for an inspired elimina-
tion of the higher notes of life : the very highest. That
saying of Tony's ripened with full significance to Emma
now. Not sensualism, but sham spiritualism, was the

meaning ; and however fine the notes, they come skilfully evoked of the under-brute in us. Reasoning it so, she thought it a saying for the penetration of the most polished and deceptive of the later human masks. She had besides, be it owned, a triumph in conjuring a sentence of her friend's, like a sword's edge, to meet them ; for she was boiling angrily at the ironical destiny which had given to those Two a beclouding of her beloved, whom she could have rebuked in turn for her insane caprice of passion.

But when her beloved stood-up to greet Mrs. Percy Dacier, all idea save tremulous admiration of the valiant woman, who had been wounded nigh to death, passed from Emma's mind. Diana tempered her queenliness to address the favoured lady with smiles and phrases of gentle warmth, of goodness of nature ; and it became a halo rather than a personal eclipse that she cast.

Emma looked at Dacier. He wore the prescribed conventional air, subject in half a minute to a rapid blinking of the eyelids. His wife could have been inimically imagined fascinated and dwindling. A spot of colour came to her cheeks. She likewise began to blink.

The happy couple bowed, proceeding ; and Emma had Dacier's back for a study. We score on that flat slate of man, unattractive as it is to hostile observations, and unprotected, the device we choose. Her harshest, was the positive thought that he had taken the woman best suited to him. Doubtless, he was a man to prize the altar-candle above the lamp of day. She fancied the back-view of him shrunken and straitened : perhaps a mere hostile fancy : though it was conceivable that he should desire as little of these meetings as possible. Eclipses are not courted.

The specially womanly exultation of Emma Dunstane in her friend's noble attitude, seeing how their sex had been struck to the dust for a trifling error, easily to be over-looked by a manful lover, and had asserted its dignity in physical and moral splendour, in self-mastery and benign-ness, was unshared by Diana. As soon as the business of the expedition was over, her orders were issued for the sale of the lease of her house and all it contained. ' I would sell Danvers too,' she said, ' but the creature declines to be treated as merchandize. It seems I have a faithful servant ; very much like my life, not quite to my taste ; the one thing out of the wreck !—with my dog ! '

Before quitting her house for the return to Copsley, she had to grant Mr. Alexander Hepburn, post-haste from his Caledonia, a private interview. She came out of it notice-ably shattered. Nothing was related to Emma, beyond the remark : ' I never knew till this morning the force of No in earnest.' The weighty little word—woman's native watchdog and guardian, if she calls it to her aid *in earnest* —had encountered and withstood a fiery ancient host, astonished at its novel power of resistance.

Emma contented herself with the result. ' Were you much supplicated ? '

' An Operatic Fourth-Act,' said Diana, by no means feeling so flippantly as she spoke.

She received, while under the impression of this man's honest, if primitive, ardour of courtship, or effort to cap-ture, a characteristic letter from Westlake, choicely phrased, containing presumeably an application for her hand, in the generous offer of his own. Her reply to a pursuer of that sort was easy. Comedy, after the bar-baric attack, refreshed her wits and reliance on her natural fencing weapons. To Westlake, the unwritten No was conveyed in a series of kindly ironic subterfuges, that played it like an impish flea across the pages, just giving the bloom of the word ; and rich smiles come to Emma's

life in reading the dexterous composition : which, however, proved so thoroughly to Westlake's taste, that a
second and a third exercise in the comedy of the negative
had to be despatched to him from Copsley.


## CHAPTER XL

### IN WHICH WE SEE NATURE MAKING OF A WOMAN A MAID AGAIN, AND A THRICE WHIMSICAL

ON their way from London, after leaving the station, the
drive through the valley led them past a field, where
cricketers were at work bowling and batting under a verti-
cal sun : not a very comprehensible sight to ladies, whose
practical tendencies, as observers of the other sex, incline
them to question the gain of such an expenditure of energy.
The dispersal of the alphabet over a printed page is not less
perplexing to the illiterate. As soon as Emma Dunstane
discovered the Copsley head-gamekeeper at one wicket,
and, actually, Thomas Redworth facing him, bat in hand,
she sat up, greatly interested. Sir Lukin stopped the carriage at the gate, and reminded his wife that it was the
day of the year for the men of his estate to encounter a
valley Eleven. Redworth, like the good fellow he was,
had come down by appointment in the morning out of
London, to fill the number required, Copsley being weak
this year. Eight of their wickets had fallen for a lamentable figure of twenty-nine runs ; himself clean-bowled the
first ball. But Tom Redworth had got fast hold of his
wicket, and already scored fifty to his bat. ' There !
grand hit ! ' Sir Lukin cried, the ball flying hard at the
rails. ' Once a cricketer, always a cricketer, if you 've
legs to fetch the runs. And Pullen 's not doing badly.
His business is to stick. We shall mark them a hundred

yet. I do hate a score on our side without the two 00's.'
He accounted for Redworth's mixed colours by telling the
ladies he had lent him his flannel jacket ; which, against
black trousers, looked odd but not ill.

Gradually the enthusiasm of the booth and bystanders
converted the flying of a leather ball into a subject of
honourable excitement.

' And why are you doing nothing ? ' Sir Lukin was
asked ; and he explained :

' My stumps are down : I 'm married.' He took his
wife's hand prettily.

Diana had a malicious prompting. She smothered the
wasp, and said : ' Oh ! look at that ! '

' Grand hit again ! Oh ! good ! good ! ' cried Sir Lukin,
clapping to it, while the long-hit-off ran spinning his legs
into one for an impossible catch ; and the batsmen were
running and stretching bats, and the ball flying away, flying back, and others after it, and still the batsmen running,
till it seemed that the ball had escaped control and was
leading the fielders on a coltish innings of its own, defiant
of bowlers.

Diana said merrily : ' Bravo our side ! '

' Bravo, old Tom Redworth ' ; rejoined Sir Lukin.
' Four, and a three ! And capital weather, haven't we !
Hope we shall have same sort day next month—return
match, my ground. I 've seen Tom Redworth score—old
days—over two hundred t' his bat. And he used to bowl
too. But bowling wants practice. And, Emmy, look at
the old fellows lining the booth, pipe in mouth and cheering. They do enjoy a day like this. We 'll have a supper
for fifty at Copsley's :—it 's fun. By Jove ! we must have
reached up to near the hundred.'

He commissioned a neighbouring boy to hie to the booth
for the latest figures, and his emissary taught lightning a
lesson.

Diana praised the little fellow.

' Yes, he 's a real English boy,' said Emma.

' We 've thousands of 'em, thousands, ready to your hand ' ; exclaimed Sir Lukin ; ' and a confounded Radicalized country . . .' he muttered gloomily of ' lets us be kicked ! . . . any amount of insult, meek as gruel ! . . . making of the finest army the world has ever seen ! You saw the papers this morning ? Good heaven ! how a nation with an atom of self-respect can go on standing that sort of bullying from foreigners ! We do. We 're insulted and we 're threatened, and we call for a hymn !— Now then, my man, what is it ? '

The boy had flown back. ' Ninety-two marked, sir ; ninety-nine runs ; one more for the hundred.'

' Well reckoned ; and mind you 're up at Copsley for the return match.—And Tom Redworth says, they may bite their thumbs to the bone—they don't hurt us. I tell him, he has no sense of national pride. He says, we 're not prepared for war. We never are ! And whose the fault ? Says, we 're a peaceful people, but 'ware who touches us ! He doesn't feel a kick.—Oh ! clever snick ! Hurrah for the hundred !—Two—three. No, don't force the running, you fools !—though they 're wild with the ball : ha !—no ! —all right ! ' The wicket stood. Hurrah !

The heat of the noonday sun compelled the ladies to drive on.

' Enthusiasm has the privilege of not knowing monotony,' said Emma. ' He looks well in flannels.'

' Yes, he does,' Diana replied, aware of the reddening despite her having spoken so simply. ' I think the chief advantage men have over us is in their amusements.'

' Their recreations.'

' That is the better word.' Diana fanned her cheeks and said she was warm. ' I mean, the permanent advantage. For you see that age does not affect them.'

' Tom Redworth is not a patriarch, my dear.'

' Well, he is what would be called mature.'

' He can't be more than thirty-two or three ; and that, for a man of his constitution, means youth.'

' Well, I can imagine him a patriarch playing cricket.'

' I should imagine you imagine the possible chances. He is the father who would play with his boys.'

' And lock up his girls in the nursery.' Diana murmured of the extraordinary heat.

Emma begged her to remember his heterodox views of the education for girls.

' He bats admirably,' said Diana. ' I wish I could bat half as well.'

' Your batting is with the tongue.'

' Not so good. And a solid bat, or bludgeon, to defend the poor stumps, is surer. But there is the difference of cricket :—when your stumps are down, you are idle, at leisure ; not a miserable prisoner.'

' Supposing all marriages miserable.'

' To the mind of me,' said Diana, and observed Emma's rather saddened eyelids for a proof that schemes to rob her of dear liberty were certainly planned.

They conversed of expeditions to Redworth's Berkshire mansion, and to The Crossways, untenanted at the moment, as he had informed Emma, who fancied it would please Tony to pass a night in the house she loved ; but as he was to be of the party she coldly acquiesced.

The woman of flesh refuses pliancy when we want it of her, and will not, until it is her good pleasure, be bent to the development called a climax, as the puppet-woman, mother of Fiction and darling of the multitude ! ever amiably does, at a hint of the Nuptial Chapter. Diana in addition sustained the weight of brains. Neither with waxen optics nor with subservient jointings did she go

through her pathways of the world. Her direct individuality rejected the performance of simpleton, and her lively
blood, the warmer for its containment, quickened her to
penetrate things and natures ; and if as yet, in justness
to the loyal male friend, she forbore to name him con-
spirator, she read both him and Emma, whose inner bosom
was revealed to her, without an effort to see. But her
characteristic chasteness of mind,—not coldness of the
blood,—which had supported an arduous conflict, past
all existing rights closely to depict, and which barbed her
to pierce to the wishes threatening her freedom, deceived
her now to think her flaming blushes came of her relentless
divination on behalf of her recovered treasure : whereby
the clear reading of others distracted the view of herself.
For one may be the cleverest alive, and still hoodwinked
while blood is young and warm.

The perpetuity of the contrast presented to her reflections, of Redworth's healthy, open, practical, cheering
life, and her own freakishly interwinding, darkly penetrative, simulacrum of a life, cheerless as well as useless,
forced her humiliated consciousness by degrees, in spite
of pride, to the knowledge that she was engaged in a
struggle with him ; and that he was the stronger ;—it
might be, the worthier : she thought him the handsomer.
He throve to the light of day, and she spun a silly web
that meshed her in her intricacies. Her intuition of
Emma's wishes led to this ; he was constantly before her.
She tried to laugh at the image of the concrete cricketer,
half-flannelled, and red of face : the ' lucky calculator,'
as she named him to Emma, who shook her head, and
sighed. The abstract, healthful and powerful man, able
to play besides profitably working, defied those poor
efforts. Consequently, at once she sent up a bubble to
the skies, where it became a spheral realm, of far too fine
an atmosphere for men to breathe in it ; and thither she

2 F

transported herself at will, whenever the contrast, with its accompanying menace of a tyrannic subjugation, overshadowed her. In the above, the kingdom composed of her shattered romance of life and her present aspirings, she was free and safe. Nothing touched her there—nothing that Redworth did. She could not have admitted there her ideal of a hero. It was the sublimation of a virgin's conception of life, better fortified against the enemy. She peopled it with souls of the great and pure, gave it illimitable horizons, dreamy nooks, ravishing landscapes, melodies of the poets of music. Higher and more celestial than the Salvatore, it was likewise, now she could assure herself serenely, independent of the horrid blood-emotions. Living up there, she had not a feeling.

The natural result of this habit of ascending to a superlunary home, was the loss of an exact sense of how she was behaving below. At the Berkshire mansion, she wore a supercilious air, almost as icy as she accused the place of being. Emma knew she must have seen in the library a row of her literary ventures, exquisitely bound ; but there was no allusion to the books. Mary Paynham's portrait of Mrs. Warwick hung staring over the fireplace, and was criticized, as though its occupancy of that position had no significance.

' He thinks she has a streak of genius,' Diana said to Emma.

' It may be shown in time,' Emma replied, for a comment on the work. ' He should know, for the Spanish pictures are noble acquisitions.'

' They are, doubtless, good investments.'

He had been foolish enough to say, in Diana's hearing, that he considered the purchase of the Berkshire estate a good investment. It had not yet a name. She suggested various titles for Emma to propose : ' The Funds ';

or ' Capital Towers ' ; or ' Dividend Manor ' ; or ' Rail-holm ' ; blind to the evidence of inflicting pain. Emma, from what she had guessed concerning the purchaser of The Crossways, apprehended a discovery there which might make Tony's treatment of him unkinder, seeing that she appeared actuated contrariously ; and only her invalid's new happiness in the small excursions she was capable of taking to a definite spot, of some homely attractiveness, moved her to follow her own proposal for the journey. Diana pleaded urgently, childishly in tone, to have Arthur Rhodes with them, ' so as to be sure of a sympathetic companion for a walk on the Downs.' At The Crossways, they were soon aware that Mr. Redworth's domestics were in attendance to serve them. Manifestly the house was his property, and not much of an invest-ment ! The principal bed-room, her father's once, and her own, devoted now to Emma's use, appalled her with a resemblance to her London room. She had noticed some of her furniture at ' Dividend Manor,' and chosen to consider it in the light of a bargain from a purchase at the sale of her goods. Here was her bed, her writing-table, her chair of authorship, desks, books, ornaments, water-colour sketches. And the drawing-room was fitted with her brackets and étagères, holding every knick-knack she had possessed and scattered, small bronzes, antiques, ivory junks, quaint ivory figures Chinese and Japanese, bits of porcelain, silver incense-urns, dozens of dainty sundries. She had a shamed curiosity to spy for an omission of one of them ; all were there. The Cross-ways had been turned into a trap.

Her reply to this blunt wooing, conspired, she felt justi-fied in thinking, between him and Emma, was emphatic in muteness. She treated it as if unobserved. At night, in bed, the scene of his mission from Emma to her under this roof, barred her customary ascent to her planetary kingdom. Next day she took Arthur after breakfast for a walk on the Downs and remained absent till ten minutes before the hour of dinner. As to that young gentleman, he was near to being caressed in public. Arthur's opinions, his good sayings, were quoted ; his excellent companionship on really poetical walks, and perfect sympathy, praised to his face. Challenged by her initiative to a kind of language that threw Redworth out, he declaimed : ' We pace with some who make young morning stale.'

' Oh ! stale as peel of fruit long since consumed,' she chimed.

And so they proceeded ; and they laughed, Emma smiled a little, Redworth did the same beneath one of his questioning frowns—a sort of fatherly grimace.

A suspicion that this man, when infatuated, was able to practise the absurdest benevolence, the burlesque of chivalry, as a *man*-admiring sex esteems it, stirred very naughty depths of the woman in Diana, labouring under her perverted mood. She put him to proof, for the chance of arming her wickedest to despise him. Arthur was petted, consulted, cited, flattered all round ; all but caressed. She played, with a reserve, the maturish young woman smitten by an adorable youth ; and enjoyed doing it because she hoped for a visible effect—more paternal benevolence—and could do it so dispassionately. Coquettry, Emma thought, was most unworthily shown ; and it was of the worst description. Innocent of conspiracy, she had seen the array of Tony's lost household treasures : she wondered at a heartlessness that would not even utter common thanks to the friendly man for the compliment of prizing her portrait and the things she had owned ; and there seemed an effort to wound him.

The invalided woman, charitable with allowances for her erratic husband, could offer none for the woman of a

long widowhood, that had become a trebly sensitive
maidenhood ; abashed by her knowledge of the world,
animated by her abounding blood ; cherishing her new
freedom, dreading the menacer ; feeling, that though she
held the citadel, she was daily less sure of its founda-
tions, and that her hope of some last romance in life was
going ; for in him shone not a glimpse. He appeared to
Diana as a fatal power, attracting her without sympathy,
benevolently overcoming : one of those good men, strong
men, who subdue and do not kindle. The enthralment
revolted a nature capable of accepting subjection only
by burning. In return for his moral excellence, she gave
him the moral sentiments : esteem, gratitude, abstract
admiration, perfect faith. But the man ? She could
not now say she had never been loved ; and a flood of
tenderness rose in her bosom, swelling from springs that
she had previously reproved with a desperate severity :
the unhappy, unsatisfied yearning to be more than loved,
to love. It was alive, out of the wreck of its first trial.
This, the secret of her natural frailty, was bitter to her
pride : chastely-minded as she was, it whelmed her.
And then her comic imagination pictured Redworth
dramatically making love. And to a widow ! It proved
him to be senseless of romance. Poetic men take aim
at maidens. His devotedness to a widow was charged
against him by the widow's shudder at antecedents dis-
tasteful to her soul, a discoloration of her life. She wished
to look entirely forward, as upon a world washed clear of
night, not to be cast back on her antecedents by practical
wooings or words of love ; to live spiritually ; free of the
shower at her eyelids attendant on any idea of her loving.
The woman who talked of the sentimentalist's ' fiddling
harmonics,' herself stressed the material chords, in her
attempt to escape out of herself and away from her
pursuer.

Meanwhile she was as little conscious of what she was doing as of how she appeared. Arthur went about with the moony air of surcharged sweetness, and a speculation on it, alternately tiptoe and prostrate. More of her intoxicating wine was administered to him, in utter thoughtlessness of consequences to one who was but a boy and a friend, almost of her own rearing. She told Emma, when leaving The Crossways, that she had no desire to look on the place again : she wondered at Mr. Redworth's liking such a solitude. In truth, the look back on it let her perceive that her husband haunted it, and disfigured the man, of real generosity, as her heart confessed, but whom she accused of a lack of prescient delicacy, for not knowing she would and must be haunted there. Blaming him, her fountain of colour shot up, at a murmur of her unjustness and the poor man's hopes.

A week later, the youth she publicly named ' her Arthur ' came down to Copsley with news of his having been recommended by Mr. Redworth for the post of secretary to an old Whig nobleman famous for his patronage of men of letters. And besides, he expected to inherit, he said, and gazed in a way to sharpen her instincts. The wine he had drunk of late from her flowing vintage was in his eyes. They were on their usual rambles out along the heights. ' Accept, by all means, and thank Mr. Redworth,' said she, speeding her tongue to intercept him. ' Literature is a good stick and a bad horse. Indeed, I ought to know. You can always write ; I hope you will.'

She stepped fast, hearing : ' Mrs. Warwick—Diana ! May I take your hand ? '

This was her pretty piece of work !  ' Why should you ? If you speak my Christian name, no : you forfeit any pretext. And pray, don't loiter. We are going at the pace of the firm of Potter and Dawdle, and you know they

never got their shutters down till it was time to put them
up again.'

Nimble-footed as she was, she pressed ahead too fleetly
for amorous eloquence to have a chance.  She heard
' Diana ! ' twice, through the rattling of her discourse and
flapping of her dress.

' Christian names are coin that seem to have an indifferent valuation of the property they claim,' she said in
the Copsley garden ;  ' and as for hands, at meeting and
parting, here is the friendliest you could have.  Only
don't look rueful.  My dear Arthur, spare me that, or I
shall blame myself horribly.'

His chance had gone, and he composed his face.  No
hope in speaking had nerved him ;  merely the passion to
speak.  Diana understood the state, and pitied the naturally modest young fellow, and chafed at herself as a
senseless incendiary, who did mischief right and left, from
seeking to shun the apparently inevitable.  A side-
thought intruded, that he would have done his wooing
poetically—not in the burly storm, or bull-Saxon, she
apprehended.  Supposing it imperative with her to
choose ?  She looked up, and the bird of broader wing
darkened the whole sky, bidding her know that she had
no choice.

Emma was requested to make Mr. Redworth acquainted
with her story, all of it :—' So that this exalted friendship of his may be shaken to a common level.  He has an
unbearably high estimate of me, and it hurts me.  Tell
him all ;  and more than even you have known :—but for
his coming to me, on the eve of your passing under the
surgeon's hands, I should have gone—flung the world
my glove !  A matter of minutes.  Ten minutes later !
The train was to start for France at eight, and I was
awaited.  I have to thank heaven that the man was one
of those who can strike icily.  Tell Mr. Redworth what

I say. You two converse upon every subject. One may
be too loftily respected—in my case. By and by—for he
is a tolerant reader of life and women, I think—we shall
be humdrum friends of the lasting order.'

Emma's cheeks were as red as Diana's. ' I fancy Tom
Redworth has not much to learn concerning any person he
cares for,' she said. ' You like him ? I have lost touch
of you, my dear, and ask.'

' I like him : that I can say. He is everything I am
not. But now I am free, the sense of being undeservedly
over-esteemed imposes fetters, and I don't like them. I
have been called a Beauty. Rightly or other, I have had
a Beauty's career ; and a curious caged beast's life I have
found it. Will you promise me to speak to him ? And
also, thank him for helping Arthur Rhodes to a situation.'

At this, the tears fell from her. And so enigmatical had
she grown to Emma, that her bosom friend took them for
a confessed attachment to the youth.

Diana's wretched emotion shamed her from putting any
inquiries whether Redworth had been told. He came re-
peatedly, and showed no change of face, always continu-
ing in the form of huge hovering griffin ; until an idea,
instead of the monster bird, struck her. Might she not,
after all, be cowering under imagination ? The very
maidenly idea wakened her womanliness—to reproach her
remainder of pride, not to see more accurately. It was
the reason why she resolved, against Emma's extreme
entreaties, to take lodgings in the South valley below the
heights, where she could be independent of fancies and
perpetual visitors, but near her beloved at any summons
of urgency ; which Emma would not habitually send
because of the coming of a particular gentleman. Dresses
were left at Copsley for dining and sleeping there upon
occasion, and poor Danvers, despairing over the riddle of
her mistress, was condemned to the melancholy descent.

'It 's my belief,' she confided to Lady Dunstane's maid Bartlett, 'she 'll hate men all her life after that Mr. Dacier.'

If women were deceived, and the riddle deceived herself, there is excuse for a plain man like Redworth in not having the slightest clue to the daily shifting feminine maze he beheld. The strange thing was, that during her maiden time she had never been shifty or flighty, invariably limpid and direct.

## CHAPTER XLI

### CONTAINS A REVELATION OF THE ORIGIN OF THE TIGRESS IN DIANA

AN afternoon of high summer blazed over London through the City's awning of smoke, and the three classes of the population, relaxed by the weariful engagement with what to them was a fruitless heat, were severally bathing their ideas in dreams of the contrast possible to embrace : breezy seas or moors, aërial Alps, cool beer. The latter, if confessedly the lower comfort, is the readier at command ; and Thomas Redworth, whose perspiring frame was directing his inward vision to fly for solace to a trim new yacht, built on his lines, beckoning from Southampton Water, had some of the amusement proper to things plucked off the levels, in the conversation of a couple of journeymen close ahead of him, as he made his way from a quiet street of brokers' offices to a City Bank. One asked the other if he had ever tried any of that cold stuff they were now selling out of barrows, with cream. His companion answered, that he had not got much opinion of stuff of the sort ; and what was it like ?

'Well, it 's cheap, it ain't bad ; it 's cooling. But it ain't refreshing.'

' Just what I reckoned all that newfangle rubbish.'

Without a consultation, the conservatives in beverage
filed with a smart turn about, worthy of veterans at parade
on the drill-ground, into a public-house ; and a dialogue
chiefly remarkable for absence of point, furnished matter
to the politician's head of the hearer. Provided that their
beer was unadulterated ! Beer they would have ; and
why not, in weather like this ? But how to make the
publican honest ! And he was not the only trickster
preying on the multitudinous poor copper crowd, rightly
to be protected by the silver and the golden. Revelations
of the arts practised to plump them with raw-earth and
minerals in the guise of nourishment, had recently knocked
at the door of the general conscience and obtained a civil
reply from the footman. Repulsive as the thought was
to one still holding to Whiggish Liberalism, though flying
various Radical kites, he was caught by the decisive ultra-
torrent, and whirled to amid the necessity for the inter-
ference of the State, to stop the poisoning of the poor.
Upper classes have never legislated systematically in their
interests ; and quid . . . rabidæ tradis ovile lupæ ? says
one of the multitude. We may be seeing fangs of wolves
where fleeces waxed. The State that makes it a vital
principle to concern itself with the helpless poor, meets
instead of waiting for Democracy ; which is a perilous
flood but when it is dammed. Or else, in course of time,
luxurious yachting, my friend, will encounter other reefs
and breakers than briny ocean's ! Capital, whereat
Diana Warwick aimed her superbest sneer, has its instant
duties. She theorized on the side of poverty, and might
do so : he had no right to be theorizing on the side of
riches. Across St. George's Channel, the cry for humanity
in Capital was an agony. He ought to be there, doing,
not cogitating. The post of Irish Secretary must be won
by real service founded on absolute local knowledge. Yes,

and sympathy, if you like ; but sympathy is for proving, not prating. . . .

These were the meditations of a man in love ; veins, arteries, headpiece in love, and constantly brooding at a solitary height over the beautiful coveted object ; only too bewildered by her multifarious evanescent feminine evasions, as of colours on a ruffled water, to think of pouncing : for he could do nothing to soften, nothing that seemed to please her : and all the while, the motive of her mind impelled him in reflection beyond practicable limits : even pointing him to apt quotations ! Either he thought within her thoughts, or his own were at her disposal. Nor was it sufficient for him to be sensible of her influence, to restrain the impetus he took from her. He had already wedded her morally, and much that he did, as well as whatever he debated, came of Diana ; more than if they had been coupled, when his downright practical good sense could have spoken. She held him suspended, swaying him in that posture ; and he was not a whit ashamed of it. The beloved woman was throned on the very highest of the man.

Furthermore, not being encouraged, he had his peculiar reason for delay, though now he could offer her wealth. She had once in his hearing derided the unpleasant hiss of the ungainly English matron's title of Mrs. There was no harm in the accustomed title, to his taste; but she disliking it, he did the same, on her special behalf; and the prospect, funereally draped, of a title sweeter-sounding to her ears, was above his horizon. Bear in mind, that he underwent the reverse of encouragement. Any small thing to please her was magnified, and the anticipation of it nerved the modest hopes of one who deemed himself and any man alive deeply her inferior.

Such was the mood of the lover condemned to hear another malignant scandal defiling the name of the woman

he worshipped.   Sir Lukin Dunstane, extremely hurried,
bumped him on the lower step of the busy Bank, and said :
' Pardon ! ' and ' Ha ! Redworth ! making money ? '

' Why, what are you up to down here ? ' he was asked,
and he answered : ' Down to the Tower, to an officer
quartered there.   Not bad quarters, but an infernal distance.   Business.'

Having cloaked his expedition to the distance with the
comprehensive word, he repeated it ;  by which he feared
he had rendered it too significant, and he said : ' No, no ;
nothing particular ';  and that caused the secret he contained to swell in his breast rebelliously, informing the
candid creature of the fact of his hating to lie : whereupon
thus he poured himself out, in the quieter bustle of an alley,
off the main thoroughfare.   ' You 're a friend of hers.
I 'm sure you care for her reputation ;  you 're an old friend
of hers, and she 's my wife's dearest friend ;  and I 'm fond
of her too ;  and I ought to be, and ought to know, and do
know :—pure ?   Strike off my fist if there 's a spot on her
character !   And a scoundrel like that fellow Wroxeter !—
Damnedest rage I ever was in !—Swears . . . down at
Lockton . . . when she was a girl.   Why, Redworth, I
can tell you, when Diana Warwick was a girl—— ! '

Redworth stopped him.   ' Did he say it in your
presence ? '

Sir Lukin was drawn-up by the harsh question.   ' Well,
no ;  not exactly.'   He tried to hesitate, but he was in the
hot vein of a confidence and he wanted advice.   ' The cur
said it to a woman—hang the woman !   And she hates
Diana Warwick : I can't tell why—a regular snake's hate.
By Jove ! how women can hate ! '

' Who is the woman ? ' said Redworth.

Sir Lukin complained of the mob at his elbows.   ' I
don't like mentioning names here.'

A convenient open door of offices invited him to drag his

receptacle, and possible counsellor, into the passage, where immediately he bethought him of a postponement of the distinct communication ; but the vein was too hot. ' I say, Redworth, I wish you 'd dine with me.   Let 's drive up to my Club.—Very well, two words.   And I warn you, I shall call him out, and make it appear it 's about another woman, who 'll like nothing so much, if I know the Jezebel. Some women are *hussies*, let 'em be handsome as houris. And she 's a fire-ship ; by heaven, she is !   Come, you 're a friend of my wife's, but you 're a man of the world and my friend, and you know how fellows are tempted, Tom Redworth.—Cur though he is, he 's likely to step out and receive a lesson.—Well, he 's the favoured cavalier for the present . . . h'm . . . Fryar-Gunnett.   Swears he told her, circumstantially ; and it was down at Lockton, when Diana Warwick was a girl.   Swears she 'll spit her venom at her, so that Diana Warwick shan't hold her head up in London Society, what with that cur Wroxeter, Old Dannis-burgh, and Dacier.   And it does count a list, doesn't it ? —confound the handsome hag !   She 's jealous of a dark rival.   I 've been down to Colonel Hartswood at the Tower, and he thinks Wroxeter deserves horsewhipping, and we may manage it.   I know you 're dead against duelling ; and so am I, on my honour.   But you see there are cases where a lady must be protected ; and anything new, left to circulate against a lady who has been talked of twice—Oh, by Jove ! it must be stopped.   If she has a male friend on earth, it must be stopped on the spot.'

Redworth eyed Sir Lukin curiously through his wrath.

' We 'll drive up to your Club,' he said.

' Hartswood dines with me this evening, to confer,' rejoined Sir Lukin.   ' Will you meet him ? '

' I can't,' said Redworth, ' I have to see a lady, whose affairs I have been attending to in the City ; and I 'm engaged for the evening.   You perceive, my good fellow,' he resumed, as they rolled along, ' this is a delicate business. You have to consider your wife. Mrs. Warwick's name won't come up, but another woman's will.'

' I meet Wroxeter at a gambling-house he frequents, and publicly call him cheat—slap his face, if need be.'

' Sure to ! ' repeated Redworth. ' No stupid pretext will quash the woman's name. Now, such a thing as a duel would give pain enough.'

' Of course ; I understand,' Sir Lukin nodded his clear comprehension. ' But what is it you advise, to trounce the scoundrel, and silence him ? '

' Leave it to me for a day. Let me have your word that you won't take a step : positively—neither you nor Colonel Hartswood. I 'll see you by appointment at your Club.' Redworth looked up over the chimneys. ' We 're going to have a storm and a gale, I can tell you.'

' Gale and storm ! ' cried Sir Lukin ; ' what has that got to do with it ? '

' Think of something else for a time.'

' And that brute of a woman—deuced handsome she is ! —if you care for fair women, Redworth :—she 's a Venus jumped slap out of the waves, and the Devil for sire —*that* you learn :—running about, sowing her lies. She 's a yellow witch. Oh ! but she 's a shameless minx. And a black-leg cur like Wroxeter ! Any woman intimate with a fellow like that, stamps herself. I loathe her. Sort of woman who swears in the morning you 're the only man on earth ; and next day—that evening—engaged !—fee to Polly Hopkins—and it 's a gentleman, a nobleman, my lord !—been going on behind your back half the season !— and she isn't hissed when she abuses a lady, a saint in comparison ! You know the world, old fellow :—Brighton, Richmond, visits to a friend as deep in the bog. How Fryar-Gunnett—a man, after all—can stand it ! And drives of an afternoon for an airing—by heaven ! You 're out of that mess, Redworth : not much taste for the sex ; and you 're right, you 're lucky.  Upon my word, the corruption of society in the present day is awful ; it 's appalling.—I rattled at her : and oh ! dear me, perks on her hind heels and defies me to prove :  and *she 's* no pretender, but hopes she 's as good as any of my " chaste Dianas."  My dear old friend, it 's when you come upon women of that kind you have a sickener.  And I 'm bound by the best there is in a man—honour, gratitude, all the list—to defend Diana Warwick.'

' So, you see, for your wife's sake, your name can't be hung on a woman of that kind,' said Redworth.  ' I 'll call here the day after to-morrow at three P.M.'

Sir Lukin descended and vainly pressed Redworth to run up into his Club for refreshment.  Said he roguishly : ' Who 's the lady ? '

The tone threw Redworth on his frankness.

' The lady I 've been doing business for in the City, is Miss Paynham.'

' I saw her once at Copsley ; good-looking.  Cleverish ? '

' She has ability.'

Entering his Club, Sir Lukin was accosted in the reading-room by a cavalry officer, a Colonel Launay, an old Harrovian, who stood at the window and asked him whether it was not Tom Redworth in the cab.  Another, of the same School, standing squared before a sheet of one of the evening newspapers, heard the name and joined them, saying : ' Tom Redworth is going to be married, some fellow told me.'

' He 'll make a deuced good husband to any woman—if it 's true,' said Sir Lukin, with Miss Paynham ringing in his head.  ' He 's a cool-blooded old boy, and likes women for their intellects.'

Colonel Launay hummed in meditative emphasis.  He stared at vacancy with a tranced eye, and turning a similar

gaze on Sir Lukin, as if through him, burst out : ' Oh, by
George, I say, what a hugging that woman 'll get ! '

The cocking of ears and queries of Sir Lukin put him to
the test of his right to the remark ; for it sounded of occult
acquaintance with interesting subterranean facts ; and
there was a communication, in brief syllables and the dot
language, crudely masculine. Immensely surprised, Sir
Lukin exclaimed : ' Of course ! when fellows live quietly
and are careful of themselves. Ah ! you may think you
know a man for years, and you don't : you don't know
more than an inch or two of him. Why, of course, Tom
Redworth would be uxorious—the very man ! And tell
us what has become of the Firefly now ? One never sees
her. Didn't complain ? '

' Very much the contrary.'

Both gentlemen were grave, believing their knowledge
in the subterranean world of a wealthy city to give them
a positive cognizance of female humanity ; and the substance of Colonel Launay's communication had its impres-
siveness for them.

' Well, it 's a turn right-about-face for me,' said Sir
Lukin. ' What a world we live in ! I fancy I 've hit on
the woman he means to marry ;—had an idea of another
woman once ; but he 's one of your friendly fellows with
women. That 's how it was I took him for a fish. Great
mistake, I admit. But Tom Redworth 's a man of morals
after all ; and when those men do break loose for a plunge
—ha ! Have you ever boxed with him ? Well, he keeps
himself in training, I can tell you.'

Sir Lukin's round of visits drew him at night to Lady
Singleby's, where he sighted the identical young lady of his
thoughts, Miss Paynham, temporarily a guest of the
house ; and he talked to her of Redworth, and had the
satisfaction to spy a blush, a rageing blush : which avowal
presented her to his view as an exceedingly good-looking

girl ; so that he began mentally to praise Redworth for a
manly superiority to small trifles and the world's tattle.

'You saw him to-day,' he said.

She answered : 'Yes. He goes down to Copsley to-
morrow.'

'I think not,' said Sir Lukin.

'I have it from him.' She closed her eyelids in speaking.

'He and I have some rather serious business in town.'

'Serious ? '

'Don't be alarmed : not concerning him.'

'Whom, then ? You have told me so much—I have a
right to know.'

'Not an atom of danger, I assure you ? '

'It concerns Mrs. Warwick ! ' said she.

Sir Lukin thought the guess extraordinary. He preserved an impenetrable air. But he had spoken enough to
set that giddy head spinning.

Nowhere during the night was Mrs. Fryar-Gunnett
visible. Earlier than usual, she was riding next day in the
Row, alone for perhaps two minutes, and Sir Lukin passed
her, formally saluting. He could not help the look behind
him, she sat so bewitchingly on horseback ! He looked,
and behold, her riding-whip was raised erect from the
elbow. It was his horse that wheeled ; compulsorily he
was borne at a short canter to her side.

'Your commands ? '

The handsome Amabel threw him a sombre glance from
the corners of her uplifted eyelids ; and snakish he felt it ;
but her colour and the line of her face went well with
sullenness ; and, her arts of fascination cast aside, she
fascinated him more in seeming homelier, girlish. If the
trial of her beauty of a woman in a temper can bear the
strain, she has attractive lures indeed ; irresistible to the
amorous idler : and when, in addition, being the guilty
person, she plays the injured, her show of temper on the

taking face pitches him into perplexity with his own
emotions, creating a desire to strike and be stricken, howl
and set howling, which is of the happiest augury for tender
reconcilement, on the terms of the gentleman on his kneecap.

'You 've been doing a pretty thing!' she said, and
briefly she named her house and half an hour, and flew.
Sir Lukin was left to admire the figure of the horsewoman.
Really, her figure had an air of vindicating her success-
fully, except for the poison she spat at Diana Warwick.
And what pretty thing had he been doing ?   He reviewed
dozens of speculations until the impossibility of seizing
one determined him to go to Mrs. Fryar-Gunnett at the
end of the half-hour—'Just to see what these women have
to say for themselves.'

Some big advance drops of Redworth's thunderstorm
drawing gloomily overhead, warned him to be quick and
get his horse into stables.  Dismounted, the sensational
man was irresolute, suspecting a female trap.  But curiosity, combined with the instinctive turning of his nose in
the direction of the lady's house, led him thither, to an
accompaniment of celestial growls, which impressed him,
judging by that naughty-girl face of hers and the woman's
tongue she had, as a likely prelude to the scene to come
below.

## CHAPTER XLII

### THE PENULTIMATE : SHOWING A FINAL STRUGGLE FOR
### LIBERTY AND RUN INTO HARNESS

THE prophet of the storm had forgotten his prediction ;
which, however, was of small concern to him, apart from
the ducking he received midway between the valley and

the heights of Copsley; whither he was bound, on a
mission so serious that, according to his custom in such
instances, he chose to take counsel of his active legs : an
adviseable course when the brain wants clearing and the
heart fortifying. Diana's face was clearly before him
through the deluge ; now in single features, the dimple
running from her mouth, the dark bright eyes and cut of
eyelids, and nostrils alive under their lightning ; now in
her whole radiant smile, or musefully listening, nursing a
thought. Or she was obscured, and he felt the face. The
individuality of it had him by the heart, beyond his powers
of visioning. On his arrival, he stood in the hall, adrip like
one of the trees of the lawn, laughing at Lady Dunstane's
anxious exclamations. His portmanteau had come and
he was expected ; she hurried out at the first ringing of
the bell, to greet and reproach him for walking in such
weather.

'Diana has left me,' she said, when he reappeared in
dry clothing. 'We are neighbours ; she has taken
cottage-lodgings at Selshall, about an hour's walk :—one
of her wild dreams of independence. Are you disappointed ? '

'I am,' Redworth confessed.

Emma coloured. 'She requires an immense deal of
humouring at present. The fit will wear off ; only we
must wait for it. Any menace to her precious liberty
makes her prickly. She is passing the day with the
Pettigrews, who have taken a place near her village for a
month. She promised to dine and sleep here, if she
returned in time. What is your news ? '

'Nothing ; the world wags on.'

'You have nothing special to tell her ? '

'Nothing '; he hummed ; 'nothing, I fancy, that she
does not know.'

'You said you were disappointed.'

'It 's always a pleasure to see her.'

'Even in her worst moods, I find it so.'

'Oh! moods!' quoth Redworth.

'My friend, they are to be reckoned, with women.'

'Certainly; what I meant was, that I don't count them against women.'

'Good: but my meaning was . . . I think I remember your once comparing them and the weather; and you spoke of the "one point more variable in women." You may forestall your storms. There is no calculating the effect of a few little words at a wrong season.'

'With women! I suppose not. I have no pretension to a knowledge of the sex.'

Emma imagined she had spoken plainly enough, if he had immediate designs; and she was not sure of that, and wished rather to shun his confidences while Tony was in her young widowhood, revelling in her joy of liberty. By and by, was her thought: perhaps next year. She dreaded Tony's refusal of the yoke, and her iron-hardness to the dearest of men proposing it; and moreover, her further to be apprehended holding to the refusal, for the sake of consistency, if it was once uttered. For her own sake, she shrank from hearing intentions, that distressing the good man, she would have to discountenance. His candour in confessing disappointment, and his open face, his excellent sense too, gave her some assurance of his not being foolishly impetuous. After he had read to her for an hour, as his habit was on evenings and wet days, their discussion of this and that in the book lulled any doubts she had of his prudence, enough to render it even a dubious point whether she might be speculating upon a wealthy bachelor in the old-fashioned ultra-feminine manner; the which she so abhorred that she rejected the idea. Consequently, Redworth's proposal to walk down to the valley for Diana, and bring her back, struck

her as natural when a shaft of western sunshine from a
whitened edge of raincloud struck her windows. She
let him go without an intimated monition or a thought
of one ; thinking simply that her Tony would be more
likely to come, having him for escort. Those are silly
women who are always imagining designs and intrigues
and future palpitations in the commonest actions of
either sex. Emma Dunstane leaned to the contrast
between herself and them.

Danvers was at the house about sunset, reporting her
mistress to be on her way, with Mr. Redworth. The
maid's tale of the dreadful state of the lanes, accounted
for their tardiness ; and besides the sunset had been
magnificent. Diana knocked at Emma's bedroom door,
to say, outside, hurriedly in passing, how splendid the
sunset had been, and beg for an extra five minutes.
Taking full fifteen, she swam into the drawing-room,
lively with kisses on Emma's cheeks, and excuses, referring her misconduct in being late to the seductions of 'Sol'
in his glory. Redworth said he had rarely seen so wonderful a sunset. The result of their unanimity stirred
Emma's bosom to match-making regrets ; and the walk
of the pair together, alone under the propitious flaming
heavens, appeared to her now as an opportunity lost.
From sisterly sympathy, she fancied she could understand
Tony's liberty-loving reluctance : she had no comprehension of the backwardness of the man beholding the
dear woman handsomer than in her maiden or her
married time : and sprightlier as well. She chatted
deliciously, and drew Redworth to talk his best on his
choicer subjects, playing over them like a fire-wisp, determined at once to flounder him and to make him shine.
Her tender esteem for the man was transparent through
it all ; and Emma, whose evening had gone happily
between them, said to her, in their privacy, before

parting : ' You seemed to have been inspired by " Sol,"
my dear.  You do like him, don't you ? '

Diana vowed she adored him ; and with a face of
laughter in rosy suffusion, put Sol for Redworth, Redworth for Sol ; but, watchful of Emma's visage, said
finally : ' If you mean the mortal man, I think him up
to almost all your hyperboles—as far as men go ; and he
departed to his night's rest, which I hope will be good,
like a king.  Not to admire him, would argue me senseless,
heartless.  I do ; I have reason to.'

' And you make him the butt of your ridicule, Tony.'

' No ; I said " like a king " ; and he is one.  He has,
to me, morally the grandeur of your Sol sinking, Cæsar
stabbed, Cato on the sword-point.  He is Roman, Spartan,
Imperial ; English, if you like, the pick of the land.  It
is an honour to call him friend, and I do trust he will
choose the pick among us, to make her a happy woman
—if she 's for running in harness.  There, I can't say
more.'

Emma had to be satisfied with it, for the present.

They were astonished at breakfast by seeing Sir Lukin
ride past the windows.  He entered with the veritable
appetite of a cavalier who had ridden from London fasting ; and why he had come at that early hour, he was too
hungry to explain.  The ladies retired to read their
letters by the morning's post ; whereupon Sir Lukin called
to Redworth ; ' I met that woman in the park yesterday,
and had to stand a volley.  I went beating about London
for you all the afternoon and evening.  She swears you
rated her like a scullery wench, and threatened to ruin
Wroxeter.  Did you see him ?  She says, the story 's
true in one particular, that he did snatch a kiss, and got
mauled.  Not so much to pay for it !  But what a
ruffian—eh ? '

' I saw him,' said Redworth.  ' He 's one of the new

set of noblemen who take bribes to serve as baits for
transactions in the City. They help to the ruin of their
order, or are signs of its decay. We won't judge it by
him. He favoured me with his " word of honour " that
the thing you heard was entirely a misstatement, and so
forth :—apologized, I suppose. He mumbled something.'

' A thorough cur ! '

' He professed his readiness to fight, if either of us was
not contented.'

' He spoke to the wrong man. I 've half a mind to ride
back and have him out for that rascal " osculation "—
and the lady unwilling !—and she a young one, a girl,
under the protection of the house ! By Jove ! Redworth,
when you come to consider the scoundrels men can be, it
stirs a fellow's bile. There 's a deal of that sort of villany
going—and succeeding sometimes ! He deserves the
whip or a bullet.'

' A sermon from Lukin Dunstane might punish him.'

' Oh ! I 'm a sinner, I know. But, go and tell one
woman of another woman, and that a lie ! That 's
beyond me.'

' The gradations of the deeps are perhaps measureable
to those who are in them.'

' The sermon 's at me—pop ! ' said Sir Lukin. ' By
the way, I 'm coming round to think Diana Warwick was
right when she used to jibe at me for throwing up my
commission. Idleness is the devil—or mother of him.
I manage my estates ; but the truth is, it doesn't occupy
my mind.'

' Your time.'

' My mind, I say.'

' Whichever you please.'

' You 're crusty to-day, Redworth. Let me tell you, I
*think*—and hard too, when the fit 's on me. However,
you did right in stopping—I 'll own—a piece of folly,

and shutting the mouths of those two ; though it caused
me to come in for a regular drencher. But a pretty
woman in a right-down termagant passion is good theatre ;
because it can't last, at that pace ; and you 're sure of
your agreeable tableau. Not that I trust her ten minutes
out of sight—or any woman, except one or two ; my wife
and Diana Warwick. Trust those you 've tried, old boy.
Diana Warwick ought to be taught to thank you ; though
I don't know how it 's to be done.'

' The fact of it is,' Redworth frowned and rose, ' I 've
done mischief. I had no right to mix myself in it. I 'm
seldom caught off my feet by an impulse ; but I was. I
took the fever from you.'

He squared his figure at the window, and looked up on
a driving sky.

' Come, let 's play open cards, Tom Redworth,' said
Sir Lukin, leaving the table and joining his friend by the
window. ' You moral men are doomed to be marrying
men, always ; and quite right. Not that one doesn't
hear a roundabout thing or two about you : no harm.
Very much the contrary :—as the world goes. But
you 're the man to marry a wife ; and if I guess the lady,
she 's a sensible girl and won't be jealous. I 'd swear she
only waits for asking.'

' Then you don't guess the lady,' said Redworth.

' Mary Paynham ? '

The desperate half-laugh greeting the name convinced
more than a dozen denials.

Sir Lukin kept edging round for a full view of the friend
who shunned inspection. ' But is it ? . . . can it be ?
it must be, after all ! . . . why, of course it is ! But the
thing staring us in the face is just what we never see.
Just the husband for her !—and she 's the wife ! Why,
Diana Warwick 's the very woman, of course ! I remember I used to think so before she was free to wed.'

' She is not of that opinion.' Redworth blew a heavy
breath ; and it should be chronicled as a sigh ; but it was
hugely masculine.

' Because you didn't attack, the moment she was free ;
that 's what upset my calculations,' the sagacious gentleman continued, for a vindication of his acuteness : then
seizing the reply : ' Refuses ? You don't mean to say
you 're the man to take a refusal ? and from a green
widow in the blush ? Did you see her cheeks when she
was peeping at the letter in her hand ? She colours at
half a word—takes the lift of a finger for Hymen coming.
And lots of fellows are after her ; I know it from Emmy.
But you 're not the man to be refused. You 're her
friend—her champion. That woman Fryar-Gunnett
would have it you were the favoured lover, and sneered
at my talk of old friendship. Women are always down
dead on the facts ; can't put them off a scent ! '

' There 's the mischief ! ' Redworth blew again. ' I
had no right to be championing Mrs. Warwick's name.
Or the world won't give it, at all events. I 'm a blundering donkey. Yes, she wishes to keep her liberty. And,
upon my soul, I 'm in love with everything she wishes !
I 've got the habit.'

' Habit be hanged ! ' cried Sir Lukin. ' You 're in love
with the woman. I know a little more of you now, Mr.
Tom. You 're a fellow in earnest about what you do.
You 're feeling it now, on the rack, by heaven ! though
you keep a bold face. Did she speak positively ?—sort
of feminine of " you 're the monster, not the man " ? or
measured little doctor's dose of pity ?—worse sign !
You 're not going ? '

' If you 'll drive me down in half an hour,' said Redworth.

' Give me an hour,' Sir Lukin replied, and went straight
to his wife's blue-room.

Diana was roused from a meditation on a letter she held, by the entrance of Emma in her bed-chamber, to whom she said : ' I have here the very craziest bit of writing !—but what is disturbing you, dear ? '

Emma sat beside her, panting and composing her lips to speak. ' Do you love me ? I throw policy to the winds, if only I can batter at you for your heart and find it ! Tony, do you love me ? But don't answer : give me your hand. You have rejected him ! '

' He has told you ? '

' No. He is not the man to cry out for a wound. He heard in London—Lukin has had the courage to tell me, after his fashion :—Tom Redworth heard an old story, coming from one of the baser kind of women : grossly false, he knew. I mention only Lord Wroxeter and Lockton. He went to man and woman both, and had it refuted, and stopped their tongues, on peril ; as he of all men is able to do when he wills it.'

Observing the quick change in Tony's eyes, Emma exclaimed : ' How you looked disdain when you asked whether he had told me ! But why are you the handsome tigress to him, of all men living ! The dear fellow, dear to me at least ! since the day he first saw you, has worshipped you and striven to serve you :—and harder than any Scriptural service to have the beloved woman to wife. I know nothing to compare with it, for he is a man of warmth. He is one of those rare men of honour who can command their passion ; who venerate when they love : and those are the men that women select for punishment ! Yes, you ! It is to the woman he loves that he cannot show himself as he is, because he is at her feet. You have managed to stamp your spirit on him ; and as a consequence, he defends you now, for flinging him off. And now his chief regret is, that he has caused his name to be coupled with yours. I suppose he had

some poor hope, seeing you free. Or else the impulse
to protect the woman of his heart and soul was too strong.
I have seen what he suffered, years back, at the news of
your engagement.'

'Oh, for God's sake, don't,' cried Tony, tears running
over, and her dream of freedom, her visions of romance,
drowning.

'It was like the snapping of the branch of an oak, when
the trunk stands firm,' Emma resumed, in her desire to
scourge as well as to soften. 'But similes applied to him
will strike you as incongruous.' Tony swayed her body,
for a negative, very girlishly and consciously. 'He probably did not woo you in a poetic style, or the courtly by
prescription.' Again Tony swayed ; she had to hug herself under the stripes, and felt as if alone at sea, with her
dear heavens pelting. 'You have sneered at him for
his calculating—to his face : and it was when he was
comparatively poor that he calculated—to his cost !—
that he dared not ask you to marry a man who could not
offer you a tithe of what he considered fit for the peerless
woman. Peerless, I admit. There he was not wrong.
But if he had valued you half a grain less, he might have
won you. You talk much of chivalry ; you conceive a
superhuman ideal, to which you fit a very indifferent
wooden model, while the man of all the world the most
chivalrous ! . . . He is a man quite other from what
you think him : anything but a " Cuthbert Dering " or
a " Man of Two Minds." He was in the drawing-room
below, on the day I received your last maiden letter from
The Crossways—now his property, in the hope of making
it yours.'

'I behaved abominably there ! ' interposed Tony, with
a gasp.

'Let it pass. At any rate, that was the prick of a
needle, not the blow of a sword.'

'But marriage, dear Emmy! marriage! Is marriage to be the end of me?'

'What amazing apotheosis have you in prospect? And are you steering so particularly well by yourself?'

'Miserably! But I can dream. And the thought of a husband cuts me from any dreaming. It's all dead flat earth at once!'

'Would you have rejected him when you were a girl?'

'I think so.'

'The superior merits of another . . . ?'

'Oh, no, no, no, *no*! I might have accepted him: and I might not have made him happy. I wanted a hero, and the jewelled garb and the feather did not suit him.'

'No; he is not that description of lay-figure. You have dressed it, and gemmed it, and—made your discovery. Here is a true man; and if you can find me any of your heroes to match him, I will thank you. He came on the day I speak of, to consult me as to whether, with the income he then had . . . Well, I had to tell him you were engaged. The man has never wavered in his love of you since that day. He has had to bear something.'

This was an electrical bolt into Tony's bosom, shaking her from self-pity and shame to remorseful pity of the suffering lover; and the tears ran in streams, as she said: 'He bore it, Emmy, he bore it.' She sobbed out: 'And he went on building a fortune and batting! Whatever he undertakes he does perfectly—approve of the pattern or not. Oh! I have no doubt he had his nest of wishes piping to him all the while: only it seems quaint, dear, quaint, and against everything we've been reading of lovers! Love was his bread and butter!' Her dark eyes showered. 'And to tell you what you do not know of him, his way of making love is really,' she sobbed, 'pretty. It . . . it took me by surprise; I was expecting a bellow and an assault of horns ; and if, dear :—you will say, what boarding-school girl have you got with you ! and I feel myself getting childish :—if Sol in his glory had not been so m . . . majestically m . . . magnificent, nor seemed to show me the king . . . kingdom of my dreams, I might have stammered the opposite word to the one he heard. Last night, when he took my hand kindly before going to bed, I had a fit for dropping on my knees to him. I saw him bleed, and he held himself right royally. I told you he did ;—Sol in his moral grandeur ! How infinitely above the physical monarch —is he not, Emmy ? What one dislikes, is the devotion of all that grandeur to win a widow. It should be a maiden princess. You feel it so, I am sure. And here am I, as if a maiden princess were I, demanding romantic accessories of rubious vapour in the man condescending to implore the widow to wed him. But, tell me, does he know everything of his widow—everything ? I shall not have to go through the frightful chapter ? '

' He is a man with his eyes awake ; he knows as much as any husband could require to know,' said Emma ; adding : ' My darling ! he trusts you. It is the soul of the man that loves you, as it is mine. You will not tease him ? Promise me. Give yourself frankly. You see it clearly before you.'

' I see compulsion, my dear. What I see, is a regiment of Proverbs, bearing placards instead of guns, and each one a taunt at women, especially at widows. They march ; they form square ; they enclose me in the middle, and I have their inscriptions to digest. Read that crazy letter from Mary Paynham while I am putting on my bonnet. I perceive I have been crying like a raw creature in her teens. I don't know myself. An advantage of the darker complexions is our speedier concealment of the traces.'

Emma read Miss Paynham's letter, and returned it with the comment : ' Utterly crazy.' Tony said : ' Is it not ? I am to " Pause before I trifle with a noble heart too long." She is to " have her happiness in the constant prayer for ours " ; and she is " warned by one of those intimations never failing her, that he runs a serious danger." It reads like a Wizard's Almanack. And here : " Homogeneity of sentiment the most perfect, is unable to contend with the fatal charm, which exercised by an indifferent person, must be ascribed to original predestination." She should be under the wing of Lady Wathin. There is the mother for such chicks ! But I 'll own to you, Emmy, that after the perusal, I did ask myself a question as to my likeness of late to the writer. I have drivelled . . . I was shuddering over it when you came in. I have sentimentalized up to thin smoke. And she tells a truth when she says I am not to " count social cleverness "—she means volubility—" as a warrant for domineering a capacious intelligence " :—because of the gentleman's modesty. Agreed : I have done it ; I am contrite. I am going into slavery to make amends for presumption. Banality, thy name is marriage ! '

' Your business is to accept life as we have it,' said Emma ; and Tony shrugged. She was precipitate in going forth to her commonplace fate, and scarcely looked at the man requested by Emma to escort her to her cottage. After their departure, Emma fell into laughter at the last words with the kiss of her cheeks : ' Here goes old Ireland ! ' But, from her look and from what she had said upstairs, Emma could believe that the singular sprite of girlishness invading and governing her latterly, had yielded place to the woman she loved.

## CHAPTER XLIII

NUPTIAL CHAPTER ; AND OF HOW A BARELY WILLING
WOMAN WAS LED TO BLOOM WITH THE NUPTIAL
SENTIMENT

EMMA watched them on their way through the park, till
they rounded the beechwood, talking, it could be surmised, of ordinary matters ; the face of the gentleman
turning at times to his companion's, which steadily fronted
the gale. She left the ensuing to a prayer for their good
direction, with a chuckle at Tony's evident feeling of a
ludicrous posture, and the desperate rush of her agile
limbs to have it over. But her prayer throbbed almost
to a supplication that the wrong done to her beloved by
Dacier—the wound to her own sisterly pride rankling as
an injury to her sex, might be cancelled through the
union of the woman noble in the sight of God with a
more manlike man.

Meanwhile the feet of the couple were going faster than
their heads to the end of the journey. Diana knew she
would have to hoist the signal—and how ? The prospect was dumbfoundering. She had to think of appeas-
ing her Emma. Redworth, for his part, actually supposed she had accepted his escorting in proof of the plain
friendship offered him over-night.

' What do your " birds " do in weather like this ? ' she
said.

' Cling to their perches and wait patiently. It 's the bad
time with them when you don't hear them chirp.'

' Of course you foretold the gale.'

' Oh, well, it did not require a shepherd or a skipper
for that.'

'Your grand gift will be useful to a yachtsman.'

'You like yachting. When I have tried my new schooner in the Channel, she is at your command for as long as you and Lady Dunstane please.'

'So you acknowledge that birds—things of nature—have their bad time ? '

'They profit ultimately by the deluge and the wreck. Nothing on earth is "tucked-up" in perpetuity.'

'Except the dead. But why should the schooner be at our command ? '

'I shall be in Ireland.'

He could not have said sweeter to her ears or more touching.

'We shall hardly feel safe without the weatherwise on board.'

'You may count on my man Barnes ; I have proved him. He is up to his work even when he 's bilious : only, in that case, occurring about once a fortnight, you must leave him to fight it out with the elements.'

'I rather like men of action to have a temper.'

'I can't say much for a bilious temper.'

The weather to-day really seemed of that kind, she remarked. He assented, in the shrug manner—not to dissent : she might say what she would. He helped nowhere to a lead ; and so quick are the changes of mood at such moments that she was now far from him under the failure of an effort to come near. But thoughts of Emma pressed.

'The name of the new schooner ? Her name is her picture to me.'

'I wanted you to christen her.'

'Launched without a name ? '

'I took a liberty.'

Needless to ask, but she did. 'With whom ? '

'I named her *Diana*.'

' May the Goddess of the silver bow and crescent protect her ! To me the name is ominous of mischance.'

' I would commit my fortunes and life . . . ! ' He checked his tongue, ejaculating : ' Omens ! '

She had veered straight away from her romantic aspirations to the blunt extreme of thinking that a widow should be wooed in unornamented matter-of-fact, as she is wedded, with a ' wilt thou,' and ' I will,' and no decorative illusions. Downright, for the unpoetic creature, if you please ! So she rejected the accompaniment of the silver Goddess and high seas for an introduction of the crisis.

' This would be a thunderer on our coasts. I had a trial of my sailing powers in the Mediterranean.'

As she said it, her musings on him then, with the contrast of her position toward him now, fierily brushed her cheeks ; and she wished him the man to make one snatch at her poor lost small butterfly bit of freedom, so that she might suddenly feel in haven, at peace with her expectant Emma. He could have seen the inviting consciousness, but he was absurdly watchful lest the flying sprays of border trees should strike her. He mentioned his fear, and it became an excuse for her seeking protection of her veil. ' It is our natural guardian,' she said.

' Not much against timber,' said he.

The worthy creature's anxiety was of the pattern of cavaliers escorting dames—an exaggeration of honest zeal ; a present example of clownish goodness, it might seem ; until entering the larch and firwood along the beaten heights, there was a rocking and straining of the shallow-rooted trees in a tremendous gust that quite pardoned him for curving his arm in a hoop about her and holding a shoulder in front. The veil did her positive service.

He was honourably scrupulous not to presume. A right

2 H

good unimpulsive gentleman : the same that she had always taken him for and liked.

' These firs are not taproots,' he observed, by way of apology.

Her dress volumed and her ribands rattled and chirruped on the verge of the slope. ' I will take your arm here,' she said.

Redworth received the little hand, saying : ' Lean to me.'

They descended upon great surges of wind piping and driving every light surface-atom as foam ; and they blinked and shook ; even the man was shaken. But their arms were interlinked and they grappled ; the battering enemy made them one. It might mean nothing, or everything : to him it meant the sheer blissful instant.

At the foot of the hill, he said : ' It 's harder to keep to the terms of yesterday.'

' What were they ? ' said she, and took his breath more than the fury of the storm had done.

' Raise the veil, I beg.'

' Widows do not wear it.'

The look revealed to him was a fugitive of the wilds, no longer the glittering shooter of arrows.

' Have you . . . ? ' changed to me, was the signification understood. ' Can you ?—for life ! Do you think you can ? '

His poverty in the pleading language melted her. ' What I cannot do, my best of friends, is to submit to be seated on a throne, with you petitioning. Yes, as far as concerns this hand of mine, if you hold it worthy of you. We will speak of that. Now tell me the name of the weed trailing along the hedge there.'

He knew it well ; a common hedgerow weed ; but the placid diversion baffled him. It was clematis, he said.

' It drags in the dust when it has no firm arm to cling to.

I passed it beside you yesterday with a flaunting mind and not a suspicion of a likeness. How foolish I was ! I could volubly sermonize ; only it should be a young maid to listen. Forgive me the yesterday.'

'You have never to ask. You withdraw your hand—was I rough ? '

'No,' she smiled demurely ; 'it must get used to the shackles : but my cottage is in sight. I have a growing love for the place. We will enter it like plain people—if you think of coming in.'

As she said it she had a slight shock of cowering under eyes tolerably hawkish in their male glitter ; but her coolness was not disturbed, and without any apprehensions she reflected on what has been written of the silly division and war of the sexes :—which two might surely enter on an engagement to live together amiably, unvexed by that barbarous old fowl and falcon interlude. Cool herself, she imagined the same of him, having good grounds for the delusion ; so they passed through the cottage-garden and beneath the low porchway, into her little sitting-room, where she was proceeding to speak composedly of her preference for cottages, while untying her bonnet-strings : —'If I had begun my life in a cottage ! '—when really a big storm-wave caught her from shore and whirled her to mid-sea, out of every sensibility but the swimming one of her loss of self in the man.

'You would not have been here ! ' was all he said. She was up at his heart, fast-locked, undergoing a change greater than the sea works ; her thoughts one blush, her brain a fire-fount. This was not like being seated on a throne.

'There,' said he, loosening his hug, 'now you belong to me ! I know you from head to foot. After that, my darling, I could leave you for years, and call you wife, and be sure of you. I could swear it for you—my life on it !

That 's what I think of you. Don't wonder that I took
my chance—the first :—I have waited ! '

Truer word was never uttered, she owned, coming into
some harmony with man's kiss on her mouth : the man
violently metamorphozed to a stranger, acting on rights
she had given him. And who was she to dream of denying
them ? Not an idea in her head ! Bound verily to be
thankful for such love, on hearing that it dated from the
night in Ireland. . . . ' So in love with you that, on my
soul, your happiness was my marrow—whatever you
wished ; anything you chose. It 's reckoned a fool's part.
No, it 's love : the love of a woman—the one woman ! I
was like the hand of a clock to the springs. I taught this
old watch-dog of a heart to keep guard and bury the bones
you tossed him.'

' Ignorantly, admit,' said she, and could have bitten her
tongue for the empty words that provoked : ' Would you
have flung him nothing ? ' and caused a lowering of her
eyelids and shamed glimpses of recollections. ' I hear you
have again been defending me. I told you, I think, I
wished I had begun my girl's life in a cottage. All that I
have had to endure ! . . . or so it seems to me : it may be
my way of excusing myself :—I know my cunning in that
peculiar art. I would take my chance of mixing among
the highest and the brightest.'

' Naturally.'

' Culpably.'

' It brings you to me.'

' Through a muddy channel.'

' Your husband has full faith in you, my own.'

' The faith has to be summoned and is buffeted, as we
were just now on the hill. I wish he had taken me from a
cottage.'

' You pushed for the best society, like a fish to its native
sea.'

' Pray say, a salmon to the riverheads.'

' Better,' Redworth laughed joyfully, between admiration of the tongue that always outflew him, and of the face he reddened.

By degrees her apter and neater terms of speech helped her to a notion of regaining some steps of her sunken ascendancy, under the weight of the novel masculine pressure on her throbbing blood ; and when he bent to her to take her lord's farewell of her, after agreeing to go and delight Emma with a message, her submission and her personal pride were not so much at variance : perhaps because her buzzing head had no ideas. ' Tell Emma you have undertaken to wash the blackamoor as white as she can be,' she said perversely, in her spite at herself for not coming, as it were, out of the dawn to the man she could consent to wed : and he replied : ' I shall tell her my dark girl pleads for a fortnight's grace before she and I set sail for the West coast of Ireland ' : conjuring a picture that checked any protest against the shortness of time :—and Emma would surely be his ally.

They talked of the Dublin Ball : painfully to some of her thoughts. But Redworth kissed that distant brilliant night as freshly as if no belabouring years rolled in the chasm : which led her to conceive partly, and wonderingly, the nature of a strong man's passion ; and it subjugated the woman knowing of a contrast. The smart of the blow dealt her by him who had fired the passion in her became a burning regret for the loss of that fair fame she had sacrificed to him, and could not bring to her truer lover : though it was but the outer view of herself—the world's view ; only she was generous and of honest conscience, and but for the sake of the truer lover, she would mentally have allowed the world to lash and abuse her, without a plea of material purity. Could it be named ? The naming of it in her clear mind lessened it to accidental :—

By good fortune, she was no worse !—She said to Redworth, when finally dismissing him ; ' I bring no real disgrace to you, my friend.'—To have had this sharp spiritual
battle at such a time, was proof of honest conscience, rarer
among women, as the world has fashioned them yet, than
the purity demanded of them.—His answer : ' You are
my wife ! ' rang in her hearing.

When she sat alone at last, she was incapable, despite
her nature's imaginative leap to brightness, of choosing
any single period, auspicious or luminous or flattering,
since the hour of her first meeting this man, rather
than the grey light he cast on her, promising helpfulness,
and inspiring a belief in her capacity to help. Not the
Salvatore high raptures nor the nights of social applause
could appear preferable : she strained her shattered wits
to try them. As for her superlunary sphere, it was in
fragments ; and she mused on the singularity, considering
that she was not deeply enamoured. Was she so at all ?
The question drove her to embrace the dignity of being
reasonable—under Emma's guidance. For she did not
stand firmly alone ; her story confessed it. Marriage
might be the archway to the road of good service, even as
our passage through the flesh may lead to the better state.
She had thoughts of the kind, and had them while en-
couraging herself to deplore the adieu to her little musk-
scented sitting-room, where a modest freedom breathed,
and her individuality had seemed pointing to a straighter
growth.

She nodded subsequently to the truth of her happy
Emma's remark : ' You were created for the world, Tony.'
A woman of blood and imagination in the warring world,
without a mate whom she can revere, subscribes to a likeness with those independent minor realms between
greedy mighty neighbours, which conspire and undermine
when they do not openly threaten to devour. So, then,

this union, the return to the wedding yoke, received sanction of grey-toned reason. She was not enamoured : she could say it to herself. She had, however, been surprised, both by the man and her unprotesting submission ; surprised and warmed, unaccountably warmed. Clearness of mind in the woman chaste by nature, however little ignorant it allowed her to be in the general review of herself, could not compass the immediately personal, with its acknowledgement of her subserviency to touch and pressure—and more, stranger, her readiness to kindle. She left it unexplained. Unconsciously the image of Dacier was effaced. Looking backward, her heart was moved to her long-constant lover with most pitying tender wonderment—stormy man, as her threatened senses told her that he was. Looking at him, she had to mask her being abashed and mastered. And looking forward, her soul fell in prayer for this true man's never repenting of his choice. Sure of her now, Mr. Thomas Redworth had returned to the station of the courtier, and her feminine sovereignty was not ruffled to make her feel too feminine. Another revelation was his playful talk when they were more closely intimate. He had his humour as well as his hearty relish of hers.

' If all Englishmen were like him ! ' she chimed with Emma Dunstane's eulogies, under the influence.

' My dear,' the latter replied, ' we should simply march over the Four Quarters and be blessed by the nations ! Only, avoid your trick of dashing headlong to the other extreme. He has his faults.'

' Tell me of them,' Diana cooed for an answer. ' Do. I want the flavour. A girl would be satisfied with superhuman excellence. A widow asks for feature.'

' To my thinking, the case is, that if it is a widow who sees the superhuman excellence in a man, she may be very

well contented to cross the bridge with him,' rejoined
Emma.

'Suppose the bridge to break, and for her to fall into
the water, he rescuing her—then perhaps ! '

'But it has been happening ! '

'But piecemeal, in extension, so slowly.  I go to him
a derelict, bearing a story of the sea ; empty of ideas.  I
remember sailing out of harbour passably well freighted
for commerce.'

'When Tom Redworth has had command of the " derelict " a week, I should like to see her ! '

The mention of that positive captaincy drowned Diana
in morning colours.  She was dominated, physically and
morally, submissively too.  What she craved, in the absence of the public whiteness which could have caused
her to rejoice in herself as a noble gift, was the spring of
enthusiasm.  Emma touched a quivering chord of pride
with her hint at the good augury, and foreshadowing of
the larger Union, in the Irishwoman's bestowal of her
hand on the open-minded Englishman she had learned
to trust.  The aureole glimmered transiently : she could
neither think highly of the woman about to be wedded,
nor poetically of the man ; nor, therefore, rosily of the
ceremony, nor other than vacuously of life.  And yet, as
she avowed to Emma, she had gathered the three rarest
good things of life : a faithful friend, a faithful lover, a
faithful servant : the two latter exposing an unimagined
quality of emotion.  Danvers, on the night of the great
day for Redworth, had undressed her with trembling
fingers, and her mistress was led to the knowledge that
the maid had always been all eye ; and on reflection
to admit that it came of a sympathy she did not
share.

But when Celtic brains are reflective on their emotional
vessel they shoot direct as the arrow of logic.  Diana's

glance at the years behind lighted every moving figure to
a shrewd transparency, herself among them. She was
driven to the conclusion that the granting of any of her
heart's wild wishes in those days would have lowered
her—or frozen. Dacier was a coldly luminous image ;
still a tolling name ; no longer conceivably her mate.
Recollection rocked, not she. The politician and citizen
was admired : she read the man ;—more to her own discredit than to his, but she read him, and if that is done
by the one of two lovers who was true to love, it is the
God of the passion pronouncing a final release from the
shadow of his chains.

Three days antecedent to her marriage, she went down
the hill over her cottage chimneys with Redworth, after
hearing him praise and cite to Emma Dunstane sentences
of a morning's report of a speech delivered by Dacier to
his constituents. She alluded to it, that she might air
her power of speaking of the man coolly to him, or else
for the sake of stirring afresh some sentiment he had
roused ; and he repeated his high opinion of the orator's
political wisdom : whereby was revived in her memory
a certain reprehensible view, belonging to her period of
mock-girlish naughtiness—too vile !—as to his paternal
benevolence, now to clear vision the loftiest manliness.
What did she do ? She was Irish ; therefore intuitively
decorous in amatory challenges and interchanges. But
she was an impulsive woman, and foliage was thick
around, only a few small birds and heaven seeing ; and
penitence and admiration sprang the impulse. It had
to be this or a burst of weeping :—she put a kiss upon his
arm.

She had omitted to think that she was dealing with a
lover a man of smothered fire, who would be electrically
alive to the act through a coat-sleeve. Redworth had his
impulse. He kept it under,—she felt the big breath he

drew in. Imagination began busily building a nest for him, and enthusiasm was not sluggish to make a home of it. The impulse of each had wedded; in expression and repression; her sensibility told her of the stronger.

She rose on the morning of her marriage day with his favourite Planxty Kelly at her lips, a natural bubble of the notes. Emma drove down to the cottage to breakfast and superintend her bride's adornment, as to which, Diana had spoken slightingly; as well as of the ceremony, and the institution, and this life itself :—she would be married out of her cottage, a widow, a cottager, a woman under a cloud; yes, a sober person taking at last a right practical step, to please her two best friends. The change was marked. She wished to hide it, wished to confide it. Emma was asked : ' How is he this morning ? ' and at the answer, describing his fresh and spirited looks, and his kind ways with Arthur Rhodes, and his fun with Sullivan Smith, and the satisfaction with the bridegroom declared by Lord Larrian (invalided from his Rock and unexpectingly informed of the wedding), Diana forgot that she had kissed her, and this time pressed her lips, in a manner to convey the secret bridally.

' He has a lovely day.'

' And bride,' said Emma.

' If you two think so ! I should like to agree with my dear old lord and bless him for the prize he takes, though it feels itself at present rather like a Christmas bon-bon— a piece of sugar in the wrap of a rhymed motto. He is kind to Arthur, you say ? '

' Like a cordial elder brother.'

' Dear love, I have it at heart that I was harsh upon Mary Paynham for her letter. She meant well—and I fear she suffers. And it may have been a bit my fault. Blind that I was ! When you say " cordial elder brother,"

you make him appear beautiful to me. The worst
of that is, one becomes aware of the inability to
match him.'

' Read with his eyes when you meet him this morning,
my Tony.'

The secret was being clearly perceived by Emma, whose
pride in assisting to dress the beautiful creature for her
marriage with the man of men had a tinge from the hymenæal brand, exulting over Dacier, and in the compensation coming to her beloved for her first luckless footing
on this road.

' How does he go down to the church ? ' said Diana.

' He walks down. Lukin and his Chief drive. He
walks, with your Arthur and Mr. Sullivan Smith. He is
on his way now.'

Diana looked through the window in the direction of the
hill. ' That is so like him, to walk to his wedding ! '

Emma took the place of Danvers in the office of the
robing, for the maid, as her mistress managed to hint, was
too steeped ' in the colour of the occasion ' to be exactly
tasteful, and had the art, no doubt through sympathy, of
charging permissible common words with explosive meanings :—she was in an amorous palpitation, of the reflected
state. After several knockings and enterings of the bed-
chamber-door, she came hurriedly to say : ' And your
pillow, ma'am ? I had almost forgotten it ! ' A question
that caused her mistress to drop the gaze of a moan on
Emma, with patience trembling. Diana preferred a hard
pillow, and usually carried her own about. ' Take it,' she
had to reply.

The friends embraced before descending to step into the
fateful carriage. ' And tell me,' Emma said, ' are not
your views of life brighter to-day ? '

' Too dazzled to know ! It may be a lamp close to the
eyes or a radiance of sun. I hope they are.'

' You are beginning to think hopefully again ? '

' Who can really *think*, and not think hopefully ?  You were in my mind last night, and you brought a little boat to sail me past despondency of life and the fear of extinction.  When we despair or discolour things, it is our senses in revolt, and they have made the sovereign brain their drudge.  I heard you whisper, with your very breath in my ear :  " *There is nothing the body suffers that the soul may not profit by.*"  That is Emma's history.  With that I sail into the dark ; it is my promise of the immortal : teaches me to *see* immortality for us.  It comes from you, my Emmy.'

If not a great saying, it was in the heart of deep thoughts : proof to Emma that her Tony's mind had resumed its old clear high-aiming activity ; therefore that her nature was working sanely, and that she accepted her happiness, and bore love for a dower to her husband.  No blushing confession of the woman's love of the man would have told her so much as the return to mental harmony with the laws of life shown in her darling's pellucid little sentence.

She revolved it long after the day of the wedding.  To Emma, constantly on the dark decline of the unillumined verge, between the two worlds, those words were a radiance and a nourishment.  Had they waned she would have trimmed them to feed her during her soul-sister's absence.  They shone to her of their vitality.  She was lying along her sofa, facing her South-western window, one afternoon of late November, expecting Tony from her lengthened honeymoon trip, while a sunset in the van of frost, not without celestial musical reminders of Tony's husband, began to deepen ; and as her friend was coming, she mused on the scenes of her friend's departure, and how Tony, issuing from her cottage porch had betrayed her feelings in the language of her sex by stooping to lift above her head and kiss the smallest of her landlady's children ranged up the garden-path to bid her farewell over their strewing of flowers ;—and of her murmur to Tony, entering the churchyard, among the grave-mounds : ' Old Ireland won't repent it ! ' and Tony's rejoinder, at the sight of the bridegroom advancing, beaming : ' A singular transformation of Old England ! '—and how, having numberless ready sources of laughter and tears down the run of their heart-in-heart intimacy, all spouting up for a word in the happy tremour of the moment, they had both bitten their lips and blinked on a moisture of the eyelids. Now the dear woman was really wedded, wedded and mated. Her letters breathed, in their own lively or thoughtful flow, of the perfect mating. Emma gazed into the depths of the waves of crimson, where brilliancy of colour came out of central heaven preternaturally near on earth, till one shade less brilliant seemed an ebbing away to boundless remoteness. Angelical and mortal mixed, making the glory overhead a sign of the close union of our human conditions with the ethereal and psychically divined. Thence it grew that one thought in her breast became a desire for such extension of days as would give her the blessedness to clasp in her lap—if those kind heavens would grant it !—a child of the marriage of the two noblest of human souls, one the dearest ; and so have proof at heart that her country and our earth are fruitful in the good, for a glowing future. She was deeply a woman, dumbly a poet. True poets and true women have the native sense of the divineness of what the world deems gross material substance. Emma's exaltation in fervour had not subsided when she held her beloved in her arms under the dusk of the withdrawing redness. They sat embraced, with hands locked, in the unlighted room, and Tony spoke of the splendid sky. ' You watched it knowing I was on my way to you ? '

' Praying, dear.'

' For me ? '

' That I might live long enough to be a godmother.'

There was no reply : there was an involuntary little twitch of Tony's fingers.

**THE END**